LOOKING FOR A KINGDOM.

Also by Christine Mangala

The Firewalkers
(short-listed for the Commonwealth Best First Book Prize
and for the Deo Gloria Award)

Transcendental Pastimes

LOOKING FOR A KINGDOM

Christine Mangala

AQUILA
2014

First published in 2014

by

Aquila Books U.K.,
26 Richmond Road, Cambridge CB4 3PU, England

www.aquialabooks.uk.com

Cover design by Claudia Asimionoaei

ISBN 978-1-872897-1-34

To Lance and Jenny

for their heart-warming friendship and love

1

Mr Maharajah

Gangadar Rao lifts the edge of his top-towel, delicately sponges his glistening dome, flings the doors of the library open and proclaims:

'His Royal Highness Maharajah Krishna Deva Raja of Ratnapuri! — Welcome, gentlemen!'

I shall always be 'His Highness' to Ganga Rao, my loyal secretary of some forty years of service. He has been waiting for my signal, waiting patiently for me to lift my eyes off this newspaper so that he can usher in today's visitors. A trade-mission, I am told, from Australia. My son Jayadev, who for some peculiar reason likes that country, has set this up. He should be here: but polo, as always, takes precedence.

In come the two gentlemen from 'down under'. One gives me a vigorous handshake from a plump hand, the feel of a pond-frog, quickly followed by the other, a lingering, leathery paw:

'G'dday, Mr Maharajah! Dick Clayton. Pleased to meet ya.'
'G'dday, Mr Maharajah! Reg Horne. Pleased to meet ya.'

'— Good afternoon to you both, sirs!'

Silence. They seem dumbfounded, as all visitors are at first: awed, not by me, but by the imposing array of weaponry on the walls of this library. Swords, daggers, pistols, lances, shields, and muskets with polished bayonets: souvenirs from the Mysore

Wars in which the Rajahs of Ratnapuri, my ancestors, had fought; first, alongside Tippu and the French; soon after, alongside the British, against Tippu and the French. Before and also after they yielded to the treaty that Lord Wellesley had discharged at them with the force of a blunderbuss, they had fought, my ancestors, bravely and cannily, with sword and pen, and kept their state, their titles, their honours and their dignity, whereas I ...

That bayonet (the one above the bust of Julius Caesar) had once sought the heart of Tippu – might have been Wellesley's – it still glints proudly in the afternoon sun. It fills my heart with shame and pain.

Stripped of my state, my titles, my purse and my privileges, what am I now but a mere Mister? Or so it would seem.

Except for Ganga Rao, my loyal secretary: for him I shall always be 'His Royal Highness'.

Mr Clayton edges forward. 'Shall we start, Mr Maharajah?'

I wonder what it feels like to plunge glowing steel into warm flesh.

'– Reg and I put together this presentation, Mr Maharajah. We're sorry Dr Crawley isn't here yet to give her views which we're sure she'd want to when she gets here. Meantime we'd like to project these charts. You'll see how our company's doing. She's right up there. Zodiac's signs are good.' He laughs.

Zodiac? – Zodiac? What does the man mean? Yet I'll not give him the pleasure of my failing memory. The way he blathers on, it's bound to emerge sooner or later.

'– Pharmaceuticals, our latest venture; we took over Ixion, dusted her down, cut off here and there and now she's doing real nice.'

Ah! *Zodiac International.* Now I remember. Fertilizers, that's what they are into. Not long ago I remember doing something with them. Rather sorry we did. So now they've moved onto chemicals for humans. I let him drone on. Spread-sheets and flow-charts and peak-performances, the same dreary waffle year in and year out.

I do not like the cut of Mr Clayton's collar, a skimpy piece of cardboard that sags under his well-layered chin; nor do I like the way the man sits on my Regency mahogany, legs splayed at an unseemly angle, to let his bulging belly hang over the edge of the blue velvet. His face is puffy, breath short and his girth speaks of many good dinners. I wonder what pills he is on. For all this, tubby Mr Clayton, I suspect, is harmless; whereas his sidekick, the tight-lipped, hollow-cheeked Mr Horne, he's the one to beware of. No doubt he is a mung-bean-and-mineral-water fitness-freak. I dare say he jogs on the beach and sweats in the gym every day. I must warn Jayadev about him: *Yon Cassius hath a lean and hungry look.*

Enter Jayadev, with a scrawny white female at his elbow. Young she must be, no more than thirty or so, yet you wouldn't think so looking at her skin; parched by too much sun or, more likely, by too much brain-work. Her navy-blue trouser-suit does little to flatter her gangly figure but certainly makes her look 'one of the boys'. Perhaps that's the idea. Jayadev cautiously steps towards me, smiling a moustachioed smile to cover up I know not what.

'Sorry to be late, father. This is Dr Crawley. Senior Lecturer in Leisure Studies at the University of Tumbi-Umbi. Consultant to *Zodiac.*'

Before I can put my palms together in *namaskar* she grabs me by both hands; bony, limp and elastic, her palms hang down like a plucked partridge. 'Delighted to meet you! Please just call me Margaret. I was watching Dev at polo. What a fine rider he is! I grew up with horses: I never tire of them. My father keeps a great stable at Scone. Dev must visit us — so must you! You'll love it out there.'

She talks fast or rather jerks about, greasing her words with abundant zest.

Mr Horne vacates his chair for her. 'Hi, Maggie! Just in time. We've nearly finished. Your turn now.'

'Okeydo.' She puts on an outsize pair of spectacles that fit her face like a riot-shield. More graphs, more charts, more statistics. She moves about like an animated skeleton, yet her voice has a pleasant Irish lilt to which I succumb until it hits me what she's on about. Despite years of practice I cannot keep my countenance serene, and my ears burn with shame.

Demagogic research in penis-size: that is this woman's chosen field of research. Apparently she prepares the questionnaires, sends them out all over Australia, to native-born and ethnic-immigrant alike, asks the men to measure up ... before ... and at the peak of their performance ... and after; she then solemnly collates the findings, feeds them into yet another computer and comes up with ideal designs for the most reliable rubbers. This she does, day in and out. *Zodiac* funds the project and therefore she is treasured by her university as an eminent researcher.

I cannot look at the woman. I set my face firmly towards the men, much as I dislike them.

Condoms. That is what all that preamble was about. They may have talked about starting a Pharmaceuticals Division in my territory for the benefit of our people but what they are really after is quality condoms for their people, produced here with cheap Indian overheads and cheaper Indian labour. They can't quite trust our brands; they may be good enough to export to Canada but not to Australia, it seems. So they want my land, my money, my personnel to help them set up a company, ostensibly to supply our poor people with affordable drugs, yet in truth, to manufacture vast quantities of condoms for their home-market.

Once that Crawley woman stops, Dick Clayton goes full steam ahead.

'Our government is backing us in this scheme of ours. P.M. Jim assures us his personal support. He's dead set to deliver his election promise: free condoms for every man and child and a clean, healthy, AIDS-free country.' He beams at me, expecting me to beam back.

I return a stony glare. Unperturbed, he continues, with what I can only call a triumphal smirk.

'– And Dev here showed us round the valley. We've picked a beaut spot for company HQ. Jobs, research, new markets – we have a great future ahead together. Dev's right behind the scheme: he has seen to all the paper-work, all ready to sign. We just wait for you, Mr Maharajah, to come on board.'

So I see. I have been betrayed from within. That's why Dev skulked off to polo. He knows me. He has little time for my sensitivities, even less for my nostalgia. He wants me to move with the times. Why, he may even erect a stupa in his father's honour and inscribe on it: 'Krishna Deva Raja, defunct Rajah of Ratnapuri, celebrated King of Condoms, divine dispenser of reliable rubbers to Asia and Australasia.'

Oh what a fall there was, my countrymen!

I rise to leave. Mr Clayton stalls me while Mr Horne dives towards the door: 'Just one moment please, Mr Maharajah. We have something for you.'

Enter Mr Horne, bearing a caged koala-cub. 'A present from P.M. Jim Rafferty. When he heard about your fabulous nature-reserve, he immediately rang Taronga Zoo – and here he is.'

I feel sorry for the poor creature. 'Will he survive here?'

'Sure. Little buggers are fussy eaters but we've taken care of that. He comes with P.M. Jim's greetings and best wishes for our lasting partnership.'

I blink at the sleepy cub, huddled in a corner, munching. I myself could do with whatever it is in those gum-leaves that keeps the koala in so benign a stupor. My mind is a veritable tornado at sea. Body and soul, I feel as if I have been dragged through the ruts of a monsoon-sodden alley.

2
Ziggy

At the age of thirty eight, on my birthday that is not the day of my birth, I, Ziggy Martin, once again face my sandstone-visage in the shaving mirror and recoil in shame and disgust. Once again I find myself straining to pull out the trident of a question that has speared into me ever since I quit the killing-fields of Cambodia: Who am I, why hither, where hence?

'A man who does not know who he is, and what he is for, is a machine without a manual, a ship without a chart, a seeker without a goal.' I can hear the genial voice of my father who is not my father, but nonetheless revered Reverend Jerome C Martin: he would stoop slightly over the pulpit's edge as he wafted these words in lieu of incense over his spruce congregation, who seemed to know all too well where they were heading and what for, all too ready to consume their pre-cooked life, packaged and promoted by the media – whereas I ...

It was exactly twenty years ago, on my eighteenth birthday, they told me, my parents, Reverend Jerome C. and Mrs Monica T. Martin of Butterfield parish, that I, Ziggy, was not the son I thought I was. Not a son but more than a son, a gift from God, a sign from heaven, an answer to prayer, a response from the Great Silent One whom Reverend Jerome and Mrs Monica had been badgering ever since their little Ezekiel perished in the waves off Fingal Bay. One minute he was there, their darling

Ezekiel of shining golden curls, playing in the sand, chasing the waves off his castle, the next minute he was gone, abducted by a freak wave. So five years later, still raw with grief, one night when they were walking their aged Labrador 'Tippu' in Birdwell Park, walking in silence, concentrating hard in the dark to divine the will of God as to the 'call' they had had that evening from a bishop in the north, and just as Mrs Monica tugged hard at Tippu's leash, forcing by proxy the Great Silent One to yield a yea or a nay: – Should Reverend Jerome C. Martin of St. Paul's, Butterfield, abandon his flock of devout Sydney-siders and sojourn in alien Queensland, in distant Toowoomba? It happened just then, as Tippu broke loose from Mrs Monica's grip, making her run and pant, it happened as it always happens in Reverend Jerome's reckoning – a sign of God hits you when you are least prepared and from an angle that you least expect, always a tricky drop-shot you're not quite ready for, especially after your own best back-hand. Between Tippu's barks, they heard the whimper of a child, of a weak abandoned child, clearly a sign from heaven, not written in the skies or stars but flashing in fluorescent-green right in their path.

They found him in the sand-pit: four or five or six, difficult to tell; a small under-nourished child with fine golden head and saucer-blue eyes, clad in a lime-green dungaree, eyes smarting with sand and whimpering. And no one else beside him or within whistling distance.

Monica picks up the waif and hugs him close: 'Poor darling! Fancy leaving a child this late in the park! Poor dear! There, there!' Damp from the dungaree seeps into her finely-pressed red cashmere cardigan.

A grave Reverend Jerome flashes his torch on the dungaree. 'My dear Monica, listen to this!' He reads out the words scribbled with a felt-tip pen on the back-bib.

PLEASE TAKE ZIGGY HOME. I CANT DO NOTHINK. ME COLD TURKEY. ME NO GOOD FOR HIM HE NO GOOD FOR ME. THANKS YOUS.
p.s. He wets hisself. Nappy inside T-shirt. Ta.

Monica sucks her breath in. 'Oh, Clarence!' It's only in very extreme situations that Mrs Monica invokes the Reverend's middle name. And so does he: 'Shh, my dear Teresa!' With a slight wave of his hand Reverend Jerome calms her. 'Can't you see what I see?' His bushy eyebrows shoot upward and his eyes dilate with the intensity of a dawning vision. Monica understands. The crisis is clearly over.

'I see. I see it now, Jerome. This waif – answer to our prayer.'

'Precisely.' His eyebrows level.

'Our little Ezekiel returned to us. Ziggy for Ezekiel – our child Ziggy.' By now the child has flopped onto her shoulders and begins to fall asleep, sucking his thumb.

Reverend Jerome drops to his knees and lifts his eyes to the clear night sky. 'Thank you, Lord! You do move in mysterious ways, wonders to perform. We accept.' He rises, singing *The Lord is gracious and of great goodness'.*

Monica, swaying from side to side with the sleeping child, tugs at his sleeve: 'What should we do? What if –?'

'– "Sufficient unto the day", Monica.' He takes a quick look around. Not a soul about, only a distant bark from a chained dog on someone's veranda. Must be something on the television, keeping everyone in. 'No need to agitate, my dear. The Lord has provided us this child. There's no question of what we should do. We take him home. Indeed, we'll do as asked by his mother. Tomorrow I'll ring the bishop with my yea. We pack and we leave as soon as we decently can. From then on, this Ziggy is our Ezekiel. No police, no orphanage, no foster-homes, no welfare nosey-parkers, no lawyers, no courts. Come, let's go!'

That was how I came to be Ezekiel Ziggy Martin, of indeterminate age, picked up from wet sand in a park. And why did they tell me, on my eighteenth birthday, this story of my life's shady start? Whatever possessed the genial Reverend and his ever-smiling wife to so quietly take me to the brink and dangle me over an abyss? It was not guilty conscience: no one had ever looked for me, claimed me or fought over me, and they had lavished on me all care and attention, as only the Reverend and Missus can — yet why pull the carpet from under my feet so thoughtlessly?

— Not without thought, as it transpired, but impelled by the weight of too much thought. It was with hushed expectancy that I was told, in words wafted like incense, heady with promise and vision: 'Ziggy, my son! You are no ordinary mortal, you are a gift from God: you, a wayside waif we picked up and have brought up as our own, you do not belong to us. We have no more claim on you than Elizabeth and Zechariah had on John the Baptist. You must be launched into the very city you came from, and for which you, no doubt, have a mission. Ziggy, we send you with our blessing. Wait for the word of the Lord! Watch and wait!'

Bewildered and furious as I was — and still am — I can never get away from the watching and waiting.

3

Katarina Mia

The hand of the Lord was upon me, and he carried me out in
the spirit of the Lord, and set me down in the midst of the
valley; and it was full of bones:
And he caused me to pass by them round about:
and behold there were very many in the valley;
and lo, they were very dry.
And he said unto me,
'Son of man, can these dry bones live?'
And I answered, 'O Lord God, thou knowest.'

I do not know how my namesake in the O.T. coped with his visions,
given that he was prone to staging them as street-theatre. I guess he
got a buzz out of being a spokesman for the Lord Almighty. No
such luck for me — though I, in my own humble way as a photo-
journalist, have given the world some 'sneak-previews' of the Last
Judgement. And I can't get away from those pictures, day or night.

I'm back in Phnom Penh. On the path leading to the Red Cross
Centre, I see a pile of limbs: arms, legs, thighs and broken ribs.
Someone has harvested them off a minefield in the outskirts of
the city, and unloaded a truck-full on this path for the whole
world to see. And it is my job to make sure that the world does
see. As I adjust my camera, I hear singing. The mighty Jessye
Norman is leading a troupe of purple-clad black singers. Her
voice soars above a phalanx of basses and baritones:

Dem bones, dem bones, dem dr——y bones,
Now hear the word of the Lord!
Leg bones ... connected to the ... knee-bones
Knee bones ... connected to the ... hip-bones
Hip bones ... connected to the ...
Now hear the word of the Lord ...

— Hang on! I see no leg-bones, dry or otherwise, to connect to the knee-bones on the young man before me: where the left leg should be there's scrunched-up skin, knotted over an ugly stump. Nor do I see any arm-bones to connect to the shoulder-bone on the little girl beside him: the sleeve of her dress flops from an absent arm that has been blown off by a very efficient mine, to bleach in the sun somewhere in a paddy field. Nonetheless, this broken china-doll of a child smiles at my camera. With a sick feeling in the pit of my stomach, I click away. From behind, someone lays a hand on my shoulder. I turn around. A faceless young woman, skeletal-thin from drugs, pushes a snivelling youngster before me and vanishes. And the child's clothes glow fluorescent-green: it is I, and my ghost of a mother.

I wake, shivering. The phone is ringing. I cannot tell if it is day or night, nor how long I have been dozing in my deck-chair on the balcony. I came out here sometime in the afternoon to plane-spot: unlike the other residents of this ugly block of flats that attracted me by its preposterous name, 'Ascension Towers', I do not mind the noise. Quite the contrary: I enjoy watching them swoop down over Leichhardt Town Hall, align themselves along the Norton Street cappuccino-route as they head out towards Botany Bay. — Welcome home, all ye lucky bastards, and farewell all ye wise escapees!

The phone is still ringing. Few of my friends know that I am back in the country and fewer still my whereabouts. Perhaps just a wrong number. I pick up the receiver.

'Hello! ... Ah, Katarina, I'm sorry ... I seem to have fallen asleep.'

'You amaze me, Ziggy! How can you sleep in that infernal noise? — Look! It's imperative I see you this evening!'

'Must you, mighty Katarina?'

'Stop mocking me, you sour gherkin! I'll be over there in half an hour.'

'What is it about, this time?'

'I'll tell you when I get there. It's an emergency. You've got to help, for old times' sake. See you soon! Ciao!' She rings off.

For Katarina Rossi, or KooriKat, as she now prefers to be called, life is a lit-chain of Chinese crackers, spluttering and bursting with crises, large and small. It's some ten years since I first met Katarina at the Café Gregorio: Café Gregorio, of all the coffee-and-pasta havens in Norton Street the least pretentious and most dependable. I haunt the place still, not just to enjoy Signor Rossi's exquisite sea-food, but as much to revel in his lyrical musings over past haunts where his memories lie anchored: Capri, Sorrento, Napoli, Vizzini and Palermo. One late afternoon, I was in the café as usual, sitting by the window, waiting for Signor Rossi to emerge from the kitchen. After an especially querulous editorial session, I was in dire need of my café macchiato. I find myself, however, confronting a cappuccino I had not ordered. I stare at the loathsome froth for a minute or so, then decide to send it back. The moment Signor Rossi hears of the mishap, it's match to touch-paper. His stocky frame quivering from top to toe, he launches into a lament Siciliana:

'– Why you do this to me, cara Katarina ? Why you give this thing, this rubbish to Signor Martin? Signor Martin, my good friend, he is a beau-di-ful gentle-man, Signor Martin is so in-telli-gent, he drink the right thing right time—he no drink cappuccino now. Why you do this stupid thing, Katarina mia?' He stops to exude a deep sigh and grows more lachrymose. 'Ah, Signor, I tell you, she break my heart, this daughter. She is my beau-di-ful daughter but she don't know nothink about Italia food, she care nothink. I wish she be like her mamma. My poor Felicia, she Australiana but she make such beau-di-ful Italia things always, such beau-di-ful ravioli salmone, such love-ly risotto pescatore – but Katarina? She reading, reading all the time – I don't know what! A girl must know to cook, no? But

Katarina?' He shrugs his shoulders in total despair. 'Katarina? What she do when she marry? When she has kids? I don't know. Maybe she feed her kids McDonald-garbage? Ah Katarina, she break my heart –'

Katarina returns with a glass, half-filled with the dark essence: café macchiato, with its distinctive, discreet line of creamy foam.

'– Enough, Dad! Mum's awake. She's calling you. You better go.'

Signor Rossi shuffles through the salon doors that lead to the kitchen and beyond. Katarina turns to me with undisguised hostility. '– Satisfied?'

'Sorry to have caused you trouble. – How come I haven't seen you before?'

'I don't work here. Not my scene. I can't stand the smell of seafood. Dad goes crook at me all the time. Mum's been sick. I came to see her, got roped-in.'

'So you don't live here? What are you studying? Where?'

'Do I have to tell you my life-story just to make up for a coffee mix-up?'

'No, you don't. I couldn't resist asking. Who in his right mind would?'

Suddenly, the sullen clouds that had obscured her handsome features vanish. She drags a chair close and sits, facing me.

'Hey! – I thought I'd heard your voice before. Don't you work at the *Herald* too? I started there just last week. Aren't you the guy that brings in those gruesome stories from God-knows-where? The girls were talking about you. You are leaving us or something?'

'Nothing unusual, just a routine assignment. I go away now and then. Have to.'

'Ah!' Her face sags. I see Signor Rossi in her hangdog expression.

'What have they given you?'

She shakes her head, lighting a cigarette. 'What d'you think they give someone like me? – Social column, wog-gossip, you know, tit-bits.'

* * *

She is right. Katarina Rossi is quite a titty-bit herself: bright dark eyes, fine aquiline nose, a mass of glossy reddish-black hair, and a strong, shapely Aphrodite of a figure. Perhaps it is her bearing or the dark-mauve lipstick and nails she favours – but whenever I see Katarina, I think of a Gymea lily: a succulent brandy-glass of a lily in full bud, rising imperiously from a rosette of leaves on its tall green, notched stem, high above the surrounding bracken. Breathtakingly luscious while still in bud. Once in bloom, I have seen many a Gymea in the Hawkesbury wilderness wither quickly and droop, its juicy petals shrivelling to charred-black, leathery remnants. I do not wish to be around when that happens to Katarina. For the past ten years, I have waited for that moment with apprehension. So with the old familiar dread, I open the door for her.

She is dressed in a slinky black number, slits down the side and tight as tight can be. An embroidered sulphur-crested cockatoo curves round her waist and up towards the left shoulder.

'– Hi!' Unusually tongue-tied, she extends a braceleted hand towards me. As I take it, she trips her high-heels over the door mat and falls into my arms. She straightens up, and arches her head for me to kiss her cheeks. Thank God, she is as soft and strong as ever. The nemesis is yet to come.

Some years back, during a prolonged sulk against her father, Katarina took to power-dressing, flattening and toughening her image in grey suits. Gone now are the superman-pads: her shoulders bustle up, not in power-mode but to enhance her full, firm breasts. Her hair is a maze of serpentine coils and smells deliciously of gardenia.

'Welcome to my hovel, Katarina! You look stunning as ever.'

'You're not bad yourself, a bit more weathered'. She looks me over and smiles. '— Sandstone improves with weathering, doesn't it?'

She inspects my Spartan furnishings, barely hiding her distaste: a red futon and a few well-worn cushions covered in Thai fabrics.

'Hasn't changed much.'

I clear some space for her. 'Can I get you something?'

'No, Ziggy. I absolutely must not. Not before the party. God knows, I'll get tiddly soon enough. — Get some togs on. You have to take me.'

'Party? What party? Where? Are you sure I'm the person you want?'

'Oh Ziggy! Do I have to beg you? I'm partner-less at the moment and I have to go to this blasted party. It's imperative I have some muscle with me. The place'll be crawling with ad-men and arty-farts. I can't face it alone. If my magazine's to succeed I need to impress them, you know, surprise them. If I turn up with you, that'll do the trick. Since your last stunning exhibition, no one's seen you. I know they're dying to.'

'Hold on! — What magazine? I thought you were with *Oz-Vogue*.'

'Heavens, no. I quit that some time ago. I've got my own rag now: *Koori-Chic*, edited by KooriKat.'

'Now I get it. I've been wondering how you came to be KooriKat. — Come off it, Katarina! You're no Koori.'

'That's what everyone says — even *I* thought it can't be. Then my mother died and I learnt the truth. You remember my batty old grandma? Maybe you never met her. She hated wog-food, never came near the café. It turns out she was no grandma. My mother was adopted. As she lay dying, she made me promise I'd track down where she came from. She'd put off asking questions for fear of Dad. You know him. Can you imagine?'

I can. Signor Rossi would have hit top C in his wailing if he had had to face being married to a Koori. Yet Katarina is clearly thriving on her new identity, be it fact or fiction. The possibility of an aboriginal ancestry has injected fresh sap into her system: this Gymea may yet last a little longer and may even dry gracefully.

'—Don't stare at me so doubtfully. I've got proof. I can show you the papers if you like.'

'I believe you.' I put on a tie and grab a jacket. 'Tell me more about this *Koori-Chic*. I didn't know there was one.'

'Let's move on. I'll tell you on the way. — Shsh! What's that noise? Someone's crying.'

I look at my watch. 'She's right on time. It's my neighbour, Mrs Yurisch. She cries every evening. Usually starts after the SBS News, goes for a while. Sometimes keeps it up through the night. In the morning she trips off to the markets bright as a button, returns with her basket loaded with peppers and cucumbers. A neat, trim little woman.'

'Poor thing! Does she live by herself?'

'No, no. She has a husband. I rarely see him, a lugubrious man much older than her, it would seem. A car-mechanic, I gather. He looks permanently depressed.'

'What a gloomy, weird set-up! Why do you live here? Are you that broke?'

'No, not really.'

'Why torture yourself? You're welcome to move into my pad any time. Million-dollar views and masses of room. — Don't look alarmed! I'll leave you well alone, if that's what you want.'

I remember the last time we were together. In our studio-flat in Paddo we were wrapped in a cocoon of sensuousness. I have never felt so strong or confident, before or since that interlude. With so much passion going through my blood and bones, I felt as if I had tapped into the secret of life, somehow tuned into the ancient and inexhaustible energies of rocks and gorges. I could make Katarina happy: her lithesome body thrived on our scented nights of giddy sex ... Then began the rows. At first, intermittent and easily patched over, they soon became frequent and swelled to operatic dimensions: hysterical, acrimonious and prolonged. Our thrill-filled tropical paradise of a flat shrunk to a stifling hot-house. I couldn't breathe or think clearly within the ambit of her psyche. She rent herself in fury over my mood-shifts, my silences. *The mind, alas, has many, many mountains, cliffs of fall, frightful, sheer, no-man-fathomed. Hold them cheap may who never hung there ...* I needed to roam among them unimpeded, by myself. Katarina couldn't comprehend, I couldn't explain. In a desperate bid to understand, she took to Tarot and tea-leaves. I couldn't cope with her absurd fixations. We parted after six months. It has taken six years to arrive at a manageable friendship. I now prefer to love and admire Katarina from afar. She knows it, yet the nesting instinct is overtaking her pride. She is twirling her keys expectantly:

'— Well?'

'I'm sorry, Katarina. No, thanks. I quite like it here.'

'Suit yourself. — We better hurry.' Somewhat piqued, she drives fast and furiously.

I look for a way to restore her buoyancy. 'OK. Tell me about your magazine.'

Her animation returns. 'Oh, yes! It was two years ago. I think you were still out in bad-lands somewhere.'

'Phnom Penh.'

'That's right. Some hell-hole, I remember. Things were getting pretty ratty at *Oz-Vogue*. And Mum was dying, getting skeleton-like day by day. And there in the office I was promoting these skinny zombies. I woke up. What was I doing with these bulimics, anorexics and cocaine-addicts, when I would have given anything to see my mum back in proper flesh? I packed it in. Mum died peacefully with me holding her hand, the least I could do. Then I started the search. Dad hated me doing it: "You, my Italia daughter, why you want to be Koori?", he kept wailing. He couldn't get it out of his head that I was being wilful, betraying him in some way.'

'Perhaps he was afraid of losing you.'

'Maybe you're right. It never occurred to me. Anyway, he needn't have worried. I found my tribe. The Bundjalung-Clarence River people. I'm a city girl: I can't go back to any tribe, even if they'd have me. But it's nice to know you belong, truly belong somewhere in this country. I want to do all I can to help my people. So the magazine. Something to lift our image beyond politics. The only thing I know well is fashion. So, *Koori-Chic* to promote Koori culture.'

'Sounds good. Going all right?'

'So-so — I wish you'd work for me. Why don't you, Ziggy? I could do with some brains. The blokes I work with, to be frank, are real dills. Lots of agro and passion for the cause but not much upstairs. I'm trying hard to lift the action above whinging polly-talk. I want to dazzle them out there, and there's so much to dazzle with. Why don't you come on board? — Come on, Ziggy, why don't you join me? Help our people?'

'Not really my scene, Katarina. I know so little, I'm ashamed to say.'

'All the better, you can learn. Besides I have some gorgeous designs, gorgeous girls. Real women, not your fantasy skeletons.'

'My Tuol-Sleng skeletons are no fantasy. I have my records, just as you have.'

'I'm sorry, Ziggy. I wasn't talking about Cambodia, but size 0 models. If I may say so, you are in danger of getting stuck in one track. Haven't you had enough of war-pictures? How many more limbless, cute children can we take? For God's sake! the world is beautiful. Look around! Open your eyes. Why spend all your energy on the dead? Can't you spare a little for the living? You can do it. Do it for me!'

'I'm sure you're right, Katarina. When the moment comes, I'll do what I can.'

She stops the car before a modernist mansion, set high on a rocky ledge in dense bush land. As she reverses to park, she continues:

'Why not right this moment? Try pretending you are working for me. I'd love that. It'll boost my image. I need it badly. At the moment, I'm a bit of a joke to these money-bags. I need to get more ads. God knows I need those bastards. Help me!'

For once, she is not trying for effect: her plea is sincere.

I weaken. 'Who'd believe me? I've done no work on aborigines, let alone in the fashion-line.'

'Leave that to me. We can make them believe anything we choose to. We're in the make-believe business, after all.'

Katarina Rossi prepares for attack. She takes her make-up case out and re-defines her eyes and lips.

4
The Party

Konrad Kristian made his millions with balls: countless little steel balls that coursed in the grooves of machinery, large and small. 'My ballerinas,' Konrad liked to call them; 'all manufacturing dances to the tune of my petite ballerinas.' No matter what size they came in, nifty little beads or large as owl's eyes, without Konrad's ball-bearings no machine could turn, no industry function, no commerce flourish, across Australia or even across the world. The map on the wall of his factory up north in steel-city, covered in coloured pin-heads, witnessed to that.

His ballerinas, his sugar-plum fairies, nestled in little boxes on shelves stacked high up to the ceiling, and they hatched him his millions. They did that in the seventies; for since then Konrad has moved on, but always pursuing a most mathematical route: from spheres to squares, from squares to cubes, from cubes to cones, from cones to cylinders. 'Beautiful forms,' Konrad would croon, invoking Le Corbusier. 'As our great master of abstraction so rightly says, they are the most beautiful forms, which light reveals to advantage, so distinct, so tangible.'

Right from the start, when he bought an anaemic company and transformed it into a sprinting athlete, Konrad had more than money in his mind. He despised the dark-suited, grey-faced big-business brigade. 'Monopoly-players,' he dubbed them; 'no better than casino-gamblers. They have lost touch with the grit and grandeur of manufacturing; they have no soul, no passion for the mathematical beauty of industrial products. Ah, the beauty of it, the sheer style and sheen of it all.' So Konrad chuckled over the goods that he designed and that his companies produced: conical kettles, tubular tables, spherical beds, cylindrical work-stations – a whole gamut of wares for the home and the office to tease the readers of *Vogue Living*. It was Konrad's dream to be to industry what Picasso was to art – original, strong and spare; but also what Yves St. Laurent was to fashion – sensuous, elegant and stunningly beautiful.

So when Konrad Kristian built his mansion on a steep rocky ledge that Lane Cove Council had written off as unbuildable on, it was to be a parable of mathematical perfection. But he had to fight hard. When the Council objected to his colour-scheme for the outer walls – bold bands of yellow and black, dotted with discs of red – he took them to court and lost. That didn't deter Konrad. He settled for plain white walls only to get his own back. Much to the fury of his sedate neighbours, who hid behind timid pastel shades, Konrad installed large square windows framed in black metal and festooned them with blinds in brilliant hues, not one 'matching' another. So his mansion straddled energetically up ragged ledges, a set of Rubic's cubes joined by connective decks. Amidst the cones and pyramids that formed the zigzag roof-line, one could see the occasional Jodhpur-hat of a domed roof, for Konrad had not entirely forsaken his first passion for spheres. He even set a mock-Medici shield over one of the entrances, studded with round balls – but steel balls from his factory.

The evening sun, deflected by the Medici balls, dazzles Ziggy as he scrambles out of Katarina's Ford Cortina. A strong wind has started up, throwing long shadows of scrabbling branches on Konrad's multi-coloured blinds, like the scrawny hands of children reaching for sweets.

Liquorice Allsorts!

Ziggy stretches, yawns, and bursts out laughing.

Katarina, still at the driver's seat, focussing on her war-paint, cranes her neck towards him. 'What's so funny?'

'You've surprised me, Katarina! Of all places, I wouldn't have dreamt that we'd end up at Liquorice Allsorts.'

Katarina, now concentrating on re-arranging her hair, and with a tortoiseshell clasp clenched between her teeth, hisses: 'What sorts? Can't hear you!'

'Liquorice Allsorts', shouts Ziggy against the wind. 'Didn't you know? That's what locals call this mansion.'

'Oh!' Katarina snaps her bag shut and locks the car. Pushing her sun-glasses up to keep her hair back, she squints. 'I see. I see what you mean. How cute! I love liquorice allsorts – all except the little black stumps. – Can't wait to see the great man.'

'Does she know?' Ziggy wonders. He cannot but admire her courage in venturing into Konrad's domain, but does Katarina really know what she's in for? Should he obey the old protective urge and warn her? Or should he leave her to fend for herself? – Yet what could he say?

He casts a quizzical look at her. 'I didn't know you were a friend of Konrad Kristian.'

'Heavens above, no! I don't know him at all. I know of him, like everybody else. No, no, I got an invite through a friend of a friend – Tilley, I don't think you've met her. Well, Tilley knows Tony. – Remember Tony? Tony Abraham? Haven't seen him for ages.'

'Nor have I, not since his Oxford Street gallery went bust. Weird bloke.'

Katarina giggles. 'Tilley tells me Konrad likes collecting weirdos.'

'That might explain why he asked me to visit him –'

Katarina's eyes grow saucer-size. 'You! You've met the great K.K.?

You know him? Why didn't you tell me?'

'You never told me where you were taking me. Had I known, I'm not sure I'd have come.'

'Everyone's dying to get a toe in here and you, you alone can be so huffish! Don't be a spoilsport. Just imagine: you, a friend of Konrad and I had no idea.'

'No, Katarina, I can't call myself his friend — an acquaintance perhaps. Met him at the Opera House, during an interval. He spilt wine on me as we stepped out onto the balcony. He seemed to recognize me, apologized profusely, we got talking. He took my address: — and lo and behold, a new jacket arrives the next week! — It was an All-Russian programme I recollect — and the S.S.O. trying hard to be Slavic, but the conductor wasn't up to it, so the orchestra just trundled on! — the less said the better. Konrad *did* say a lot, raged on against them, against the city skyline, and against a whole host of things, like some demented prophet.'

'I can't wait to meet him. Now that you know him, it's even better than I'd hoped.'

'Katarina — '

'No, not a word. I won't take any nonsense from you. Sounds as if we're in for a full-scale rave.'

As they reach the front door they hear a pounding of heavy metal.

A tall woman in a flowing white silk dress, with a cigarette holder in one white-gloved hand, meets them at the door. Her bony face and cavernous eyes seems to perch uneasily over some very muscular shoulders.

'Come in, my darlings! Tanya: I am your fairy godmother for this fabulous evening. You'll need me to guide you through the madhouse.' She grabs Katarina and squashes her in a tight embrace, while extending an elegant hand for Ziggy to kiss.

'— That feels better!' She loosens her grip on Katarina. 'My, what great tits! Tilley told me I'd recognize you by them. Fabulous! How I envy you! Look at me! I have to pay a whack, not speaking of the pain of all that medication. Nevertheless I mustn't whinge — where did you get this gorgeous outfit?'

'My own label. Koori Fashions. We've just started.'

'You must tell me more.' And encircling Katarina's waist, she drops her voice to a purr. 'And who, I pray is this hunk?'

'Ziggy Martin. You know — '

'Ziggy! Well, I never! — How stupid of me not to recognize you, you juicy crustacean! Where have you been hiding all this while? Don't you remember me? Of course, you wouldn't! What a silly question! Tony? Tony Abraham? Well, I'm Tanya now. Didn't Tilley tell you? I've had a change.'

'Pardon me, Tony — I mean Tanya. I ... I didn't know ... I ... I'm sorry.'

'Don't say that. Absolutely not. Whatever for? I feel on top of the world. Never felt better. — You should try it. Is your Dad still going strong? Boy, couldn't he lash out, come February! What would the gays have done without him? His effigy was one of the best, I'd say, at the Gay Mardi. He was a brave man, mind you. Braving that lot with his Sodom and Gomorrah jazz. We had great fun. — Look at you, Ziggy! You look positively fun-starved. Am I right?'

'I suppose you could say that. It's hard for me to find 'fun' in my line of work.'

'What a shame!' Tony-Tanya lets go of Katarina and grabs Ziggy's hands. Closing her eyes, she feels him all the way up to his shoulders. 'I get it. I can feel a huge block of black energy.' Opening her eyes widely, mascara glittering, she edges closer. 'What's your favourite colour?'

'Red, I suppose.'

'Thought so. You see, Katarina, how right I am, about our friend Ziggy. Tanya's always right. Tony used to get things wrong, but Tanya? - never! Sure you like red, the colour of passion, of anger, of wonderful energy – but boy, when it starts to somersault inside you with nowhere to go, it turns black. Black, black, black. Let me tell you something, something I can see with my third-eye. You are going to have an important experience, a mind-blowing experience soon.'

'Oh, I'm sure – I'll probably get dead-drunk by the end of this evening.'

Tony-Tanya pouts, offended. 'Seriously! – Don't give me that old cynic-routine. I don't usually predict, unless I feel compelled as I do now.' She pauses, waiting for Ziggy. He stays silent.

Katarina hastens to make amends. 'What d'you see, Tanya?'

Tony-Tanya resumes cheerily: 'Underneath our friend's corrugated exterior, I see a female lurking. How else can you explain so much sensitivity?'

Katarina looks away, embarrassed. Tony-Tanya continues, peering earnestly at Ziggy. 'Take my advice, my friend! Drop your Yahweh-fixation. Be changed, like me! I can recommend a darling of a doctor who performs miracles. Be transformed and discover the Goddess Within!'

Tony-Tanya moves her hands away from Ziggy with a dramatic sweep and sighs. Katarina gives Ziggy's hand a squeeze, suppressing her smirk. A group of young revellers in party-hats sweep past them. As they swing open a side-door, shrill strains of a fairground organ wash into the *boom-thud* of disco-beat.

Tony-Tanya shrugs her muscular shoulders. 'Sorry, darlings! I do get carried away. Mustn't keep you one minute more from the fun, Konrad'll never forgive me. – To the right, you'll find the Fair. Konrad has brought in a merry-go-round, specially for all you kiddies.'

Katarina brightens up. 'Wow! I haven't been on one for years!'

'That's the girl!' Tony-Tanya brushes flecks of glitter off Katarina's dress. 'This is a party with a difference, you'll find. Konrad calls it "Pilgrim's Progress". Uncle K. wants everyone to have loads of fun, so you start with kiddies' stuff, you get to ride geegees, suck lollies, gorge yourself on junk-food – '

Ziggy pulls a wry face. Tony-Tanya taps him with her cigarette-holder. 'Don't give up so soon! Hear me out. To the left, in the garage, there's dodgems galore for hyperactive kids like you. – See! I'm right again! I see you smile, do I not?'

'Dodgems sound fun, I confess.'

'There! When you've had enough of that, you can move up to level two. Disco-land. You can booze and bop till you drop.' Tony-Tanya winks at Ziggy, putting an arm around Katarina. 'If he abandons you, darling, do let me know. I'll dance with you anytime. He can go straight on to the upper deck.'

'What's up there?'

'D, E and F.'

Katarina finds it hard not to look puzzled.

'My, sweet child, how refreshingly naïve! You do need your fairy godmother. Dope, Ecstasy and F. F is what F always is, and more – Konrad has put a special fetish on today's menu. I won't spoil the fun, telling you what it is. Really ingenious, our Konrad, as always! K. has excelled himself this year. Life as a progress-party, or a party-as-progress through life. – Brilliant concept, don't you agree?'

Katarina seizes the chance. 'Tanya! Can you do me a favour? Introduce me to Konrad? I'm dying to meet him.'

Tanya's eyes arch. 'Sweet pet! What a shame I have to disappoint you. Konrad isn't here.'

'– Whenever he arrives?'

'He won't.'

'"Won't?" Why?'

'You really don't know him, do you, my poor dear? Konrad Kristian is giving this party for all his friends to have fun, and so they are. It proves his point. You don't need a host to be present for a great party such as this. Konrad loves to play *deus absconditus*. Mind you, everything is being recorded – so beware!'

Ziggy interposes. 'The author's dead, here the host is dead, so to speak. How very post-modern indeed!'

'Ziggy, my genius, you've twigged it, Konrad would appreciate it. He's ever so PoMo, though he hates what some of them do in the C.B.D. You should *hear* him on the subject.'

'I did once.'

Ziggy puts on a thick middle-European accent: 'Boxes and crates, boxes and crates, curses upon dem, crates and containers tarted up with glass and chrome, dey think dey have a masterpiece. Cretins! Pathetic, provincial hacks! Who do dey think dey are, kidding with der Kitsch?'

Tony-Tanya claps daintily. 'Bravo!'

'– Shall we?' Katarina arm-locks Ziggy and firmly steers him towards the fairground music.

They meet Tilley by the merry-go-round. A short, thin woman in a spruce black suit, straight grey hair and sparkling, beady eyes, Tilley reminds Ziggy of a low-diving magpie. Katarina embraces her:

'Hi, Tilley!'

'So you made it. I'm glad.'

'Meet my friend Ziggy.'

Tilley inspects him as she shakes hands. 'I know your work. Delighted.'

Katarina, still restlessly searching the room, explodes. 'Tell me. Tilley, is it really true that Konrad doesn't attend his own party?'

'Most certainly, my dear.'

'I can't understand it. I've been wanting to meet him so badly.'

'I think you're better off not meeting him. To tell you the truth, it's too much of a risk.'

'Risk? – I'm quite capable of looking after myself.'

'Not what you think. Konrad wouldn't even touch you, perhaps, gorgeous as you are. On the contrary, he'll smother you with compliments. But I guarantee that every one of them will carry a poison-tip and you'll quietly choke to death.'

'My! He does sound dangerous. But why?'

'Too difficult to explain. All I know is that our Konrad is a great devotee of Abstraction, some esoteric branch of it.' Tilley turns a cool, inquisitorial eye towards Ziggy.

Ziggy returns her stare and adds, 'Rondo-Cubism. A School of Abstraction that seems to have had a brief life in Konrad's native Czechoslovakia. He's keen to revive it here, that is what I gathered from what he said. Didn't sound very esoteric but it struck me as yet another dead-end.'

Katarina gives him an approving smile. 'What has all this got to do with women?'

Tilley steps forward to bat. 'Precisely! Nothing. "All civilization is the victory of logism over biologism" – one of Konrad's maxims. He truly believes that man must abstract or perish.'

Katarina pouts. 'What *bull!*'

Tilley resumes her patronizing tone. 'Not entirely, my dear! Nothing our friend Konrad says ever qualifies for that epithet.'

She turns a beady, bright gaze at Ziggy. 'There's a lot in what Konrad says, don't you agree? We need to transcend our conditioning, learn to levitate above necessity, don't you think? Or else, as Konrad says, we'll be lost in the amorphous bountiful womb of nature, never to surface.'

Ziggy stands frozen for a moment; then quickly swirls round to grab a glass of whisky from a black-suited attendant who is rushing past them. 'I think I am ready to drown myself right now.' He gulps the contents and reaches for another.

The merry-go-round slows down. Katarina niftily hoists herself onto a horse, and waves. '– And I'm going to fly from it all. See yous! Ciao!'

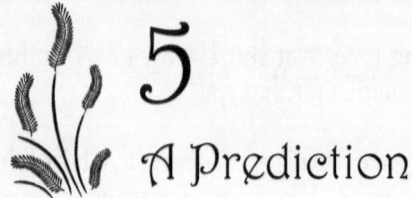

5
A Prediction

Vembu, my priest-and-astrologer is not much to look at: a dried prune of a scholar. He has, I must admit, a five-metal-bell voice that is sheer joy to listen, even when he is spreading gloom, as he is now, declaiming funerary verses from the *Yajnavalkya Samhita.*

'He is foolish, who considers as eternal the existence of human beings, which is worthless as the trunk of a plantain tree and as transient as bubbles.'

'If this body, originated from the five elements by the fruit of the deeds acquired by one's person, should be dissolved into five elements, what is there to repent for?'

'The earth shall meet with destruction, so shall the surging deep and the deities. Why then shall not the world of mortals meet with destruction?'

'The departed person shall, reluctantly, eat the phlegm and tears discharged by his own people. Therefore, one should not weep, and one should perform funeral rites proportionate to one's powers.'

Well may the sage speak so: this puja-room, charged with sadness this morning, bears witness to his truth. I could have spared myself the ordeal. Years ago, on the banks of Mother Ganga, I performed all that was needed to bid final farewell to the departed spirits of my ancestors. My obligations to them were well and truly discharged and the safety of their onward journey assured; yet I cannot bring myself to ignore the day of my beloved Queen Uma Devi's departure. So each year, in this week preceding Navaratri festival when her anniversary falls, I get Vembu to conduct a simple ritual. With his guidance I have poured libations not just for my queen but also for other ancestral spirits, should they be still lingering: for my father Vijaya Deva Raja who acquired the throne by default, as it were, when his twin-brother, my uncle Vikram Deva Raja, was snatched away in the prime of his life; for my cousin-brother Indra Deva Raja who lost his life fecklessly in a car-crash, leaving me to tend his precious treasure, my niece and ward, Rajakumari Indrani. She lights up the autumn of my life:

That time of the year thou mayst in me behold
When yellow leaves, or none, or few, do hang
Upon those boughs which shake against the cold:
Bare ruin'd choirs, where late the sweet birds sang.
In me thou see'st the twilight of such day
As after sunset fadeth in the west;
Which by and by black night doth take away,
Death's second self, that seals up all in rest ...

The bard never fails to make me moist-eyed, always with his right words for the right mood ... Indrani is my joy; whereas my son Jayadev, who ought to be the staff of strength for me to lean on, is daily becoming a weight that drags down my soul: Jayadev and the sordid schemes he is hatching with those pinguid Australians.

Vembu coughs significantly to draw my attention. He shuffles some yellowing papers in his hand.

'About this other matter, my Lord?'

'Ah, yes.' I had forgotten. My monthly horoscope reading. I hope he is not too verbose. *Brevity is the soul of wit.* Vembu ought to know that. I may not be the Prince of Denmark but Vembu is my Polonius.

Vembu prostrates before the statue of Krishna and settles down.

'Hear, O hear, Your Royal Highness, what the light-bestowing science of astrology has to say to you who are blessed with a most blessed horoscope. Having consulted sacred records for both Your-Highness's horoscope and for our precious Princess, according to Highness's instructions –'

Vembu pauses to check if I am paying attention. '– This is what I humbly seek to put before Your Highness, my reading of the current situation. May I?'

'Yes, yes – you may proceed.'

'First, Your Royal Highness may be well aware, for your humble servant spoke most recently, as recently as yesterday only, we are, I mean, Your Royal Highness is, at last emerging from the second-cycle of that accursed Saturn's seven-and-a-half-year dominance. As your humble servant reminded Your-Highness with a view to comforting Your Royal Highness and quelling undue alarm, this reign of Saturn was but the middle and second one and much damped down by the good gazes of other "friendly planets" from "friendly houses". Still, we may rejoice that the Saturn of the seven-and-a-half-year plague is moving on, and, nothing but auspicious things can come of that. Well –' Vembu pauses to check if his pronouncement has made the desired impact.

I find him more than usually tiresome this morning.

'Anything new? All this I have heard before. If you have nothing more, you may leave.'

'Most certainly I have, my Lord.' Vembu adjusts his glasses, re-crosses his legs in the lotus-position to ease pins-and-needles. 'As Your-Highness is well aware, one must, when studying one's fortunes, look not just into what the reigning planet of your horoscope's house-of-birth is doing but also take much care to ascertain what are the reigning planets of other houses which are duly and clearly marked in relation to one's house-of-birth in our scriptures. When I was thus perusing these other houses, my eyes fell on something significant. I discerned that the reigning planet of your second house is currently sojourning in the eleventh house –.' Vembu pauses again, arching his bristly brows to underscore the importance of his discovery.

I must bat accordingly.

'– So? What has our astrologer to say about that?'

'A great deal, Your Royal Highness, a great deal indeed of auspicious predictions which follow as always from Your Royal Highness's auspicious   predilections. Let me read what the sacred books say! According to Parachara, who expresses your predilection in most masterly words, when the reigning planet of the second house is sojourning in the eleventh house, auspicious results ensue: by skill of tongue, acquiring wide-ranging wisdom, he will be doing much lending-borrowing (i.e. banking business) and such like, making much profit. Brotherly, sisterly support too he will be having, acquiring many lands, homesteads, mansions and many properties, he will be busying in household affairs with peace, plenty and prosperity.'

'Nothing really new in it, is there?'

'Ah! At first perusal, perhaps not. But when read in conjunction with Her Royal Highness Rajakumari Indrani's, something gleams in the distance.'

'A gleam, you say? I could do with a shaft, or, even a lightning-bolt. Anything to lighten my darkling-soul.'

'Most certainly, Your-Highness. As Your-Highness may know I have taken steps to ensure the dispelling of gloom, most certainly a remnant, an aftermath of Saturn's exit. Now perusing Rajakumari's horoscope, I am becoming aware, once again, of that young lady's extraordinary star-conjunctions. Notably – how can anyone with the merest brush with the science of horoscoping fail to appreciate such conjunctions? – Most notable is the position of the reigning planet of her ninth house.'

'Well, what of it? Remind me.'

Eyes glittering, Vembu leans forward. 'Well, the reigning planet of her ninth house from the house-of-birth is occupying that very house-of-birth. Hence her predilection which is so true to life, as we can all witness: an auspicious person displaying great devotion and faithfulness towards elders, parents, teachers and God. Much ancestral property will befall that person. Once again in Guru Paracharya's masterly words, such a person will possess a magnanimous character, of charity. This person will be disbursing wealth according to sacred dicta. Such a person will be much attracted to penetrating mysteries; a devout student of devotional rules, such a person will be a possessor and enjoyer of mansions, carriages, vehicles, crowds of attendants, and be occupying positions of exalted status in society with prosperity, peace and joy and live to see burgeoning progeny.'

'Mmm. – Is that all?'

'Your-Highness sounds a little disbelieving today. Bearing that in mind, I am now paying extra attention to today's conjunction of planets.'

'Did you consult the *Ephemeries* and make the necessary adjustments, as I instructed you?'

'Most certainly, Your-Highness. Foreign m'leccha book *Ephemeries* may be: but very useful in ascertaining the exact whereabouts of our planets today.'

'And they are ...?'

'All pointing to a very significant turn of events: sea and air travel, to distant lands, but curiously, not west nor north but a southwards journey. At first I was a little concerned, needless to say why, south being the domain of Yama – but we have nothing to fear from the god of death. No need for alarm, for the beneficial gazes of many friendly planets are enough to counteract any mischief from that quarter.'

A gentle tap on the door comes as welcome relief from my Polonius.

'— Who's there?'

'Hari only, my Lord.'

'What brings you here, Hari?'

'The postman, my Lord. A very important letter, registered letter for Your-Highness. Secretary sahib is out with Yuvaraj's visitors. Your-Highness must sign or postman is not delivering.'

'Tell him I'm coming. Give him some sherbet. I shan't be long.'

'Yes, Your-Highness.'

The registered letter for which I duly sign is from Messers Rowlatt and Roy, Solicitors, Wahroonga, N.S.W., Australia.

Who are these solicitors writing to me from an address totally unfamiliar to me? My suspicions at once turn to Jayadev. What has he been up to behind my back?

As I step into the sunlit courtyard outside the puja-room I tear the envelope open and read.

I am wrong about Jayadev. The contents astonish me. After all my efforts, now from a total stranger — this!

My head begins to swim with a thousand thoughts, like petitioners clamouring for attention. I stop and turn.

'Hari!'

Hari is not far behind. He comes running.

'Go and tell Rajakumari to come to the library. At once.'

I feel kindly towards Vembu who is dogging my steps, bursting with curiosity. I put a hand on his shoulder.

'Well, my dear friend. This time you may well have got it right. For once, your predictions may indeed be pregnant with truth.'

6
Lizzy Rani

What's in a name?

— I hear that often enough from my beloved guardian and uncle Maharajah Krishna Deva Raja. Uncle KDR adores Shakespeare. I assure you, he has a picture of him hanging in his puja-room, next to Lord Krishna. And every day without fail, Uncle honours the bard with a fresh rose-garland, for as far as Uncle is concerned, Shakespeare is the true rose of England. So Uncle celebrates the bard's birthday as a feast, inviting select Shakespeare-wallahs from all over the country. Only those who unreservedly adore the bard get invited and they are pampered with rose-garlands, rose-water and treated to the most exquisite *gulguntu* made with the tenderest of pink-rose petals and crystal sugar. And they read, declaim, and perform all day long; free copies of the bard's works are distributed to high-school students, competitions are held, prizes given and the day finishes with fireworks in honour of the greatest genius that ever lived. So you shouldn't be surprised to hear that Uncle knows the plays well and can't resist citing them, especially when he is disenchanted with people.

What's in a name?

Uncle KDR says that to console himself, whenever they call him 'Mister Maharajah'.

— It doesn't work. I can see that. He knows and I know that the true answer to that question is EVERYTHING.

Take my formal name. Who, in this day and age, would want to be Sowbhagyaratnavijayalakshmi — sure to be ignominiously reduced, to a sow or a bag or a rat?

Fortunately, my mother had the sense to insist on an alternative. She named me Indrani: she must have known in her heart of hearts that I would be sole offspring-daughter-heir to Indra Deva Raja, my car-crazed father who crashed out of life when I had just turned six. I didn't know him well, except as someone over whom there was a great lot of head-shaking and tut-tutting, especially after he defied unwritten palace-codes and gave me the forbidden name of my foreign grandmother, Alice.

So I am now Rajakumari Indrani Alice. RIA: it has a certain ring — Persian, I like to think. I can live with that. For the palace-staff — my ayah started it — I am Lizzyrani. I am more than happy to live with that; even happier to bury the other one, the Sow-what-not, in some safe, down in the palace-vaults which is where it belongs. Let it fade to a brown smudge in a codicil to the will that charts the line of succession to the throne of a kingdom that is no more a kingdom, here in Ratnapuri.

Of all the rooms in the eastern-wing, which is where we live — the rest of the palace is tourist domain — of all the glittering rooms along that sun-lit corridor, my favourite is the ivory room. No one would venture into it until I chose it as my study — I needed a large, uncluttered space in which to display and test my model-house projects, and I find this room perfect. I am alone in thinking that: for all the servants, and my relatives, even uncle KDR, believe that this ivory-studded paradise is *poisoned*. It was here, on this very divan, that my grandmother Alice lay dying of typhoid. Her ghost is said to haunt this room. I wish I could see her and also Grandpa Vikram. — Alas, no such luck!

I love the smell of polished rosewood and the feel of its intricate ivory inlay. My complexion, they say, is that of ivory. The patterns that surround me are so intricate, so rococo, that if I lie on the divan and follow them on a cool afternoon I can get deliciously tangled in a maze of ivory lace. — And I often do, searching for fresh inspiration for my dream-project. I am not too happy with the one I finished yesterday and badly need a second opinion. I can't get Uncle KDR, he is still locked up in the puja-room. I'll have to humiliate myself before my ayah once again, for she has nothing but scorn for a girl who aspires to be an architect. She is standing by the window that overlooks the entrance to the palace, her eyes glued to a pair of binoculars which I much regret giving her. I have been calling her for the past ten minutes at intervals but she is too absorbed in counting the tourists to pay attention. Now I have no choice but to try an old ruse.

'Jeevesamma! Jeevesamma! Come at once away from that window! I see a little scorpion right above you, on the window-ledge.'

It works. Ayah jumps back, agitated.

'Where, where, little Princess?'

'I was only teasing, Jeevesamma. Come, I want you tell me what you think of what I have built.' I grab her hand and drag her to the billiard table, where my precious model-houses are assembled to form my dream-town.

Ayah peers at the table vaguely, while several frowns concertina on her ebony dark forehead. 'Jeevesamma, Jeevesamma! What stupid name you call me! My good name is Janaki, why you are mangling it always?'

'Because Jeeves is the cleverest, wisest, and most tactful of all butlers — and a very good companion too. He's a great chap and I want you to be my Jeeves. Now tell me what you think of this. This time I have redesigned all the interiors so that there is plenty of air-circulation in the summer. And I have narrowed the streets a bit so that people aren't tempted to drive cars there. What d'you think? Jeeves would know what to say.'

'"Jeeves, Jeeves!" I am sick of this nonsense. Those orange-books are curdling your pretty head. What's that writer's name? Some no-good-name I'm sure. How can it be otherwise when a man's name is pig-in-house-full-of-holes.'

'Now who is mangling names, Ayah? P.G. Wodehouse is a very funny man. I wish he could hear you now.'

'Come, it's nearly eleven o'clock. You still with hair in disarray. Time to comb and plait. So *dry* it has become! All this shampoo -pampoo you are using, your hair is getting like some muslim girl's henna-horror. O Rama! Rama! — One of these days I am going to give you a proper oil-bath, with hot chilli-scalded gingelly oil.'

'Not on my life!'

'Oh yes — hot chillies in hot oil. Only then this evil-eye will be going. And you will be finding a proper husband, not playing with Lego like a child.'

'I'm not playing, Jeevesamma! This is hard work, hard thinking — hours of it. Building an ideal town with ideal houses in it for our hot climate, how can you be so flippant? You don't understand. I should have waited for Uncle KDR — *he* understands.'

'Ah, the Maharajah! I am worrying for him too. He looks bilious to me. If Rani Uma Devi were here, it would break her heart to see him as I saw him this morning — looking so sad — like Vishnu himself carrying the weight of this world on his back. Maharajah is very upset. Or very angry — I don't know which — Cook Chari tells me that Maharajah ate nothing last night nor this morning —and this morning he is locked up in the puja-room with astrologer Vembu only with him. I hope very much it's horoscopes for *you* they are looking at.'

'I hope not. I don't want to marry. They are all nincompoops, these horoscope-prospects. I don't want to be tied down. I want to build, like great grandfather Rama Raja. No one has done anything good since him. I want to do it.'

'How you talk! Enough of this nonsense! What has a girl to do with rubble and cement? You should be thinking of bangles, jewels, silk-sarees — and a handsome young man.'

'How tedious! I want to travel, freely, adventurously, like grandfather Vikram did.'

'Travel, travel, that's what everyone thinks of nowadays. What good does it do? These travel-travel people, don't I see them every day here, stomping all over our palace? They have the same bad bellies, bad headaches, and they go home with more. Sitting in a tin-box, flying around, eating bad food, making wind, no fresh air for days, swallowing God knows what germs — I don't see what good travel-travel does to anyone.'

'Come off it, Jeevesamma, you do carry on so! People do get *off* planes, see wonderful things, meet interesting people.'

'Don't I know what evil comes of that? — Vikram Maharajah should never have crossed the black-water — he might still be living.'

'Poor Grandpa! I love this photo! — He looks so young, so lively! I can never think of him as dead or as Grandpa. It's so odd having a grandfather so much younger than Father.'

'Raja Vikram was very, very handsome. No wonder that English lady stole him!'

'*Off* you go again, Jeevesamma! So prejudiced! Grandma Alice did *not* steal him. How many times do I have to correct you? They met on board ship, they danced, they were a perfect pair, Raja Vikram and Alice Gordon. No wonder they fell in love and married! — *He* stole *her* if you like. You are never fair to Grandma Alice.'

'What do you know about that? All that trouble she caused. — She cost him his crown.'

'That's just palace-malice. Uncle KDR says that Raja Vikram would have been king if he had returned. How can you blame Grandma Alice? She was so brave to come here at all when Raja Vikram went off to fight. Be fair! It was Grandpa who caused trouble, joining the Japs, like that! — Always blame the woman, never mind what the truth is!'

'I am knowing the truth as well as you, young lady. These white hairs on my head can tell you more truth than you can ever take. Rajah Vikram was brave – he was a mighty warrior – he went to fight, not like some who hid in their harems.'

'But he chose the wrong side!'

'Are you blaming him for joining Bose? What else can a young tiger like him do? Sit in a maidan, fasting, chanting 'Rama-Rama' like cicadas in summer and hope the British go away getting sick of all that noise? Rajah Vikram could fight like Arjuna; you can't cage a tiger and not make him angry. If that white lady hadn't trapped him, who knows he might still be here. It makes me cry.'

'Leave off, Ayah! Have some pity on Poor Alice. Look at her! Isn't she beautiful? – People tell me I have her eyes.'

'Nothing of the sort. You have good Indian eyes. Like a gazelle's.'

'But they are amber, like hers, Jeevesamma.'

'Who says amber isn't Indian? – Enough of that! Sit down!'

Ayah pushes me onto the velvet stool before the mirror and starts disentangling my hair, running her fingers through the tangles. I stare hard at the mirror, as always, hoping to invoke the ghosts of Grandfather Vikram and Grandmother Alice. Instead I see a wrinkled old face.

Hari. Uncle KDR's oldest and favourite retainer has crept into the room. There's a strange smirk about his leathery lips.

'What is it, Hari?'

'Maharajah wants to see Lizzy Rani in the library. Soon, His Highness says, very important, very very important, miss.'

'Oh, good!'

I yank my hair free of Ayah's steely grip, grab my dupatta and run.

7
The Aftermath

'Ziggy Martin, our celeb photographer, I presume?'

I feel a slight pressure on my elbow and swing round. Two figures seem to have materialized from the smoky barbecue-area beside Konrad's octagonal swimming-pool, where I have taken refuge. A tall heavy-shouldered, ginger-haired man in his mid-forties extends a hand.

'Rowlatt. Ray Rowlatt.' And gesturing theatrically with his bejewelled right hand towards his olive-skinned companion: '— And this is my partner, Roy — Rohan Roy. We're honoured to find you.'

'I beg your pardon. I don't think we've met.'

'Now we have. Haven't we, Roy?' He giggles faintly. 'It must be fascinating to do what you do. We saw your exhibition last month in Paddington. Wow! What scenes! What horror! Yet so beautiful! So unreal! — I don't know how you do it. Mind boggles, stomach churns. My friend Rohan is of course used to such things. He comes from —'

'Ray!' The peeved young man interjects. 'Don't give him that shit! I'm a Sydney-sider like you. Never been to Bangladesh, never will.'

'OK! OK! I'm sorry. I was just making a point. — Sorry, Mr Martin — or dare we call you Ziggy?'

I must escape. I have seen enough of human folly and perversity for one evening; and I'm not prepared for yet another invasion of my booze-battered psyche. I lost Katarina early on in the evening, some four hours ago. My morose reluctance to shake and bop with her in the disco-room finally cracked her patience. She was taken over by a black-bearded body-builder with a permanently-etched grin, and I saw them disappearing together to the top-deck, where Tanya had indicated that Konrad had some special fetishes on offer. For ice-cream fanciers, there was a dispenser in the shape of Marilyn Monroe. It was one of Konrad's proudest re-designs. He had picked up a life-size plaster figure of Monroe of the swirling skirt from Flash-Trash, then fitted her boobs with an ingenious ice-cream dispenser: press the pad of your choice on her bottom, and ice cream, pink, vanilla or chocolate, would ooze out of her nipples. The bubble-gum blonde had gathered quite a throng – but no Katarina. Sick with too much whisky and my head ricocheting between the inane conversations around me, I had made one last attempt to locate Katarina. I found her at last in the chocolate-painting room, well and truly doped, stripped to the waist and stretched out on a marble table. The black-bearded hunk, equally bare, was painting her breasts with melted chocolate and licking it off, much to the delight of the cheering crowd around. I had no option but to retreat.

I stare at my latest unwanted invaders. A thought strikes me.

'– Did you say "Roy"?'

The ginger head pushes forward. 'Yeah! "Rohan Roy". That's my friend here.'

'I vaguely remember something about a Roy'.

'Good!' The ginger-head beams. 'I'm sure you do. – Rohan! Don't be shy! Tell him.'

The surly Eurasian deigns to smile.

Rowlatt prompts. 'Remember Jayadev? Prince Jayadev?'

'Jayadev? You mean Prince Jayadev of Ratnapuri. Yes, indeed. We were at uni together.'

Rohan turns to me. '– That's it. He used to talk about you and your work. You see, we shared rooms for a while. He liked my mum's cooking. She used to fill my fridge every week. Jay and I, we watched Indian movies.' Rohan gets quite flushed at the recollection.

Rowlatt presses his friend's hands reassuringly and turns to me with a knowing look. 'See? I knew it. I knew we know you. I knew it the moment we saw you.'

Memories of my Indian friend peek faintly through my alcoholic haze: a handsome, sporty bloke, very popular with the girls. We had met through the Film Society. He was fascinated with anything to do with films and cameras and had followed me around, even though he seemed bored by the sordid street-scenes I was filming. Apart from his princely pedigree, there wasn't much to him – or if there was, I never saw it. – But why are these two clowns pursuing me? What do they want?

Rowlatt waves a ringed finger at me. 'You see, Rohan and I are partners – in every sense. You may have heard of us: Rowlatt and Roy, Solicitors. Wahroonga. Believe it or not, we have had to deal with your friend Jayadev's dad recently. Most extraordinary business. Strictly confidential, of course.' He pauses, waiting for a cue from me.

I rise to leave. 'Confidential it better be then. Goodbye.'

They move alongside me. 'Who knows, we may meet again.'

'Perhaps.'

'Are you leaving? So are we. We can talk as we go. Where did you park your car?'

'Park? No. I came with a friend. She's still partying. I'm walking home.'

'Where to?'

'Leichhardt.'

Ray Rowlatt looks aghast. 'You must be joking! Walking to Leichhardt from here? At this hour? — We can't let him do that, can we, Rohan?'

So I get a lift to Chatswood; at Chatswood Station I insist on parting from them. As I board the train, I retch. I have eaten nothing all evening. Sure, there was food, food of all kinds — dainty party canapes and plenty more junk-food: party-pies, yeeros, and plutos dripping with ketchup. And sculpted food for those who dared; an Asian artist — Mexican-Indian-Japanese — had set up noodle-sculptures on the kitchen island, draping black and white capillaries of noodles on utensils and spilling them onto plates and bowls, with prawns, mussels, clams and octopus dangling from them like so many sea-flowers, and all pulsating with a glutinous sheen under carefully focussed spotlighting. I had passed them all by, refilling my glass yet again. Now I am to pay for it. Retch, retch. I must avoid sicking-up in this train.

I stagger towards the door and run into a group of 'Night-lighters'. I had heard of them from the Reverend: eager, young folk with a marvellous idea for spreading the Word. — So he had commended them, with just the faintest hint that I might look upon them as model evangelizers. As usual, they are patrolling the night-trains, singing choruses, which they compose as moved by the Spirit; and as the Spirit goads them, they bear down with their message on the drunks, the homeless, the streeters. the ferals and the crinklies. Each of them carries a sturdy Ever-Ready black torch, emblazoned with a fluorescent-orange sticker with the slogan 'JESUS IS THE LIGHT OF THE WORLD'. They encircle me and start singing:

'Are you looking? Are you looking?
Are you looking for the king—dom of God?
Are you ready? Are you ready?
Are you ready for the coming of the Lord?
Are you saved? Are you saved?

Are you saved from the wrath that is to come?
Have you chosen? Have you chosen?
Have you chosen the Light of the World?'

How I escaped from the clutches of the Night-lighters I can barely remember. I staggered out at the Central and down the escalator to Eddy Avenue and was heading towards George Street to catch a Night Owl bus or hail a taxi.

Then it happened.

Somewhere between Pitt Street and Eddy Avenue, under one of those monumental arches: a black tramp, swaggering with a sherry-cask in hand, waylays me.

'How you going, mate? – Felix. Say Hullo to Felix!'

I try to side-step. He bars my way. 'Can't say "Hullo", mate? What's wrong? Say "Hullo, Felix!"'

'Hullo, Felix!' I mumble.

'Say it proper. "Hullo, Felix! Hullo, Australia Felix, how d'you do?"'

His reddened eyes glower at me menacingly. I repeat duly. He guffaws. '– Just a joke! Like my name: Australia Felix, mate, Australia Felix. Just call me Felix. Want a swig?'

So I swig.

He waves his forefinger at me. 'Don't do it! Not worth it!'

'Don't do *what*?'

'I sees you. I can tell. I knows.'

'What did you see?'

'Ah!' He taps his nose. 'Let's keep it a secret, eh? I won't dob you in.

You was going to jump, wasn't you? You was looking at them tracks, looking at them with death in your eyes, Felix sees, Felix says, 'Don't even think about it, mate, I knows that look. I knows that feeling. But listen to me, mate, listen to A-u-s-t-r-a-l-i-a Felix, why give the Big-Bugger the satisfaction? Why? That's what I says to meself, "Bugger me if I give the Big-Bugger the satisfaction." — Spare a dollar or two, mate?'

'If I can find any.' I search my pockets. — My wallet's gone. Damn those Night-lighters! Could they have? Couldn't catch my soul, so took my wallet? Perhaps I dropped it, maybe left it in Katarina's car. My mind can't grip onto any notion for more than a second.

Felix watches me with mournful eyes. 'Take your time, mate. I've got all night.'

I find some loose notes floating around in my back-pocket. I hand him a fiver.

'God bless you! Don't let the other Bugger get you! He hasn't got me yet. See ya!' He vanishes down an archway. And I hear the sound of a steady stream of piss.

I am desperate myself, I start looking for a loo.

8
'I AM that I AM'

'Ezekiel!'

I look around. I can see no one.

'Ezekiel!'

There it goes again, clear as a bell yet deep and strong. No one calls me by that name except my father and that too on rare occasions, when he has had to bite back some rage.

'*Ziggy*, if you must!'

The tiles of the Museum Station loo vibrate with the echo. This time the call is mellow, like the voice of a loved one at the end of a telephone. I search the loos. Not a soul about. Silence, rippling velvet silence, pulsates from the yellowing white tiles. —It must be Felix's sherry, rebelling against Konrad's whisky. I must be hallucinating — but isn't one supposed to see something if you hallucinate? I see nothing except the tiles, the loo doors, stained floors and walls, washbasins, mops, brooms and buckets. My mind is as lucid as can be — or is it? I must be going out of my mind, hearing voices in a public loo. Sure sign of schizophrenia setting in. Oh, God! What's happening to me?

'There, now you know who I am.'

All the doors of the loos are open. There's no one beside me in the whole building. I brace myself and retaliate. 'Whoever you are, wherever you are, come out! Who *are* you?'

'I am.'

'What kind of an answer is that?'

'Sufficient.'

'Hang on! If you are who I think you are ...'

'I AM that I AM.'

'Oh, no! I've read that — not lately, I must admit, but surely I remember where it comes from. — It can't be, no, not in this day and age — and certainly not here!'

'Why not?'

'Don't fool me! — Why don't you show yourself then?'

'I did once. Didn't do much good. Better as it is. You either believe or you don't. It's every man's choice. Choose!'

Those blasted Night-lighters! Their silly jingles have got to me. I must be going crazy, standing here holding this conversation with an invisible X. I must douse my head and wake up sober.

'— Please yourself. I'll wait. I am used to waiting.'

I turn the cold tap full on and fill the sink and plunge my head for a good while. I lift my face up and take stock. No, I am not drunk. I spewed out all that sometime back. I feel remarkably clear-headed. I can recollect everything and in sequence: Katarina taking me to the party at Konrad's, meeting Tanya, Tilley, and that ice-cream vending Marilyn; Katarina covered in chocolate, the comic duo, Rowlatt and Roy, those insistent Night-lighters — and last of all, Australia Felix. Surely I can walk out of here, sane and sober. Yet something or someone is stopping me. I feel hemmed in by an invisible magnetic barrier.

I mop my face and search again. Nothing has changed. Still the same weighty silence, and warm vibes pulsating from the tiles.

Again that clear deep voice that could chisel granite.

'— Well? Feel better?'

'So you're still here.'

'I am, you might say, ever-present.'

'OK. I give up. What do you want from me?'

'That's better. I'm glad you are willing to co-operate.'

'Co-operate with *what*? For*what*?'

'You have a mission.'

'No, no, not that again, *please*. I've had enough of that from the Reverend.'

'He is just an agent. Now you meet the boss.'

'What am I supposed to do?'

'Speak.'

'Speak *what*?'

'Speak out as you feel, speak out on what you will see!'

'What will I see?'

'You will see.'

'I will see?'

'Yes, You will see, and fairly soon. Be alert. – That's all, for the time being.'

9
A Fire Sermon

I dash out of the bathroom to quell the insistent ring of the phone. I am not ready yet for Katarina's fireworks nor in the mood for playing father confessor to her.

It was a relief to hear an older voice, soft, care-worn, yet with enough power to tweak my conscience.

'– Hullo, Monica! How are you?'

'I'm all right, son. It's your father. He's in the back garden. He is starting it again. Can you come?'

'Don't worry! Just say you're having a barbecue.'

'Ten in the morning? Who'll believe me? You know your father. He won't stop at burning a few papers. He'll start looking for other things. Soon there'll be a mighty blaze. You promised to take all that stuff under the house to the dump. You never called.'

'I'm sorry, I did mean to call. My car has broken down. It's still at the garage.'

'I'm very worried. I fear this time he will really go too far. He looks so intense. The neighbours have let him off so far, but they won't this time, I'm sure. Someone is bound to ring the Council.'

'Don't be so alarmed, Monica.'

'Please come quickly and stop him. I don't know what to do. He won't listen to me, not on this.'

'Call him to the phone. I have something to ask him, I need his help.'

'Oh! He'll be ever so pleased, son. You live so close, yet we hardly see you.'

Reverend Jerome C. Martin has a sermon-block. It is particularly galling, since the invitation to preach is from the new rector of his former parish at Butterfield. Much as Reverend Jerome has resigned himself to retirement and to caring for the elderly in the Golden-Gate Nursing Home at Lewisham, much as he has resolved to exude faith, hope and *caritas*, no matter what state of decay and decrepitude he encounters in the senile inhabitants of the Home, his heart is far being from full of the joy of the Lord these days. So when the long-awaited invitation to preach at his old church came, he leapt up, so to speak, like the paralytic. – And then this cursed block! No matter how hard he tries, how deep he reflects, no matter how steadily he paces his study, he cannot get the sermon going. The words come and go, vapour-thin and lifeless, tired dead clichés about faith and works, about caring and sharing: churning-out pap he has no heart to serve.

What he really wants to tell them is something quite different. No more placing cushions under men's elbows: he needs to blast them out of their quilted complacency – yet how? He has always abhorred the fire-and-brimstone style – though he can see now why some are driven to it. Day after day of trying to bring light into dead-fish eyes, to call forth some sparkle from the crevices of crumpled old faces, failing, day after day, to unblock the blocked arteries or soften the hardened hearts of wilful old hags who are clinging to life, to a mere semblance of life, yet clutching tight their handbags and their petty little egos – he wants to speak forth: he can see where they are heading, clearly see it. Still, he cannot roar and thunder. That has never been his style, nor shall it be now. But strong and scriptural as his sentiments are, the words refuse to flow, as if afraid of buckling under the weight of such prophetic utterance. Yet he *must* speak, if only to save himself from getting crushed by the burden of so much unexpressed truth.

There is only one thing to do. He must light a fire.

He must light a proper fire, not just a little fire in the fireplace, but a blazing, roaring, grand bonfire in the back garden.

No doubt Monica will panic. Poor frail woman! She is convinced that Council officials will come and get him and cart him away, especially now that there is a fire ban – and she might well be right. What of it? Perhaps a spell in some lock-up is what he needs: after all it didn't do the Apostles any harm, being imprisoned from time to time. Anything would be better than this dampening of the spirit.

Reverend Jerome rises from his desk, muttering to himself: 'No, never mind Monica, never mind Council regulations, I must light this fire: a spirit-reviving fire, a word-sparking fire! – Now I must search for some combustibles; no doubt Monica has hidden away all things burnable.'

Half an hour later, Monica pushes the patio door open, phone in hand, excited. Her face drops as she sees her husband prizing out a loose piece of four-by-two from the side fence and throwing it on top of an already roaring volcano of a bonfire.

'Jerome, dear! It's Ziggy on the phone! He wants to speak to you.'

'Ah! Tell him I'll ring back in a moment, my hands are filthy.'

Her alarm deepens. 'Can't you speak to him now, dear! It's ages since we heard from him.'

'I did say I'll ring him back as soon as I have cleaned my hands.'

'He says he's coming over.'

'Good! In that case I can talk leisurely.'

* * *

By the time I arrive it is too late. The Reverend has had his way. He is lucky once again. No one has complained – or so it seems. I find him seated at his desk, writing away. He lifts up his flushed face and with a twinkle in his eye waves a greeting. 'Just in time, you're just in time, son! At last it's coming! I expect you know: I had to do it. Poor Monica! I know I must spare her but there are times, as you know, my son, when one cannot please a woman! – Listen to this! I hope you don't mind. It's not often I get a chance to try out something. It's such an intellectual Siberia here.' He pushes his bifocals down and almost pleads. 'I hope you don't mind.'

'Not at all. Go on!'

'Well, this is what I have in mind to say to them – who knows, some of my old parishioners may still be there; if they are, they are in for a shock. Here it goes.' He clears his throat. 'Just a few notes, mind you ! I shall, of course, speak as the Spirit moves, but nonetheless the Spirit never objects to a little premeditation:

The Budhha, I believe, preached a Fire Sermon. I do not know why it is called so, but I must confess fire is a most inspiring element. Often I sit in my rocking chair watching the logs burn and glow in the grate, I say to myself, isn't it a marvel? Isn't it a marvel that all is fire, as it were; isn't it a wonder that everything is burning constantly in this life? No wonder human beings are made of 80% – or is it 90%? – of water, or else we'd combust, given all that metabolic burning that goes on in our bodies. If you take the earth –calm, serene and majestic as the wilderness and mountains are – the belly of the earth is still burning. We forget that, most of the time, until a volcano erupts in Iceland, or in Italy, or Mexico or Java, then there is no way we can escape that knowledge. There's no holding back those streams of fire that gush out from the wounds in the mountains. The stars burn; the black holes, I believe, explode when they can no longer bear the weight of what they suck in.

Awesome universe, awesome God, our God who has created it all. Always at the heart of it all: FIRE! Frightening, isn't it? Yet we are safe, we are protected, most of the time. How? Why? Because as John (etc.) says: GOD IS LOVE. God's love burns at the core of everything that there is. For those who repent and turn to Him, He is light, and His light lightens our lives, our souls and bodies, and we are ushered into heaven. – And yet, there are so many barriers, so many walls, so many blocks we put between us and Him. And when we do, and if we choose to remain locked in our little bunkers, in our own little puny selves, if we choose darkness, if we reject Him, His love becomes a laser beam that scorches, a fire that burns and sears ... And that, my friends, is Hell.' – What do you think? You think it is too strong?'

'No, not at all. Quite the contrary. Ever so gently you take us to the brink.'

Reverend Jerome allows himself a little twitch of a smile. 'I am not one for roaring and thundering. But I had to say it. It's choking me not to.' His face sags into its habitual weariness.

'– How are things?'

'As usual.' He stops, seeing Monica enter with a tray. '– Ah, tea! About time! And salmon sandwiches too.' He helps himself and passes the plate to me. As Monica leaves to refill the teapot he leans across, conspiratorially. 'She's angry with me. I had to do it, you understand, don't you? – Are you free? I've to visit the old folk midday. I'd like you to come with me. Can you?'

'Sure.'

As he opens the front gate to the Nursing Home, Reverend Jerome stops and faces me.

'You wanted to talk about something, Monica said.'

'Yes. – No. Well, I don't know how to put it. I think ...' It is proving harder than I had imagined to broach the subject.

He waits, patiently holding the gate half open, head down as if he were expecting the buffalo-couch underfoot to continue. In that tone and posture I see years of training, in listening and putting at ease awkward confessors. I am not quite ready for him, not yet. I change tack and slip into a brisk professional tone.

'— Tell me, Father, I have been wondering about a passage in the Gospels, the one where the disciples hear the voice of God, proclaiming Jesus to be His Son. "This is my beloved Son" and so on. What do you think really happened? Did they actually hear those words or is it just some conviction that they dressed up in those words?'

Reverend Jerome lets go of the gate, lifts his head up and, smiling, puts a hand on my shoulder. 'Difficult, isn't it, for us to believe that they could have heard anything like that? — I must admit I am surprised but pleased that you should be pondering such a question. My answer is 'yes'. I believe that they *did* hear those words. No doubt Biblical scholars would pooh-pooh the whole idea, but then they dismiss most of the Gospels anyway. No doubt you'll get some clever sophisticated explanation. I am a simple believer. As far as I am concerned, if the Gospel writers say something happened, it happened.'

'Mmm ... You are quite *sure?*'

'I am. I have to believe that those disciples heard those words. I am not alone in thinking such things are possible. Saint Theresa, for instance. She writes about "locutions", meaning divine messages or words one inwardly hears but clearly hears as words.'

'So you believe it is possible for a "message" to be so audible?'

'For rare gifted souls, yes. Alas, most of us are not, our hearts are too blocked up for such grace. Besides, we are all too ready to believe some psychiatrist who will no doubt convince us that it is all fantasy, sheer self-delusion.'

'What if that's right?'

'Mind you, it is true of most of the cases any psychiatrist sees. "Hearing voices" is a sure sign of mental illness. Besides, even if one is sane and sound, one must be careful. The Scriptures warn you: the Devil can whisper too. It all depends on what one hears and how one acts.'

He pauses to give me a searching look. 'May I ask, why your sudden interest in this?'

I stare back and begin to feel ridiculous at the mere thought of my 'voice' in the Museum Station loos.

'It's nothing. I have been interested in it, thinking about it on and off.'

'I see.' He opens the gate fully. 'Anything else you wanted to talk about?'

'No, nothing. Thanks, anyway.'

'You needn't. As I said before, I am a simple believer. I know I can't offer you much; for that matter, not much to any of them in there either. I do what I can, God willing.' His voice sags. 'I am grateful for your company this morning as I walk into that "valley of desolation". – My daily cross, as you'll see.'

And I do.

I begin to see.

I see more than I want to see, more than I have heart to see.

The dining-room of the Nursing Home glows pale pink as the sun streams through large French windows, casting a coquettish glow on the old folks' cheeks. Reverend Jerome moves around among the geriatrics with consummate skill: an impresario spreading solace, albeit a thin layer of solace, before a final performance. He stops by a beady-eyed woman almost bent double over her plate.

'– How are we today, Mrs Beecham? Enjoying your dinner?'

'Corned beef again. I hate corned beef.' She prods the food as if raking manure.

'I'm sorry to hear that, my dear. I'll have a word with the nurse. Perhaps she can get you something else.'

'What'll she get me? Cheese sandwiches? I don't want no more cheese sandwiches. Cheese doesn't agree with me. And it's plastic cheese.'

'Oh, dear, we are in a fix, aren't we?' Reverend Jerome tweaks the lapels of his jacket, assuming a Pickwickian benevolence. 'Perhaps you'll get something you like at tea-time.'

'Fat chance!' Growling, Mrs Beecham glowers at other more passive diners with furious envy.

As we move away from Mrs Beecham, the Reverend whispers. 'Poor dear, she broke a leg, getting out of bed. Had to have a hip operation. It hasn't been successful, keeps giving her trouble. She is angry, permanently angry, with everything and everyone. Perhaps it is better that way –'

We pause by a table where an old man in a tweed jacket and baseball cap is sitting by himself with a pack of cards spread before him.

'– How are you today, Mr Linton? Enjoying your game?'

Mr Linton stares stolidly ahead, ignoring the question. He could be deaf. The Reverend doesn't give up: not with wooden Mr Linton, not with the totally senile Mrs Crawford, nor with the bewildered Mrs Mead, nor with the twitchy Mr Brent. Depression, dementia, Alzheimer's, Parkinson's – is this all there is to old age? Why is he badgering them with good cheer? What is there for them to be cheerful about? How can he carry on this charade after writing that sermon? Why doesn't he speak up? –Tell them the truth? – Shock them into life?

Just as the veins on my forehead tighten, the Reverend puts out a hand as if to hold me back. We are blocked by a short, fat woman. He bends down to her.

'What can I do for you, Connie?'

She casts a furtive glance towards me as she tugs his sleeve. 'Is he from my Bruce? Has he come for me? Where's me ticket?'

The Reverend pulls something from his jacket pocket and hands it to her. A red Travel Ten, expired. 'No, my dear. I am afraid not. But I'm sure your Brucie 'll send someone soon. Let's keep our fingers crossed, shall we?'

'Fingers crossed, fingers crossed.' She mutters as she tucks the ticket away in her handbag and looks up smiling. 'I'm ready. My suitcase is packed and everyfink. I've got me hot-weather gear an' all. It gets scorching in Adelaide, Brucie tells me.' She turns to me. 'I am going to Adelaide, you know, for me birthday. They're expecting me: Bruce, Cheryl, Norman, Linda and the twins. Ta, Ta!'

As she moves away, the Reverend sighs. 'Poor dear! This is a daily routine. Her son sent her here and the whole family moved down to Adelaide. That was years ago. She has no visitors. I give her these tickets, keeps her happy. – You've probably had enough. We'd better go.'

Just as we head towards the exit, a large lady with a mop of white hair zooms alongside in her wheelchair. 'Just a moment, Reverend! You haven't said hullo to me this morning!'

He stops and turns round. 'I'm sorry, Mrs Booth. I beg your pardon.'

She puts aside her bag of wool and gestures towards me with a pair of knitting needles. '– Who is this young man with you? Our new Physio? Never seen him before!'

'My son Ezekiel, Mrs Booth.'

I extend a hand. 'Hullo!'

She doesn't take it. Instead she gives me a steady look. 'Ezekiel, eh? —Didn't know you had a son named *Ezekiel.*'

She puts extra emphasis on my name, with more than a touch of scorn. Her eyes grow dark and fearful. 'Why have you come here? What do you want from us? Isn't it enough we are like this? Why did he bring you here? To torment us?'

For once Reverend Jerome stands speechless.

Mrs Booth continues to look at me as if I were a policeman about to handcuff her. Her voice ascends to a screaming pitch as she continues. 'Go on, then! Do what you've come to do! Say what you like! I shan't listen, you know. I *know* what you're thinking, don't think I don't.'

An athletic-looking Tongan nurse interposes. 'What's all this, Mrs Booth? — screeching like the lorikeets out there?' She grabs the back of the wheelchair and pats a cushion behind the old lady's back. 'Now you behave yourself! We'll have none of your rantin' and ravin'. You say nice goodbye to the gentlemen! If you are good I'll wheel you out into the garden to see the birds. Not if you carry on so!'

She niftily twiddles the brake lever with her toes, pushes Mrs Booth towards the French window and looks back, smiling. 'Don't get upset! She doesn't talk for days, then she gets like this. She means nothing. Don't take it to heart!'

I cannot help taking it to heart. Something in me has needled the poor old woman. But *what?* Even the Reverend has gone quiet all of a sudden. The way he strokes his chin and glances at me now and then, he too must be wondering. Finally, as he shuts the gate behind, he speaks.

'It's strange. That woman, Mrs Booth. She's usually one of the more bearable inhabitants. She doesn't say much — but when she does, she usually talks sense, can even be witty. I wonder what got into her today?'

'Shock, perhaps, and resentment. After all, why should she be polite to a total stranger like me? '

He shakes his head. 'No, no. I don't think so. There was something odd in her manner, something disturbing in her tone.'

As we walk towards home, he begins telling me the story of Mrs Booth. I miss most of it. He looks up and sees that I have.

'– That's my reading of the situation. What do you think?'

'I beg your pardon – I don't have an answer.'

He pats my shoulder. 'Don't worry! We can talk about it another time. – Staying for lunch? Monica'd be pleased.'

'No. – No thanks. I have a few things to do. I've lost my wallet. Need to arrange for a new licence, credit cards and so on.'

'Pity ! Where did you lose it? When?'

'Last night. Somewhere between Chatswood and Leichhardt.'

'Tiresome, losing a wallet. Hope you can sort it out.' He takes a step forward and embraces me warmly. 'Thank you for keeping me company. I appreciate it. See you soon, son. Don't leave it too late. God bless!'

I think I can feel a tear-drop down the sleeve of my shirt. He turns his back briskly and enters the house.

Should I have told him?

Dare I come out with it? Dare I tell him what was really going on when that Mrs Booth started raving on?

I could feel it, there was no mistaking it, though it was my first taste; as we stood by that wheel-chair I could feel my heart yielding suddenly, as when a plane hits an air-pocket: a dizzy dip followed by a sensation of a membrane dissolving and something opening up within me, from where I could see Mrs Booth. I could see the struggle inside her: a struggle that was taking place deep down those layers of fat and flesh and at a furious pace: an insane Punch-and-Judy show. A lifetime of disappointments, grief, and resentments were clubbing her spirit, which nonetheless kept rearing up, striving to surface above the blows, reaching for some air, for some invisible helping hand. Yet she was being tugged down and was drowning in fear. And it was from that whirlpool of despair, of drowning hope, that she saw me; and saw that I had seen her as she was.

10
'Strong-Eye'

As my key clicks open the lobby door of my Ascension Towers, I hear a clatter and a thud. A black figure rears up beside me. Australia Felix.

He must have been hiding among the bins in the alcove underneath the front step.

'G'day, Zig!' His teeth glint in the dark porch.

I can barely hide my surprise. 'What are you doing here? How the hell did you –?'

'Find ya? Easy.'

He raises his left palm, twirling a card between his thumb and forefinger: my driving licence. His grin broadens and the massive brown-black ringlets that frame his face seem to titter as he whips out something from his pocket, as though he were some magician on a Talent Quest Show. My wallet.

'How on earth –?' I stop. Better not ask how he came by it, in case ...

He catches my eye and wags a finger. 'No mate, not me. I swear. A Felix is no thief. Bloody drunk, pissed blind, yes. Thief? Never. Beg, ask, take. Never bloody steal.'

'Thanks, anyway.'

I find myself grappling with his implied distinction between taking and stealing. Perhaps he has picked up my wallet from somewhere I had dropped it. Yes, that must be it. He grabs me by the shoulder.

'Got a beer, mate?'

'Sure.' I have no option but to ask him in. I switch on the stair-well light. 'I live on the top floor.'

Perhaps because he is sober, or, perhaps, because his clothes are cleaner: he seems to have spruced himself up for this visit. He looks younger than before: thirty plus, I surmise, couldn't be older than that, the way he bounds up the stairs ahead of me. He stops on the landing of the top floor, waiting for me to catch up, grinning more than ever.

'Hey, mister Zig! You're the asking-kind. Why you don't ask?'

'Ask what?'

'The wallet.'

'I guess you found it.'

'Na, na.' He wags a finger again. 'Sure I found it. Not on the tracks, not on the platform. Guess where? On a bloody blackfella! No mate of mine, that bugger. His mob come from Taree. I see him partying in the park.'

'Which park?'

'Central Station, where I sleep. I see this bloody bastard dancing round, cask in hand, his mates cheering him on. Right behind 'em Felix is there, on the bench, not hearing nothink, so this fella reckons. Then he reckon'd wrong, the dickhead! Pissed out sure I am, nothin' wrong with me ears. I hear him all right, bragging he'd nicked this fancy wallet off some dumb gubba. I raise me head, I rub me eyes, I see ya, first like I get me strong-eye back, then I see ya in that bloody driving licence he's flashin' about. The bloody bastard is flashin' about more: photos, credit-cards, dollars. "Hey, man", says I, "What's up?" "Come and join the party", says he. "Sure", says I. When I's get close, I get cool-like. "That wallet" — I fix me eyes on it — "That wallet, it belong a mate of mine. Hand it over." He pulls back, laughing. "You kidding?" I grab him. "Hand it over or I'll twist your bloody arm off!" I roar, me eyes spitting fire, my foot on his foot. "You get me? Gimme it or I'll bloody kill ya." — Lucky I am a bigger bugger than him! He go quiet. "OK, OK. Take it!" he says. "— Out with it! All of it", I says. I reckoned he'd tucked a tenner or two away. "Spill it out or I'll thump ya. You want to party with the cops?" "No man, no cops, man". He's shakin' like a bloody starving dingo. "That's all, man, honest!" He's begging me. I let him go. — You count it, Zig! Every bloody bottom dollar there, OK.?'

I count. 'Seems I've got more than I remember.'

Australia Felix laughs out loud. 'I must've scared the shit out a' that bastard. No worries, mate! Let's have a party.'

'Sorry! I forgot your beer.' I hand him a Heineken.

'Ta.' He grabs the can. As he pulls its ring off, he surveys my flat in a proprietorial manner. 'Nice place you've got here, Zig.' His words are drowned by the roar of a low-flying United Airlines. Felix sniffs the air.

'Bloody bastards! Smell it, can't ya?'

'— Dumping fuel as usual. I bet they home-in on the coffee-route down Norton Street, they come down so low. From seven to ten each evening. Still, I don't mind.'

'Where I hang about, they roar all the time, like bloody cockies after the grain-trains. That's Redfern for ya. Who cares a shit about Redfern?' His wild eyes dart past my bedroom door towards the verandah. 'You're a lucky bugger. Beaut view.' He gulps, waving his beer can towards Leichhardt Town Hall.

'You think so? Not much to look at.'

Without further ado, he walks past my bed to the verandah. 'You've got the whole bloody sky, Zig! With all them million stars up there, what more d' ya want, mate? Sleeping with th' stars, can't beat that!'

He has a point, I have to admit. The flat is not much to boast about, but come to think of it, I have never felt confined here.

'Hey! Come, look!' he shouts, leaning over the parapet. 'What a *beauty*!"

I join him. He's pointing to a red Porsche that has pulled up by the kerbside. A couple of sleek-haired Italian youths get out.

'Great street for fancy cars, this one,' Felix chuckles. 'Didn't I tell ya? I used to work near here.'

'Where? What were you doing?'

I look at his face in the light of dusk and foresee a saga of labyrinthine interest. He is no common drunk.

'Flood Street. Cars. Trucks. Bloody good mechanic, I am. Tech-trained. Want yours done? Just gimme.'

'I'll bear it in mind.'

'Where's she? Take me to her, I'd love to have a poke around.'

'In the garage. Canterbury Road.'

'That mob? They'll rip ya off! Come, Zig! Let's go get her. I'll fix her. Any crook car, Australia Felix can get her back on the road bloody quick!'

'Thanks. But I can't. They've nearly finished. Just some spraying to do.'

'What's wrong with 'er?'

'Some bloke bumped into me at a stop-sign. Rear light gone. Exhaust's bust.'

'Piece a cake! Shame I can't do her for ya. — Look!' He swirls round to draw my attention to a tall, buxom brunette. '*What* a sheila! — Hey, Zig, she's looking at us!' Seeing my face tauten, he stops grinning. 'What's up, mate? *Yours?*'

'Not exactly. An old friend.'

Sure enough, five minutes later, I hear the clickety-clack of Katerina's high heels. Felix opens the door to her. Her eyebrows arch. Dressed in a demure black dress and veiled, she looks as if she'd just been to mass. Before I find my voice to explain the presence of my unusual companion, Felix introduces himself.

'Hi! Felix. Australia Felix.' He extends a hand. 'Nice to meet ya.'

'Katarina ...' She looks bemused, but only for a few seconds.

'— Hullo, Ziggy!' She gives me a peck, then turns towards Felix. '— And where're you from?'

Felix laughs. 'Where else? Redfern.'

'No, I mean, your tribe.'

'Awabakal. Up Newcastle-way. My mob hangs about the Lake. — And you?'

Katarina flashes a quick, angry glance towards me. I shake my head in the negative.

She turns to Felix, smiling. 'How did you guess?'

'I've got the strong-eye, haven't I?' He guffaws. 'Na, I'm kidding. — Just the way you asking me, "your tribe". You don't look the book-writing kind. Got to be personal, I reckon'd.'

'I'd love to meet a real medicine-man, one who really has the strong-eye. I hope I do when I get to see my mob.'

'What's yours?'

'I believe I belong to the Bundjalung, Clarence River way. One eighth, I figured out. And you? You look the full works, if I may say so.'

'Na! Maybe half and half. Bloody fruit-salad, you could say. My Grandma, full-blood and bloody good fisherwoman, she come from pineapple-banana country up North. My Grandad was Koori-Irish-Kiwi. That makes me Dad half and half, I reckon, maybe three-quarters. Mum is quarter from Wangi. – Mix it all up, give it a shake, an' you get me, Australia Felix, the Superblackfella.' He guffaws.

Wide-eyed Katarina joins him laughing. 'Fantastic name you have. Were you really called Australia Felix?'

'Mum called me Felix, she was hooked on James Bond movies. Dad called me Abel. I changed it. That was when I was with the band. All the other blokes got themselves fancy names, went tribal, I says to misself that's too easy, too damn easy for white folks to put yous in a basket an' forget, what you need is a name to make the gubbas sit up an' take note. So: Australia Felix.'

'Cheers! Let's drink to that! – Got any bubbly, Zig?'

'Sorry! Just lemonade.'

'That'll do fine.'

She grabs the Schweppes I pass her and raises it elegantly towards Felix. 'To Australia Felix!'

Katarina's new-found chumminess with my drunken acquaintance begins to irk me. I feel a surge of venom: 'Katarina didn't tell you, Felix, her new name. She's now KooriKat.'

'Beaut, mate! Let's drink to that!'

He opens the fridge and helps himself to another Heineken. Peering into the fridge like a foraging squirrel, he swings round. 'Hey, Zig! No tucker in there! I'm starvin'. Let's have a party.' He picks my wallet from the coffee table and takes out two twenty-dollar bills. 'Come, Kat! Let's go get some grub!'

* * *

Several hours later, I wake up with a start. There's a steady, penetrating drone of a twin engine overhead. — Dawn already? Or have they cut short the curfew hours yet again? Perhaps an emergency? Someone in trouble? Aeropelican? I push my duvet aside to check. Just past 3 a.m.: so flashes the green glow on my Mickey-Mouse alarm, an erstwhile gift from Katarina. Ah, Katarina! Her perfume still lingers in my room, despite other competing odours: salami, beer, pizza. I spy a half-finished pavlova on the coffee table, cream oozing like an ice-cap melting. CDs and tapes lie scattered round the room. Quite a party she and Felix managed to stage, without any assistance from me!

The drone overhead gathers momentum. I keep still, muscles taut, waiting for a bang and a crash.

No, not tonight.

Spared again. Surely one of these days it is bound to happen, somewhere here or hereabouts in the inner west, a plane will explode, hurling hot metal and bodies wrapped in sheets of flame and we shall all be engulfed in one great bonfire. I grope in the dim recesses of my half-awakened brain, desperate to grab the thread of a dream or a vision, something that had filled the screen just moments before. Phrases from the Reverend's sermon, inscribed on sooty bunting, had risen off a roaring fire and blown in the wind, slapping against my face as they whizzed past. I feel seared. Perhaps it's just the vodka. Felix and I had moved from beer to vodka as we got heated, swapping tales of wars and war-crimes, massacres and genocides. Katarina had sat quiet, sipping mineral water. When Felix urged her to 'have a go' and dared her to taste the liquid fire, she had snapped, every word dripping with righteous indignation. 'No thanks, no drinking bouts for me. I leave that to him.' I was well away, yet felt stung. I couldn't help laughing.

'Who's talking? After what *you* got up to last night?'

She had put her Schweppes down firmly and in a tear-laden voice, burst out:

'Whose fault was it? Who drove me to it? You – you – you are responsible for everything, everything I do –'

Floods of tears.

'Come, come! Be fair.'

'Fair? How *dare* you ask me to be fair? Oh, Ziggy, how can you be so thoughtless, so cruel to me?'

'Katarina, please. No arguments. I'm not in the mood.'

'"Not in the mood"? Do you think *I* am? To think I came here to apologize! Stupid me – stupid, stupid me! Always hoping! Stupid, really stupid!'

More tears.

– Could I claim innocence? Acquit myself? Was I really guilty? She convinced me for the moment.

'I'm sorry. I'm not sure what I am accused of. Whatever it is, I am sorry.'

Awkward silence, punctuated by her sobs.

Felix picks up a box of tissues from my desk and sits next to her. 'Hey, Kat ! There! Zig says "sorry". You hear? "Sorry" he says. Great! Beaut word, this "sorry"! Come, clean up!'

She gives him a sidelong glance, pulls out some tissues from the box and her sniffles subside.

'I must be going.'

'— Let me see you to the car. Where is it?'

'Renwick Street.'

We walk in silence. Just as she gets into her car, she turns to me.

'I need to talk to you, a proper talk. I couldn't do it with that abo mate of yours around.'

'No mate of mine.'

'He seems quite at home. Be careful! You shouldn't be so trusting. Give an inch, you'll have his whole mob moving in.'

'But Katarina! I thought you *liked* him. You two were getting on like a house on fire!'

'That's different. I don't dislike him. But I still think you need to watch. — When can I see you?' She is smiling. 'No surprises, no parties, no scenes, I promise.'

'How about dinner sometime? I'll give you a ring soon.'

When I get back, I hear snores drilling through the doors. I find Felix stretched out on my red futon, lying sideways, his head resting on a folded arm and sleeping just as he might on a park bench. I switch the light off, lie on my bed and start counting the stars. *You never never know if you never never go!* I cannot stop that Northern Territory Tourism jingle rattling through my brain. I sit up, squashing my pillows to make a nest for my head. Through the open bedroom door I can see Felix; still in the same posture but his snores have subsided to a gentle rumble. I watch him.

'See?'

That voice again.

Startled, I look around. As before, no one beside me, only Felix, and he is well away.

'What do you see?'

There is no mistaking that tone, strong, quiet, and avid for an answer. I have to respond.

'I see ... I see a face like sedimented rock. Layers and layers of stories there. I see a quick-witted, spaniel-eyed youngster, keen to please, keen to get on; I see a high-spirited youth bent over a car bonnet, baited, bullied and taunted; I see an aimless wanderer, roughing it out on park benches and drunken sprees — but there's nothing new in all this, if I may say so. There are thousands like him.'

'I am aware, burningly aware: contrary to what most human beings imagine.'

'What am I supposed to do? I've let him invade my flat. He sleeps here tonight. But tomorrow? I can't see myself tolerating him. What about Katarina's warning? I admit I didn't like it. Still, it's common-sense, isn't it? What should I do? Suppose he just stays on, should I just let him?'

'You are free, like me.'

'Free? Shackled to a conscience and ineffectual? Is that freedom?'

'Would you rather I left you alone?'

I opt for silence.

'Take heart. You are doing well. Are you ready for more?'

'More of what?'

'Just concentrate.'

The props vanish: the bed, the solid objects that fill the room, then the room itself.

All that remains is a shadowy outline of Felix' sleeping body, suspended as it were against a blue-black night sky. Then the outline becomes mobile and Felix surfaces like an animated cartoon. I can only see him in silhouette. His gestures are precise and exaggerated, at times breaking into dance mode. He stands poised, ready to run, his ears tuned to pick up the faintest rustle or rumble in the bush. I see a mob of black faces by a camp-fire, eating, laughing, and singing. I hear the thud of horses' hooves, and musket-fire; I see a pack of mounted police driving the drowsy campers into a swamp; bodies falling, women and children screeching like birds trapped in a bushfire. Silence descends while the river turns red.

Felix wakes up, stretches, gets up, looking vaguely for the bathroom. I am grateful that he hasn't fouled my futon. Bleary-eyed, he emerges from the bathroom and staggers towards my bed.

'– What's up, Zig? Didn't ya sleep?'

'Not really.'

'You OK? You look like you've been seeing spirits.'

'I have, in a manner of speaking.'

'I can tell. I knows it the first time I saw you. You sure have the "strong-eye", like me Mum's uncle. Gee, he was scary. He could see straight through you like x-ray.'

'And you? Do you have the "strong-eye" too?'

'I could have, but I'm a lazy bugger, you know me. My Mum's uncle, he come to me in this dream. He says to me "Felix! Go down to the waterhole, I am waiting for you there." I know what that means. My Mum told me. "He wants you to be the next medicine-man", she says. That's when I left Wangi. Bloody bugger that I am, I want to be a city boy, not a bloody medicine-man. Not much future in that, says I to misself. Maybe I was wrong. Look at me now! A no good-for-nothing bugger.'

His eyes fill with tears. He wipes them and brightens up.

'Got a guitar?'

'An old one, haven't touched it for months. Look under the bed.'

He pulls it out. 'She'll be fine.' As he thrums and tightens the strings, his face acquires a reverential solemnity, completely erasing all traces of drunkenness.

'– I wrote a song about the old man. He saw things, not just people and spirits. My old Gran told me the story over and over, how he saw the chief of chiefs in burning clouds.'

I sit up. 'You mean –?'

'Yeah! He saw the white man's god, Jehovah. He told the old missionary who'd come to the Lake. The Reverend couldn't get over it. I wrote a song about it. The only good thing I ever did. Want to hear it?'

'Sure, go ahead.'

He tunes up. 'Mind you, it's not the same without my backing-group.' He stops, and addresses me as if I were an audience of hundreds. 'This song. It come to me when I was camping near Erraring. I see this flock of pelicans take off, so sudden, it's like the buggers peeled the blue off the Lake, you know, just like paint under blowtorch. That's when I got this song. It tells the story of my Mum's uncle, I only knew him when he got to be a close-up-dead old man; this song is about when he was still an elder, when he saw this vision in a dream. I dedicate this song to him. The song is his, because I take it he's singing through me.'

Felix sings. His voice is strong; he pauses now and then,

underscoring the refrains, in a softer mode, giving them a country-western lilt. Each phrase is charged with an intense emotion that makes me uneasy:

'Lying on the shores of Nikkinba
'I am dreaming of the night on the mountain
'Still dreaming—
'Still dreaming of the night on the mountain
'Sugar-Loaf Mountain,
'Where we fell
'Where we fell, where we fell
'From the burning red clouds
'Where we saw, where we saw where we felt
'The sweep of eagle-hawk's wings
'Of a man in a clothing of fire
'When we stood in the burning red clouds
'Where we saw and trembled
'At the sweep of his fiery wings
'At his searching scorching eyes
'Then we fell from the burning red clouds
'If you have ever seen
'What we had seen
'If you have ever shook
'As we had shook
'At the sweep of those fiery wings
'At those searching scorching eyes—
'Lying on the shores of Nikkinba
'Dreaming, dreaming, trembling
'Dreaming, dreaming, trembling
'Till your dying day —'

He stops and rises abruptly. 'Got to go. Thanks, mate. See ya.'

He fumbles around in his trouser pocket and not finding whatever he is looking for, turns to me. 'Shit! I've lost it.'

'Lost what?'

'Kat's card. She give it to me.'

I can barely contain my surprise. 'Are you seeing her?'

'Sure. She's is a beaut kid. I am helping her out. You know. Mr Odd-Job.'

One would have thought I was jealous, the way questions rushed out from me.

'When? Where?'

'She's going up to the Myalls for a photo-session, didn't she tell ya? I know the mob up there. Lot of gear to lift too, I said I could help. But shit, I don't know where I lost the bloody card!'

He starts shifting things from off the coffee table and finds the card under a beer-can.

'See ya! Take care!'

Felix departs, slamming the door.

11

East-South-Eastward Ho!

Uncle KDR hates flying.
Not that he has any fear of flying.
No, no, not at all. He has his own helicopter, JATAYU.
And when the mood takes him, he flies JATAYU with great aplomb.

'On the eagle-wings of my JATAYU I can soar and sweep down on whatever or wherever I choose. Soaring aloft on a helicopter is a sport fit for a prince, one better than hunting a tiger, chasing a buck with cheetahs, or even sticking a wild pig. What is there to be gained by being *cabin'd, cribb'd, confin'd* in a tin box, cosseted like an invalid by unctuous attendants with their polystyrene smiles? No! Jet travel is not for me! No, definitely not!' — So Uncle would silence any member of the family who dared to suggest air-travel to any destination. He would not hear of it, not Uncle KDR.

Mind you, he was only telling part of the truth; not even telling the truth, more like disguising it. We all know the real reason why he refuses to board a plane, if he can possibly avoid it.

It is a feud, a vendetta, a long drawn-out bout with the gods of the air, a smouldering quarrel with a nameless enemy.

It was a plane, so Uncle KDR is convinced, that took his beloved uncle and my grandfather, Vikram. Handsome, brave Prince Vikram, so fired up with visions of a glorious rejuvenation for our perishing kingdom of Ratnapuri, who was snatched off by some evil god of the air in the prime of his life.

It was a plane that killed our beloved Netaji whom Prince Vikram adored. Who knows, they might even have been together when that plane burst into a ball of fire!

No one knows for sure how or where Prince Vikram died. All we know is that he had joined Bose's forces in Burma and had been the beloved leader's confidant. Doesn't it naturally follow that Prince Vikram would lay down his life for his Netaji and our country's freedom?

For Uncle KDR, planes have become abhorrent for yet another reason: an irksome factor, but nonetheless a constant reminder of his sad fate. If jet-travel hadn't become so popular, we would not have to put up with the hordes of tourists that have no taste, no glamour, no grace, no discrimination and who fill the sacred precincts of our palace with their inane chatter, and leave behind a trail of empty cans, paper cups, sweets-wrappers, and disfigure our marble pathways with blobs of abominable gum. It makes me livid, much as I try to be tolerant ...

Still, I wouldn't be telling you the truth if I didn't confess that I envy those tourists. At least they can get out. As for me, I am trapped; in a silken cage, but nonetheless, a cage. The only path to freedom is an arranged marriage to some nincompoop and I cannot tolerate even the idea of it. So I fret and fume, dreaming of distant lands.

— But then that letter comes, by special delivery, from somewhere in Australia called Wahroonga, and from a firm of solicitors we never heard of and with names that make me hysterical: Rowlatt and Roy. What kind of an unfortunate person must he be who has to go around with that infamous name? For God's sake, how can anyone ever forget the Rowlatt Act and the massacre at Jalianwalabagh?... As for Roy, he could be Scottish — but more likely to be Bengali. Come to think of it, my cousin Jayadev used to know a Bengali Roy in his student days, yet Bengali Roys are not hard to find in any part of the world. Whoever these solicitors are, it doesn't matter much: with names like that and being solicitors to boot, I'm sure they are dull as tepid tea at an embassy garden-party. What the letter brought us, brought me, to be specific – no point in being coy about it – was the news that was indeed a surprise, a monumental surprise I should say, to me and to Uncle KDR.

An *inheritance*.

I have been declared heiress to a vast property somewhere in Northern New South Wales – a 'station' as they call it there, with homesteads and such things – all left to me by someone we didn't know existed, but whose name made him instantly recognizable: Robert Gordon, a descendant of the Gordon family of my much maligned grandmother, Prince Vikram's consort, Alice Gordon. This Robert Gordon, 'the deceased' in law-speak, was an artist of some repute, who lived in a commune of dubious reputation, had made a great deal of money with his paintings – I heard Ganga Rao, whom Uncle set to work on fact-finding, gasping at the sums that a Gordon landscape could fetch at Sotheby's ... Well, rich this Robert Gordon was, but married he was not. He seems to have extended his property as far as he possibly could, a vast stretch that sprawls somewhere north of a river named Clarence – I looked it up in my atlas, it has ever such attractive curves and twists, I think I shall adore it. I already adore its name: Clarence. I expect it has nothing to do with that unfortunate Duke of Clarence who was drowned in a butt of malmsey, but I cannot help thinking of this river flowing with red wine – though from what a grim Ganga Rao told Uncle, it was more likely to have been blood. Still, from what we can see from Gordon's paintings (Ganga Rao managed to round up some exhibition catalogues) my river looks beautiful, just like our Kaveri, serene and sacred. No wonder the inmates of the commune don't want to leave. Everyone in the commune – it seems that our cousin Gordon had a fair number of hangers-on – they must all have had a very nasty shock when the will was read. Their bohemian patron, whom presumably they had always revered as an exemplary communist in a country of crass capitalists, turned out to be a covert royalist! What else would they think when they heard that Comrade Gordon, who had professed the commune to be his family, nevertheless had made sure that all his wealth went to a blood-relative, to a distant Princess in India whom he had never met or even corresponded with, but who, by the tortuous logic of history, happened to be his only living descendant?

When Uncle KDR read the letter out to me, he went very silent at first, as if he were taking a deep dip in our temple tank. Then he emerged, refreshed by a dive into his storehouse of memories. His face brightened, floodlit by a sudden vision. 'Well, my dear Indrani!' He spoke gently and with an energy in his voice that I had not heard for a long while. 'My dear child! God is indeed good to us, the stars are certainly benevolent. This is indeed an auspicious new beginning for us – for you and for me. After all those fruitless searches of mine during my sojourn in Europe – Bhagvan knows how hard I tried to make peace with those Gordons! And I had to do it secretly, my dear, for the elders had never really accepted that marriage. But, alas, no success: bitterness on both sides! Your grandmother's relatives were either too snobbish to bother with a brown face, even a Prince's, or those who knew something of the circumstances of Alice's death and Prince Vikram's war efforts were too livid even to speak to me. I cannot tell you how this letter overwhelms me! After all these years to hear a friendly voice – alas, no voice but just a relayed message! I would have very much liked to have met this Robert Gordon. What a sad loss! So rare these days to find a man with true *pietas*.'

'I wonder why he didn't contact us?' I ventured. 'He could have. Clearly, he knew all about us. Why didn't he then?'

'That we shall find out, shall we not?' Uncle KDR's eyes were twinkling. I could see some Shakespeare surfacing and I wasn't wrong.

'– *There is a tide in the affairs of men* – and so forth . . . Are you ready for a little travel, my dear – a voyage, East-South-Eastward Ho?'

'Uncle!' I jumped up and hugged him. 'You mean, we are to go to Australia?'

'Yes, I do indeed. But the usual stipulation applies.'

*   *   *

That was about six months ago. Little did I think that when old Hari brought that message and I ran to the library, with my dupatta flying and Jeevesamma cackling after me, comb in hand, little did I dream that I would be standing on this scorching deck and gazing at this limitless span of blue.

Not just the sea but everything else seems to have become stretched. Time too. It must be just a week ago — it feels like aeons — since we boarded this ship, predictably named *Orient Empress*, at Bombay. I had to wait till we got to Penang to step ashore, for Uncle KDR had vetoed any foray into Colombo: 'I have no wish to tempt any of their Tigers' was all he had said and Ganga Rao relayed the message in plainer terms: 'Too risky, Little Princess! Too, too dangerous for any of us, and most of all for your beautiful highness! You cannot, you must not step ashore, totally out of the question! I beg you not even to think of it, Little Princess!'

So bang went my dreams of a trip up to Kandy to pay my respects to the Buddha! While all the other passengers tripped out, I had to sit it out in my cabin, chafing at the bit. Penang was OK but hearing so many Tamil voices in the background made me feel that I hadn't yet left home. Singapore should have been better; I ought to have rejoiced at the tidiness of the place and the briskness of the people — yet I felt sad. Something was awry, as if the whole city had got tetchy with its own success and needed a catastrophe or a nervous breakdown or something to regain some feeling. I was not sorry to leave Singapore yesterday. I hope we have something better at our next port of call. The least I hope for is a chance to see a sun-bathing Komodo dragon. I have heard so much about them.

Now we are cruising somewhere on the South China Seas. Could be anywhere as far as I am concerned, for all I can see is water and more water. Nothing in sight, unless you count the odd bit of plastic rubbish that bobs up even here. Just a vast stretch of nothingness; nothing much happening, or is expected to happen — unless, of course, we run into pirates, for these seas, so Captain Souros tells us, are awash with pirates. – As for all those cheap CD players, ghetto-blasters, computers and VCRs that our passengers were frantically buying up in Orchard Road and some of them dumb enough to wonder why the guarantees were missing – well, shall we say, strictly speaking, those goods had no business being in those stalls at all?

To be frank, this voyage so far has been rather dull. It is not what I had in mind at all. I had hoped – foolishly, now that I think about it – I had hoped that we might be on a tall ship, something like the *Cutty Sark* or at least a *Søren Larsen*: on some elegant brigantine where I could play sailor, stand watch, take a turn at the helm, even climb the rigging to hoist a sail or two. Why not? – Alas, no such luck. Not a chance in a million of anything daringly romantic or adventurous in this floating resort. There is nothing empressy about this utterly safe tub. – It doesn't bother Uncle KDR, because all he has to do is channel-hop from the present to the past: out from the incredible treasury that is his memory comes story after story about the exotic days of sea-voyaging – all lovingly recollected to regale our captive captain and to refurbish this dull dowager of a ship. Uncle KDR is totally immersed in the world of the great liners; he talks about the 'three-stackers' and the 'four-stackers', knows the tonnage and speed of each and every one, and who carried the blue-riband, when and how long, and what precisely happened to the likes of *Mauritania*, *Lusitania* and *Aquitania*. And he turns positively reverential when he talks about his favourites: the 'Great Queens', as he likes to speak of *QE I* and the *Queen Mary*.

No, it doesn't trouble Uncle KDR that we are actually marooned in glorified suburbia, a floating playground, buzzing with an unusually ugly bunch of humans: a motley crowd of paunchy middle-aged men, hard-faced, flabby females and over-painted oldies, faces like furrowed fields with powder in the cracks. There are a few younger couples, honeymooners or 'good-timers' by the look of them, but no one that I feel any inclination to talk to. Except the captain.

Captain Alex Souros is an Australian – Greek Australian, he says. He is as handsome as a captain should be, and his manners are impeccable. Uncle likes him so much that he has accepted his invitation to visit him in Sydney and meet his wife and children. If it were not for Captain Souros, our evenings would be unbearable. I would rather listen to him or Uncle than attend any of the so-called 'entertainment' that is laid on. Thank God our cabins are a haven. Once we are enclosed within our wing and surrounded by our entourage, it is as if we were back in our palace. Ganga Rao starts fussing around, Vembu mumbles prayers and the other attendants buzz about, making sure of this and that — and if it were not for the slight dip and sway, I could almost forget we are on the high seas. Jeevesamma is so sea-sick — or so she says — that she has taken to her bed and refuses to leave her cabin. I suspect that she is so much enjoying being waited-on all the time, that she has decided to carry out her protest against this whole trip by lying prone — which, however, gives her enormous energy to devise and discharge ingenious gastronomic challenges to the kitchens. Since she is in too delicate a state of health to bother me, let her play her own version of being a maharani on holiday!

— Ah, there goes the sun, dipping down the horizon like an orange football that a weary tropical day has at last kicked between the goalposts. This is the moment I have been waiting for, to see this magical, fiery *plop* — it never ceases to amaze me.

Sundown means cocktail hour. If I don't hurry, Uncle will send out a search-party — or worse still, I might be summoned through a pager, like a lost child at a fair. I shouldn't dawdle, especially as it is our turn to play host to Captain Souros. And I must dress suitably for the occasion — the blue saree, I think.

*   *   *

'Come in, my dear!' Uncle KDR greets me without looking up. He is bent over the desk, a relief-map of India spread out before him. Uncle is busy sticking pins, ribbons and flags.

Captain Souros holds the door open for me. Lifting his cap ever so lightly, he stands to attention, eyes lighting with faint amusement.

'— Good evening, Princess! It is a pleasure to see you again. I hope you had a pleasant day.'

'Yes, thank you, Captain.'

Captain Souros is solidly built yet gives the impression of being swift and agile. Perhaps it is his naval training, or perhaps he is an avid sportsman — maybe even a fanatical swimmer or tennis player. I could ask, but that would make me seem overly interested. Besides, I have no intention of being dragooned into playing tennis.

But I do find it fascinating to watch him. When he smiles, as he does now, his thick, dark eyebrows meet in the middle and knit and twist like a braid. However closely he shaves — he seems to have done so recently — his face looks overcast like a monsoon sky: irrepressible bristles form a patina of bottle-green. If he didn't smile, he could look dour and intimidating — as he might, I suppose, to his staff. I catch a whiff of something subtle and expensive, a CK or Dior aftershave that exudes from his green chin like vapour from moss. The perfume reminds me of my cousin Jayadev, who is also given to dousing himself with such things. — Thank God, Jayadev is not on this voyage with us! Cousin Jayadev, just because he is my cousin-brother, still treats me as if I were a child in pigtails, someone he can tease, bully and patronize. Whereas Captain Souros — well, it is such a pleasure to be treated as an adult. The Captain seems to have perfected the art of being warm and friendly, without being too familiar.

'I am curious to learn about your kingdom,' he is saying. 'You must forgive me, Princess. I cannot say the name. You must help.'

'Ratnapuri.'

'Thank you. I know so little about your country, your kingdoms. Your uncle is enlightening me.'

'— Take a look, Captain!' Uncle summons him to his side with an imperious wave of his magnifying glass. Catching sight of me, Uncle stalls for a fraction, as if he has forgotten something. '— Ah, here you are. I was explaining to the Captain how the British gobbled up our Princely States. Old hat to *you*.' He pauses, clearly wishing to spare me yet another retelling of that sad tale. 'Why don't you assist Ganga Rao ? See to the drinks and so on?'

I edge past them towards the far end of the cabin (which is rather like a motel-room) to where Ganga Rao is ceremoniously arranging snacks on a tray as if for evening puja. I hear Uncle in full-flow once more, having assured himself of the Captain's undivided attention.

'– This is the State of Deccan, the Nizam'a domain – he certainly had a big piece of the cake – and this is Mysore. They were the big league – also Baroda, there in the Northwest. Sayaji Rao of Baroda and his friend the Wodiyar of Mysore were progressive rulers, the British couldn't fault them, hard as they tried, nor could they swallow them, as they did Oudh up there. Great pity that the big three didn't join the Chamber of Princes. It was left to lesser ones like us. – Mind you, Ratnapuri is not inconsiderable, as you can see here: if anything, our lineage is as ancient and unbroken as any they can boast of. All in all, if you add up all the states, large and small, we, the Princes of India, amounted to quite a big presence. There were six hundred of us. Between us we occupied two fifths of the country, well over seven hundred thousand square miles: our subjects formed nearly one third of total India, twice the size of the population of Britain.'

'I had no idea. It must have been quite a challenge for the British.'

'Indeed it was. They courted us, nevertheless: we were a thorn in their flesh. We should have resisted them. We could have, if only we had been in tune with the times. Had we united, had we been of one mind, one accord, one commitment to a grand, progressive vision of the future! – Alas, no, it was not to be.'

'Unity is always a problem. Few people have vision.'

The Captain knows what is needed, and what is more, he sounds sincere. It is easy for Uncle to continue.

'We nearly did succeed, you know. Had the big trio been with us, we would have, I am sure. But they kept out, Mysore, Baroda and Hyderabad, they didn't need the Chamber of Princes. What they forgot was that the Chamber needed *them.*'

'Suppose they had joined you?'

'A very different scenario. We might have had a Federation. Certainly we would have had more backbone, more clout, more bargaining-power. We could have sent the British home, instead of trusting them, as most of us did. Promises were made, you know, almost set in stone – the great Queen's compact, "to respect the rights, dignity and honour of the native princes as our own". No one imagined it would be so easily forgotten. We were naîve enough to believe that the British were an honourable nation!'

'It seems governments make promises only to break them. We see this every day.'

Ganga Rao arrives at Uncle's side noiselessly, bearing a tray of drinks and snacks. Captain Souros pulls out a chair for me.

'– Hullo again! Your uncle's perspective is fascinating. You know, in Greece, there are still people who want our king back.' He hands an orange-juice to me and takes a whisky for himself.

'Thank you. Will that happen? Will Greece accept monarchy, after the colonels?'

'Maybe. The colonels still have sympathisers, I'm sure. Maybe not: we Greeks are passionate about freedom.'

'And how about you, Captain? Do you want your king back?'

I have caught him in a trap. I can tell by the way he takes time to sip his drink. I am not sorry to have caused some discomfiture.

'It's not for me to say. I am Australian. My grandparents came out, started a fruit farm near Griffith, so did my wife's family, only they

94

bought a vineyard. My children are Aussies through and through. You must come to my home, meet my children: Theo is ten and Helen is eight. It will be great for them, to meet a real Princess, and a real king.'

That did it.

I could see Uncle getting moist-eyed. When he gets lachrymose, he reaches for the bard, as others might for a handkerchief.

'*Do not mock me, fellow student.*' To put the Captain at ease, Uncle adds: '– Hamlet to Horatio. What right do I have to call myself a king or speak of my kingdom, when a scoundrel government has deprived us of everything? First they took away our privy-purses, then our privileges – out went the gun-salutes, our right to run our own radio-stations, our hunting-fishing privileges – all snatched away! It's not the loss that hurts most but the crass betrayal! *Ingratitude, how sharper than a serpent's tooth thou art!*

Uncle pours himself another whisky. He is bound to get more maudlin. I must somehow stop him falling into the pit.

I rise and push the tray of snacks towards him. 'Uncle!'

He mechanically picks a potato crisp. 'Yes, my dear?' His glazed eyes brim with a rush of melancholy.

'Uncle! Surely not all is lost. Our people are still loyal to you, Uncle.'

'True, true indeed. But is that enough?'

Rising from his chair, glass in hand, he begins to pace up and down, his lecturing mode:

'Take your case, Captain. You are captain. Of what? Of this ship, of the *Orient Princess*, no less. Suppose they made you redundant, suppose they take your ship away from you, pension you off, everyone still calls you "captain", because they remember. But is it the same? I ask you, is it?'

The Captain shrugs his shoulders.

Uncle continues. 'Of course not. Why? What's the difference? A great deal. A great deal is missing: your ship, your badge of honour, your command, your team, your responsibilities – the trust of those who travel under your protection. A Captain without a ship is only a shadow of a captain. So it is with me. I am just a shadow of a maharajah, a mere *Mr* Maharajah!'

'No, Your-Highness!' Ganga Rao's voice from behind us cuts in. 'Your-Highness is always Your-Highness.'

Uncle laughs; but the tinge of hysteria I detect makes me nervous. I wish Ganga Rao hadn't intervened. As I fear, Uncle relapses further, dredging out darker quotes from the bard.

'*That way madness lies. I shall not be mad, fool! I shall not be mad.* – Recognize that, Captain? King Lear. Need I remind you what happened to him when he gave up his kingdom?' He laughs again, this time normally: sympathy for Lear dampens his own sense of injury. 'Don't worry! I am not King Lear. I shall not give up. Quite the opposite!'

He sits down and refills the Captain's glass. 'Let bygones be bygones. Let us drink to the future!'

'– To the future!' We raise our glasses. Uncle has come full circle. He is positively merry now.

'Ratnapuri is on the move! We shall found a new kingdom, a new Ratnapuri, on the banks of Clarence River, in Northern New South Wales. Bhagvan willing, our kingdom shall be a model, a paradigm for all kingdoms to come, for truly I believe the pendulum is swinging back again. Democracy will die of mediocrity, and monarchy will return all over the world, and Ratnapuri shall be the harbinger of that new dawn! Let us toast the kingdom to come: Ratnapuri, revised edition!'

As he raises his glass and we clink glasses together, Uncle's face is suffused by a golden light from the setting sun.

12

Suppose it Really Happens ...

A wailing melody from an elderly Chinese busker's *erhu* reverberates down the railway tunnel that takes me from George Street to Surry Hills. My eyes have barely recovered from the impact of the psychedelic mosaic-murals that cover the walls of that tunnel, when a cocktail of odours hits my lungs: chemical residues from clothing factories and leather-goods outlets, diesel fumes, ground coffee, fried fish and falafel. The address on my slip of paper turns out to be a dingy building sandwiched between a Thai noodle-bar and a grimy-glamorous Lebanese restaurant that offers a belly dancer for Saturdays and special functions. I follow the rainbow-serpent that sprawls up the wall along the stairs; its flickering tongue points towards the door of Koori Chic.

'Come in! The door is open.' Katarina's voice is tinged with weariness. She is seated on a swivel chair, with her back to the door; she swings round, and starts as if she had seen a ghost.

'– Ziggy! Well, I'm damned! You look –,' she stalls, '– You look so hollow, so *scooped out*! You're not on some zany diet or something, are you? Where have you been? It's been months and months!'

'I was called away on an assignment.' – I should have thought ahead. Now I have to brew up an instant lie, some plausible tale to cover my tracks.

'You could have told me.'

'I know. But you know how it is: rush of the moment – and once I get away, I get so involved.' My voice, unusually hectic, might give me away, but she seems ready to swallow anything.

'Where did you go this time?'

'Vanuatu, following the tracks of the rebels.' I don't know why I conjured up Vanuatu: somehow its proximity to our shores makes it seem less of a lie.

'Oh! – I wondered. I suppose you don't know about Dad.'

'I'm sorry, Katarina. I just discovered. My feet take me to Café Gregorio automatically, after a spell away. I'll miss the old man. He was a fine character, and such an excellent storyteller. I loved listening to him. He always seemed so well, almost indestructible. What happened?'

'True. He never missed a day at the Café, still his ticker wasn't too good. His doctor sent him for a by-pass. Things went wrong after the op. A week later he was dead.'

'I'm sorry, deeply sorry. Must have been hard for you.'

Guilt-twinges begin to bite, despite my resolve to keep them at bay. Already at the Café, I had a foretaste of them when I first heard of Signor Rossi's death: from some surly youth, who was wrestling with a jammed cash-register.

'Dad's death was bad enough, worse was the funeral. Bloody awful Sicilian circus! They came out of the woodwork, all those uncles, aunts and cousins I'd heard about but never seen. None of them had come to Mum's funeral! They hated her – she was Aussie, not of their *blood*. Do you know, they even argued with Dad about letting Mum share their precious bloody family-tomb? Now they turn up, all black up to the hilt, *Cara-Katarina-mia*-ing me, and all the time sharpening their claws for the pickings. You'd think Dad was some mafia-millionaire, the way they poked and prodded. Yet it's they who live in Maroubra-Beach mansions! Dad never managed more than a hovel in Leichhardt! I've had enough of their sentiment and hypocrisy. I'm sick and tired, bloody exhausted!'

'I bet you are. – Shall we go for a drink? Better still, it's past noon, why not a leisurely lunch on the waterfront somewhere? I haven't forgotten my promise.'

'Made six months back?' She pushes her chair back and stands up, facing me, arms akimbo. 'Ziggy Martin! I don't understand you. You promise to take me out, then you disappear, not a word from you; it's as if I don't exist. Then you march in and ask me out, just like that?'

'Is that wrong? Better late than never, as they say.'

'Don't you see? Perhaps you can't. I don't want your pity.'

'Pity? Heaven forbid! I am not pitying you, Katarina, I am pleading. Give me a chance to make amends. I feel terrible about missing the old man's funeral, not being there to help you. I'm sorry. You look worn out, so am I. A dinner might set us right. Won't you accept?'

She drops her arms and shrugs her shoulders. 'OK. Maybe you're right.'

'Where shall we go?'

'Wherever. I don't care.'

'What about Doyle's? I love the harbour view. But I forget – you don't care for sea-food.'

'I dare say I'll find something I can't smell, even in Doyle's. It's worth it for the waterfront. – Give me a sec.'

She disappears into a side room.

I have never visited her office before. It is ominously deserted. Perhaps it is the day off for her staff. Looking around, I see tell-tale signs: bare walls, half-filled cardboard cartons, piles of unsorted papers, sketchbooks, charts, fabric-samples, design cut-outs and heaps of glossies. I can smell imminent removals.

Katarina returns: her skin glows and her hair shines in bright coppery coils. She ventures a smile, seeing my eyes running over her. 'OK. Lead on.'

'Are you moving out?'

'Yeah! Winding-up, in fact. I can't make it. It's tough in the fashion-business. I'm losing too much money. With no Dad at the Café, I'll soon be totally broke.'

'Who's running the Café?'

'Antonio. My nephew. He's leasing it.'

'A little dour, isn't he, for the job? Couldn't get much out of him.'

'That's because he's a recent arrival. The poor bugger hasn't got much English. But he's not yet poisoned by the black-brigade. He was in some trouble, after some street shoot-out. Dad got him out of Palermo. You could say I'm stupid, handing the Café over to him. But least he's keen and he can cook, Dad had trained him.'

'Glad to hear that. Café Gregorio is still the best place for a marinara. But I'm sorry about you having to pack up this venture. I thought it was exciting, adventurous, worthwhile.'

'Did you? – Why didn't you help me then?'

'You know –'

'Yes, yes. I know. Not your line of work, etcetera, Strange! I'm not sorry to see it go. It was like a game. And I got hit from both ends. My Koori staff said we were playing up to white-folks' fantasies. And I had trouble persuading my white buyers that Koori could be "chic".'

'What are you planning to do?'

'Don't know. Might head north. Now that Dad's gone, there's nothing to hold me here. A friend of mine is opening a gallery-café up at Byron Bay, wants me to join her. I might give it a go. What about you? I still can't believe it, you looking so gaunt. How did you do it?'

'Let's eat first. I'll tell you.'

Doyle's at Circular Quay is bustling with the latest shipment of tourists disgorged by the *Oriana*. A shaven-headed waiter who recognizes me flounces towards us and, with great flourish, seats us at a table overlooking the water. As I run my eyes down the menu I suffer another twinge of guilt.

'It's not too late, if you'd rather eat somewhere else.'

Katarina picks up her menu, gives it a cursory glance, and flings it down. 'Don't worry. There's always something crumbed and smothered for the likes of me.' Throwing her head back to let the breeze caress her tresses, she takes a deep breath. 'It's heavenly to sit here. I haven't been out much, too busy, cooped up with my creditors and account-books. – It's no joke, mate: what is there to smile about?'

'Just thinking how lively your hair looks in this autumn sun, whether I could get that same effect with my lighting.'

She smiles. 'Thanks. I'd forgotten how lovely it is just to sit and watch the boats, listening to the water going plop-*plop*. It makes me so relaxed I could go to sleep. But, I'll keep awake, since I have the rare pleasure of your company.'

The waiter returns with our orders: a chilli-crab salad for me and something indistinguishable in a mornay sauce for Katarina. After he departs, I refill our glasses with the Wyndham's Verdello that sits chilling in a bucket. Katarina clinks glasses.

'Cheers! So, tell me. What was it like out there?'

'Where? – Oh, you mean Vanuatu? Fine.'

I pick up a crab claw, crack it open and busy myself with teasing out its tenacious white flesh.

She watches me for a few seconds.

'Is that all you can say? You look shattered. What happened to you? Did they torture you or something?'

Dare I risk it? Dare I tell her what has been really happening for the past few months, what or Who has been torturing me? Shall I tell her that this dinner out is a brief interlude, which might get interrupted by summons from that inexorable voice?

'Well, in a manner of speaking, I *was* tortured. Seeing people suffering, being just a witness, feeling the pain yet unable to do anything about it – all that is torture in itself, wouldn't you say?'

'But you must be used to it by now, like nurses in intensive-care wards.'

'Some hospitals have "screaming-rooms" for nurses. You never quite get used to it. I still get nightmares about Phenom Penh.'

'Surely Vanuatu isn't as bad as Cambodia?'

'Pain is the same wherever you see it, whatever the cause. We're never far from it, if only we choose to stop, listen and see. That's what I am discovering. The other day, I saw this woman when I went for a walk –'

'Hang on! Didn't you say you had just returned from Vanuatu? How long have you been back?'

Bad slip. Besides, I am getting tired of covering-up, and the isolation.

Seeing me silent, she continues, in a surprisingly calmer tone.

'You were lying, weren't you? You didn't go to Vanuatu at all.'

I put the claw down. 'You're right. I didn't go anywhere. Something has been happening to me. I can't talk about it without sounding crazy.'

'Go on! Take the risk. I won't certify you. More to the point, I won't laugh, I promise.'

'Not here. Let's go to my flat. I'll make you some coffee. And I'll try. — Waiter!'

'Good!'

* * *

While I pour steaming espresso into two cups, Katarina calls out from my bedroom.

'I see you've been busy. What a fantastic collection!'

'You think so? — Your coffee is ready. Sugar?'

'Yes, please.'

I join her. She is arched over, half-bending and stretching, in some aerobic-exercise posture, while apparently absorbed in studying the smaller figures that cover the lower part of the wall. I am tempted to prop the coffee cups on her shapely, jutting behind, tight in black lycra pants. While I linger, savouring the moment of desire, she straightens up.

Her face wears a look of total innocence as she picks up her cup.

'Thanks! I must say I'm glad to see whole bodies for a change. Incredibly interesting faces! Where did you take them?'

'Right here, in central Sydney.'

'I can't put my finger on it, they look normal enough, yet there's something eerie about them, something unnerving. It's as if – I don't know.'

She turns back towards my portrait gallery which covers an entire wall.

'– Go on! Tell me what you see.'

'Grief? Despair? Fear? Loneliness? They all look crushed: yet there's something strong, something spiritual about them. Your lens has caught them waiting, waiting for – I don't know what. Like people outside law courts. For all I know, they might be. Are they?'

'No.'

'What are you doing with them? A doco?'

'No. Maybe a book. There's a story to each one of them. That's not the reason why I took them. I had no choice.'

'They sure look chosen. I love this one, this woman with her dog. Beaut Labrador ! I'd love one like that.'

'That's Leila and Bruno. She was the first. It happened soon after that party you took me to.'

'KK's ? Don't wish to remember it. I was a disaster. You weren't much better, either. Stings my brain even to think about it.'

'I felt sick for days afterwards. Not just the booze I'd had but everything I had seen and heard made me sick to the core. I wished I were back in Cambodia, back with life in the raw – brutal, bizarre, unpredictable and painful but alive, alive all the time.

'You press-guys are all the same, you glamorize horror.'

'Do we? Or do we just give a kick in the butt to the smug and the affluent at what they choose to forget? Anyway, I'm not here to defend the press. I felt lousy. I needed to defoliate, to shed the scum of so-called "civilized" life.'

'Now you sound like a drum-beating, male-bonding, New-Age nutter.'

'Nutter I am, no doubt, but not that kind of nutter. You know very well I'm barely sociable, let alone clubbable.'

'Sorry.' Suddenly she darts towards me and plants a quick peck on my cheek.

She moves away but I pull her back, seek out her lips and kiss thirstily. She relaxes in my arms, nestling her head against my chest. I tighten my grip. She resists and wrenches herself free.

'– Don't! Don't do that to me. Don't let me be a fool again. I know you don't want to.'

An awkward silence fills the space between us. I feel angry: with her or with myself, I cannot tell. She seizes her handbag and starts rummaging.

Perhaps she is right. Perhaps I should let her go, and once again retreat into a corner of my lonely den and lick my sores.

I flop on my bed. '– Would you rather leave?'

She looks up, having composed herself. 'No, no. A promise is a promise. I'm here to listen, listen I shall. I don't have to say it but I do care about you. So, *please!*'

She looks prim and proper, her back upright against the chair, hands folded on her lap. I feel like an errant, spotty teenager who has been sent by the head-teacher to a school counsellor. The taste of her lips is still fresh. If I shut up now I might lose her forever.

'Where was I? – Yes. I set off to see this journo friend of mine, Josh. He had given it up, married a Thai girl and opened a spice-shop in Rozelle.'

'Which one?'

'*Rama-Aroma*. I chose the name.'

'That one. *The Herald* gave it a plug in "Short-Black".'

'Deservedly. — Isn't it ridiculous?: I needed to sniff the aroma of that shop: galangal, lemon-grass, dried fish, holy basil. It did the trick. A bowl of noodles with Josh and Lily, sitting among the sacks of rice, crates of spices, it was wonderful. I raced home, picked up my camera and wandered aimlessly, just glad to be alive again. It was a beautiful afternoon, windy but glorious spring light, with jacarandas shedding purple confetti. I ended up near the old power station in Balmain.'

'Is it still there? I thought they'd knocked it down. Dad used to rave about it. He said he found the best wild fennel there, in the grass around. I wonder if it still grows!'

'Sure does. When I got there the grass had just been cut. I saw clumps of crushed fennel all over the place — the smell was heady. Then I saw *her*.'

'What did you say her name was?'

'Leila. She was sitting on a ledge, knees pulled up, chin resting on them. She was very still — except, every few minutes, she would throw a stick for her dog to fetch: her hand moved mechanically, otherwise she was totally abstracted. Then it happened. Something snapped shut inside me, like a door being closed. I felt locked in. And I heard this voice.'

'Voice? Whose voice?'

'I've heard it a couple of times before, this voice. It is not anyone's, not mine either, yet it speaks to me, clear as a bell. And there's no escaping it. It is a voice with authority.'

'What does this "voice" say?'

'Commands me to see her story, her anguish.'

Katarina's eyebrows arch.

'– I know I sound crazy. I warned you. I'd better stop.'

'No, no. You can't stop now, not allowed to. Go on! *Please!*'

'It was as if I'd been given the key to her psyche. I could tell what was going on there. – It was no pleasure-trip, I assure you.'

'Glad to hear it. What did you "see"?'

'At first it was vague. She seemed all tangled up, like someone trying to unravel a ball of knotted twine. She was being hideously looped and strangled. As I clicked away, I could see better. I could tell she was or had been a ballet-dancer. Married. Perhaps two children. Clearly well off. There was a legal aura about her. Her husband, I was convinced, was some big-wig in a city law firm. Dream-couple, envy of Balmain yuppies. Yet something was rotten at the core, so rotten that she was on the brink of suicide.'

'Do you mean to say that you photographed this woman and she poured out her secrets to you?'

'Not at all. I wish it was that simple. No. I told you before, I saw her secrets before I exchanged a word with her, like a preview. It wasn't just plain seeing but feeling the agony she was going through. Rough trip.'

Katarina goes quiet, starts inspecting the state of her nails.

'– Did you talk to her?'

'Eventually. She realized I had taken pictures of her and was very annoyed. I apologized. She mellowed, and wanted a copy, especially of Bruno, the dog. She didn't want it sent home, so we arranged to meet at the same spot.'

'How nice for you!'

'I shall ignore that. – I met her, gave her this photo. Then I ventured to ask her if she was O.K, if the crisis was over. She turned red: embarrassment, anger, I couldn't tell. Instead of saying, "What crisis?" she bursts out. "How do you know? *What* do you know? Are you a snoop? Has he sent you? I could scream rape."'

Katarina laughs.

'I'm not surprised. Serves you right!'

'I calmed her down. I bluffed. I told her that a friend of a friend had said something about a Leila and her marriage running aground.'

'Sure someone hadn't?'

'Of course not.'

'Then?'

'She bought it. I got bolder – rather, I was prompted. You see, I had to test it.'

'You mean –'

'The voice. Whether it was genuine, whether I was going bananas. So I said to Leila: '"Why suicide? Why don't you just leave him?"'

'Did she slap you in the face? She should have.'

'I'm sure I deserved it, but she didn't. Her response was: "Strange! When I caught you taking my picture, I felt pulled back, preserved, at least for the time being. I know I should leave him, but I have no obvious excuse and I'm a Catholic. Then there are the children. How can I? I feel paralyzed. I feel frozen alive."'

'– Bugger you! You've got me feeling sorry for her.'

'I felt I ought to cheer her up somehow, but I couldn't. What I saw confirmed her sense of doom.'

'What a miserable seer you are! What did you do?'

'Nothing. Just stroked the dog.'

'Stroked the dog? Sure it wasn't Leila?'

'Please, Katarina! This is no time for jealousy. I wasn't involved, not in the way you think.'

'Oh yeah!'

'Honest. Believe me!'

'— Is that the end?'

'Not quite. A few days later the phone rang. It was Leila. Her voice came from the depths of hell; "I told you I couldn't. Now I am doomed". Her son had run after his football and been hit by a speeding car. He was in intensive care, fighting for his life.'

'My God! Did he make it?'

'He was in a coma. She thought he'd pull through. Husband didn't.'

'So you met him?'

'At the hospital. Leila introduced me as the dad of one of her ballet-pupils. The husband looked strangely detached. He looked at his son as if he were just a vegetable: he didn't seem to care if he pulled through or not.'

'Come on! That's horrible! Aren't you a bit biased? Poor bloke! He must have been in shock. You can't always tell how people feel.'

'True. Yet when he spoke, my spine froze. He was so callow, indecently impatient. The law, or rather, *success* at law had got to him. His eyes were glazed as if he couldn't see people, only cases. His son was a "case" with no mileage. He would rather it was over — verdict given, judgement pronounced, damages assessed, court dismissed. He was totally locked-in. All he could think about was the law. He had defended some appallingly nasty cases, was proud of it. I tell you he was so brined in defending the indefensible that he seemed to have lost all sense of right or wrong.'

'My, my! – How can you be so hard on someone you don't know?

'Because I could see quite clearly: and it was true.'

'True? Who says so? This Leila?'

'She didn't say a word about him. She didn't have to. All I had to do was listen to the voice and see.'

'So you keep telling me. As far as I know the only people who hear voices are either prophets or schizos. You don't seem schizoid. I hate to admit it, but I have to believe you: you are a small-time liar – not over something big like this.'

'Thanks!'

'Are you seeing her still?'

'No. Nor do I wish to. I couldn't, anyway. Leila was just the beginning. Every face you see on this wall is there for the same reason. I could go on for days and nights if I told you what happened with each of them. Barely had I coped with one "seeing", another would happen. Always the same pattern, but different stories. I even started praying, pleading to be released from this – I didn't want to see any more.'

'Did it stop?'

'Now and then, I'd get a respite. I want it to stop altogether.'

Katarina gives me a searching look.

'Are you sure?'

'I do and I don't. I have been thinking. Suppose we have to answer to our Maker, supposing He exists — how do we account for ourselves with all these complications of guilt and pain? What sort of a Judgement can there be when we are all so mangled up? — I can't stop going over this.'

'Mmm. — Shouldn't you talk to your Dad?'

'I can guess what he'll say. Too neat. It'd be no help, yet I can't go on like this. I feel seared inside.'

She rises from her chair and sits beside me on the bed. She strokes me as if I were a sick cat.

'Poor you!'

I close my eyes. Her tenderness seeps into my sore tissues, like water trickling down a dried-up creek. She bends down, her hair falling over my face.

'— Glad to see me after all?'

'I had to see you. I saw you too — tired, sad, immensely sad. I rang the flat: got the machine. I didn't have your office address. So I rushed to the Café. A day later, you might have gone.'

Her eyes moisten. 'I might have. The fact is, I am still here.' She rustles my hair. 'You have changed. Remember when I read tea-leaves? You went ballistic. Look at you now! A regular clairvoyant!'

'I don't know how clairvoyants work. I can't see anything by willing it or thinking about it, only when I hear that voice.' I take her hand, and kiss her fingers one by one. '— So you don't think I need a quack?'

'Quacks? I've no faith in them, not after what they did to Dad. Maybe you need a change of scene. Why don't you come with me to the north?'

'I can't just run away. What's the point?'

'Maybe you can get some help. — Let me come clean. This gallery job of mine, that's nothing. I'm going north, really, to find out more about my tribe.'

'The Bundjalung?'

'So you *do* remember! You believed me after all.'

'Why shouldn't I?'

'That makes it easy. You come with me and we'll find a medicine-man. They're bound to have one. He'll sort you out.'

'I don't know if I want to be "sorted out". It's hard: but I am, so to speak, addicted now.'

'No wonder you look shattered! You are burning your innards out, bingeing on people!' She runs her palm over my pulsating forehead. 'And you are hot! What you need is – '

'You.' I pull her down beside me and cover her with kisses. As I sink myself into her warm, soft flesh, I breathe in her loveliness. She smells of orange-blossom. Her thighs grip around me and I feel like a drowning man winched up from a storm-tossed sea.

'What a fool I've been to neglect you, Katarina: *cara Katarina!*'

13
Awakenings and Arrivals

Saturday morning, 10 a.m. New Town is barely awake.

Apart from the few cafés that do breakfast, King Street is as reluctant to stir into life as is Rohan Roy, snugly asleep between cool, black satin sheets in his new home, 'Aloha'.

'Aloha' it had to be: so his partner Ray had decreed, the moment he set his eyes on the three palm trees in front of the house. Palm trees or not, Rohan could see nothing remotely Hawaian about that black-and-white, paint-peeling, three-storied terrace tucked away in a back street of New Town. But his partner's word was law. So he has to live with, live in, 'Aloha'.

They had to move from Wahroonga, so Ray had insisted, when the firm was restructured and relocated in brand-new premises in Pitt Street: a flashy chrome and glass container of a block that had already earned the title of 'cheese-grater' to join other such CBD notables as the 'toast-rack' and the 'egg-slicer'. They were lured into the city by a client of theirs, fast-talking, fast-moving Nikos, who had got the office-block property-market sewn-up between himself and his cousins. Nikos had persuaded Messers Rowlatt and Roy into investing in his latest bid and the reward was a super-plush, sunlit penthouse.

The move to the 'cheese-grater' was just the excuse Ray had been waiting for. It was sheer torture that for five days of the week he had to stay straight-jacketed in black suit and tie, dancing attendance on his millionaire clients who were on their third or fourth divorce and fighting to guard their elusive millions from the hungry jaws of their Bulgari-jewelled, Prada-bagged piranha-wives. 'Yes, sir, no sir', 'We appreciate your dilemma, sir', 'Leave it to us, sir'; 'Yes, madam', 'No, madam', 'We understand how you feel, madam', 'Fair is fair, madam', 'Rest assured, madam'. This litany, chanted at regular intervals to cover up a multitude of dodgy deals, turned his stomach to acid: sometimes, he felt so crook that he feared he might choke on his own vomit. Come Friday evening, he had to cut loose. And where best to let go than in 'Mardigras land'?

Ray knew full well that his partner didn't share his longing. Rohan was comfortable where he was, and as he was, neither fish nor fowl. Timid Rohan would rather stay put in leafy, affluent Wahroonga, where he could camouflage himself as a solidly respectable, middle-class, square-guy. He felt no need to 'flaunt', as he put it. Wasn't it enough that he had let Ray drag him out of the closet, did he have to make a spectacle of himself?

For weeks they argued. While Ray bullied, Rohan sulked. When Rohan turned sultry-insolent, Ray got bitchy-pathetic and both indulged in emotional blackmail, followed by shaky truces. Finally, they ceased fire at Christmas and settled for New Town: near enough to the fleshpots of Oxford Street and Darlinghurst and yet gentrified enough for Rohan to carry on as he wished. And for the sake of peace and prosperity, Ray bombarded Rohan daily with projections of what they could save, in transport costs, in parking fees and above all in time, precious time – until at last Rohan surrendered.

It was the garden that did it. Little did Rohan expect to find in an inner-city suburb such a paradise. Surprisingly large, and so perfectly maintained (unlike the house) and redolent with native shrubs and trees: silky oaks, pepper-trees, grevilleas, bottle-brushes, wattles, and a fabulous ghost-gum that was sheer magic in moonlight. And all echoing to the whistles and screeches of lories, rosellas, budgies, honeyeaters and marauding packs of galahs.

Once he had set his eyes on that garden, Rohan simply couldn't hold out. Secretly he named the garden 'Paradiso'. So long as he could escape into his Paradiso, he could put up with anything.

And he had a lot to put up with. His delicate system wasn't quite ready for the fecund pond-life of the human scene around them. 'New Town has everything', his partner never tired of repeating. 'Boy, oh boy, you have everything here in New Town. What a field, what fabulous choice! Boy, oh boy!' – So Ray slavered, as he jostled amidst the motley crowd that flowed up and down King Street and Enmore Road. And Ray was right, Rohan had to admit. Here, in these crummy streets, there was room enough for every shade and type: straights, squares, gays, transvestites, transsexuals, hippies, crusties, ferals and any other mutant species. Within a few hundred metres, one could meet faces from every nation under the sun: whites, blacks, Celtic blends of both, Koreans, Vietnamese, Thai, Shanghai-Chinese, Hong Kong Chinese, Greeks, Italians, Lebanese, Portuguese, Tongans, Africans and even Bangladeshis – not that Rohan ever felt any need to fraternize with his countrymen. The streets were grubby with ingrained dirt and smelt at once acrid and sickly sweet: a stench of urine and peroxide fumes mingled with the smell of baking bread, pastries and exotic heady perfumes from the incense-strip at the heart of King Street. As for the food, 'Boy, Oh boy', Ray would chuckle: 'Where else would you find miles and miles of cafés, bars, restaurants to tickle your taste-buds? Is there nothing here to tempt you, my pretty prince?' Ray's chuckle would turn into a snarl.

Rohan Roy sticks his head out from under his white duvet, just enough to squint at the streaks of light that refract through slits in the venetian blinds.

He is annoyed.

His smooth olive forehead ripples ever so faintly with creases. Next door, in the sitting room, his partner is clashing and banging, opening and shutting doors, cupboards and chests. And he has changed the music. Gentle tabla rhythms have given way to some raucous tribal drumming. Against their barbarous assault, Rohan can no longer sustain the delicious langour of his fast-fading dream.

Paradiso had become wooded parkland. In the distance, Rohan hears yelping hounds and, as the commotion nears, he registers that he is the target of the hunt. He runs, stripping himself for speed as he darts through thorny thickets, dodging swaying vines that threaten to strangle him. After what feels like aeons, he reaches a stream and wades in; at last the hounds retreat. Exhausted, bruised and blistered, Rohan drifts down the stream which empties into a large pool, covered in bright pink lotuses. On the far side, he spies elephants bathing. He hesitates, but they ignore him and carry on siphoning water with their trunks and spraying themselves and their young. Rohan parts the plate-sized plastic-green leaves to wash himself, and is stunned by what he sees: an exquisitely sculpted taut torso, elegant supple neck, and a smooth-skinned, fine-boned, fine-toned face. No wonder Ray is crazy about him; and Ray is right, after all, to liken him to the Chola bronze they had seen in the window of *Eastern Flair*. As he stands mesmerized, he hears tinkling laughter and anklets jingling. A pair of ivory-coloured, bangled arms encircle him from behind, and slender, hennaed fingers clasp over and close his eyes. He succumbs to their luxuriantly firm grip and lets himself be crushed by a pair of warm, jasmine-scented breasts, heaving in translucent folds of silk. Just as he reaches a pitch of blissful torpor, vile drumbeats crash through and wrench him awake.

'Curse him!' Rohan mutters, 'Curse him and his bloody bongos!'

Abruptly the music stops. Ray shouts from the sitting-room.

'Wakey, wakey, my sweet prince! Come and see what I've found. Perfect for you!'

Rohan yawns. He stretches and yawns again. He repeats this routine till his irritation is fully expelled. Only then is he ready to face his partner.

'– Coming! Let me shower first.'

No doubt Ray has 'found' something 'new'; that means he has found something that in reality is old. Ray is doing what he always does on Saturday mornings: going through the contents of his camphor-chests. He bought a set of them from a Chinese Import-Export guy in Paramatta Road whose dusty-brown shop was vibrant with snarling dragons in red and gold: they writhed and twisted on everything he sold — pots, vases, screens, cupboards, lamp-stands, coffee-tables and tea-sets. For Ray, the dragons on his camphor-chests are guardians of the treasure-trove that he has amassed since boyhood: fancy-dress costumes, masks, flags, berets, caps, scarves, beads, hats, junk-jewellery galore that he pinched from his actress-mother: leather bands, tiaras, feathers, boas, and any number of sequinned shirts, jackets, boleros. Every Saturday morning the 'viewing' of these cherished treasures transforms Ray from an intimidating muscular hunk of forty plus to a vulnerable schoolboy on vacation, playing with his mother's trinkets. And each Saturday, Rohan has to play his part in the charade.

He pulls on his white towelling robe and pushes the bedroom door open.

He finds Ray, as usual, stripped down to his boxer shorts, sitting among his 'treasures' like Ali Baba in the robbers' cave. Rohan manages a smile.

'— So, what have you found this time?'

'Look!' Ray holds out a tinsel-crown and a sash of pink silk. 'Just the thing for you. With a bit of re-touching and some new jewels, and a turban to go round, it'll look perfect on you! Isn't it a great idea?'

'And what, pray, is the occasion I am to disport myself thus?'

'The next parade, of course.'

'The Mardi Gras? We've barely got over the last one, and it is only April.'

'So what? One must think ahead! — And guess what? If you don't like the turban, I have another brilliant idea for a head-gear:

something gorgeous with slit palms, sprayed gold and lacquered –
or it could be silver or gold glitter. I can't tell which will suit you, till
I've tried a few out.'

'You're not thinking of cutting from our trees, are you?'

'Of course I am.'

'Oh no. I can't let you.'

'Come on, my boy, just a few fronds. What harm will that do?'

'I know you and your trials. There will be nothing left.'

'That's unfair.'

'You will ruin the trees! It's sheer vandalism! I won't tolerate it! Not
at any price!' Rohan's voice crescendos to a shriek.

'Come, come! No need to yell at me. I was only thinking of you. I
always think only of you. And you – you–'

'I'm sorry. You know how I feel about the parade. I can't get used to
such exposure.'

'I know. I know. You are ashamed of me. That's it, isn't? And why
not ? Look at me! Look at this ridiculous flesh! How ugly I am!
Ugh! I hate myself. No wonder you hate me.'

'Ray! That's nonsense. You know it is.'

Ray glowers at him through tear-filled eyes. 'Then why are you so
beastly to me, you *bitch*?'

'For God's sake! Calm down. I've had enough.'

'Go on then! Go away, and don't ever come back!'

Rohan marches back to the bedroom. As he pulls on his jeans and

T-shirt, he takes deep breaths. Increasingly he hates the tedium of these rows. If only he had the courage to make a break – but that means tearing away the whole fabric of his life, at work, at home, and facing the harsh world out there all by himself. He is not game enough, not yet, to give up his bodyguard.

He finds Ray sitting on the floor, staring disconsolately at a sequinned scarf. Pity overwhelms him. He puts a hand on Ray's shoulder.

'Sorry, mate! I take back what I said about the palms. Take what you want.'

'No, thank you. You've spoilt it now, shrieking and carrying on.'

'Sorry if I did. I don't know what came over me.'

'Rage! You're a right spoilt brat. And I spoil you!'

'You shouldn't, should you?' Rohan attempts a laugh.

Unsmiling, Ray starts ripping out the sequins from the scarf in a frenzy. Rohan shrugs his shoulders. '–OK. Be like that if you must. I'll see to the laundry, we have a great pile-up.'

'What do I care?'

'Suit yourself.'

Rohan slams the patio door and descends the fire-stairs down to the basement.

The basement resembles a white-elephant stall at a church-fête, cluttered with junk awaiting decisions: lamps, terracotta pots, plastic boxes, buckets, ceramic dishes, plaques, cast-iron candlesticks, wire CD racks, coat-hanger sculptures, bottles, bamboo baskets, tarnished lead-light mirrors and such. But warm sunshine pouring through curtain-less windows infuses into them some glow of cheer; they look as if they are 'sitting' for a still-life session.

Another bright morning, Rohan sees: full of promise, but for the pall of melancholy that overlays his heart. As he shoves sheets and towels into the drum of the Miele, Rohan's mind flips back to other rows. He remembers too well the peace-making routine. Phase one will begin in an hour, around eleven o'clock. Ray will start making coffee, and clang the mini-gong to summon Rohan. Coffee will be drunk over a silent sulking until one 'thank you' from Rohan triggers a staccato tête-a-tête conducted to the tune of rustling newspapers: Ray will explode and explete over Fred Nile, the ABC, John Howard, the GST, his voice steadily getting more hectic as he reaches the sports pages, cussing and admonishing whoever happens to be in the ascendant, be it the Broncos, the Bulldogs, 'the bloody All Blacks' or 'the pathetic mob up North that calls itself the Knights'. After an hour or so of this, during which Rohan's monosyllabic grunts will be read as a truce-signal, phase two will commence. Abandoning their papers, both will embark on a synchronized ballet of housework, underscored by eyebrow-arching remarks aimed vaguely at the ceiling or the floor: 'The cooker is a grease-box', 'The fridge is an iceberg', 'The yard is a rubbish-tip', 'These venetian-blinds are *filthy*'. Casual and calculated bumping into each other in the course of performing tasks will pave the way for phase three. Tired, thirsty and hungry, they will flop on the settee for a beer. A little later, over a bottle of chardonay and a takeaway curry from the *North Indian Diner*, a peace-accord will be signed and sealed in a session of kiss and cuddle.

Today, the very thought of garam-masala sex nauseates Rohan. His dream has opened up a hitherto unexplored seam of his psyche; the softness of bangled arms and the firmness of warm breasts have set him afire with a new longing: body and soul, he yearns for a bone-tingling, flesh-melting, jasmine-scented ecstasy that will catapult him into a freedom that is *pure*.

His throat is dry. He can smell coffee brewing. Soon the gong will go. He is thirsty, very thirsty. He could sneak out to the corner shop for a coke and Danish. Rohan feels his pockets. Shit! He has left his wallet on the bedside table.

He looks around, seizes the bottle of distilled water he keeps for the iron and drinks from it. Then he picks up the basket of garden tools and slips quietly off into Paradiso.

With each snip and cut, each square of raked earth, his spirits revive. A couple of hours of toiling in an even rhythm gets him to the tree-lined north-end of the garden. Time for a break. His stomach is rumbling, yet he is in no mood to spoil his hard-won tranquillity. He feels secure in the garden, especially here, protected by lush bottle-brushes and pepper-trees glistening in the sun.

He stretches out on the grass, locking his arms behind to rest his head and closes his eyes; through the cackle of birds, pure peace seeps into him.

Plop!

'– Shit!'

Warm goo from birds quarrelling overhead. Lorikeets. He should have known; the buggers have got him with their liquid slime, right in his face.

He mops up, but the stink lingers. Now he has to go back to the house. Besides, the trees are getting straggly. He can't tackle them with secateurs alone. He might as well pick up the saw and ladder from the patio and finish the job properly. Rohan rises.

Ominous quiet. Where is Ray? Gone shopping? Gone out to lunch by himself?

As Rohan nears the patio, he hears a rumble of voices. Ray is talking to someone in the kitchen. By his soft, purring tones, Rohan can guess that it is to someone younger, an SBY, a 'shapely-bottomed-youth', no doubt. Rohan creeps up to the patio window, and hiding behind the shutters, listens in.

Suddenly, there is a high-pitched giggle from Ray. Rohan's heart sinks several fathoms deep: he knows too well what that giggle portends. Through the gap between the shutter hinges, he can observe the scene in the kitchen without being detected.

A boy, about fourteen or so, in khaki shorts and white T-shirt is up a ladder; and reaching over the sink, he is cleaning the venetian blinds. Ray is standing behind him, holding the ladder, his blue eyes hungrily devouring the SBY. Tall and slim, the youth has a fine head of blonde-streaked, dark hair; it has been cut high stylishly, but with a cow's lick of a front lock which the boy flicks now and then, Hugh Grant fashion, as he stoops to dip and squeeze the detergent rag. Rohan catches sight of his profile: fine aquiline nose, dark brown eyes and the barest shadow of a stubble.

Each time the youth turns towards him, Ray smiles adoringly:

'—So, where's your Mum's shop?'

'Marrickville.'

'So close! Whereabouts?'

'In the shopping-centre.'

'Great! What's it called?'

'*Hair Fantabulous.*'

'"Fantabulous!" I like that. Great name. Your hair is truly fantastic. I love the streaks, they highlight your dark hair and eyes fabulously! So — what does she charge for a cut-and-tint like yours?'

'Dunno — she's cheaper than any in King Street.'

'Don't mention them! They're shockers, positively rob you for a simple trim and colour. What's more, it doesn't last. Look at me! Look at the state of my roots! Shocking, isn't it?'

The boy turns halfway, still continuing to slide the rag across the slats.

'Dunno. Don't look too bad.'

Ray flicks his fingers dramatically over his greying ginger hair. 'You don't say! Take a proper look! you'll see what I mean. Shocking! – Do you know what Armand charges for this shitty piece of work? A fortune! I tell you honestly, a hundred bucks! Can you believe? The cheek of the man! And look at it! – I bet your Mum can do a better job.'

'Sure!' The boy turns round again, with a faint smile; his cheeks dimple. 'Yeah! Mum's good. I'm sure she won't charge a hundred bucks.'

'That's what I think. Well, my mind is made up. I must change my hairdresser this instant. Goodbye Monsieur Armand! Welcome – what did you say your Mum's name was? Something fabulous in Greek, I bet!'

'Anastasia. Everyone calls her Annie. She prefers that.'

'Annie – such a stylish, homely name. I bet she is a good cook. Your Dad is a lucky man. What does he do?'

'Drives trucks. Long distance. Dad goes to Queensland a lot.'

'You must miss him.'

'Not too bad. He's no talker.'

'Bet your mum spoils you with that lovely Greek food which I simply *adore*! What I wouldn't I give right now for a plate of *mezze*: olives, tarama, some scrumptious dolmades, and chargrilled octopus.'

'I hate that grub.'

'Never mind! You deserve a reward. Don't get me wrong. I don't mean a donation to your scout-group, but to you. You're doing a fantastic job getting the grease off these blinds. I know how hard it is. You deserve a treat! I'm starving, aren't you? I could treat you to a baked dinner, ribs, pizza or whatever you fancy. What do you say to a relaxing lunch somewhere, just you and me?'

'No thanks! I must get going. I've a few more houses to call on.'

The youth turns his back firmly and starts attacking the slats with extra zeal. The ladder shakes.

'– Steady! Take it easy. Don't you dare fall down and break your neck!'

Rohan's heart misses a beat: even as Ray hisses at the boy, he seems to be shaking the ladder.

The youth stops. 'Fuck!' There is blood on his fingers.

Ray steps upon the first rung and leaning against the boy, peers over. 'Look at you! You've cut yourself now. I warned you. These blinds are a nightmare. Come down! Let me check. So much blood! Dear, dear me!'

The youth drops the rag and steps down, with Ray helping him, almost lifting him off the ladder, ready to carry him as though he had fainted. The youth wriggles out. 'I'm OK. I better go.'

'No, no. I can't let you go, bleeding like that. Show me, let me see!'

The boy puts out his injured hand. Ray inspects the cuts; his lips close in on the lad's slender fingers as on asparagus tips and he sucks the blood off. 'There!'

The boy pulls back his hand. His lips tremble and his eyes spit venom. 'You bloody bastard! Who asked you to do that?'

'I'm sorry if I did wrong. I wanted to help. Don't be scared. Nothing to worry about!'

'I bloody well hope so, you bastard!'

'What are you getting so hot about? I meant no harm.'

'Oh yeah? You're a bloody poofter, aren't ya? What if –'

'I swear!' Ray looks steadily into the boy's eyes and his voice lilts soothingly. 'Nothing to worry about. I'm clean. I test negative.'

'Holy Mother!' The boy sighs.

Ray gets brisk. 'Now let me find some disinfectant and band-aid. Come with me, this way.'

The boy doesn't move. 'It's OK.'

'Suppose you need stitches or something. We mustn't take any chances.'

'It's nothing, just a cut. I can manage.'

'I'm sure you can. But it's better if someone else does, don't you think? Much more fun.'

Ray has edged closer to the boy and is blocking him against the ladder, his face reddening.

The boy is cool, decidedly cool. A shrewd, calculating look creeps up his handsome features.

'— Depends.'

'I'll make it worth your while.'

'What if I say I'm under age?'

'Would you?'

'Dunno. — Depends.'

'On what?'

The boy frowns. 'You shouldn't have done it, you bastard.'

'Relax. I'm OK. I'll show you my latest blood-test report if you like.'

'You can?'

'Sure!'

The boy looks around the room. 'Nice place you've got here.'

'It could be yours too.'

The boy tosses his hair back and grins. 'What's it worth?'

'Whatever you say, you name it.'

'What's the trick?'

'Up to you. Take your time.'

'I dunno. You're crazy. I'm crazy to be listening to you. I oughta be going.'

He doesn't move. After a while, he walks round the room, taking up and putting down objects on display, stopping and preening himself at the mantle-piece mirror. Something catches his eye in a magazine holder. He pulls out that morning's colour supplement: a glossy, full length portrait of Madonna in red velvet shines from the cover.

Ray watches him. 'You like Madonna? So do I. Absolutely adore her. She's my goddess!'

'Can I have this picture?'

'Of course, with pleasure.'

Ray eases the staples off and hands over the cover page. '– Are you going to see her?'

'You kidding? Sold out. Even the touts are touting for black-tickets.'

'Would you like to go?'

The boy's face flushes. 'You mean ... ? – You're crazy. Do you know what the bastards are asking for one on the bloody black market?'

'I know. I don't need them. I have a spare ticket.'

The boy's eyes nearly pop out. 'You do?'

'Yes I do. A spare ticket. And I'm in the mood to give it to you.'

'Truly?'

'Truly.'

'Go on! You're having me on.'

'No I'm not. Don't you believe me? Let me show you.'

Ray pushes up the roll-top of the desk and retrieves two tickets. He holds them up high, waving them at the boy from a distance.

'Believe me now?'

'Jesus! It's true.' The boy's eyes go glazed. 'I'd do anything for that ticket.'

'Anything?'

'Anything'. The boy dives towards Ray; but before he can touch the ticket, Ray moves away. They circle the room, Ray baiting the boy with the ticket, now raising it high, now lowering it, while the boy darts at him.

The wire-door of the patio creaks.

Rohan steps in. Ray stops, his face glowing pale and red in turn.

'— You!'

'Yeah! It's me.' Rohan slumps on the settee. 'But you can't give away that ticket. It's mine.'

'But you – you don't like Madonna.'

'Did I say that? What a shame! I do now.'

Rohan turns to the boy, who is shuffling his feet, still staring at the ticket. His eyes move from Ray to Rohan and back to Ray. 'I better be going.'

Ray pockets the tickets and moves swiftly towards the door, coughing and sputtering distractedly. 'No! Wait! – Rohan! Do something. Don't let him go!'

Rohan nimbly gets alongside Ray and pats him on the back soothingly. 'Steady, steady on, my dear chap! The young man wants to leave and I think you should let him. I am sure he is busy.' He turns to the boy. 'Aren't you? – We haven't even been introduced. I am Rohan. I live here. What's your name?' He puts out a hand.

The boy doesn't take it. 'Max.'

'Splendid! No doubt we shall see you again.'

'Maybe.'

Rohan escorts a zombie-like Ray back to an armchair. The boy is lingering by the door. 'Sir!'

'Yes?' Rohan beams at him.

'The donation for the scouts. I did do the job.'

'Of course, I beg your pardon. My friend gets a bit forgetful. Let me see!'

He picks out a ten dollar bill from the charities-tin.

'– Here! How about that?'

'Thanks!'

Once the front door is shut, Ray finds his voice.

'So you came back.'

'In a manner of speaking, yes. I decided it was time I did.'

'Did you? Why?' Ray scrutinizes Rohan. 'Nice boy, Max! Pity you scared him off. It was mean, what you did about that ticket.'

'Was it? I'm sorry.'

'No you're not. Don't fib. You did it deliberately. You wanted to spoil it. You were jealous. Admit it, weren't you?

'Perhaps. But it wasn't that. — Ray! Listen! You could get into serious trouble. The boy is under age.'

'No, he's not, he was just teasing me.'

'Are you sure? I heard what he said.'

'You did? — Did you, you sneak?'

'Listen! You won't believe this: but I was tempted, terribly tempted to let you have him. But I couldn't.'

'And pray, tell me why you couldn't, since you hate me so?'

'I don't hate you.'

'You're tired of me. You can't deny that. Tired, fed up, pissed off!'

'OK. I'm weary. It's not just you. I am sick to death of myself. I long to be something different. I don't even know if I can any more —'

'Then why did you come back? Just to spoil my fun?'

'Your fun? Do you really believe that? For Chrissake, it is another young man going the same way —'

'Thanks a lot! — Max is no saint.'

'Perhaps you're right. Still, he is young. He must have a proper chance to find himself. You can't — you mustn't do that to him.'

'Don't preach to me, buster!'

'I'm sorry.'

Rohan kneels down before Ray and kisses his hand. Ray's lips twitch in a faint smile.

'There was a time you cared.'

'I still do. And I will.'

Ray's eyes moisten. 'Oh, my dear boy! You give me a hard time. Come to me, be nice, won't you? I love you.' He raises Rohan off his feet and hugs him. Over his shoulder, Rohan catches sight of his own face in the mirror: it is the face of resignation, tinged with relief at having averted a disaster. He will have to pay a price, at least for the time being, to save the boy. Slowly and tenderly he eases himself from Ray's clasp, and speaks in lullaby-tone: 'You're fine. We're fine. Just relax. Everything is OK.'

'Is it? Really?'

'Sure!'

'OK, then.'

They sit side by side holding hands silently for a few minutes. Their stomachs rumble in turn, they burst out laughing. Rohan rises and reaches for the phone.

'I don't feel like going out. I'll order a pizza. Pepperoni for you?'

'Yes, please. I'll open a bottle of Chianti. I know you must have Chianti with yours.'

As he waits for Pizza Express to respond, Rohan checks the time.

'— Bugger! When are we due at the Sheraton? I haven't put the papers together yet.'

'Shit! I clean forgot. We've got to do shopping as well. There isn't a thing in the house.'

'Don't worry about that. Do you think this Maharajah bloke keeps Indian time?'

'I suspect he keeps Raj time.' Ray laughs. 'We'd better get there promptly by six. Cocktails, the note says. At least we'll get a drink.'

'What about the Princess? Should we take her something? A bunch of flowers?'

'Great idea !' Ray wags a finger at Rohan. 'Be careful! You've sent Max packing, don't you desert me now! Don't you dare fall in love with this Princess !'

'Fat chance! — Cheers!'

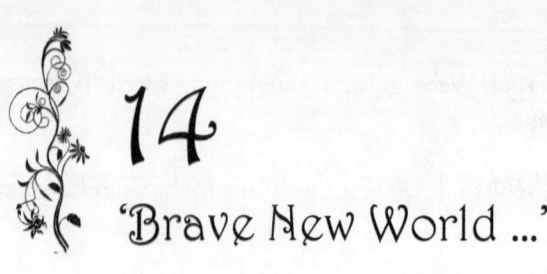

14
'Brave New World ...'

O brave new world, that hath such people in it!
My beloved niece Indrani calls to my mind that other Princess *non-pareil* whose enviable innocence found everything marvellous. Like Miranda, my Princess is all agog with wonder and delight ever since we docked at Circular Quay yesterday evening. I must confess that even I had to struggle to hold back my tears as our *Orient Princess* sauntered into the harbour just as the sun was setting. What greeted us was a veritable symphony of colour and movement: fairy-floss bales of curled clouds drifting across lofty blue skies, surging inky waters foaming white around rollicking sail-boats, agile jet-cats cutting a swathe and leaving a turbulent wake for meandering ferries to wobble in; and the white-tiled sails of the Opera House turning a mother-of-pearl pink in the setting sun – all to the tune of a myriad bird-calls from among the green belt of park and bush-land that girds the banks of the harbour inlet. – Oh, how I wish I had the bard beside me! Alas, I lack his eloquence! So much heart-warming beauty, serenity, vibrancy, vitality – I felt overwhelmed and moved to tears. So I did the only thing I could do: before we disembarked I prostrated towards the setting sun and recited the *gayatri: Tat savitur varenyam bhargo devasya dimahi ...*

We are now in the Sheraton on the Park. This suite is adequate and the view from my bedroom is pleasing enough. The floor is still swaying under my feet, as are the trees in the park that I overlook. I shall find it hard to get accustomed to the reversal of seasons, to think of April as autumn, August as winter and December as summer. Changes in perspective ordained by Mother Nature I am ready to accept, why, I even find the challenge invigorating: but I cannot dredge up any zest for what I see in the cityscape. I do not like the look of the concrete-and-glass blocks around: veritable towers of Babel and Mammon that jostle with each other to suppress light, air and men, each aspriring to new heights in their vulgar pretension. I am resolved never to allow such aberrations in Ratnapuri II. This hotel, bearable though it is with its plush decor, polished timber and soothing colours, is infected with shades of that commercial chic that dampens one's spirits. The sooner we get to the open country, our Clarence-fed territory, the better: I shall see to it that our stay here is but short. Nevertheless, I should thank Messers Rowlatt and Roy for booking us in here rather than at that grey monstrosity we passed – which I believe is the Hilton.

Messers Rowlatt and Roy are late. Clearly they do not abide by British punctuality. I am not sure what rules, if any, Australians observe. But it comforts me to think that they are a nation that plays cricket, and does so creditably: there is hope yet.

Ganga Rao enters, coughing as usual.

'Our guests are here, Your-Highness.'

'Good! – and the Princess?'

'The Princess is not back yet, Your-Highness.'

'Where did you say she went?'

'Queen Victoria Arcade, not far from here, Your-Highness. Ayah is with her and also the peon. I have instructed Ramgopal to bring her back safely, and strictly by six o'clock.'

'It's 6.20 now.'

'Yes, Your-Highness. But I am sure the Princess will be here soon. She knows we are expecting guests.'

'Summon her. I presume she took the mobile.'

'Yes, Your-Highness. I made sure.'

'One more thing before you go, Ganga Rao. I may need your help in clearing up a delicate matter. Be alert!'

'Most certainly, Your-Highness.'

* * *

At first glance my guests strike me as an intriguing pair: 'strange bedfellows', as the bard might say. Mr Roy has fine bone-structure and a smooth skin, and that easy elegance one might expect of a cultured Bengali youth. Besides, he is well-groomed and well-mannered. He wears a red rose in the buttonhole of his oatmeal, raw-silk jacket, and carries a sumptuous bunch of red roses — presumably for my niece. He is the first to greet me and I cannot but notice how deftly he avoids addressing me either by name or title.

'Welcome, sir, to our glorious city of Sydney! We very much regret that we could not welcome you at the Quay. An unavoidable board meeting kept us far too late. Apologies. We hope your long voyage was pleasant and refreshing? May we express our relief at your safe arrival and our delight at seeing you face to face at last! May we offer this bunch of roses to the Princess, as a modest token of our present pleasure and eager anticipation of all that is to come. For we are indeed looking forward to a time of creative enterprise with you, in the not so distant future!'

Mr Roy bows ever so slightly as he presents the roses. I pass them on to Ganga Rao and explain the Princess' absence.

— Did he rehearse this speech? Or, is it just dormant Bengali lyricism bursting forth? Sincere or not, I must admit this Rohan Roy is a suave fellow: he will make a fine courtier. Mr Rowlatt is of sturdier frame and looks somewhat constrained in it. He has restless blue eyes that remind me of some tropical fish in a mildewed tank, scampering around amid tangled weeds, desperate for air. He looks a shade bewildered by his friend's peroration. I guess Mr Rowlatt is not given to fine phrases or delicate manoeuvres. He is what one might call 'a rough diamond', a rock-solid lawyer: just what one might need if the going gets rough. – Hardly surprising, given the stock he must come from. One glance at him, I am convinced he has no idea of his ancestry. In fact, I don't believe he has much time for history, his, or anybody else's.

I am told that Australians set store by candour: 'all up front' is the phrase, I believe. So I think I should tackle immediately the problem that has been causing me considerable unease, ever since I first received Mr Rowlatt's letter. Once I have finished shaking hands and exchanging pleasantries, and after Ganga Rao has settled them with Scotch and soda, I take the plunge:

'– Do you mean to say, Mr Rowlatt, that you do not know who your namesake was in India?'

Mr Rowlatt shakes his head. 'I have no idea.'

'Well, well, my dear sir! Where shall I begin? How shall I put it? Your namesake Mr Rowlatt, in the heyday of the Raj was a famous man – notorious, I might say. – Ganga Rao! Please be kind enough to explain.'

'Most certainly, Your-Highness!' Ganga Rao stands behind a chair and proceeds as if addressing a class of rowdy students:

'Justice Rowlatt, an English judge, presided over a committee that made recommendations to the British government which led to the passing of the Rowlatt Acts of 1919. These infamous acts gave the Britishers drastic powers to curtail popular liberties, to arrest and detain suspects without warrant and to cast them into prisons without trial. The Rowlatt Acts were directly responsible for the atrocities perpetrated by the infamous General Dyer, who ordered the massacre of hundreds of unarmed, defenceless, innocent civilians, women and children at Jallianwallabagh; it was a most brutal, bloody outrage, forever etched in the memory of all Indians.'

Ganga Rao's patter hits my guest like a sudden shower of tropical hailstones. Poor Mr Rowlatt is left stunned and speechless. I regret my move.

'My apologies, Mr Rowlatt, for confronting you with this ugly face of history! I cannot but be amazed at this momentous historical encounter. I hope you understand why I am impelled to satify this curiosity of mine, as regarding your name. Surely there has to be a connection somewhere?'

My slow-paced words give him time to recover his voice.

'– I expect so. Come to think of it, my mother did mention some such character, lost in India.'

'Lost indeed! Thanks to the Rowlatt Acts, Sir Michael O'Dwyer secured Punjab with an iron fist: but the British lost the soul of India. On that tragic day, a sword pierced through the heart of Mother India: nothing short of *swaraj* would staunch her bleeding.'

Mr Rowlatt's lips tighten to a crease. 'I don't know if I should apologize. It is the in-thing now in Australia to say sorry for one's ancestors. Isn't it, Rohan?'

Rohan nods:

' Sure. But personally, I don't see what good it does.'

'No, gentlemen. No need for apologies, no recriminations. Far be it from me to hold you responsible for what happened in my country decades back. History is a ruthless propeller of the wheel of karma. The past is past. We must look to the future. That's why we are here. Besides, this is a land of "dreamtime", is it not? I am here to dream, to make my dreams come true. Let me proffer you my heartfelt thanks for all the hard work you, Mr Rowlatt, and you, Mr Roy, have undertaken on my behalf. I am deeply obliged to you, especially for the purchase of neighbouring properties.'

Mr Rowlatt relaxes and takes a large swig of his whisky. 'Oh, that wasn't too difficult. Too many years of drought, feral pigs running amok — the farmers were ready to sell.' He takes another swig, and wipes his mouth on the back of his palm. 'Please, just call me Ray.'

'I shall certainly try. — What has happened is most opportune, most fortunate indeed. Permit me, gentlemen, to quote the bard! I feel at the moment even as Prospero felt: *I find my zenith does depend upon a most auspicious star, whose influence if I court not but omit, my fortunes will ever after droop* ... You see, gentlemen, I have a vision —'

The door flings open and in sweeps my Princess, peon and ayah in tow, loaded with shopping bags. It is as if Diwali were here. Indrani's smiling eyes cascade sparkles of delight. She can barely contain herself.

'I'm sorry, Uncle, I am late. I do apologize, gentlemen! — But do let me introduce you to another of our guests. We met in the lift as he was looking for our rooms. — Uncle KDR, this is Mr Martin, Jayadev's friend.'

Mr Rowlatt shakes his hand vigorously, introduces him:

'Ziggy Martin, our celeb photographer. —Great to see you. I knew it. I knew we'd meet you again. —I said it that night at Konrad's party, didn't I, Rohan?'

I detect an awkward flush of recognition in Mr Martin's countenance. He disengages himself from Mr Rowlatt's grip so as to greet me:

'Welcome, sir! I'm afraid I don't know how I should address you. Jayadev suggests I call you KDR, like the family does. But I'm not sure if that's proper.'

I like Mr Martin. I appreciate his directness.

'Jayadev is right, Mr Martin. I don't mind being KDR to you. Anything is preferable to being called "Mister Maharajah". That I find highly irksome.' Everyone laughs. '– So you know my lawyers?'

'Well – I couldn't say that. We met once, briefly.'

'I see. – Please! Please sit down.'

My niece sees to that he is seated between herself and me. Like a bright-eyed kitten, she follows every move he makes. He has a remarkable head of sandy-brown hair that flips over and hides his face momentarily, as he leans over to take something from the sports bag beside him. He presents the Princess with a transparent plastic cylinder full of glittering chocolates:

'A small gift for you, Princess, comes with my best wishes. These are special to Sydney, I hope you like them.'

Indrani accepts the gift with her customary grace – except, methinks, the young lady blushes somewhat. She rises abruptly.

'Thank you. – Excuse me for a moment.' Without more ado she glides out of the room.

Mr Martin, whose eyes follow her to the door, turns to me smiling and holds out a bottle of red wine:

'My apologies. I'm sorry not to have been at the Quay last evening. I feel bad, especially as Jayadev phoned me specially to ask me to meet you. There was an unexpected crisis.'

'The crisis is past, I hope?'

'Yes – I think so. For the time being.'

Mr Martin has a most unusual face. Careworn yet youthful, he radiates warmth. His face reminds me of a freshly ploughed field, glinting in the morning light. I see in his sorrowful eyes a passion for the beautiful and the good that makes me decide instantly that I must not let him slip away, as he well might. His demeanour is of someone preoccupied in the depths of his heart: someone who

might receive you courteously and warmly enough in the outer
precincts of his abode – in the lounge, drawing room, parlour,
veranda or whatever – but he will not let you see beyond. Over the
door of his inmost chamber I see a sign that reads: 'No Trespassers.
Silence.' Given that he is 'a photographer of first rank', as Jayadev
puts it, I understand his reticence: so necessary in an artist who
must fend off unwelcome distraction. I must make sure that he
recognizes a friend and well-wisher in me; and I very much hope he
can respond to a call from the dreamer that I am.

As I pass the wine-bottle over to Ganga Rao, I catch sight of its label:

'Ah! *Hill of Grace*. What an inspired choice of a name! Thank you,
Mr Martin, so very thoughtful of you. I shall cherish this; it takes
me back to my sojourn in golden Tuscany.'

'I hope you enjoy it. It's rather a superb red. Unfortunately, the man
who made it, Mr Henschke, is no longer alive.'

Ray Rowlatt, who has been watching us with the tenacity of a seagull, butts in:

'His wife shot him.'

It makes me jump: there is an odd note of excitement in the lawyer's
tone. He continues unabashed, his voice shaking with barely
suppressed giggles:

'Mrs Henschke was caught more or less with a smoking gun in her
hands. She claimed she thought she'd shot a possum. A possum! Of
all the excuses, that's what she came up with, a possum! Unreal!'

Indrani has just re-entered the room, bearing a small basket. She
catches his last words:

'*Who* is shooting possums? Where? Why? They look so cute and
adorable! Why would anybody want to shoot them? What for?'

Her face wilts like a tender mango leaf in the midday sun.

'No one is shooting possums, my dear! Come, don't be distressed.' I signal her to sit beside me. 'This is a sad story about the maker of the wine that Mr Martin has very kindly brought us. But don't you think *Hill of Grace* is an inspired choice of a name? I take it as a very good omen.'

My Princess is mercurial in her ability to transport herself from one mood to another. One glance at her sympathetic audience and she resumes with the sweetest charm:

'Guess what I found in the Queen Victoria Arcade? – A shop selling products, with the name of the lady who sent us that postcard!'

'You mean the lady who calls herself "Tantric Rose"?'

'Yes. That's the one. Tantric Rose. I found a fascinating range of her beauty-products. Let me show you!'

Indrani casts the contents of her basket on to the coffee table as if she were throwing dice. She arranges them prettily – little tubes, bottles, jars and bars – lotions and potions that ladies, young or old, seem to adore and accumulate. She picks up each item and holds it against the light between thumb and forefinger, as though with a most dainty pair of tweezers. She bubbles away: a veritable magic show! My guests watch entranced. I wait for her to finish, then turn to Mr Rowlatt:

'Yes, Mr Ray. I have been meaning to ask you about this lady. I received from her a very strange postcard indeed! – Ganga Rao!' My secretary is swift. I pass the card to Mr Ray. 'Do read it, please! Tell me what I am to make of it.'

Mr Ray holds the card up and titters as he reads the message. *"Hi Rajah! You are a great bloke. Thanks a million. See yous soon. Love, more love and mahamudra-love! Tantric Rose."* He stops laughing. 'She must have been stoned when she wrote that.'

'What can you tell me about her? Is she young? Old? Why does she call herself by this strange name?'

'I dunno. I guess she's into yoga and sex — they all are, up there in that commune — I beg your pardon, Princess. All I know is that she's no spring chicken — but she's still a looker. She's been with our Robbie Gordon from the beginning of the commune, a life-partner, you could say. Pretty smart, runs a successful business — as Princess sure found out.'

Indrani nudges me. 'Ask him, Uncle!' Her brows arch. 'Remember? — About him, you know who —'

'Ask? — Ah, yes! — There's something that has been puzzling us, Mr Ray: why did our benefactor never contact us while alive?'

'I can't be sure. Only guess. Robbie was a hot leftie: he was always doing demos, against this or that. He couldn't let on, could he, that he had royal rellies in the nest?'

Quiet Mr Rohan wakes up, frowning: 'I dunno, Ray, I think there's more to it than just being a leftie icon. Saw a lot of him when he came to Sydney to sweet-talk buyers or fix up shows. Big bear of a bloke, white mane, white beard — looked a bit like Tagore. He was a bit odd, like artists are — went around in combat-fatigues or batik kaftans. Laughed big, talked in riddles. Always felt he was covering up something.'

'You mean, Mr Roy, that our relation had some skeleton in his cupboard?'

'No, no, sir! Nothing sinister, I'm sure. Rob was a good bloke, wouldn't hurt a fly. It's just that when I looked into his family records, there were funny gaps, things that didn't add up. Made me wonder if he really was who he said he was.'

The Princess' eyes widen with horror. 'Oh my God! What are you saying? That this Robert Gordon was a phoney?'

Mr Roy recoils.

Mr Ray pats his friend's knee as he speaks. 'Don't worry, Princess!

My friend reads too much Sherlock Holmes! There's probably nothing in it. In any case, legally it makes no difference. You're the heiress. That's all there is to it. That's what counts.'

I brace myself to speak sternly:

'My dear Mr Ray! You do not understand. It does matter — it matters enormously, to the Princess and to myself. We must know the truth.'

'Sure. Don't worry, Maharajah! We'll do a thorough investigation. I'll put a crack-team on to it.'

'I hope, gentlemen, that you can put my mind to rest — and soon. I cannot tell you what it meant to me when I heard of this Gordon and his generosity to us. After Alice Gordon, Indrani's grandmother, died, there was a total breach between our families. Nothing but neglect, contempt and anger on both sides, no prospect of understanding or acceptance. When we received your letter about Robert Gordon, my heart leapt with gladness. Believe me, it is not the size or value of this legacy: all wealth is illusion, today it is here, tomorrow it vanishes. No, it is this Gordon's evident desire, expressed in his magnanimous gesture, for peace and reparation; it is *that* which has made me embark on this dream-venture. I see a chance to make amends for my ancestors, and for the sufferings they inflicted on that unfortunate pair, Prince Vikram and Alice Gordon. I want to build bridges between the past and the present, between East and West, between the rich and the poor, between black and white. But to build well, one must make sure that the foundations are rock-solid: and that rock must be the truth. There is no room for doubt or misgiving that might white-ant our whole enterprise. You see, Mr Ray, why this is so important. Surely you understand?'

'I do, sir. I shall do my best.'

'Good!'

Mr Ray looks at his watch, and finishes his Scotch. 'If there's nothing more, we'd better be leaving. Thanks for the drink! – Nice to meet you, Princess. – See you soon, sir!'

'When are we to meet again?'

'I've kept next Wednesday morning clear for you, sir. Ten a.m., in our Pitt Street Office. Is that OK?'

'– Ganga Rao?'

'Yes, Your-Highness! I've noted the time.'

Mr Ray and Mr Roy shake our hands. Mr Roy addresses the Princess.

'In the meantime, if there's anything you need, do let me know, madam!'

'Thank you.'

She escorts them to the door. Mr Martin rises, but I stall him.

'Stay awhile, please, Mr Martin. We haven't had a chance to talk. Could you join us for dinner tonight?'

'That's very kind. I can – and I will.'

'Splendid! – Indrani! Look after our guest! – Excuse me, for a few moments.. My priest is waiting for me. Prayer-time! I shall be back shortly.'

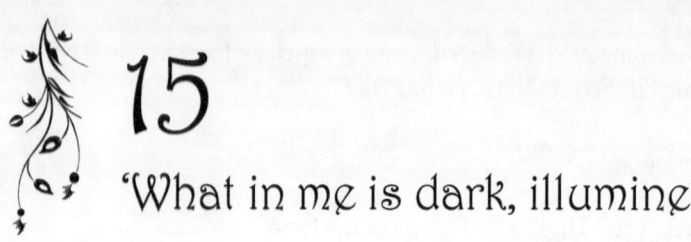

15

'What in me is dark, illumine'

Among the ill-shaped, ill-dressed, loud-mouthed, lacquered tourists crowding the lift, she stood aloof, the Princess, in regal self-sufficiency. Her ivory-slender fingers were curled round a bunch of pale yellow roses, studded with star-bright lily-of-the-valley buds, fanning out from a cluster of shiny green leaves; herself an iridescent bouquet of exotic grace, so petite, so effortlessly elegant. In the close confines of that lift – very close, couldn't have been closer, just a few plastic carrier bags shielding her delicate, perfumed body from me – our eyes met: one swift, sweet glance from those amber eyes of piercing brightness, and my heart took a dive. In that fraction of a moment of seeing and being seen, sunlight streaked into my valley of the shadow of death. A moment only, for quickly she lowered her lids, enclosing herself in regal dignity, and the flimsy barrier of plastic bags became a steel-lace grille, secluding her from the stranger that I was – that is, until we spoke in the corridor. I note that she told her uncle that we had met in the lift.

Now that her guardian has gone in, and I am left alone with her, my heart is too full for words. I have no desire to break this enchanting web of peace that holds us together.

'– Mr Martin.'

The Princess' hesitant voice rouses me.

'Yes?'

'I hope you don't mind if I ask you a personal question?'

'Well?'

She is so prettily gawky, I am suddenly moved to assume an Irish accent:

'—Well, my dear Princess! That depends on *how* personal.'

A warm red glow suffuses her pale brown face.

'I am sorry. I shouldn't have.'

'No, no, go ahead!'

'No. I don't think so.'

'I am sorry. I shouldn't tease. What is it you want to ask?' I bend towards her, almost pleading. 'Please!'

'My question is to do with the "crisis" you mentioned. It is worrying me. Is someone ill? Your wife? Children?'

'No. Thank God! It wasn't that kind of crisis. I have no wife or children.'

'Oh!'

I stay silent awhile, not without a sense of power. She folds and unfolds the ends of her saree. It is like watching an awkward puppy full of mischief, fretting to break the rules. I cannot but smile.

'The crisis was to do with a neighbour.'

'Oh?' She stops fiddling with her saree and looks up, becalmed, open-faced, ready for my tale. 'What happened? Do tell me, if you don't mind.'

'Not at all ! It is a complicated business. You see, I have these neighbours, Mr and Mrs Yurisch, migrants from what was Yugo-slavia. I don't really know them. I just say "hullo!" now and then, when we meet in the corridor. Mrs Yurisch – Anna, I now know her name – Anna did a strange thing. Every evening, come news-time on the TV, she'd cry, sob her heart out, I could hear her.'

'Poor woman! But why?'

'I guess it's because she'd lost her family in some atrocity, and the news always had new ones to report. – Just a guess.'

I have no wish to take my charming listener on a guided tour of my disturbed psyche. What would she make of me if I told her that I saw, before Anna Yurisch spoke of the turmoil she was in, how daily she revisited (as she was once forced to) and stood, zombie-like, by that snake-pit of evil outside a small Serbian town, where the shot bodies of her father, mother and two brothers lay writhing, bleeding, not dead yet, but covered over by more bodies just flung in?

I must not inflict my dark seeings on this curious child.

'Two days back, I felt there was something wrong next door. Unusually quiet. So I did what I had never done before: I knocked on Anna's door.' I pause, just to savour the flash of excitement that makes the Princess's skin glow.

'And? – You can't stop now.'

'It's a grim tale. Anna's husband, Stefan, had gone missing for a whole week. Anna went to the garage where he worked. Stefan's boss told Anna that, a week ago, her husband had had a visitor. He'd talked a while in their lingo; afterwards, Stefan left, having asked for a day off. He didn't return. The boss thought that Stefan had mentioned a death in the family, an uncle or aunt. The trouble is Anna knows of no uncle or aunt. When she told the boss, he just laughed, thought Stefan might be covering up for another woman. Anna felt furious and stupid.'

'How terrible ! I feel for this woman. Could the boss be right?'

'I wondered too. Anna is convinced there is no other lady. Her husband, who is rather morose, had been especially nice to her of late. He seemed buoyant, and was talking of big changes, of more money, of a trip to Disneyland, even buying a flat of their own. She had heard nothing to suggest another woman. No evidence at all. What alarmed her was that Stefan had taken nothing, no clothes, shaving-kit or even a toothbrush. Most worrying was that he had taken no money. Stefan apparently didn't trust the banks, so had no account, no credit cards: he kept all his money in the flat, in a biscuit-tin. Anna feared the worst.'

'You mean –?'

'Yes. She feared her husband was dead. Still she didn't go to the police. Too scared. "I can't go to them, they lock me up, they torture me, they kill me," she kept saying. People with her background don't trust anyone in uniform.'

'But she must, though. Surely, they *have* to help?'

'The NSW police? I don't want to sound cynical, but Anna had cause to be scared. It's tough for any, worse for some migrants. They'd tear her apart with their interrogation, as if she were a criminal. She was in no state to cope. Besides, she had other reasons for avoiding the police. Threatening phonecalls demanding that she "return" the money: big sum, five hundred thousand dollars. She had no idea what Stefan had got into. Panic-stricken, she'd searched and searched: but no money. Desperate and lonely, she had gone to church, to tell the priest – but didn't find him. When she got back, she found her flat trashed. – That's how I saw it: broken glass, ornaments, pictures torn apart, bedding ripped, utter chaos. The phone rang and it was the caller again. This time she was warned that if she didn't find the money within forty eight hours she would be dead.'

I do love this story-telling. Each time I pause, or stop to have a sip of my orange juice, the Princess edges closer, her agitated eyes shining in sympathy.

'—What did you do?'

'Not a great deal. I got her to take a sleeping tablet. Next morning, she called on me, better for her sleep and more coherent. She had just received an envelope in the mail, addressed to Stefan, was too scared to open it. So I did. There was a key, looked very like a locker-key. I guessed it had to do with the missing money. I made Anna some coffee, she cried and talked, and finally I persuaded her to go to the police. I had to take her, sit with her, while she made her statement. It took hours and she was shattered, poor woman.'

'And the key?'

'The police guess it belongs to some gym or health-club. They are tracking it down. The question is, supposing they find the money, where did Stefan get it from and what for? Anna is baffled and too distressed to think ill of her husband.'

'But the police do?'

'Naturally! Could be drug-money. So they can't but grill Anna. She doesn't trust them, especially now. She believes her husband is innocent. She wants me to find him. Ever since I knocked on her door she is pursuing me, pleading with me like a demented fury.'

'Oh dear! What are you going to do?'

'I feel sorry for Anna but I'm no Sherlock Holmes. First, I must find a relative or friend to look after her, or I'm stuck with her.'

The Princess's face drops.

'— I'm sorry. I shouldn't have burdened you with my messy tale.'

'No, no. It's not that. I was just thinking Uncle needs you too.'

'Does he?'

'Uncle KDR has all sorts of plans. So have I.'

'Plans for?'

'For our kingdom, in Northern New South Wales: Ratnapuri II. Of course, at present it is just an idea, a dream if you like; but knowing my Uncle, I assure you it will happen. Surely Jayadev told you?'

'I'm afraid not.'

'Typical! Jayadev is always embarrassed by anything grand. My cousin feels that Uncle and I are old-fashioned: he complains we live too much in the past. It is not true. We look to the future; why else would we be here? Uncle is serious—don't laugh!—he is very serious about our new kingdom, a kingdom as it ought to be, just as it used to be once upon a time, with all the dignity, power, beauty and care for its people. God bless him!'

She goes moist-eyed.

'And your plans?'

'Me? Oh! building. I am a student of architecture. I want to build beautiful things, just like my great grandfather did. I have been learning all I can about our territory, the Clarence River region. I have plans for palaces, temples, houses, schools, theatres, model colonies. Do you know what, so often architects don't pay enough attention to the climate and culture of the people they build for. Take the great Corbusier, for instance. What he did in Chandigarh, you know about that, don't you? – Sorry! I am boring you.'

'Not at all! I am astounded. Please do tell me!'

As I listen to her expatiate on architectural styles, ancient and modern, and expound her schemes, I realize that her butterfly-perfect daintiness is sustained by creative daring of a sculptural strength.

'– So you see!' she concludes. '*That's* why we need you. Uncle needs a companion, a good "Resident" if you like, someone who knows the country, someone he can trust. Jayadev says you are that person.'

'Does he? I am amazed. We've been out of touch for so many years.'

'Ah, but you see, he has been following your career. You are justly famous, like Sebastîo Salgado – so the reviewers say, don't they?'

'I am flattered, but I wish they wouldn't compare me to Salgado, much as I revere him. I don't feel comfortable with photography that makes suffering mystical.'

'Your work tells us how you understand people: you bare their souls. That's why Uncle – Here he is, he'll explain.'

The Maharajah looks relaxed and refreshed, his countenance aglow after a spell of prayer and meditation.

'– Indrani is right, Mr Martin. I need a counsellor and guide. Will you help us? We'll certainly make it worth your while.'

'I feel very honoured, but I am just a photographer. What use can I be to you, apart from taking some pictures?'

'That will be an auspicious start. I abhor videos. I much prefer to have a photographic record of our progress. You can be officially my court-chronicler. But that is not all. You can do much more for our cause.'

'Your cause? – I don't think I am the right person. I honestly don't think I can offer you much.'

'Let me explain. You see, Mr Martin, in my experience, whatever the undertaking, it is not one's knowledge or skill that matters, but what one is in essence. It is not what you can or cannot do but who you are. Let me be frank! My son Jayadev spoke highly of you. I listened, as I always do, to my son, reserving my judgement. Now that I have met you, I am convinced that Jayadev, for once, was not exaggerating. I know, from within, that you are the person we need. Think it over! Let us talk more over dinner. – Indrani, my dear, go, get ready! We are going out, I am tired of these hotel rooms – where shall we dine, Mr Martin? Can you recommend somewhere?'

'Indian?'

'Preferably. But not one of these pseudo-Raj set-ups with waiters in turbans! Somewhere modest and homely.'

'I think I know just the place. It's run by a Tamil lady from Malaysia.'

'Excellent!'

An hour later, we end up at *The Tanjore* in Glebe Point Road. Mrs Panch, the owner-chef, somewhat comical in her white chef's cap towering like a pagoda over her dark, buxom, saree-clad frame, emerges from among her pots of seething spices to greet us. In a short while, with her instinctive sense of occasion, she conjures up an off-the-menu feast with an eye to specialities from the Maharajah's region. The Maharajah doesn't fail to notice.

'Excellent, Mrs Panch! Mysore pepper-water, I see. Just what we need to stir us up! How do you find it, Mr Martin?'

'Hot – but welcome!'

'Splendid!'

This Mysore pepper-water is clearly potent. Nodding his head appreciatively between sips, the Maharajah gets fired up:

'It may seem strange, even foolish, Mr Martin, in this day and age of republican sentiment to speak of monarchy; but I tell you, if understood correctly, I mean, in the right spirit, our future lies in monarchy. – I see you smiling, but may I remind you that everyone thought communism was invincible, yet it collapsed, brick by brick, just like the Berlin wall itself. What guarantee is there, why should we presume that democracy can or will go on forever?'

'True!–But there's always fascism: ugly, loathsome, dangerous but nonetheless, a real possibility.'

'Precisely ! That is exactly what we must prevent. Whether it is the far left or far right, they work with the same deadly cocktail of fear, violence and oppression. If the current trend continues, and democracy sinks more and more into mediocrity, inefficiency – to be blunt, when elected governments become mere pawns to multinationals and markets, people might well turn to fascism again: it has glamour, a certain daring that even the best minds succumb to. And as our bard puts it succinctly, *Lilies that fester smell far worse than weeds.* If we are to save the world from the fascist menace, we need monarchy – by which I mean dharmic rule: responsible, compassionate, caring rule by one who willingly abides by sacred laws. Dharma , as our ancestors wisely taught us, is and should be the backbone of monarchy. Dharmic rule is the rule of truth, justice, compassion – it is the exercise of power, but with conscience and the fear of God.'

'Noble ideal, I concede. But with all due respect, isn't it a bit unrealistic to expect anyone to take monarchy seriously again, after its record?'

'I grant that. Kings have sinned and been justly routed. We, the princely rulers, some more than others, failed our people. And we reaped our just deserts. By 1972, when all our honours and privileges were taken away, we became corpses of royalty. Had we been different, what we ought to have been, India today would be a very different place. When I see what I see there – mass poverty despite progress, corruption, rank evils of communalism, caste-ism – I am more than ever convinced of the truth of what I am saying. Kings have failed: but kingship itself is not, need not, be a dead letter. To breathe into it the true spirit, make it come alive, to show what it is to hold sacred trusteeship of the world, that is to be a true rajah – by the way, do you know why we call kings "rajahs"?'

'No.'

'Not because of power, ancestry or even supposed divine authority. A rajah is a rajah because he is *ranjitah*: a king is a king because his subjects are gratified. And I don't mean "bread and circuses"! Justice, peace, prosperity for all!'

'The Isaiah agenda, I see.'

'*What* agenda?'

'Isaiah, the Prophet. Dream of ages, lion lying down with the lamb and so forth. That might be more possible than getting corporate magnates to bed down with the workers or capitalist share-holders to face the slum-slaves who make their money.'

'You see I was right! You *do* understand the battle. In my vast new territory, I don't want to be just another landlord. What I aspire is to create a small kingdom, a paradigm of sacred caring, not just of people but the environment too.'

'There's a strong green movement in that region. Will you take them on board?'

'That depends. So many of these groups get contaminated with violence and hatred. Such *adharma* has no place in what I propose.'

'Where do I come in, in all this?'

'Thank you. I am glad you haven't dismissed me as an old fool. All I need at present is your word of assent.'

I ought to know better. The Maharajah's heady words blow in like a Southerly buster into my musty imagination. But I stall.

I hear a muted ring in my jacket pocket. I welcome the chance to move away and think. I take out the phone, and go outside.

'– Hi! Ziggy!'

'Katarina! Everything OK? Where are you?'

'Where do you think? Byron Bay, of course! I came to watch the sunset, and the dolphins. What a show they put on! I can't wait for you to join me, it's so fabulous! I've found the flat. Just right for us, so near the beach! I reckon five minutes. I've signed the lease. When are you coming up? — What's that noise?'

'Someone's birthday party, getting a bit wild.'

'Whose birthday? You didn't tell me.'

'No. No. It's not our party.'

'Your party? Who are you partying with?'

'Not exactly partying. I am with the Maharajah. I told you, my old mate, Jayadev. His uncle. They arrived yesterday.'

'Dining with the Princess, I see. Take care! I don't want to have to scratch her eyes out!'

'You have nothing to fear. She is just a child.'

'Oh yeah!'

'In fact, the Maharajah's offering me a job. They're heading North.'

'Truly? In that case, they are my friends. — Will you take it?'

'I think I might.'

'Good onya! Thank him for me. And — Never mind! I love you! Ciao!'

'Ciao!'

Was it Katarina's trust? Or, the old dreamer's lure of a better world? Or, was it the enchanting eyes of the Princess gazing earnestly at me while her uncle held forth?

I agreed: I don't know to what.

16
Glenn Innes

Thank God for this eclipse!
Uncle KDR and Vembu are closeted in room 15, Uncle's room, preparing for the event: propitiatory rituals to deflect any evil that may befall us. Ayah Jeevesamma is in bed. And for the first time since we left Sydney more than a week ago, I am getting a chance to be by myself. So I have slipped out from my room to watch the eclipse from this corner of the motel-veranda.

Uncle KDR, as one might expect, decided on a slow 'progress' towards our territory. 'We must see, listen, breathe, ponder, feel and soak in the sights and sounds of this great land. It is my desire to drink deep the silence of its open spaces! Australia Felix! Land of the Holy Spirit — so it was named once, and so it should be hallowed. We are strangers, guests only at present; but you, Mr Martin, you belong. Will you be kind enough to act as our host, and assist my secretary in organising suitable transport? Thank you!"

So Uncle declared, leaving Mr Martin no choice but to oblige. After considering a cavalcade of cars, Mr Martin decided on a sturdy yet luxurious mini-bus that takes us all: that is, Uncle KDR, Ganga Rao, myself, Vembu, Ayah, the peon, with Mr Martin and his black assistant who, like his name, 'Australia Felix', is wonderfully zany. Besides being a good driver and odd-jobs man, Felix is a knowledgeable guy, full of weird stories about the places we pass. He speaks a strange sort of English which Uncle and I don't readily understand. Uncle often dozes off in the middle of a story; if Mr Martin catches sight of me listening to Felix with a frown, he deigns to 'translate'. For some reason, he seems to find this exercise highly amusing. As far as Uncle is concerned, Felix has slotted into the space left by our old retainer, Hari, who was too old to come with us. Jeevesamma is the difficult one. She cannot abide the really dark-skinned, even though she herself is no white dove. She can be annoyingly insolent: she insists on speaking of Felix as a pariah and a jungle-demon, and I have had to reprimand her sternly. Hence her tantrum.

We are travelling like a troupe of actors: Uncle KDR and Ganga Rao deliberating our 'high-serious' main plot; Ayah, Vembu and the peon hatching intrigues as befits sub-plot characters; Australia Felix ready to don the motley; myself destined to be the hapless romantic heroine buffeted about by all and sundry. Mr Martin I think of as the chorus. He just observes: observes me in particular with that faintly ironic smile which I find highly annoying. When he is not smiling, he looks decidedly sombre and tragic. I wish he wouldn't make me feel foolish just by the way he looks at me: I get confused, seize up or talk too much.

Uncle says we remind him of the travelling troupe made famous in the film *Shakespeare-Wallah*, who used to visit Ratnapuri court every year. Uncle is getting lachrymose-nostalgic about how mesmerized he was by their magic; how, with just a few meagre props and the bard's mighty words declaimed with panache, they could transform the palace courtyard into a Forest of Arden, Hamlet's Denmark, King Lear's heath, Macbeth's castle or Prospero's magical island. Uncle was a mere boy when he was captivated by the bard and has been ever since. As I expected, plans are afoot for a Shakespeare Festival in Ratnapuri II.

Right now, Vembu is centre-stage, this imminent eclipse making it his night. Our wily old priest, who normally I find a bore and a menace, has for once found something that genuinely taxes his astrological skills. 'Everything is upside down in these Southern Skies! And I am to be revising and revising all my calculations and predictions! Lord, help us! The *saptha rishis*' (the Seven Sages, our Indian name for Orion), 'the *saptharishis* are performing *shirasasana*', a headstand. If I am to be more correct, I will be saying, they are doing the crane – but in a most astonishing stretch! Everything I am seeing is in reverse! So, with Your-Highness' permission, I am finding new guidelines for our rituals.'

'So be it! says Uncle, and together they are busy devising new rules for auspiciousness. Every time we arrive at a motel – and in the past few days we have stopped at several – there is the inevitable knock on the door. Ramgopal, the peon, appears as usual with his silent, knowing grin, and starts moving the furniture around until our beds are propitiously aligned in an East-West axis so as to avoid the problematic North-South. And tonight there will be more than bed-moving.

It must be around ten and the eclipse is due in half an hour or so. Jeevesamma is already in bed, hiding herself well under the sheets, refusing to eat or drink, her dark face getting darker with fears and misgivings about this 'bad omen'. This 'eclipse curse' has given her the perfect occasion for a muted tantrum: she has been waiting to stage one ever since we left Sydney. Sydney, she loved – the crowds, the shops, the cafés, the markets, the tourists, the beaches, the parks, the bustle and colour – they were all to her liking and put her in high spirits and she was a most agreeable companion. Then, ever since we set off into gum-tree land and cattle-grazing country, and stayed in modest motels, she has been wilting and wailing. The bush and its silences give her the creeps. And to cap it all, now she feels even the moon is misbehaving.

I see her point, in a manner of speaking. All along the way from Armidale, our minibus deliciously bouncing and speeding us along the undulating road, this 'naughty' moon was with us: a bright, yellow pancake of a moon, so large and low that I could have drawn a 'smile' on it. It was certainly behaving like a cartoon character, sometimes ahead of us, sometimes alongside, now and then vanishing altogether into grey-blue clouds, then chirpily reappearing in thick indigo-blue skies. Like a child at an indoor birthday party in the monsoon season, this moon was playing reckless games while the skies were gathering their sombre momentum.

'– Penny for your thoughts.'

I was so absorbed in watching the turbulent skies I hadn't noticed Mr Martin emerge from his room. I wonder how long he has been 'observing' me.

'Oh, nothing. Just thinking why it has to be now, and here. I've never seen an eclipse before.'

'So you too think it is significant.'

'Not the way they do.' I gesture towards Uncle's door. 'It is significant for *me*. Everything has a meaning, I believe.'

'How do you decide the meaning?'

'Depends on what happens to you.'

'Before, or after?'

I have to think carefully. For once, he is not smiling that ironic smile.

'Both.'

'I see.' He stands beside me and is silent for quite a while as if he is weighing things over. 'Where is everybody? Isn't your uncle interested in seeing the eclipse?'

'I suppose he is. At present, he is with Vembu: you know, prayers and rituals for this. My ayah is in bed, she is not in a good mood.'

'I did notice.'

'I am sorry. She is really a sweetie, but can be difficult.'

'What is it? – Our driving? She looks petrified at times. I'll tell Felix to slow down.'

'Don't, please! He is fine, I'm sure. With my ayah, she is already homesick and getting a bit cranky. If it isn't the driving, it will be something else. We can't pay too much attention to her. Sometimes she fusses over me so much I feel smothered. I am so glad she is in bed. I can breathe for a while. – Isn't it a beautiful night?'

'I needed to stretch my legs, after all that driving. I was going for a walk, then I saw you. Care to join me? I have a torch, in case it gets too dark.'

'Uncle will worry. – Oh, bother! I think I will. Just a moment, I will write a note, otherwise they will think some demon has carried me off.'

'Do I rank as a demon?'

'Of course not! – I am sorry. I wasn't thinking.'   .

Mr Martin laughs, and stops abruptly:

'Your uncle is right to be concerned. This country can be very dangerous.'

'Funnel-web spiders, cane toads and venomous snakes, I know. I've been reading about them.'

'I wasn't thinking of them. Nature, on the whole, is less dangerous than man.'

'I know. I was just joking.'

'Just as well.'

We walk in silence along a side-road that slopes up towards a quarry. The moon, now entirely serious, is hovering over a ridge of trees that form a dark curtain suitable for the moon's farewell. There's a sense of being in no-man's land: Mr Martin and I could be walking into a crater of the moon itself. I stumble.

'Are you all right?' Mr Martin has been keeping a respectful distance; now he comes closer, ready to support me if needed. I steady myself quickly.

'It's nothing. My sandal-strap got caught in this piece of rock. I'm OK.'

For a few moments, he stands awkwardly offering me an arm, which I tactfully ignore. He drops it and we resume walking. Blood rushes to my forehead and I feel slightly giddy. I lose sense of where I am.

'What is the name of this town?'

'Glenn Innes.'

'I shall always remember it. It is wonderful to be free of my chains for a change.'

'Is that how you feel?'

'Most of the time. I had hoped that, leaving India, I would have more freedom. But truly I am still a caged canary, admittedly in a golden cage, very clean, very comfortable, but still a cage. The only difference is that now the cage is being aired, carried about. It is better, I confess, at least to be mobile.'

'Is it good enough for the canary to sing?'

'Me? Sing? – Oh, no. I don't sing. I suppose I could, if I tried. I love music. – I'm sorry Uncle and I have been occupying the tape-deck, playing our music all the time.'

'You needn't apologise. I am enjoying it enormously. I have never heard anything like that. My acquaintance with Indian music doesn't amount to anything more than a few twangs of the sitar. I especially liked what your uncle put on this evening.'

'You mean the Meera *bhajans*? I'm so relieved it wasn't an infliction.'

'Not in the least.'

'She also was a Princess. Shall I tell you what the song was about? Her husband, the Rana, got so fed up with her devotion to Krishna he tried to poison her. Miraculously, Meera survived, clearly saved by divine intervention. She was a caged canary too but she escaped through her songs.'

'And you? Where are you planning to escape?'

'Nowhere right at the moment. This is escape enough.'

'I'm glad to hear that.'

He wasn't laughing at me when he said that. I am sure of it. The conversation was getting awkward. I should have known when I shot my mouth off about myself. Uncle is a safer subject.

'– Do you know why Uncle is playing so much of this music? It's not just for relaxation or passing the time.'

'I guessed as much.'

'Really? What is your guess?'

'I can't be sure. But the way he puts the tape on, gazes at the landscape and meditates, I sense there's something going on. I am reminded of a priest sprinkling holy water.'

'How right you are! You see – how shall I put this? Please don't misunderstand. Uncle doesn't mean to be rude. It is just that he believes that everything needs to be cleansed, purified, to be made sacramental and revered. This is not a mere idea with him but a passion. One way of doing this is to pour out sacred music. It is to do with holy vibrations. Music, he insists, can work like mantras. As you know by now, we Indians are obsessed with purification rituals.'

'You're not alone. Some Christians use holy water and incense; the aborigines have smoking ceremonies. Ask Felix, he'll tell you. He will probably agree with your uncle that this land could do with a lot of cleansing. Music is certainly an inspired choice for it.'

'Oh, there's always a definite method in my Uncle's madness.'

'He's going to the right place. Your property is in what is known as the "Rainbow Region".'

'I've heard about Nimbin. Hippies, aren't they? We don't propose to turn hippy.'

'I beg your pardon. I wouldn't dream of thinking of you in the same company as those brain-dead morons. All I meant to say was that the farmhouse where your relation lived was once a part of a very impressive network of communes. People who laughed at them once are now stealing their ideas.'

'This Tantric Rose sounds quite practical. I wonder what she is like!'

'I'm sure you won't be disappointed.'

'Oh, look! There it goes, the moon. Rahu, the evil serpent, is starting to eat the moon, as our priest would say. I wonder how long it will take for him to spew it out? – I didn't imagine it could get quite so dark.'

'Are you afraid? Shall I switch on the torch?'

'No, no. Don't! It will spoil it.'

'I have absolutely no wish to do that.'

Uncle was not very pleased when I returned. Not that he thought I had done anything wrong, and he knows Mr Martin is a gentleman. He is troubled, I suspect, with a tinge of jealousy if I seem to be coming off the leash. All he said to Mr Martin was: 'Enjoyed your walk? Pity I didn't know. I could have done with some fresh air myself. – And,' he turned to me with a slightly hurt look, 'You, my dear, missed the blessing. Vembu had gone to a lot of trouble on our behalf.'

All I could do was apologise. Seeing that I was in trouble, Jeevesamma called off her tantrum.

17
Tantric Rose

She's a cute kid, this Princess. Cute and smart. The minute I set my eyes on her I said to myself, 'Holy Mary! You sure picked the right one, Robbie! Isn't she just a scrumptious chocolate-nougat of a girl, this heiress-Princess of yours, you bastard? Gobsmacked, are you? Got nothing to say? Lost your tongue? I'm bloody well not surprised!' So I yell at him in my heart, angry and jealous. Angry and jealous I have been, ever since those bloody pair of lawyers from Sydney told me how my sweetheart had fucked up my life with his fancy shit of a will. He just stands there, smiling like the rogue he was, gorging on her with his flinty black eyes.

'I beg yours. Didn't I tell ya?'

Robbie was with me that day: dead and gone he is for sure, and buried under the avocado tree, but his spirit hovers round this farmhouse, like he is dropping in for a cuppa and a chat. And there are moments, like on that day when little Miss Rani visited me by herself, moments when I feel his astral body so close and real I can't figure out why others don't see him. Oh, yeah, Robbie was there sure as life, when this pretty Princess stuck her gazelle of a head in, pushing the wire-door open and saying ever so sweetly, 'Are you at home, Miss Rose?' And just as well the little Miss didn't see Robbie: she is too sweet and innocent for his tricks. The old bear would have charmed the socks off her little Princessy booties. And good thing too that I was connected up to him only on plane three, that's the level at which he does his social-talk bit. Plane one and two are where we meet for minimal exchange, no more than '– Hi, Rose, how are you?' '– I'm fine, how about you? How's your astral life?' '– Not bad. Could be better. See you soon. Rose.' '– Sure you do, you bloody bastard. When I do, I'll tear your guts out, if you have any, you dickhead! Look at what you've done to me, left me begging for my bread, you son of a bitch!' '– Rose, my darling! It's not that bad, is it? Believe me, they are good folks, they'll look after you! Come on, I love you still!' So off we move on to plane four and five where we pour our hearts out, me weeping, dear Robbie saying, 'There, there, my sweet Rose, my lovely Rose', and on we soar up to plane six and seven. Cloud Nine isn't in it! Not for nothing they call me 'Tantric Rose'! All the tricks of yoga Robbie and I got up to come flooding back and we swim in light-filled bliss. Boy, oh boy, what joy!

Just as well she caught me on plane three. I don't think little Miss Riding Hood is ready for what the big bad wolf can do. She looked fresh as a poodle after a bath, bright-eyed and bouncy. I was mighty surprised to see her by herself, knowing the careful kind of bloke her uncle is. Oh, yes, we met a week ago, when the whole mob stopped by for a short while, and the rajah invited me to tea in his hotel rooms in Grafton. I can't say I've taken a shine to him nor has he to me. He's a decent sort of guy but I see dark shadows in his aura, makes me think he could be in trouble. He has been kind enough to me, letting me stay on here and run my business, though Robbie had put that in as a request, not an order. – 'We have no desire to render you homeless. The less we interfere, the better, wouldn't you agree, madam?' – I winced. He can't help that, I suppose, being royal an' all that, sounding like a poncey old sod. I got the message. He doesn't think I'm suitable company for his precious niece. I did try. I smartened myself up, put on a silk-print dress, black stockings, and a white hat and all, and sat there sipping my herbal tea ever so daintily – but he wasn't taken in. It was a charade. He knew, and I knew he knew that Tantric Rose is a daughter of Aquarius, a free spirit who might turn a nasty bitch if provoked. To be fair, he didn't try any posh tricks of polite snubbing. He seems to have found a slot for me somewhere else. I guess he is used to left-over hangers-on in his harem – that is, if he kept a harem. They all do, don't they? I could tell he thought I'm a pensioned-off concubine he wants his niece to stay clear off. So I was mighty pleased when she turned up that day, minus minders.

I take her hands, drink deeply in her lovely bright eyes, and give her a hug on Robbie's behalf.

'Good to see you, little Princess! So you got away. How come?'

'Uncle's helicopter has arrived. He is flying off somewhere along the river. Mr Martin is with him. My ayah is still down with flu. I slipped out. Felix drove me.'

'Good onya!'

'I came because there are things I want to ask you about Mr Gordon. And I want to see this house leisurely, if you don't mind.'

'You're welcome, sweetie! Feel free. It's yours, after all. I'm only here by your grace.'

'I'm sorry if you feel deprived in any way. Do let us know if you need anything.'

'I'm fine. Don't you worry about me! How about you? Settling in? How is Lockhart Lodge?'

'It's OK, for the time being. We are glad to be out of hotels and in a house again.'

'You call Lockhart Lodge a *house*? That bloody big monster of a mansion? Phew! Spooky place! I couldn't bear to be in it for a sec.'

'I see what you mean. It is badly designed. Not designed at all. Just room after room, tacked on higgledy-piggledy, as if the owner kept having afterthoughts. Pity! With a bit of proper planning it could have been a grand mansion. I can't but think that whoever built it did so automatically, as if they were in Scotland, paying no attention to the direction of the sun or wind-currents. The western side of the house must get intolerable, summer or winter.'

'That's smart, for a newcomer.'

'I should know. I'm an architect, after all. Uncle is putting me in charge of his building projects.'

'Streuth! How stupid of me! I beg your pardon. I guess you'll be putting up a palace, Taj Mahal-like?'

'The Taj is a tomb.'

'Right you are.'

'We want something, elegant, gracious and liveable. Uncle admires Italianate villas. I like Rajasthani palaces. A blend of Roman-Rajasthani, I believe, would suit the climate. As a matter of fact, Uncle, I hope, is scouting for a suitable location. I am ready to start.'

'Great! The sooner you quit Lockhart Lodge the better.'

'What do you mean?'

'You wouldn't want to stay there too long, sweetie! That Scottish-Gothic dump is custom-built for ghosts. Seen any lately?'

'Am I supposed to?'

'Sure, darling!'

'I don't think I will. I never do.'

'You soon will, if you stay there long enough.'

'Do you really believe it is haunted?'

'That's the story. If Lockhart Lodge isn't haunted, it's got to be! You know Wattle Creek? Behind the Lodge? That shit of a squatter, Ted Lockhart, he found a mob of blacks camping by the creek, and butchered them all — women, children, the lot.'

'Oh God! – It is such a beautiful place.'

'Yeah! You better get used to it, darling. How do you think this country got to be as pretty as it is? When the poms got to work, clearing the rainforests for cattle grazing, they did a thorough job, fed the land with blood and bone – abo blood and bone!'

'It's too horrible to think about. I can never understand why men have to be brutal!'

'It wasn't just the men, my pet. Their women were willing enough to mix arsenic with the flour they gave the blacks.'

'How could they? I can't believe it. It's cold-blooded murder.'

'That's not what they thought. For them, it was a matter of getting rid of some "pests". I expect you and I might have done the same. Nasty thought, but very likely.'

'Heaven forbid!'

'Heaven forbid, indeed!'

'No wonder the natives are angry. Some of our land is under Mabo-style claim. Uncle is hoping to have a peaceful settlement with their leader.'

'Good luck to him! – Now here I go yakettyyak, and you must be parched dry. What can I offer you to drink?'

'Just a glass of water, please!'

'Come, on! It's not every day I welcome a Princess into my barn. Have a tot of scotch with me, will you?'

'I don't drink whisky.'

'You don't mind if I do? Robbie loved his drop of Johnny Walker, with plenty of water. Spiritual comfort, his second muse, he said! Or he couldn't paint. So, let's drink a toast to good old Robbie who's made mates of us! To Robbie!'

So she toasted Robbie, with her glass of water; I could see the old bugger grinning, even if she couldn't. With that, he left me. I guess he knew what was coming and the cunning bastard didn't want to hang around when she popped the question she'd been holding back all this time.

'Miss Rose! Tell me about Mr Gordon's family. Does he have any relations here?'

'Family?' — I had to giggle. 'I thought you knew everything.'

'Everything? What's everything?'

'Robbie was an only child. His parents were near-wrinklies when he was a kid. Dad, I mean step-dad, was big in Dairy. When they shut down the butter company up river, they moved to Melbourne. Robbie wanted to be a painter. Dad was a four-square redneck. The only painter he cared about was Rolfe Harris with a tin of British Paints. Robbie had a tough time in Melbourne. "Pompous morons!", he used to spit. When he got a bit of money after Mum and Dad passed on, he returned here, bought back this place, their old home. He did well with his paintings, got quite a name for himself. Even the rednecks bought him, not that they cared a shit about art. Good investment, that was all. Robbie bought their properties too, when the banks closed-in on them. He got the commune going, got rich. The rest you know.'

'Why did he not contact us while he was alive?'

'Blow me if I know. It was a shitty thing to do, keep us all in the dark, even me, about this cousin — or is it cousin of a cousin? — who'd married this glamour boy-prince and lost all for love.'

'So you don't know. Pity you can't help.'

'Help with what, miss?'

'One of the lawyers, Mr Rohan Roy, you know, he has some doubts.'

'Doubts? About Robbie?'

'Yes.'

'What sort of doubts?'

'Was he really a Gordon?'

'Holy Mary ! You mean the old bugger was a fraud?'

'We don't know. The lawyer may be wrong. May be it's all un-necessary.'

'Hang on a sec!' I had to laugh out loud. 'I wouldn't put it past the bugger to pull that one on all.'

As I begin to see what my dear rogue might have done, my laughter turns to a guffaw, making the poor little thing jump somewhat.

'– I can just see the bastard! He always was a larrikin. I can just see him doing that: " Sod off commies, I am born-again royal". He was a red-hot leftie, got tired of that mob; they got boring – unforgiveable! So he does a full U-ee: out of his bag of tricks he pulls a real Princess out! What a stunt!' I laugh and laugh, till tears run down my cheeks. 'Sorry, Miss! No offence to you. I can't help it. What a joke!'

'I hope not.'

'Sorry! I shouldn't have said that. Forget it! It's just Rose after a tot or two of Scotch, that's all. As you say, there's nothing to doubt. Agreed?'

I had to do it, pretend that I didn't believe Robbie had fooled everyone. How or why, I hadn't a clue. I didn't like the way poor little Miss looked hurt. The thought of Robbie being a fraud seemed to make her real miserable. Why it should, when she's got the whole bloody lot that I should have had, I can't figure out. So I fixed her an egg sandwich and we moved upstairs. She stood a long while on the veranda, gazing at the paddock in a dreamy sort of way. It seemed to do her good. By the time we got to the bedroom, she was her old sparkling self.

We were standing by the four-poster bed, still covered in Robbie's favourite blue spread, a quilted version of Hokasai's surging seas, and I say to her, I don't know why:

'This is where Robbie died. Can you believe it, he'd just turned sixty?'

'I'm sorry for you, Miss Rose. May I ask you what he died of? The lawyers didn't give any details.'

'I bet they didn't.' I laugh. 'You don't want to know, sweetie!'

'Why not?'

'Let me put it like this: "Not fit for a young person's ear".'

'I'm not a child. I am not afraid of death. Did he suffer much? Was he in pain?'

'In pain? Na. Robbie was freaked out, darling — was right off his face.'

'Drugs?'

'Oh no! Nothing so vulgar, not Robbie. We didn't do drugs. We did a bit, way back in the seventies, then, we stopped. Just an occasional joint, that too because I had to keep up with what was hitting the markets.'

'What was it like, smoking marijuana? They say some get high, others don't. Did *you*? I've never before met anyone who actually smoked hashish.'

— She says 'hash-shi-sh' ever so daintily, hissing the word through her pearly teeth as if she was giving me a secret mantra. I would have lit up a joint with her, had I got one about me.

'—Haven't you, now? You've come to the right person. Don't get me wrong! I'm not an addict. Oh, no! It was purely professional interest. I was one of the judges for the "Weed-Quest" we held in the commune. An annual event. They'd bring them from plots and nooks from all over — God knows how they dodged the cops! Hour after hour of sniffing, biting, chewing, smoking — can't tell you what a mother of all trips it was! With some you swam to the outer galaxies, and some: — Phew! Shitty stuff! Like breathing bleach, scoured your windpipe like Drano! When you do this tasting and judging year after year, you go off the stuff, like going off chocolate if you work in a choc-factory. To top it, Robbie and I didn't like what it was doing to the kids. Day and night they'd sit, zombie-like, sucking from their orchy-bottle bhongs, slaughtering their brain cells minute by minute — strong, healthy, blokes shrinking into weedy little moronic weaklings, unfit for a day's work in farm or factory. That wasn't what Aquarians were about. Where had all the vision gone? In smoke, weed-smoke. Robbie had had enough. No more joints. No more Weed-Quests. No more Nimbin-Bus.'

'I didn't know he ran a bus-company: it is not mentioned in the will.'

'Sorry, darl, I forget. "Nimbin-Bus" is what the city-folk call the stupid morons who get brain-dead with hash. It had to stop. Robbie got mad and campaigned, hitting them with the latest research findings. Some stopped and woke up, others kept going their own sweet way to hell. The stupid thing is, they don't listen. Who needs weed when you can get natural highs in this fantastic country? Have you seen Nimbin Rocks yet? I must take you there. There's a place by Needle Rock where you can get high as a kite, just being there and breathing the air — lifts you right off this planet. Robbie loved it!'

'His death must have been very sudden.' As she says this, her eyes question me.

'You don't give up, do you, darling? OK, if you must know, it was a beautiful dawn; the phone rang. Sotheby's. They'd sold his Gibraltar Range series, couple of millions in the bank: as always, to celebrate, we broke open a bottle of bubbly and made love. Dear Robbie got so high on this, his last love-trip, he didn't land. He died in my arms, so to speak.' I can't stop the hysterical giggles bubbling up. '– to be precise, he died between my thighs.'

'Goodness me!' She blushes a plum-pink. 'I shouldn't have. I am so stupid sometimes.'

'It's OK, pet. It's time you learnt some facts of life.'

'I am not ignorant. I read books.'

'I bet you do. I bet you know the *Kama Sutra* back to front.'

'It's a very boring book. So technical, like reading a machine-manual.'

'Is that so?'

Blow me! I threw that in about the *Kama Sutra* just to tease; lo and behold, she trashes the world's most-perved-over classic with the slightest toss of her pretty little Princessy snout. She did surprise me. It's time I gave her a surprise or two.

'Now, Miss Rani, would you like to see the great man's studio?'

'Yes, please!'

'To the paddock then.'

'You mean those railway-carriages I saw. I wondered what they were doing there. Uncle loves trains, especially the old-style ones.'

'Robbie was hooked on steam trains and trams. He bought these cars off Goninan's, when they went all electric. He loved working there, even in the hot weather. He kept the fans whirring, made him feel as if he was just halting at some station. Always on the move, that's our Robbie!'

So I show her round. 'Car One, the Alpha – this is where he keeps his old work, things he didn't want to sell. Look at this one, "Ebor Falls at Twilight", his favourite.'

'It's so beautiful, just as it looks, yet so ethereal. I recognize the scene. We stopped there a while. Uncle instantly fell into deep meditation. He said it reminded him of home, the Falls of Courtallam.'

'For Robbie, painting Ebor was like praying. Came from deep inside him, this light, the way it bounces off the black granite, throwing up sprays of diamond-glitter. Yeah, he couldn't sell it, even when a German buyer offered him seventy thousand for it.'

'I can understand.'

'It's yours now, sweetie!'

'I don't know how to thank this extraordinary man! Such a stranger to all of us!'

It was then I had the idea. It came to me like a nudge from Robbie.

'There is something you can do for him, you know, sweetie.'

'Really? – What is it?'

'Come this way!' So I take her to the fourth car, the Omega. 'This is where he kept work-in-progress. He kept it locked – he wouldn't let anyone see, not even me, till he'd finished a painting. It was quite a surprise to me when I got here and found this – there!' I whisk off the cotton drape over a canvas on the easel to reveal a half-finished nude. 'Recognize her?'

'Oh my God!'

Little Miss stands dumbfounded. I can almost feel her goose-pimples.

'– Alice, my grandmother? 'She moves closer, and touches the canvas as if she were fingering a delicate piece of silk.

'– It is incredible, so like her – yet how could he?'

'– Know what she was, nudie? Robbie was trained in the old way, not in one of these chicken-shit abstract art kindergartens. He sees the bones beneath the clothes, he knows what the flesh looks like. Brilliant, isn't it? I had no idea who she was or how he'd conjured her up, till the will was read. Then I searched and found this sepia-print of your Grandma, carefully hidden away. You know what? You look so like her.'

'Do I?'

'I bet. Robbie agrees.'

'Robbie?'

'Yeah! He's here. I can sense his aura. He wants to finish this, with your help.'

'Me? What are you talking about?'

'He wants you to sit for him, then he'll work through me. Heard of automatic writing? This will be automatic painting. Promise you'll sit for him, won't you?'

'Sit for you, you mean?'

'No sweetie. I mean for him, for Robbie. I'm no painter. Oils, essences, that's my line.'

'I know. I bought some of your brand.'

'Truly? Like them?'

'Yes. Especially the jasmine oil.'

'Good! – Believe me, Robbie is serious. You can't refuse him, after all he has done for you.'

'I'm sorry, Miss Rose. I don't understand how you can paint when you don't know how.'

'Robbie will guide me. I trust him. If he says I can, I can. If he says I must, I must. I have no option. He could be trouble if we don't do this.'

'You bewilder me!'

'Don't be scared! Nothing to worry about! It's very simple. You have a lovely body, shame to hide it. Robbie was getting good at nudes. I promise you, you'll be his best. We'll put it in for the Archie. Sure to win!'

'No, no. I can't possibly do that.'

'Can't you? Why not? What are you afraid of?'

'Afraid? I am not afraid of anything. It just doesn't seem right.'

'Really? All those bosomy belles in your temples, not just nudie neither, getting up to all sorts of tricks, with such ecstasy in their faces! – Are you ashamed of your culture?'

'Of course not!'

'Then what's the big deal?'

'What will Uncle say? He'll be shocked.'

'Only if you tell him. Why not keep quiet till it's done, and then see? Why not a secret between us girls? Let's keep it that way, shall we? Do it for Robbie. I sense that his spirit won't rest till he's done his last great painting. You do no one any harm. Beauty for beauty's sake! Let's celebrate life, as Robbie would say. – OK?'

'I'll think it over.'

'Good girl.'

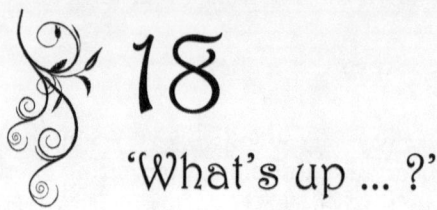

18

'What's up ... ?'

'Ziggy!'

Katarina stands immobilised at the open door, her fingers tightening round the hanger of the dry-cleaning she is carrying, her lips twisting bitterly as she bites back her anger:

'I thought you'd gone for good. Why didn't you ring?'

'I wanted it to be a surprise.' I take the jacket away, throw it over a chair, and kiss her. 'Happy birthday!'

She stays still in my arms, eyes closed; tears run down her cheeks.

'You, remembering my birthday – this is too much!'

'Don't be upset! – I did warn you! Being a "guide" to this Maharajah is utterly bizarre. I never know what he'll get up to when. The other day he took me on his helicopter, prospecting suitable locations for his residence. Hair-raising trip! Lucky I'm still here.'

'Tell me all about it! – Let me get you a drink! It's my Martini-time.'

'Open this first!'

'What is it?'

'A prezzie, of course, for my birthday-girl.'

She tears at the wrapper like a toddler at first Christmas. 'An opal pendant! I can't believe this! This is not like you, Ziggy! What's up?'

'We went to White Cliffs, to inspect the mines – the Maharajah has shares in opal. Stayed overnight in one of those underground motels, never done that before. Wonderfully soothing experience, I thought I might become a cave-dweller. KDR offered me "a choice of opals for the lady of my choice". So here you are!'

'KDR? – And the Princess, what do you call her?'

'Princess.'

'I see.' She fingers the pendant thoughtfully, twisting it round to flash glittering filaments of light from its turquoise-and-pink face.

'–I shan't pretend I'm not a wee bit jealous. – Still, this lovely gift! I'm overwhelmed! You've never done anything like this before. This rajah's clearly good for you.'

'Clearly.'

'Tell me everything. I've so much to ask.'

'First things first. Dinner out. We might even go dancing, if you'd like that.'

She gives me a searching look, kisses me on the forehead. 'We might, on the other hand, we might not. Don't disappear while I shower, promise?'

'Promise.'

The flat is quiet, except for the running water, and Katarina singing. *Questa regia*. Her voice resounds with the passionate hauteur of Turandot, yet how unlike the ice-maiden is my Katarina! She has done well with the flat: airy, light-filled and sparsely furnished, a pair of bamboo basket-chairs, white cushions and a few low, black-lacquer tables: I suspect she has gone Zen.

The Bay looks breathtakingly picturesque. There is something eerie about the light, filtering through puffs of dark clouds: relentless shafts of sharp brightness from the cliffs down to the rock-strewn sand. Picture-perfect setting for an Annunciation. I expect to see an angel or two with a dove in train.

No dove. Only an abrasive seagull squawking past the window, splashing the glass with its droppings.

I feel duly chastised. I shouldn't have come. Certainly not on her birthday, bearing gifts. Given her KooriKat instinct, she is bound to catch me out: how long before she discovers that this visit is a desperate alibi? What right do I have to play with her feelings, exploit her trust, simply to stop myself skidding further into my reckless, somnambulist romancing of the Princess? With avuncular attention and courteous interest, I am skidding fast; and I know I have no right to lure an innocent-abroad into my bat-infested den.

The bamboo-chimes tinkle in a rapid flurry. In them, I hear the Princess' sparkly laughter: it is not as easy to disengage as I had hoped.

I had decided to leave Lockhart Lodge quietly. After all, KDR had been informed, and as for the Princess, it was best to leave a note. That's what I had settled on, till I saw her on the lawn from my bedroom on the first floor.

She was reading, swaying in her hammock, her clothes dotted with ferny leaves, her brow knitting and face clouding over now and then. I watched her a while, then decided that I could not possibly leave without saying farewell. I took care to stroll across the grass quietly: a childish whim to surprise a child, I told myself. My squelchy tread on the buffalo-couch gave me away.

The Princess hopped off her hammock, hastily pulling down her scarf over her loose-fitting top that clung to her white-laced, petite breasts.

'Mr Martin! You startled me.'

'My apologies, Princess! Good afternoon!'

'Please! Why don't you just call me Indrani or Lizzyrani? No need to be so formal.'

'I prefer to call you "Princess".'

'So be it!'

'I've come to say goodbye. I'm off early morning.'

'Oh! —Why goodbye? Aren't you coming back?'

'Sure I am. But I don't know how long I'll be away.'

'I see. May I — I know I shouldn't ask — but may I know where?'

'Byron Bay. To see a friend I've neglected.'

'A lady friend?'

'A longstanding friend. I haven't seen her since a brief visit a month ago.'

'What's her name?'

'Katarina Rossi.'

'Nice name. Is she Italian?'

'Her father was. She believes her mother was part aborigine.'

'How interesting! She must be very beautiful. I hope we meet sometime. She is most welcome to visit us. Do tell her.'

'Most certainly I shall. —What are you reading?'

'Same again: *Venomous Beasts of Australia.* The pictures are fantastic. Such horrible creatures, yet so beautiful! I can't keep wondering how anyone survives in this country. I have a good mind to pack up and leave!' She laughs, tinkling like a set of cowbells.

'Please, don't talk of leaving. On the whole these beasts don't bother you, if you don't bother them.'

'Really? I find it hard to believe – but then, how would I know? Uncle doesn't let me go anywhere without my bodyguards. Neither he, nor Ayah, nor the peon is keen to go bush-walking. So far, all I have seen of the bush is from safe lookouts. I dislike being just a tourist, on the fringe, as it were. I can't even go down to the river as much as I'd like to.'

'Would you like me to take you to the river? It's a fine afternoon.'

'If you don't mind – and, please, can we go through the jungle?'

'You mean the rainforest. I don't see why not, except –'. I size up her flimsy white cotton outfit. '– You need some proper shoes, and sturdier clothes, to keep the leeches off.'

'I'll go and change. I shan't be long.'

She returns, looking faintly comic yet winsome, in camouflage trousers, black beret and hiking boots; give her a rifle, she'd be ready for combat.

Our 'jungle' begins at the south-east of the property: a rough path flanked by blue gums, wattles and coachwood trees that soon tapers into a narrow track through densely canopied wet-forest. From among the clusters of king-ferns and broad-leaved lillipillies, giant strangler-figs rear up, like disconsolate ancient warriors with elkhorn-ferns for headdress. We wade into a soupy silence that breaks out in melodic whistles and atonal shrieks: an invisible ensemble of birds testing their vocal chords in haphazard rivalry. A sudden fugue of cacophonous braying from the kookaburra section makes the Princess jump.

'— Are you frightened?'

She shakes her head. 'It was so sudden. And I keep fearing I might step on some creature.'

'They can hear our steps metres ahead. — Stop!' I whisper. 'Hush!'

'What is it?' she whispers back.

'There!'

She looks around bewildered. I grab her hand and direct her towards the nearest strangler.

'This way! Behind those lillipillies! Here comes our soloist, by the look of him. A lyrebird! Keep very still. We may be lucky.'

We stand, I don't know for how long, the Princess's petal-like palm enclosed in mine, while the bird, a fine-tailed Superb, carries on his work, seemingly oblivious to our presence. He rakes up leaves, branches and dirt with his long-curved claws, thrusting them back and forth, scraping the earth and trampling all over it, till a sizeable, firm mound emerges. With one swift imperious glance, he scatters the yellow robin that has been hovering around for cast-off worms. The Superb hops onto his mound, and preens lazily, stopping midway to eye the Princess. She is in freeze-mode, barely breathing. The bird struts across his stage, testing, as it were, invisible microphones; he stops, and flicking his long tail over his whole body, launches into song: a churring vibrato of a prelude, arching upwards into a vigorous outpouring of melodies. His feathers quiver in a silver shimmer as he varies his song, interspersing Mozartian cadences with Offenbach, parodying snatches of other birdcalls. He sings and sings as if he were the sole voice in the wilderness, reaching out to the whole world from the dawn of creation.

The bird-song grips me, and sweeps me out from my lacerating visions into fathomless goodness. Like a trapeze-dancer, instinct with an impeccable sense of timing, I do a backflip and dive into velvety silence. Layers of fatigue scale off, and, my whole body feels recharged with myriad filaments of emerald light.

The music stops. My grip tightens. The Princess looks up, expectantly, her amber-eyes bright as polished jewels. I kiss her hands and whisper:

'Let's wait. He may dance for us.'

The Superb hops off his mound, scrabbles around among the trees and reappears, more animated. He springs on to his stage, and ceremoniously sways back and forth and sideways, hopping from one foot to another. A female emerges from the undergrowth, joins him on the mound and lets him cover her. The Princess looks away:

'– Let's go.'

We make our way back to the track. The Princess disengages her hand.

'Thank you. It was so beautiful! He deserves his name.'

'Thank the bird, not me. I wish we'd had him as our national emblem, instead of the clumsy emu and the bulky kangaroo.'

'This bird reminds me of our palace-peacocks. Peacock is also our emblem. We have two as well – the peacock and the elephant.'

'Why don't you adopt the lyrebird as your emblem for Ratnapuri II? You couldn't do better. After all, KDR has chosen, I believe, four sites along the river.'

'For four new "display-mounds" you mean to say, don't you, Mr Martin?'

'Not necessarily all new. Sometimes lyrebirds renovate old ones too.'

'As we might, if the sale of the Castle comes through. You can just see us strutting, singing and dancing, can't you?'

'– Stop!'

We stand still: just a few feet ahead, a green python slithers across the path, leaving a track, as if of bicycle tyres.

'– OK. Traffic's cleared, we can go now.'

'How could you "hear" him, with all these noises, not to mention my chatter? You are amazing, Mr Martin.'

'I'm only a learner, not an expert like Felix.'

'Felix is such an interesting guy. I really like him. And he has so many stories, some so funny!'

'As a matter of fact, he now has a story about your uncle.'

'Has he? Is it funny? I am guessing correctly, no?'

'No offence meant. Felix likes you all but he can't help making things up.'

'Oh, please! Do tell me!'

'I am not sure I can tell it as well as Felix.'

'Please! I must hear it.'

'We are almost near the river. Let's find somewhere to sit.'

'I love this Clarence!' The Princess runs towards the water's edge. 'I love the way this river look and flows, I love especially watching the waters swirl round those outcrops of granite.'

I find a log, and after turning it over and inspecting it thoroughly, I call her back.

'Your throne is ready, Your Royal Highness!'

She smiles. 'Thank you! Now, my story, please!'

'"A Bush Conference": story by Australia Felix, retold with some additions by Ziggy Martin.

'Says the one-claw crab to the goanna: "what's up, mate?"
Says the goanna to the crab: "Been fighting? Lost a claw again?"
Says the one-claw crab again: "So what? I'll soon grow another. What's up?"
"Dunno," says the goanna. "Let's ask froggie. He's so bloody puffed up, bet he's busting with news." The giant tree-frog puffs and puffs before he croaks: "What do I care? Ask the Major up there!"
Together they shout, one and all, the one-claw crab, the goanna, and the giant tree-frog: "WHAT'S UP, MAJOR?"

'The Major Mitchell, a fine specimen of a pink cockatoo, doing his sentinel duty on the topmost branch of a skeletal gum, turns around:
"Hmm? Did someone call me?"
Once again the trio shout: "What's up, Major? All this busy-busyin' around us, all this diggin' an' loppin' an' sawin', what's up, what's up?"
"Steady, steady!"

'The Major cocks an eye towards up-river, swivels his neck right round to check down-river, stretches his pearly-pink feathers, first a left stretch, then a right stretch, sharpens his beak on the bark, unfurls his orange-red crest, shakes the powder off his feathers, and tightens his claws :
"A stranger I spy. A dark, brown, rich stranger I spy."
"A stranger," croaks the giant tree-frog; "A brown stranger", lisps the goanna; "A dark brown stranger", mutters the one-claw crab.
"Yes," the Major continues, "a dark brown stranger and his flock. They are coming our way. I am yet to find out, for what?"
"For what? For what?"
"For what? Precisely my question. We have had the blacks, we have had the whites; we have seen the blacks fighting the blacks, we have seen the whites fighting the blacks, now the brown ones are here. Are they fighters too? I ask myself," says the Major.

"'Not more fighters," grunts the feral-pig, who has just joined the conference. "I've had it up to my snout, these human swines chasin' an' shootin' and killin' us, in our home ground. Up to my snout, I've had it! So have the 'roos, the wombats, and all our bush-brothers; "Move on, stranger," we cry. We must fight for our bush-space. Bush brothers all! I call you to unite and fight, fight to the death for our bush-rights!"

"'Steady, steady!"
Chairman Major flaps his wings. "Calm down, my friends!" The Major stretches his neck to deliver a magisterial squawk: "Calm down, all of you! Rumour has it – what our friend white cocky picked up on the grain-train from Port Hunter, and I might remind you, the grain-train cockys are a reliable source – rumour has it that this brown stranger is a royal chief, that he is no fighter but a planner. And he has plans, mighty big plans."
"Sure does!" In waddles the wombat. "Sure he does, hacki' an' sawin' an' clearin'. Bet he has plans for a bloody golf course!"

'In flies a lyrebird, and perches on a branch near the Major: "Listen ye all! I heard somewhat different."
The Major turns to the lyrebird deferentially: "And, what did you hear, I pray?"
"They say, this royal brown chief is here, not to wreck us but to save us. And no golf-courses, most certainly not: his flock play polo, not golf – that I am sure of."
Silence for the space of three seconds.

'The one-claw crab crawls up a little. "What about our river? What is he doing to our river? He is there every day. I see him sitting there, thinking, thinking. It's dangerous when humans think so much."

'The lyrebird flutters up to a neighbouring tree, on to a leafier branch: "Search me! All I know is he owns this place, he likes it and he means to stay, and he likes our river and he has plans for things by the river."

'The goanna slithers to the water-edge. "Did you hear that, crockies? He likes the river, and he has plans. He wouldn't want you

185

lot squatting there and messin' about, would he? Watch out! He likes your river!"

The crocs muster: "We'll make sure he doesn't."

"Good onya, crockies! You do just that. I see he comes down to the river often. How come you guys missed him?"

"Yeah?" grumble the crocs. "Must've been siesta-time. Has anyone seen him?"

"I have," trills the lyrebird. "I have seen him bow down to the river, sprinkle water over his head, sit down under the giant-strangler, eyes closed. I s'ppose he prays."

"Prays? We'll make sure he is here to pray not prey." The crocs open wide their jaws in silent guffaw. "Or, else, snip, snap, off he goes to his Maker."

'The red-bellied black snake slithers in. "If I can be of any assistance. One quick nip, you know how tactful and reliable I can be. My record speaks for itself."

"Order! Order!" the Major shrieks. "Quiet, you bloodthirsty lot! Not guilty until proven. Get it? If what our friend Superb says is true, we have nothing to fear from this dark brown chief. So I suggest we wait, wait and watch, and be true to our motto: 'Live and let live.' Now, pass the word down, 'Live and let live.' Meeting dismissed!"

The Major folds his wings, gives a little shrug, and closes his eyes.

"Live and let live," says the lyrebird to the wombat; "Live and let live," says the wombat to the feral pig, the feral pig to the goanna, the goanna to the giant tree-frog, the giant tree-frog to the one-claw crab, the one-claw crab to the crocodiles. "Live and let live", they all shout.

End of story.'

The Princess claps.

'Wonderful! You must tell it to Uncle. He would readily agree. Do you know he is planning to have an eco-conference as soon as we are ready?'

'Then we must get Felix to tell his story. It could be a keynote address.'

'Brilliant! This bush is so rich, so full of life, it makes me giddy. I fear I'll never be able to tell what's what.'

'Don't worry! There's an easy way to learn. When I am in Byron Bay, I'll get you a "seek-and-find" poster. They sell them to schools.'

Her face drops. 'You're right. I am no better than a school kid.'

'I'm sorry. I didn't mean to sound patronising.'

'No, no. You can make fun of me, I don't mind. I am an ignorant foreigner, after all.'

'We are all ignorant foreigners in this land.'

'That is very kind of you. But I don't think that can be true. Sometimes I wonder if Uncle and I — if we are not being plain silly with our schemes.'

'Of course not! They are splendid schemes.'

'Do you really think so?'

'Why wouldn't I?' I give her a hand and raise her up from the log.

'Because, because —' She shakes her head '— you seem to be laughing at me all the time. I get confused.' Her eyes sadden and her voice grows solemn. 'Please take me home the quick way. I've been away too long, I'll be missed.'

*　　*　　*

And already, just a day away, I am missing her. I take out the poster I have bought, spread it out on the window-seat and search for our Superb, hidden somewhere in the greenery.

Katarina returns, fresh and elegant in blue silk dress which sets off the opal.

'What's that?'

'Just a poster.'

'May I?' she looks at me questioningly.

'For the Princess. She is trying hard to learn the names of our birds and beasts. I thought she might find this useful.'

'Oh! – Will I ever see her?'

'Of course! She has invited you to come any time. Certainly you must be there for the Coronation.'

'Coronation? You're not serious!'

'Indeed I am. KDR is planning a full-scale traditional Coronation ceremony. He is inviting representatives from all sections of the community, besides dignitaries from the government and overseas. It is going to be a spectacular. You can't miss it.'

'Who is going to be crowned, him or your Princess?'

'*My* Princess, Katarina?'

'Yes. *Your* Princess.'

'Katarina!'

She moves away and stands looking out into the dark sea. 'I think there's going to be a storm. Let's dine in and watch. I'll order something.'

Later, the window-panes of our blue bedroom judder as storm-winds whistle through. Slanting rain lashes against the clouded glass. I feel trapped as in a car-wash.

'Stop!' Katarina pushes me off, switches on the bedside lamp, and lights a cigarette.

'What is it?'

'You know very well.'

I lie back, hands over my head. 'I'm sorry.'

'What were you thinking about?'

'A lyrebird.'

She props herself on an elbow, stubs her cigarette, inspects me with a bemused expression.

'A lyrebird? There you do surprise me.'

'Saw one yesterday. A magnificent Superb.'

'A real one? Not one of your "seeings"?'

'A very real one.'

'Lucky you!' She looks at me steadily, drawing on her cigarette. 'You had company, right?'

I don't reply.

'The Princess?'

'I was escorting her to the river. She isn't allowed to go anywhere without a bodyguard. We saw this lyrebird. He sang and danced.'

'How nice!'

'It was beautiful.'

I remember the discreet, unconfused way in which the Princess moved away when the male covered the female. She was so natural, so matter-of-fact that I wondered if she understood what was happening. Surely she can't be that naïve? Was she aware of what I was doing when I kissed her hand so lingeringly, or was she still in freeze-mode? For that matter, was *I* aware of what I was doing? A momentary impulse? Or, as Katarina suspects, am I falling in love?

The winds get menacingly louder. The window-panes give out a death-rattle. With pressure building up inside the room, the glass is ready to shatter. I rise and open the window just enough to avert disaster. Lightening reveals wall-high breakers lashing about like angry beasts, foaming at the bit, ready to wreak havoc on the shore.

Katarina returns from the bathroom wearing a Tai-Chi robe. She lights another cigarette, and sitting on the edge of the bed, faces me. Her voice is uncannily steady.

'I think, Ziggy, it is better if you leave.'

'Katarina!'

'Rather you went back than brood over her here.'

'Come on, I'm not brooding.'

'Aren't you?'

'Just a passing thought.'

'Am I a passing thought too, when you are with *her*?'

'Katarina! Please! Don't start an argument. I have come to be with you.'

'Sure! – But *can* you? Be honest!'

'In so far as I can be with anyone – and if I am allowed.'

'What's stopping you? – Why is it that you've never asked me to marry you?'

'Marry? – I didn't know you wanted marriage.'

'Yes, marriage, children. Suppose I do – will you?'

I know the answer. I don't have the guts or the heart to say it. There is something holding me back; there has always been something holding me back, long before the advent of my Princess. Oh God, what am I doing?

'– I fear it won't work.'

'You fear wrong. If you love me as I love you, why shouldn't it work?'

'I do love you, but –'

'But what? – Are you planning to hook this Princess?'

'Good heavens, no!'

'Then what?'

'Things happen to me. You know what I mean, I am not myself.'

'Does your "voice" still bother you?'

'"Bother" isn't the word. I am better; but not in the clear yet: I am not sure if I ever will be. It happened again. I was with KDR in his 'copter. He was at the controls, I had the map. We were somewhere over the Gibralter Range. He was intoxicated by what he saw. Got talking about his schemes, growing more and more grandiose. He got so excited we had several near misses: we could have easily crashed into some boulder or tree. How we survived is a miracle in itself. All through the trip I had a queasy stomach. At first, I thought nothing of it; just nerves, or the kedgeree at breakfast I should have skipped, I kept telling myself. Yet deep within me I had this sense of foreboding building up. Strangely enough, it wasn't about a crash. I knew we'd be OK, despite KDR's reckless flying. It was something far more sinister. It was as if, while he was plotting out his earthly paradise, I had had news of the serpent's whereabouts. I fear something is going to go horribly wrong.'

'Why don't you tell him to get real?'

'I can't. There's nothing sinister in his plans. He wants to reverse the trend, from globalisation to localisation. Strip his talk of oriental lingo, what he proposes is feasible: improving conditions for workers, humanizing industry, sacralising the land, fair-deals etc. – nothing vicious or dangerous about that.'

'Then what are you getting worked up about?'

I cannot go any further. My alarm over the Maharajah's euphoria was genuine enough, but there was something else. Plunging through light-edged dark clouds over the Gibraltar, with mountains undulating beneath us and tree-tops dancing in the wind, I was reminded of the old man in Felix's song:

...Where we saw ... where we felt ... the sweep of eagle-hawk's wings ... of a man in clothing of fire ... in the burning red clouds ... where we saw ... where we saw and trembled ... at the sweep of his fiery wings, at his searching scorching eyes ... where we fell ...

It was as if I had felt the sweep of those fiery wings, and crashed through the threshold of earthly reality into a chasm of ever-pulsating light and life. One foot in paradise, I had caught a whiff of life beyond life. And, for the first time, I had an inkling of where my "voice" was urging me to. What can I say to Katarina, who is dreaming of domestic bliss and children on the beach?

Katarina lifts her head up, tossing her hair back.

'– So? What's *really* bugging you? Fear of commitment?'

'To be fair, so long as I keep hearing this "voice" and "seeing" things, I don't believe I can settle into ordinary life.'

'In that case, you clearly need help. – Are you willing to see a "clever-man"? I can find you one through my cousin Zelda.'

'Your cousin? Bundjalung cousin?'

'No such luck!' Katarina laughs. 'Bloody Sicilian! I didn't know I had a cousin till I visited New Italy. Met Zelda, who runs the Arts Centre shop. Soon found out that she belongs to the Rossi clan, to a healthier branch of the family tree, it turns out. Her folks grow olives. Zelda buys stuff from the local Bundjalung. She gets on with the grey-hairs. I am sure she can fix you up with a "clever-man".'

'Thanks!' I take her hand and put it to my lips. 'So you're not throwing me out into this storm?'

'Not yet.'

19
A Crypto-King Dreaming

If I, as yet a crypto-king, fix the sharp point of a pair of compasses at our current seat at Baryulgil, and draw an arc from Glenn Innes in the west towards Tooloom Falls north of us, curving past Murwillambah, then halt at some solitary island off Byron Bay, I shall be shaping a domain studded with saphhire, diamond, topaz, silver and beryl. And if I complete my circle, swinging my compass southwards, starting near Llangothlin and gliding past Cathedral Rock to pause at the mighty Ebor Falls, then trekking through dense-wet Dorrigo, emerging from its sky-high canopies somewhere near Woolgoolga to confront the bracing winds off the Pacific, I shall be taking in yet more treasure-laden terrain: gold, quartz, sapphire and topaz. *Ratnam, ratnam,* jewels everywhere, not a sparkle to be lost! So rich is this territory in jewels galore to please the heart of any king that I cannot but marvel how providential it is that our new kingdom is to be a Ratnapuri, a kingdom of jewels! And once my beloved niece Indrani is crowned as queen of Ratnapuri II in a ceremony that shall be a coronation in all but name, and I am installed as her Regent, and our newly-designed crest of lyrebird-on-elephant is set upon all our properties, farms and factories, schools and hospitals, upon all that we own and run — then we shall aspire to be, as it were, an exquisite paradigm of sacred trusteeship.

We are well placed here at Baryulgil, in this elegant ruin of a palazzo which the locals call 'the Castle'. Indrani and I took to it instantly. Indrani, with her expertise in *vastu shastra*, confirmed what I had instinctively surmised: that this palazzo, much in need of restoration, is charged with auspicious vibrations. At the height of its glory it had been the seat of a pioneer squatter, and if we are to believe word-of-mouth reports, he had been a benign autocrat who treated the natives as human beings, even wrestling with one in a friendly bout. By all accounts, written and oral, he was a true gentleman of civilized disposition, so rare in these parts in those days.

The plight of the native aborigines is grim indeed. No longer shot, or killed by arsenic hidden in flour, but still dying a slow death, bitten by the poisonous fangs of rapacious trans-national corporations who stalk this sacred land in giant, ugly strides, seeking whom they may devour. Such is the menacing advance of *Vulcan* who swallowed up *Zodiac* who had ingested *Ixion*, who had munched away at lesser fry such as *Meridian* (who were in sugar), *Lucan* (in woodchip), and *Zephyr* (in cotton).

Vulcan is ever on the move, taking in all it can, to feed the bellies within its bloated belly. I have been re-reading the *Panchatantra* – where else would I find inspiration for wise strategy but in these ancient fables? Very soon I have to hatch a scheme or two, if I am to rescue the oppressed of this land from *Vulcan*'s greedy clutches. So far I have lulled *Vulcan* into thinking that I am no more than a harmless old eccentric, keen on renovating ruins. May they continue to slumber, whilst I dream and scheme!

For scheme and plot I must – and in secret, whilst I make friendly, 'business-as-usual' overtures to the enemy. Commerce, as history proves time and again, is the most tried and tested pathway to conquest. Was it not commerce that paved the way for the mighty Cholas when they set about conquering the eastern seas, and held sway over Kadaram, now Kedah, Sri Vijaya (or Cambodia), and Champa (otherwise Vietnam)? My heart leaps with pride when I recall the Chola embassies to China, when I read of the entrepreneurs of old whom the Emperor of China courted with strings of copper dollars, receiving in turn glassware, camphor, brocades, rhinoceros horns, ivory, incense, rose-water, borax, cloves and other opulent and aromatic articles. It brings tears to my eyes to dwell on the grandeur of our commerce with the Sung Dynasty Emperors, even as I am moved to laughter by the mighty Cholas suffering such gross mutations of their Sanskritic names! Who would even recognize Rajaraja in Lot'sa-lot'sa, or Sri Rajendra Chola in Shi-lo-cha-yin--to-lo-chu-lo, or Kulottunga in K'ie-lo? Laugh as we may, those were the days of open conquest and decorous trading, conducted with grace, courtesy and dignity. – So unlike the fast-moving, fast-talking, furtive mendacity of our modern transnational corporations! To be sure, the agents now flourish chequebooks at their bamboozled victims (mind you, with one eye still on their calculators): yet sordid and devious are their ways, compared to the humane gestures of yore! When the King of Khamboj sought the friendship of Rajendra Chola, did he not do so by sending him his own victorious chariot in which he had overcome many a hostile army?

Imperialism, sneered at by some as 'organized loot', is well and truly alive. Who needs armies, ships and soldiers when the likes of *Vulcan* can conquer through a team of grey-suited, briefcase-bearing lawyers and accountants with their laptops? So, you see, I need to scheme and plot, to match their cunning with my craft.

– Where has Ganga Rao laid my file on *Vulcan*? For that matter, where *is* my secretary?

The outer room where he normally busies himself is ominously quiet. Just as I reach for the bell, Ganga Rao appears, bearing a silver tray: my morning coffee and the day's mail.

'– Good morning, Your-Highness! I am sorry I am late. There was a bad accident on the road to the post office.'

'How bad?'

'The driver was lucky. He is alive. Foolish man! A kangaroo jumped on his car and he had no guard over the windscreen! Clear case of gross negligence.'

'Anyone else injured?'

'Thank God, there was no else in the car!'

'And the kangaroo?'

'The animal was bleeding very badly. They were debating whether to shoot it or not. I think they shot it.'

'Mmm – I do not like this incident. Not a good omen when you were undertaking our auspicious task. I presume the invitations have been posted?'

'Yes, Your-Highness.'

'Call the driver! I must personally tell him to take extra care when he drives the Princess.'

'Mr Felix has already left, Your-Highness. The Princess had an engagement at the Women's Co-operative. But there is no need to worry, Felix is a first-class driver.'

'Yes, but there are times when I fear he may forget the road. He is a dreamer. Still, one must grant that he does understand the vagaries of the roads here. – I see you have our mail. Anything interesting?'

'Here is a cover marked "Personal and Confidential".'

'Ah! From Messers. Rowlatt and Roy. About time they found the truth about our benefactor.'

'I hope what they say brings comfort to Your-Highness.'

Ganga Rao froths my coffee while I read the letter.

Dear Sir,
An update on our latest findings with regard to the Princess's benefactor, the late Robert Gordon. Our researchers have filed the following report:

Robert Gordon, painter, farmer, entrepreneur, political activist, conservationist, was the only son of Amy Gordon, and stepson of Dan Burkett, her second husband. Amy Gordon's first husband, and Robert Gordon's father, seems to have been one William Richter, who, at some stage in the Depression years changed his name to William Wright.. Unemployed and travelling north in search of work to avoid being a 'susso', William Wright had arrived at Bluegum Farm, Camira Creek, which belonged to the Gordon family. There he was employed for a few years as a farm-mechanic, met and married Amy, whose precise relation to the family is not as yet clear. She was governess to the Gordon children, including Alice Gordon, our Princess' grandmother. We have as evidence a charming hand-made birthday card from one of the Gordon children, which reads: 'To dear Amy, whom we tease and torment and who loves us best.' Unfortunately, William Wright met with a violent death (cause unknown) and Robert was born soon after his death; one Edward Gordon stood as godparent.

If we are to solve the mystery that shrouds Amy Gordon's identity, and thereby set your mind at rest, we need access to letters and papers, which we believe were left by the late Robert Gordon and which are currently in the care of Miss Rose. We have approached Miss Rose with a request to release the said letters, and as yet have not met with a positive response.

From our researches so far, we are moved to conclude that there was a strong, if somewhat ambivalent connection between Mr Robert Gordon via his mother Amy, and the well-respected Gordons of Blue Gum Farm, Camira Creek, who were famous for bringing out Highland cattle from their native Scotland.

If further clarification is required, Miss Rose must be persuaded to release relevant letters and any other records in her possession.

I wish to add that Roy and I have ourselves approached Miss Rose several times but met with a hostile response. So there the matter rests. We await your instructions.

Yours sincerely,   Ray Rowlatt.

'Well, well, well! – Ganga Rao! Call Indrani! She must be informed of this at once.'

'The Princess is out, Your-Highness!'

'Ah, yes. So you told me. – Where has she gone?'

'She is opening new premises we have secured for the Women's Cooperative. And –'

'And what?'

'She is proceeding from there to visit Miss Rose, staying overnight perhaps.'

'With Miss Rose?'

My harsh tone makes Ganga Rao blink rapidly. '– Allow me to remind Your-Highness, our Princess did seek permission.'

'Did she? Did I grant it? I must have. Did she give a reason for this visit?'

'I believe the Princess is also wanting to find out more about her benefactor from Miss Rose.'

'Playing Miss Marple, I see. I fear she is too young to be meddling with skeletons in cupboards. Yet, from what the lawyers say, we may well need her charm-offensive. As for Miss Rose, I must confess I do not care for that lady: she altogether lacks refinement.'

Ganga Rao ventures a smile. 'She is a jolly lady. If I may say so, Your-Highness, I believe the Princess is working hard, and feeling lonely. She needs a companion.'

'I know, I know. I ought to find her a husband. I am fully aware of that, Ganga Rao. But there is a time for everything. A marriage for the Princess at this moment would jeopardise our plans. You see, Ganga Rao, in my vision I see our Princess as Gloriana, the Virgin

Queen, holding sway over the hearts of many and not the captive of any one man. A husband will be clearly an impediment to the fulfilment of our dream.'

'Your-Highness knows best.' Ganga Rao bows, and stooping low, busies himself polishing the silver tumbler with excessive zeal.

'Of course,' 1 continue, '1 am not opposed to her marrying eventually, once our kingdom is well and truly set up.'

'Of course!' Ganga Rao puts the tumbler down and smiles.

'Why, 1 may even organise a *swayamvara,* so she can choose for herself. What do you think? Invite suitable candidates, suitors 1 mean to say, to our Pan-Princes Conference, let the Princess choose, like Damayanti of old.'

'Most wonderful idea, Your-Highness. There are already many suitable matches in our Coronation guest-list, Your-Highness.'

'Good! That will give her a chance for a preview.'

'Damayanti chose Nala. It was a love-match.'

'1 take your point. There is no reason why the Princess shouldn't fall in love with someone suitable. By "suitable", 1 mean he must be coming from the right family, horoscopes agreeing; and it has to be someone who knows how to be a Consort: he cannot do better than learn from the illustrious example of the Duke of Edinburgh.'

Ganga Rao shakes his dome emphatically. 'Very true.'

'It's all in the stars, in any case. Vembu gives me such puzzling readings, 1 cannot be sure if our Indrani is destined to marry at all! Who knows, she may be destined to reign as Gloriana, Virgin Queen, such as Shakespeare served! If the powers above ordain such a thing, who are we to argue?'

'Most certainly, Your-Highness. "Man proposes, God disposes".' He chuckles. 'Our little Princess is very strong-minded. She will not be easy to please.'

'That too I am aware of, Ganga Rao. Enough on this topic – is there anything else?'

'Vembu is wanting to talk about the Coronation ceremonials.'

'When are the elephants due?'

'Any time this week, Your-Highness.'

'Tell Vembu, I'll talk to him after evening puja. I am a little tired at present. You may leave.'

'Thank you, Your-Highness.'

'One moment! Before you go, get me the Princess! I must speak to her at once.'

'Yes, Your-Highness.'

He has got me agitated, my secretary, in his sly, sneaky way, nudging me to face what I have so far avoided. Dream as I may about Indrani being the Virgin Queen of our kingdom, it will be gross selfishness on my part to expect her to be my life-long companion. I am her guardian, I shall be her Regent: and reluctant as I am to part with her, one day I must let go. I must find her a husband. Dharma demands it, and far be it from me to swerve from dharma.

I wish Uma Devi, my gentle queen, were alive still. Much as I busy myself with dreams and schemes, at the end of the day I dread that dark cavern of sleep where loneliness awaits to gnaw my soul, where I know myself to be a journeyman to grief. After Uma Devi's untimely demise, they told me I should marry again, or, at least take a concubine or two. I could have, so easily. There was that Princess from Kamalapuri, a little over the boundary-line, but attractive enough: short, plump, with doey, docile eyes, she would have been a warm companion indeed – and quite a dowry she would have brought with her too! Vembu ruled her out, having spied a dark speck in her horoscope which – he put it bluntly for once – might mean my early demise. One cannot marry a woman knowing that she bodes death. I gave up after that, allowing myself an occasional indulgence: those film-stars whom Ganga Rao vetted could not but be ephemeral fancies, gaudy flowers that bloom a while in the glare of limelight, with no enduring grace to appease soul-ache. I could have searched further but when I reflected on the consequences of imposing a new 'mother' on Jayadev and Indrani, I pulled back. I have seen the most docile of women turn into the most cunning vixen or ferocious tiger once they have entrapped their men in the coils of passion. I couldn't risk that, not when my amber-eyed beauty looked up to me, her guardian-uncle, to protect her from the wickedness of this world. And how right I was: it has been my joy to see her grow, and blossom into the finest flower of a Princess.

Suddenly, a great commotion below; the noise seems to emanate from the portico. Ganga Rao rushes in, excited and puffing:

'They are here, Your-Highness – the royal elephants: Jaya and Vijaya are already here, a week earlier than expected. And Mr Martin too! He has escorted them. And there is a lady with Mr Martin.'

Laud we the Gods! Even as King Cymbeline might say, *laud we the Gods!*

I join Ganga Rao at the window. There they are, my beauties, Jaya and Vijaya, a right royal pair splashing their trunks in the fountain. I am rather proud of our fountain, a replica of Bernini's 'Leaky Boat', which, more than all the baroque fountains of Rome, spoke to my heart: for me this ever-filling, ever leaking boat is the very image of our transitory life. As I said to Indrani, 'In the midst of all our pomp and circumstance we need a humbling reminder of the vicissitudes of fortune'.

Then I see her, Mr Martin's lady friend. She must be fearless, to be sitting so near the elephants, on the ledge of the 'Leaky Boat'. She has taken her shoes off. Fine legs. She is dangling her feet in the gushing water, her movements teasing Jaya, and her handsome body is tremulous with laughter. I can only see her back. What a fine head of hair! Luxuriant coppery-red coils dance around her slender ivory column of a neck. Mr Martin certainly chooses well.

He senses my presence at the window, looks up, removes his hat and waves. His companion jumps off her perch, somewhat skittishly for a tall, buxom woman, and gazes at me, elegantly lifting purple-nailed fingers to shield her eyes against the light. Her lips, also of a deep purple hue, part slightly as if she is about to say something, but no words come out.

Am I such a shock to her? Or do I detect a deepening flush in her cheeks? It could, of course, be just the rouge or sunburn. Or, could it be that my appearance is not what she might have expected?

I linger by the window a while before moving back.

'Ganga Rao! What did Mr Martin say her name was, this lady friend of his?'

'Miss Rossi, Your-Highness. Miss Katarina Rossi, I believe.'

'Ah, Katarina! There is a certain Mozartian ring in such a name, don't you agree?'

Ganga Rao blinks. I forget that Mozart does not figure in his musical horizon, supposing he has one.

'Go and look after them! I'll join you shortly.'

'Yes, Your-Highness!'

I pause before the mirror. For one touching sixty, I am told often enough I am well-preserved. Thanks to years of meditation, I am blessed with a wrinkle-free countenance. As for my receding hairline, it lends a certain Shakespearean gravitas, which some ladies find appealing. And I do believe that my luxuriant moustache more than compensates for my waning mane.

What a good omen! My trusted adviser and his lady friend arriving at the same time as our auspicious royal elephants!

GAJA LAKSHMI: Goddess of Wealth and Well-being, flanked by adoring elephants.

That is it! Miss Katarina Rossi reminds me of Ravi Varma's painting of just such a scene.

Most certainly, an auspicious sign!

20
A Touch of *Courtesia*

'Please, Miss Rossi! Take, take!' I stretch out my hand towards our guest.

'What is it?"

'Jaggery only. Elephants love it. Do give Jaya a lump – she is looking towards you. She clearly likes you!'

'Thanks.'

Katarina Rossi takes the ball of jaggery I am offering on her right palm and holds it out to Jaya, who greedily devours it. Jaya's trunk so undulates in affection to Katarina's strokes that the lady and the elephant seem to be bound in mystic harmony.

'You certainly have made a friend there!'

'She's great! Ever since we met her she's been like this. Poor things! I felt sorry for them, cooped up in a crate and jolted about on our roads. She's so cute, isn't she? And so friendly! I can't believe it.'

'My late Queen, Uma Devi, was a favourite with her. She is used to receiving tender care from her, and her daily jaggery!'

'She certainly loves this stuff.'

'It is very sweet. Like me, my elephants have a sweet tooth, so to speak.'

'I thought I knew all about sugar: but I've never seen sugar like this before.'

'Do you want to try? Do, please!'

'No, no! It's OK. Jaya might get crook if I take hers.'

'No, no. You don't have to take hers. Please let me – if you don't mind – open, please!'

I try as far as possible to sound like my dentist. She obliges, laughing a little as she munches. Her mouth, her teeth – *pearly bright as a split pomegranate.* I now know what the poet means.

'Well? How do you find it?'

'Mmm. Delicious! Slightly salty.'

'A touch of salt always makes sweetness sweeter, like tears in beautiful eyes. If I may say so, you have beautiful eyes, Miss Katarina! Your presence will do much to make these halls resound with cheer. My niece is a little lonely, she needs a young companion.'

'Ziggy says the Princess is as clever as she is beautiful. I can't wait to meet her.'

'She shouldn't be long. I have summoned her. Mr Martin has been a good mentor to her, but I am glad he has brought you to us. You are welcome to stay as long as you wish: our home is your home.'

'It is very kind of you.' She pauses, and tossing her hair back, looks me straight in the face. 'How should I address you? Ziggy says you hate being called Mr Maharajah.'

'That's correct. For you, as for Mr Martin, I am KDR.'

'Thank you. – Where is Ziggy? He promised he wouldn't be long. But then, I'm used to him not keeping his promises.'

'Please, don't be hard on Mr Martin. The fault, my dear Miss Katarina, is wholly mine. My secretary is getting very anxious about our Coronation Day. He is briefing Mr Martin on all that needs to be done. I am afraid Ganga Rao is a "details man". He will be keeping our friend busy for quite a while. My apologies! In the meantime, while the servants prepare your room, may I invite you to have some refreshments in my library? Perhaps I could show you round our palazzo afterwards?'

'That'll be great! Thanks.'

I was not sorry that Ganga Rao kept Mr Martin occupied. After all, Mr Martin needs no introduction to this palazzo: he has been supervising the renovations and building up a photographic record of progress, he knows every nook and corner, every crack and crevice. And if I am not wrong, Miss Katarina was not averse to a touch of *courtesia*. She sparkled and bubbled as we sauntered down colonnaded arcades, through courtyards, banqueting rooms, reception-halls, pausing now and then to have discreet glimpses of bedrooms. She was thrilled that I had assigned them rooms which bear panels of mother-of-pearl inlay work – she must have enjoyed my guided tour, why else would she hang on every word I uttered with such rapt attention? Within half an hour, she seemed to feel perfectly at ease in my company, as I certainly did in hers.

We had just stopped at the summer house. I stood by the entrance, while she sat down. She took off her shoes and began shaking them to be rid of the gravel that had irked her. Her moist, bare arms, glistening in the sun, took me back. Uma Devi, my beloved queen: she too was given to such vigorous shaking when she was folding a saree or a shawl. It brought a lump to my throat.

Katerina looks up, smiling. 'Where next? I'm ready now. – Are you OK?'

'Fine, fine.'

I look away as she continues to scrutinize me, clearly disbelieving. 'If you're sure? I hope I haven't tired you with my chatter.'

'Not at all. Something from the past. Memories, as you know, sometimes flood one.'

'They sure do! I hope yours are good ones.'

We resume our walk across the fresh-cut lawn. Something gives way within me. Until that moment I did not know how much it had been weighing on me, my promise to my father, Vijaya Deva Raja.

'He made me promise, you know, my father. He made me promise that I would fight that demon-woman.'

'Streuth! Who is she?'

'Mrs Gandhi, of course. She was the real culprit. It was she who struck the death-knell of our Princely States, she who stripped us bare, taking everything away, all our privileges. In 1970, the day she committed this crime, my father went into depression and never came out of it. He made me promise, the day he died. It was also the day little Indrani was born.'

'Amazing! What timing!'

'Indeed! Exquisite timing. We didn't know whether to weep or rejoice. Such an adorable baby Princess, so bright-eyed, chubby-limbed, full of life. Surely my father's soul had found a new home in her.'

'You mean the Princess is his reincarnation?'

'It may sound strange, yet look at what she is destined to, to be the Virgin Queen of this domain, Ratnapuri II. Only when I launched the scheme did I begin to feel that I am fulfilling my promise to my father.'

'Sure. I see what you mean. Does this mean that the Princess cannot marry?'

I detect more than a dispassionate query.

'No, no. The Princess may marry, but I do believe it is not sensible at this juncture.'

'I see. — What if the Princess is in love?'

'As yet Indrani has given me no cause to believe that.'

'Oh!'

'She is not a sentimental girl. If and when she does marry, I am confident that it will be a well-considered choice. She is well aware where her duties lie, and I am pleased that she is ready to respond to the ancestral call. — Did I tell you? They were twins, my father and Indrani's grandfather. I am definitely seeing in her the spirit of those twins: Uncle Vikram's daring and my father's resolute will.'

'And her parents? What were they like?'

'Alas, she lost them young, you know. Indradev loved cars and cars had to be his undoing. Her mother Lakshmi was with him when they crashed. Tragic, very tragic for the child, just turned six and orphaned in an instant. Yet I envy my cousin-brother; he was lucky to die without sickness and take his companion with him. Not like me! When Uma Devi died, I felt as if I had lost a limb. I still do.'

'I am very sorry.'

'No, no. I should apologize, burdening a beautiful young lady like you with my sadness — no, no, you are here to rejoice with us, to celebrate, not to commiserate. May I confess something? I find your company exquisitely refreshing. You will stay a while, won't you?'

'Thanks! I must check with Ziggy.'

'Ah, here comes Mr Martin, released at last! — I was just saying to Miss Katarina —'

'I heard. Kat doesn't need my permission: she's free to do as she pleases.'

'Excellent! That's settled then. Shall we toast this happy occasion with champers? I do hope Miss Katarina likes our champagne: *Omar Khayyam* – aptly named, I believe.'

Mr Martin puts an arm around his companion, squeezing her with what struck me as excessive pressure. 'Katarina loves bubbly, in any form, any time – isn't that so, my dear?'

* * *

Tantric Rose flings the wire door open, her pink kaftan ballooning in the breeze.

'Hi! Miss Rani! Good to see you! Like a drink or a bite to eat, before we start?'

'No thanks! I'm full. They laid on a big spread at the Women's Co-Op. I had to sample everything to please the ladies. Now I feel drowsy.'

'That's just fine by me. Couldn't be better. Robbie always liked his models a bit dopey, gave them a glass or two, or a joint, to get that languorous look he was keen on – shall we go? This way!' She slams the door behind her; a sleeping cat squeals and follows her, wailing. 'Cut it out, Joany! Stay where you are. Robbie won't like you in his studio, you know that very well. Bad luck!'

She kicks the cat back into the house and steps down the verandah; and hitching up her kaftan, strides across the paddock towards the railway carriages. The Princess follows her.

'I do love these carriages, but it's so hot in here.'

'You bet it is. Just drape yourself over the chaise-longue and relax, dearie.'

'Is that all?'

'Sure!'

'Well, I thought you might –'

'Want you to strip? I'm not dumb. I know that's too much to hope, but if you want to –'

'Oh no. No, no. I can't do that.'

'Can't you? Shame to hide what you've got. Never mind. We shan't worry about that. Robbie's an expert. He can manage, I'm sure.'

'Robbie?'

'Of course, Robbie. You don't think I'm doing this by misself, do you?'

'Did he paint many girls?'

'Didn't he just?'

'Nude?'

'What d' you reckon?'

'Didn't you mind?'

'Why should I? – He was a painter. He had to do what he had to do.'

'Did he paint *you*?'

'Over and over. I got bored sitting for him, hour after hour, starkers and starving – it was never perfect enough. Shit, I said to misself, I could be doing something better. – Now, if you don't mind, I must focus. I must tune into Robbie. I shan't say very much. That doesn't mean you can't. You carry on. I can listen on another track. – Tell me what you did today.'

'I was at Lawrence, opening the new premises for our Women's

Co-operative. Pretty place, Lawrence, isn't it?'

'A bit of a relic now. It was a dirty fight between Lawrence and Grafton. Lawrence lost.'

'So I hear. But it's so peaceful there, that's why we relocated there. The women like it too. Most of them are mixed blood. This lady Olga I met, she's so unusual looking, red hair, blue eyes, dark skin and a sort of Mongolian look – she says there's some Hungarian, Tartar blood in her aboriginal veins. She does fantastic work – tapestry, ceramics – she showed me how they bake the dots in. It was fascinating. – Miss Rose?'

'Mmm.'

'Are you OK?'

'Sure I am. Are you?'

'It's so hot in here. I'm drenched.'

'For Chrissake, take that top off! There's no one here to spy on you.'

'Maybe you're right.'

'Of course I am. I know you're shy. Keep your scarf on, if you like.'

'I shall.' The Princess takes her top off and attempts to cover her breasts with her muslin scarf.

'Isn't that better? – What beauties you have, my pet – a right pair of turtle doves! Now relax and carry on. You were telling me about Olga.'

'You were listening then.'

'Of course I was.'

'I thought – the way you looked, your eyes going trance-like – I thought you were off.'

'That too! I can be on *and* off.' She laughs. 'Don't forget, I can be in the body and out of the body. Not for nothing they call me "Tantric Rose".'

'I feel so sleepy. May I?'

'Please yourself. The stiller you are, the better for Robbie and me.'

The pedestal fan hums on, and soon the Princess slips into deep sleep. Her scarf slips to the ground.

'Good girl! – Robbie! Are you with me?'

'Rose!'

'How am I doing?'

'Not bad, not bad at all. – Lighten a bit the left breast, or she'll look like she's got cancer.'

'You bastard!'

'OK. OK. You're doing fine, Rose! I couldn't do better.'

'Am I? Truly ? It's aeons since I picked up a brush.'

'My fault. You should never have given it up.'

'I couldn't compete with you.'

'Why did you tell her you couldn't paint?'

'Don't be a dill, Robbie! Would she sit for me? For you, her great sugar-daddy, she'll do anything. Look at her!'

'Beautiful child! So innocent, Lord preserve her!'

'If only she'd take it all off!'

'She will, eventually. Don't worry.'

'I don't have your charm.'

'You have a better trump-card.'

'True!'

'Go for it, Rosie! Go for the Archibald! Good luck!'

'Stay ! Don't vanish yet! – I can't do this if you abandon me.'

'I won't. I'm on call, whenever you need me.'

Muffled tone from a mobile starts the Princess awake. Rose drops her brush.

'Shit! Damn these mobiles! – Yours or mine?'

'Mine!' The Princess pulls out the phone from her handbag. 'Yes, Uncle?'

Her brow creases through a range of 'yes' and 'no' until she puts the phone back with a final 'I understand! I *promise*.'

'– Miss Rose!'

'What's he after? Don't tell me, I can guess.'

'Those papers. It is very important we have them. We can't solve the mystery otherwise.'

'You really go for the frontal, don't you, dearie?'

'There's no point in beating round the bush. You know why I'm here today –we must know the truth about Amy Gordon.'

'Must you?'

'Absolutely!'

'Some truths should be left well alone. Why dig in that muck-heap?'

'Is it *really* a muck-heap?'

'In my opinion, all search for ancestral roots ends in some muck-heap or shitty midden.'

'Whatever it is, we must have the papers.'

'What's it worth?'

'How much do you want?'

'I'm not talking money.'

'What then?'

'Suppose you go bare for this –'

'Miss Rose!'

'Look, Miss Rani! What's the big fuss? You know you're pretty. You know it is perfectly safe. And I know you want to do it. Why pretend? You strip and I hand over the papers. That's a deal.'

A long silence. Then a giggle from the Princess.

'You're right! I'm a coward. I'm only thinking of what Uncle will say if he finds out.'

'Is my little Princess afraid of the big bad wolf?'

'Certainly not!'

'What's stopping you then? He doesn't need to know. I won't be telling him.'

'I won't either. After all, it's Grandmother Alice in the painting! Who's to know it's me as well?'

'Now you're talking! Good girl!'

'Next session perhaps. I can't stay. Uncle expects me back by dinner-time. We have guests. And our elephants have just arrived. I must go.'

'OK, pet! Next session then. A deal is a deal, right?'

'Right.'

21
A Royal Picnic

I tap out my cigar on the balcony ledge and take in a deep draught of the scented smoke. KDR is right about this. As my nasal sensors get sharpened in the wake of a puff or two, there follows a distinct alacrity of mind. Quite a turnaround for me, considering how relentlessly I have hounded Katarina to give up her cigarettes. But then, as KDR would say, one moves to a different plane when one graduates from cigarettes to cigars.

A moonless, still night. Silent, but for the ineffable humming of a billion-trillion stars in a squid-ink sky, pulsating with I know not what from the far corners of the universe – which, they say, might stretch for ever and ever. A never-ending nightmare of emptiness? Or an ever-pressing bid to face the One who reveals everything and nothing in an irrevocable 'I Am'?

A merciful respite from that voice for a few weeks. – Only, I suspect, because I am being shunted towards someone from whom I must find a clear directive. How can I possibly take it as mere coincidence that the spot chosen by KDR for tomorrow's picnic is in the vicinity of the very man I am to meet: Boonoo Boonoo Billy?

I can hear Katarina in her bedroom, pottering about, humming to herself. She is happy, happier than at any time with me at Byron Bay. At dinner this evening she shone: glamour-queen par excellence, wrapped in one of her KooriKat spectaculars, a strapless, pearl-studded black and silver outfit that etches her contours. Katarina could reign supreme: the Princess was delayed; and when she did arrive, wan and weary, she had to retire early. She seemed barely to notice the lavish attention her uncle was pouring over his favoured guest. Our eyes barely met; and when I did catch her, there was something troubling about her evasiveness.

The humming stops. Katarina pads across the short corridor that links our bedrooms and knocks on my locked door. She pauses and knocks again.

I could ignore her, let her think that I am still with KDR, sipping cognac. I could postpone her inevitable questioning, gain a brief respite till the morning.

Is it worth the hassle?

'— I'm out here, Kat! It's a magnificent night!'

'Just a sec!' She pads back to her room, and when she steps through the French doors on to our common balcony, she is draped in shimmering blue. She glides behind me, and locking me in an embrace, plants a light kiss on my crown. Her breasts, warm through the silk, press against me.

'Thanks a lot, Ziggy, for bringing me here. I wasn't at all keen to leave the Bay.'

'I'm glad you like it.'

'It's great! — Ouch!' She slaps her neck, crushing a whopper of a mozzie. 'The bastards! How they love my flesh! I'm sorry, I must get back in. If you want to talk, you have to come in. My room or yours, I don't care which.'

'Yours, then.'

I close the doors and draw the curtains. She flings herself onto the bed, ready as for a catalogue-shoot of dressing gowns. Arms akimbo, I face her. 'What do you want to talk about?'

'What a question! Everything! Wasn't that a beaut dinner? Is this what you do here every day? No wonder you weren't in a hurry to come down to the Bay.'

'Every other day we fast.'

'Truly?'

'Tonight was exceptional. Tonight was in your honour.'

'Thank you very much! Silver service, chandeliers with real candles, white-gloved butlers, cordon-bleu cooking, sorbets, champagne! A Parisian hotel in the middle of nowhere!'

'Never mention hotels to KDR, he abhors the very word. If you go to India you'll know why: every crummy corner café calls itself a hotel. For KDR, the acme of gracious living was to be found in the great ocean-liners, the Cunards, and the P & Os in their heyday. That's what he wants to recreate here.'

'I don't care where his ideas come from. I think I can get used to this life-style. – This picnic tomorrow, what will it be like, what should I wear?'

'Anything you like. You don't need my advice for that.   But be prepared, KDR never does anything just for fun.'

'What do you mean?'

'This royal picnic is as likely to be a royal progress. I bet there's a hidden agenda. I'm surprised he didn't tell you. You seemed to be getting on exceedingly well with him.'

'Whose fault was that? You can hardly complain. No sooner we get here, you desert me.'

'I didn't desert you, nor am I complaining. I'm glad you got on with KDR. It makes it much easier.'

'For what?'

'For you to stay on till the Coronation. You do want to stay, don't you? Surely you can take time off – you don't seem to be enjoying that gallery job.'

'Yeah, sure! I wasn't thinking of that.'

'What then?'

'The Princess. Wouldn't she mind? She seemed moody.'

'She was late. And she knew her uncle wasn't happy with her. She was expected to grace the occasion as a Princess should. Instead, she had spent too much time with Miss Rose.'

'I see.'

'KDR doesn't care for that lady.'

'That explains it then.'

'Explains what?'

'Why he was pressing me to stay. And all that talk about being a companion to his niece. Am I expected to chaperone her?'

'Would you like to?'

'No thanks. I'm not a girl's girl. Besides, I bet she'd rather you were her minder. That's what you have been, haven't you? She seemed pretty crook with you. I could see it in her eyes. Now I get the full picture.'

'There's no picture to get.'

'You want me to believe that?'

'I certainly don't want you to spoil a good day. Let's not quarrel over the Princess!'

'Who says I want to quarrel?'

'I think it's better if we both drop the subject. I'm tired and we have an early start. Good night! Sleep well.'

*   *   *

Next morning we don't make the early start we were meant to. KDR is in his military mode, pacing up and down the gravel path, twirling his moustache. He stops under the portico.

'Ganga Rao! Where is Indrani? Why is she keeping us waiting?'

'The Princess is almost ready, Your-Highness. She is not altogether well this morning, Your-Highness.'

'Why didn't you tell me before? We should postpone this trip.'

'Now only I am learning this, Your-Highness. Ayah says it is not anything serious. The Princess is not wishing to cause any disruption to the programme, Your-Highness. Here she is.'

Indrani trips down the hallway stairs, her yellow sash fluttering like butterfly wings. She halts by the portico pillar, as she struggles with a failed sneeze; her dainty face contorts to a squashed peach.

'Sorry, Uncle! I seem to have picked up some allergy. Makes me want to sneeze all the time. Just a bother, nothing more. No need to change any plans. I could do with the fresh air. So, please!'

KDR brightens up. 'Right then, let us proceed!'

And proceed we do. Animals entering the ark two by two: KDR and the Princess, myself and Katarina, Jeevesamma and Ganga Rao and countless servants in our wake. Australia Felix is already at the wheel. A string of servants, in an ant-like procession head towards the van and load it with tents, tables, umbrellas, chairs, *dharis*, boxes and blueys, with enough food and gear to last us a long while, were we to be trapped in the bush.

Ganga Rao darts out from the van, phone in hand. 'Your-Highness!

Prince Jayadev is on the line. He has arrived safely in Sydney; he wishes to report.'

'Jayadev? He certainly knows how to interrupt. I better hear what he has to say. — Please, excuse me! Take your seats, I shall not be long. And Miss Katarina, may I have the pleasure of your company?'

Katarina flashes a quick glance towards me and catches me smirking.

'Sure, delighted!'

As KDR moves away from the van, talking to Jayadev, the Princess turns to us, her eyes lighting up with a mischievous smile.

'Good morning, Mr Martin, Miss Katarina. I hope you slept well. I apologize for last night. I was so fatigued, and this allergy must have been on the way, I could not be properly sociable. But I gather that Uncle more than made up for my failure.'

Katarina, pushing up her sunglasses over her luxuriant hair, beams a gracious smile: 'Don't worry about last night. We have plenty of time to get to know each other. I've decided to accept your uncle's invitation: I'll be staying till the Coronation. If I can be of any help, please don't hesitate!'

'Thank you very much. I dare say we'll need all the help we can get.'

KDR re-joins us. 'Well, all is well that ends well. Jayadev will report in a week. I have given him some tasks to complete in Sydney. Now, where were we? Ah, yes, seating arrangements. Now Indrani, I'd like Miss Katarina to have the seat behind the driver. And as for you, Mr Martin —'

'Don't worry, Uncle. Let the servants take the middle seats. I prefer the back window, that way I can see better.'

'Excellent! Excellent! Let us proceed!'

Jeevesamma takes her place between us, seating herself with an air of determination, a school matron making sure her charges don't come to blows. Like me, she has sensed that the Princess' apparent high spirits and good humour barely conceal some indefinable anger. Angry with me? With Katarina? Her uncle? Or herself? Conducting a conversation across Jeevesamma turns into veritable ping-pong match, with the ball going astray more often than not.

'Oh, Mr Martin! Look at these tree ferns lining the road. Don't you think they are standing as guard of honour for someone?'

'I'm sure they are. And surely for you.'

'And these boulders! You won't guess what they remind me of!'

'Why wouldn't I?'

'Because you are always serious, whereas I think of silly things.'

'What silly thing are you thinking of now?'

'I think these boulders look like comic cartoon-beasts. Like a bunch of crouching beasts ready to pounce upon the Flintstones.'

'It is possible that some *are* fossilized beasts.'

'There you see! I make a joke, you turn it serious.'

'Is that a crime in your book?'

'Of course not!'

Seeing her ward indulge in apparently harmless banter, Jeevesamma dozes off. Soon she is snoring. The servants, sitting behind us, jabber away in their lingo, their excitement carrying their voices to a pitch that acts as a useful barrier. I seize the moment.

'How's Miss Rose? How did you get on?'

'OK.'

'"OK." Is that all you can say? Has she handed the papers over?'

'Not yet. But she will.'

'You sound confident.'

'I have reason to be confident. It's really up to me. We've struck a deal.'

'What might that be?'

'I can't tell you now, maybe later – when I've got the papers.'

'You should be careful.'

'Should I? Why?'

'It is no secret your uncle doesn't approve of your friendship with Miss Rose.'

'Must I always be my Uncle's little girl?'

'I didn't mean that.'

'In any case, Uncle is preoccupied. Your lady friend is charming. Watch out! Uncle might steal her.'

'Katarina is free. I am not her jailer.'

'Truly! I don't understand. I never will. How can you –?' She slumps back exasperated. 'It's none of my business.'

'You are quite right. The truth is Katarina loves me or thinks she loves me. She wants to get married.'

'When are you getting married?'

'We are not.'

'Oh!'

Why do I have to justify myself to this naïf? What does she know about these things? Yet I cannot stop. '– Katarina should know. She doesn't want to know.'

'If I may say so, Mr Martin, that sounds cruel.'

'Cruel? Perhaps I am cruel. Believe me, I'm sparing her. I won't make her a good husband. She knows that too.'

'I'm sorry. I shouldn't be asking these questions.'

'Not at all. I'm glad you did. It shows –'. I have to stop. I dare not voice what I recognize.

'Shows what? That I am a foolish busybody? From now on I shall keep mum. Strict silence from me, I promise.'

'Pity! I was enjoying our conversation. I missed you when I was away.'

'And I thought you'd had enough of our company.'

'I shall never have enough of your company.'

The Princess bows her head and her cheeks turn a delightful hibiscus-red.

It is noon by the time we arrive at our destination: the Falls.

KDR is ecstatic. 'What a holy, what a *mighty* sight! A veritable down-pouring of celestial waters! My Hardwar! My Ganga! Praised be to Bhagvan who has ordained these holy falls here! – Excuse me, I must have a closer look.'

Abruptly, he leaves us, and strides towards the edge of the cascade. Soon we see him silhouetted against the rocks, hands upraised in prayer, his forehead glistening with water spray.

The servants begin setting up our lunch, and the Princess decides to supervise. The air fills with spicy aromas.

Katarina, who has been standing on a rock, observing KDR, re-joins us.

'– Care for a drink, Katarina?' I offer her a lemonade.

'Thanks!' Sipping her lemonade, Katarina approaches the Princess.

'– Anything I can do?'

'Thanks, but we are almost ready. Just waiting for Uncle now.'

'Your uncle is a very religious man, isn't he?'

'Yes. He is so happy to have this waterfall on our Northern boundary. He has found his Hardwar.'

Seeing Katarina's blank look, the Princess continues. 'I'm sorry, I should explain. Hardwar is where the river Ganges – Gangama we call her – descends from the locks of Shiva, that is, from the Himalayas, down to the plains. Hardwar is very sacred to us. – Ah, here he is. I am sure Uncle will explain better. These Falls are our Hardwar, isn't that so, Uncle?'

KDR puts an affectionate arm round the Princess. 'How right you are, my dear. You see, Miss Katarina, how my little Princess can read me like a book.'

'But Uncle!' the Princess interposes, her eyes glinting with mischief, 'Felix tells me these Falls are not at all sacred to the aborigines. In fact he says the name has something to do with lice.'

'What a pity! I am sorry to hear that. But must one be guided by a mere name? Look at them! Not a thousand sparkling diamonds can match the brilliance of this water-spray. I think it is our duty to give these falls a properly auspicious name.'

'Will they let us?'

'We shall see. It will, of course be politic to discuss the matter with the Elder. I shall bring it up at our meeting.'

As I had guessed, KDR's picnic was a mere prelude to far more important tasks. Hard to tell whether the meeting with the aboriginal Elder, Boonoo Boonoo Billy, was pre-arranged or just happened by chance, but there we were, by 3 o' clock, sitting on benches outside his workshop, which is littered with finished and unfinished wood carvings of every shape and size. His ancient face is itself like a prime block from a gnarled pepper tree, etched with aeons of story-lines. A young black assistant who might be his son hovers around, opening bottles of coke, while the Elder sits facing KDR, doling out his responses with measured silences.

Ganga Rao produces, as it were by magic, a bundle wrapped in tissue-paper.

KDR hands it over. 'We are very honoured to be your guests in this country, Mr Billy. Please accept a small gift from our country which, I believe, may well have been the home of your ancestors long, long ago.'

'They reckon we go back 60 million years. And we roamed all over this land. And where are we today? Today we are refugees in our own land.'

'It shall not be so — we must make sure of that.'

The Elder looks away, passing the bundle to his assistant.

'Please!' KDR's tone is exceptionally deferential. 'It would give me great pleasure if you were to open our gift, Mr Billy.'

The Elder nods. The young man tears off the tissue and uncovers a grey shawl wrapped round a set of wooden logs.

The Elder's face crinkles in a smile.

'What kind, mate, this wood?'

'Sandalwood, from Mysore.'

'Bloody good wood.'

'I hope you'll enjoy carving it.'

'You bet I will. Thanks, mister.' He rises. 'Let's go in. We can talk better.'

We pick up the signal and stay outside. KDR follows the elder into the workshop. Ganga Rao goes back to the van and returns with a file of papers.

'His Highness needs this, his Mabo file. Don't you think I should take it in, Little Princess?'

'Definitely not.' The Princess is in a distinctly imperial mode. 'I don't believe Mr Billy is a "files-man". Certainly no papers at this stage! Uncle will manage, don't worry. The deal we are offering is very generous. I doubt if Mr Billy will get anything better.'

Katarina yawns, arching her arms in an outward stretch. 'I'm tired. I'm going for a walk. Anyone cares to join me?'

Her invitation is vaguely pitched. The Princess rises.

'I will, if you don't mind.'

'Of course not. And Ziggy – hadn't you better escort us?'

'Ziggy? I don't believe it!' The Princess can barely suppress her giggle. '– Is that your real name, Mr Martin?'

'Why not? Is it that strange?'

'No, no. I can't think of you as that rock star – what's his name? David Bowie?'

'Nothing to do with him. My parents are very pious folk. Ziggy is short for Ezekiel, an Old Testament prophet.'

'I know that. He was very visionary, wasn't he?'

Katarina butts in before I can re-route our conversation.

'— Sure was. What's more, our Ziggy is quite a visions-bloke himself. Don't you know? As a matter of fact, he sees and hears such stuff, he can be quite scary.'

'Katarina!' My cheeks burn in anger. 'That's enough.'

'Don't go crook at me, Ziggy. I think it's better if the Princess knows the truth. My dear Princess, our Mr Martin is not — how shall I put it? — he is not quite *well*. He suffers from, let us say, bouts of vision-sickness.'

If looks could strangle, mine would. The Princess looks at me with profound solemnity. Katarina continues, in a merry tone:

'Don't get me wrong. I'm not saying he's neurotic or psychotic, or any of those things. No, no. He's fine. I am sure he doesn't need a shrink. What he needs is a healer. As a matter of fact, he needs to see the very man your uncle is with right now.'

'Boonoo Boonoo Billy?' The Princess turns to me, her face suffused with anxious concern. 'Is he a medicine-man? I hope he can help you, Mr Martin.'

'— I don't know yet. I am sorry. Katarina shouldn't have bothered you with this.'

'On the contrary,' says Katarina, with more than a touch of spite, 'I think Ziggy should explain. He owes it to you, considering —'

'Considering *what*?'

The sudden sharpness in the Princess' tone arrests Katarina in mid-flow. She pauses before resuming. 'Considering — if I may, my dear Princess, speak plainly — considering how concerned you are — we all are — about our friend here.'

My forehead pulsates with rising pressure. 'Thank you, Katarina! — My apologies, Princess. Katarina is right. I will explain, not right now, not here.'

'It's OK.' The Princess smiles. 'Let's go back. I know Uncle would want a photo session. Ready for it, Mr Martin?'

We walk back briskly and in silence. We find KDR and the Elder outside the workshop, exchanging parting greetings.

KDR looks at his watch. 'Good timing, Mr Martin! — Now, Indrani, if you could join us and help hold this this magnificent gift which Mr Billy has kindly given us.' He points to a large wooden plaque in the shape of Australia, with dotted etchings marking tribal territories.

'If you, my dear, stand in the middle, it would make a perfect picture, don't you agree, Mr Martin?'

'Perfect!' I click away. The Elder deigns to smile: the meeting must have gone well.

One final farewell and we return to the van. Just as we resume our seats, the Princess hops down. 'Excuse me, Mr Martin! I must speak to Uncle.'

I see her conferring with him for a short while; and KDR gives new instructions to the driver. When she returns, her face glows with a new excitement. 'Good! Uncle says we have time. We are going to see Resort Raja at last. You may remember I drew up the plans months ago. We have been so busy, I haven't visited it yet. I hope the builders are not messing up my design.'

'Dare they?'

'They better not.' She laughs. 'If they mess up, I shall decree "Off with their heads!"'

22
Boonoo Boonoo Billy

'Come in, mister! Come right through!'

Boonoo Boonoo Billy calls out from somewhere in the dark interior of his workshop. I pick my way through chunks of red gum, planes, chisels, saws, hammers, roughly in the direction of his voice.

I find him seated on a tree stump; his head is bent sideways against what looks like a sturdy branch. How can he work in this light – or rather, in this lack of light?

'Now you can turn the switch on! There it is, right behind you!'

I fumble and find the switch of a desk lamp on a long lead.

'– Checking on what the little buggers done in there.' He taps the end of a twisted piece of gum. 'Got to do it in the dark, like them poor buggers.'

It dawns on me slowly that he is referring to the white ants that have hollowed out the wood destined to become a didgeridoo.

'So you come at last. Been waiting for you.'

'Really? – I couldn't get through. I did try.'

'Bloody phones. Don't want no phones when I work with this bugger. – Come close!'

I edge towards him.

Come on, close close! – Here, put your ear to this, right here.' He points to the blow-hole.

I do as instructed. His gnarled face looms above me like an overhanging rock. His eyes glisten.

'– Hear it?'

I pause. 'Can't say I hear anything, unless – the tube is very silent but very alive.'

'You're not wrong. I knew you'd come good. – A didge is no didge if the little fellas didn't get to feed in there.' He rises. 'I go crook when I see what the bastards sell in fancy shops. – Bloody murder, I tell ya, nothing but bloody murder, cutting green bleeding trunks, and for what? For shitty souvenirs for tourist-buggers! – And take a look at this. Isn't she a beauty? They do a great job, the little whiteys, chump chump chump they go day and night, and I get this tube. That's Mother Nature for you: treat her with respect, learn to wait, and she give you all you need. Forget respect, she bloody well kill ya! – So, you come at last. Raja-business or yours?'

'Bit of both.'

'Like a beer?'

'Love one. Thanks.'

He opens a couple of Fosters, froth streaking over his rugged hands.

'– Been seeing things, I hear.'

'What did Zelda tell you?'

'Never mind Zelda, she know nothing much. *You* tell me.'

'I don't know where to start.'

'Start a story where a story starts. When did you get it?'

'Get what?'

'The strong-eye.'

'So you know. — Some six months back.'

'Go on!' He listens, clutching the didge, his ear close to it as if he were conferring with the ghosts of the white ants, while I dredge up episode after episode of my 'hearing' and 'seeing'. As I reach the end of my story I cannot resist pulling back:

'I could, of course, be simply deluded. This thing, the "strong-eye" you call it, I can't even tell if it's a gift or a curse.'

'Come clean. You want it or not? You've got to decide.'

'It's not that simple. I don't have any control. Besides, how do I know I'm not just sick? After all, I did spend many years in war-zones. My imagination has got sick, perhaps.'

He rises and takes a step towards me, didge in hand, and stares straight into my eyes. 'Mister, you don't come here, make no shitty excuse. You know what it's about. You come here so I tell ya: "Get on with it, mate!"'

'What exactly *am* I to get on with?'

'You wanna to find out, right?'

He puts the didge down very carefully on the work-bench, his head bent over it, muttering; then straightens up, smiling — the first smile of the day. 'Come, let's get outta here. Walk good for talk.'

So we set off, following a steep, curvy dirt road and soon find ourselves entering a patch of rain-forest that begins where the gums end. A different world: dark, moist, vibrant with sounds that bubble up from a rich silence. It seems sacrilegious to speak. My companion has no such qualms.

'— Hear them, can ya?'

I strain my ears to catch the latest bird-whistle. 'What bird is it?'

'Bird? Don't mean no bird. Listen close to what's under here.' He gestures towards our feet as we squelch our way through dense undergrowth. 'Can't see the buggers but they're there all right, busy busy busy, millions billions of them, waste-workers, work real good. Turn all this stuff to beaut compost. Reclamation work. Just join the team. You've got real work to do.'

'Real work?'

'I talk plain, don't I? — Strong-eye's for healing.'

'Beg your pardon. How can I heal when I feel sick myself?'

'We'll see to that. — You been a watcher and a collector till now. No more watching, time to get started with healing.'

'How? What?'

'Don't be a dill! There's plenty to do in the muck-heap. First we must "make" you, set you right.'

'That's what I came to you for.'

'Ya, I know. I don't forget. Let's see where we are. — You're a lucky bloke. You're more than halfway there, you've been taken up to the clouds, shown things, you've even got your dreaming.'

'You mean the lyre-bird I told you about.'

'Sure — good! You're learning. When did you see him?'

'When I was out walking with the Princess.'

'She's a good one, your woman.'

I stumble over a log. 'Sorry! What did you say?'

'That pretty Princess, your sheila, she take you to your dreaming.'

He speaks as if he was a witness. Complex truth simply put.

A rush of exhilaration makes me feel light-headed. 'That lyre-bird brought us close, very close but I couldn't say anything to her. Come to think of it, I fell for her the first time I set my eyes on her. I've been saying no to myself ever since.'

'Lying to yourself. —Never does no good — nor lying to the other woman.'

'Poor Katarina!'

'Don't ya worry about her. She'll be right. She's movin' on . — The Princess, she loves ya. — Now we got that sorted, back to basics. You must find your country, where your mob come from.'

'Impossible. I know nothing about my father or mother.'

'Mother 'll do.'

'No chance!'

'She'll tell ya if you let her. —Ask around. No harm in that.'

'Whom shall I ask?'

'Start at home.'

'Monica? The Reverend? — They know nothing.'

'You sure?'

— Is it possible that they may have held back information from me? It had never dawned on me before that they might have. I'd always accepted their story of my foundling status without question. And it had always tapered off at the edges. Did my mother ever know where I ended up? Did she ever try to find out? I'd always assumed that, having dropped me into the sandpit, she'd vanished. Who was she? Where did she vanish? And then there was that skinny-ghost of a figure in my dreams, always wearing dark glasses — if only she had lifted them once, maybe I'd know who she is.

A sudden shaft of bright light falls across our path. We have arrived at a clearing, a bora-ring. Billy stops.

'This is where our mob meet. They listen to me, an old fool — not close-up dead yet, just grey hairs. They listen 'cause I tell the truth. Believe me, you'll get there.'

'I have to believe you. I want to believe you.'

'Good! Let's turn back — reckon we need another beer, then the Raja-business.'

We are on our third Foster. It is more than an hour since we returned from our walk. Billy is again pottering about the workshop, which has turned a magical pale-yellow in the late afternoon light. He has been ignoring me, except to keep me supplied with beer. I am not sure how many more cans I have to down before he resumes conversation.

A gust of westerly sweeps in a heap of dry leaves, wood-shavings and sawdust. Billy rises and shuts the door, plunging us once more into semi- darkness. I look at my watch.

'I must be going. Don't fancy driving back in the dark.'

'Welcome to stay, mister.'

'Thanks. I must get back. They're expecting me at dinner-time.'

Billy laughs. 'What you tell the Raja, if you go now? We haven't talked his business yet.'

'I thought you didn't want to.'

'Na! – Got to do a bit of thinking, don't I? When you start thinking, things come flooding, an' bloody well choke ya. You know what I mean.'

'Of course.'

'– You play cricket?'

'A little, at school. The Raja is mad on cricket.'

'Ya, he told me. We talk a lot of cricket when he came. Did ya know a crack team of blackfellas went to England long before white fellas came out to play here?'

'I didn't know that.'

'They sure did. Forty-seven matches they played. This Raja, he know all about it. Bloody good game they played! Bloody smart fellas!' He laughs and laughs, till his eyes fill with tears. 'What a joke! – Cunning bastards! First get the black fellas playing white man's game, then you beat them at it, crush them right underfoot till there's nothing left, no dignity, no self-respect, no life to speak of.'

He crushes the can in his hand and flings it across the room. The beer is quite clearly taking over. I am not sure if I should allow him to make any commitments in this state.

'Perhaps we should talk another time.'

'You think I'm drunk. No no no!' Wagging a finger at me, he pulls his stool close to me. 'Just pissed off with the whole bloody situation.'

'I'm sorry.'

'"Sorry?" —Sure you're sorry. But,' He rises and stretching his arms out, yawns. 'Boonoo Boonoo Billy had enough of this sorry shit. Had enough of the talk talk fellas. — We've filed our claim. Tell him this time we're going to fight till the last drop of life to get our land back. This time there's no giving up. This time we catch the white man in the courts with his own white law-tricks. This time we win. Tell him all that.'

'He knows, and he understands. That's why he sent me.'

'We've got them scared — scared shit, putting in that claim. Lismore, Byron Bay, Bellina, Grafton, all the way from Tenterfield to Tweed Heads. — We're after the government. What's this Raja after? Why's he chasing me? What for?'

'He is not chasing you. He wants to help.'

'What the bloody hell can he do for us?'

'As you know, he now owns large part of the land in your Mabo claim. He wants to work out a just deal for you, set an example for others.'

'Oh ya! He told me that.'

'So, are you willing to negotiate? He's keen to get a deal done before his big function.'

'The one he call "Coronation"? That don't bother me. Big kid's birthday-bash — He's welcome to his bittafun.'

'So what do you say?'

'Why should I trust him?'

'He came to see you. You know if you can trust him or not. Besides, the Princess is the owner, not the Raja.'

'Something in that — but he pull the strings.'

'True. But she can speak for herself. As you say, she is a good one.'

'The good don't always get what they want.'

'We've got to start somewhere.'

'Sure. – Can they deliver?'

'That's what I'm here for. To find out precisely what your demands are.'

'Right! I'll deal plain with you. The government is running scared an' scaring people – they tell the poor city-buggers black fellas 're after their backyards, their semis and detacheds – bloody liars! – First get the white fellas scared like in the good old days an' count on them to mow down the blackfellas, that's what the government reckon. We ain't falling for that. We put ads in the papers, we make clear what we want. Fishing, hunting, mining-rights, full control over our traditional land, our sovereignty back.'

'I don't see any problem with that. The Raja is more than willing to do that.'

'The mining-rights. How can he deliver that? He's one of them, right?'

'Yes – and no. How shall I put it? He's working on that from inside. Not easy to get the companies to relent, but he is determined to get results. He's put in a lot of money, they've got to listen to him.'

'This like Christmas come early all at once. Too good to be true. Too easy. Gimme a minute.'

He sits on a log rubbing his stubbly chin for a few moments.

'– Ah, I got it. I'm not wrong. There's a problem.'

'What sort of problem?'

'Supposing you're right – supposing this Raja do as he say, it will be the end of us if we settle with him.'

'Why should that be?'

'The bloody government will get the wrong idea. They'll think we've dropped our claim. The bastards will do anything to get off the hook.'

'The Raja has thought of that. That's why he is keen to do a proper deal with you – set a model. He wants to help you fight, join you, work with you, especially the Princess. You trust her, don't you?'

'She's a smart kid. Good heart.'

'What's there to lose? You get what you want and go on fighting in the courts, and with big backing.'

'Sound good. Real good.'

'So you agree?'

'Dunno. There's something not quite right about all this. I feel it in me bones. Some trouble. I smell it, like rotting flesh.'

My heart sinks. He catches my eye, sees a shadow passing. He grabs me by the shoulders and shakes me.

'You know! You know what Billy's talking about. You smell it too, don't ya? Out with it! Can't keep no secrets from old Billy your mate, not after we done all that talk talk. Spit it out! What d'ya see?'

'Nothing. I can't say I see anything. – Yet, like you, I fear something. I wish I didn't.'

'There ya go.'

'Perhaps it's just nerves. I first felt it when I went on that 'copter ride with the Raja. More recently, last week —'

'When the Raja come here?'

'Ya. But not here. After we left you, we went to inspect Resort Raja. It's a holiday-conference complex we're building south of here. The Princess has designed much of it. She has put in a lot of work. She wanted to check how the work was coming on —'

'We don't need no more bloody buildings in the bush.'

'The complex is on old clearing. It's set in the mango plantation by the river.'

'You don't mean Georgi's?'

'The Raja owns it now. But Georgi's still the manager.'

'Strange fella. White Russian, they say.'

'I don't think so. More like a Serb or Croat. Do you know him?'

'Who? Georgi? Na. He keep to hisself. They reckon he got a millionaire brother down South. Wog-gossip.'

'Interesting. What else does wog-gossip tell you?'

'Reckon this brother put up the money. Georgi keeps losing them mangoes. The fruit-bats get to them before he does. This Georgi no good manager. Why the Raja keep him?'

'It is KDR's policy. Not to displace people as far as possible.'

'Don't care for him. Him and his killer-dogs. Got one of our kids. Dogs still there?'

'Yes. For security. Georgi's assistant Ben handles them now. He's better at it.'

'Ben? Never heard of him.'

'He hasn't been there long. I met him last week for the first time. He made an impression and —'

'And what?'

'I sensed something between them, something odd.'

'You don't mean no bloody poofter business?'

'No, no, Not at all.'

Big burly, snarling Georgi and stocky, stooping, bearded Ben? Even the thought makes me laugh.

'—Definitely no poofter business, I assure you. It's something else. It struck me that this Ben is more like a serf or a slave than an assistant. He never lifted his eye — kept his baseball cap pulled right down.'

'That fella bother ya?'

'Why he should I can't tell. He never said anything. And he is good with those dogs. Yet it is when I saw him with Georgi I got this sick feeling in my guts.'

'You keep watch, keep listening. Never put aside what the gut says.'

Billy closes his eyes and hums a tune. A great weariness spreads from him.

I rise to ward it off.

'— Thanks for everything. I better get going. It's getting dark.'

'OK, mate! See ya again soon. Take care. And take care of your Princess.'

'I shall. Thanks. See you later.'

23
A Necklace

'Hi!' Katarina greets my reflection in her dressing-table mirror, her fingers struggling with the clasp of a necklace round her neck. 'Perfect timing, Ziggy! I need some help.'

'Sure.' I click the clasp and she adjusts the pendant to sit snugly in her cleavage.

She smiles: 'Well, what do you think?'

'Looks lovely on you. Suits you, rubies and pearls. – Let me guess, a gift?'

'Not quite. At present, it is lent. KDR wants me to wear it for the ceremony. He thinks that as the Princess' Lady-in-Waiting I may not have the right piece of jewellery. He is right, of course. How can I say no?'

'Sure.' I watch her as she turns her neck sideways to catch the light of the sun.

'– And if I like it, I may keep it.'

'*Do* you like it?'

'Who wouldn't? It's beautiful. I've never got to wear anything like this, nor likely to.'

'Will you keep it?'

'I'm not sure. — It was his wife's.'

'I see.'

She watches me in the mirror as she removes the necklace.

'—Pity! It suits you. Why take it off?'

'I can't possibly attend this meeting wearing rubies in the middle of the day!'

'Before we go, there's something I want to tell you.'

'Yes, of course. I meant to ask you last night but couldn't in front of all our guests. Then you boys disappeared for your cigars! — How did you get on with the medicine-man? Was he any help?'

'I like Billy. He's clarified a few things. Set my mind at rest somewhat.'

'That's wonderful news!'

Her tone is gushy. I flinch.

'Kat!'

'Yes?'

'Do keep the necklace, if you would like to. Don't hesitate on my account.'

She places the necklace back on its velvet-bed in the case very carefully and looks up.

'— It's not about the necklace, is it? What you really mean is that it's over between us, don't you?'

'As I said to Billy, I'm tired of lying to myself. Let's face it. We're stuck in a cul-de-sac. We both need to get out and go our different ways.'

'Cul-de-sac! You're not wrong there.'

'There's no reason why we can't continue as friends.'

'I suppose not.'

'You don't need me to tell you. Your presence is much appreciated here and your talents.'

'Don't, Ziggy! Don't try to buck me up. I don't need it.'

'You will stay on, won't you?'

'If I am to keep my word to KDR, I have to. He's asked me to run the Press Conference, shield the Princess from the press-hounds.'

'Good! – I think we better go. It's nearly noon.'

'Where are we meeting?'

'The balcony of the library.'

'You go ahead. I need a few minutes.'

'OK. And –'

'Yes?'

'Thank you for making it easy.'

'I'm tired too – of not facing the truth.' She laughs. 'Strange! I never imagined it would happen like this, over a ruby necklace. On reflection, I think I'll keep it.'

As I reach the top of the landing, I see the Princess below, pacing up and down the patio, her turquoise saree billowing in the breeze. Her hair hangs loose. I have an insane impulse to bungee-jump; instead I skip down the stairs, heart pounding.

'– Good morning, Princess!'

'Ah, Mr Martin! I'm glad I caught you before our meeting. – Can I have a word with you?'

'Sure.'

'This way, please!'

I follow her along a side-corridor and into her work-room. Two billiard tables occupy the whole room, their tops covered with drawings, plans and balsa-wood models of Resort Raja. She walks round the tables, her brows crinkling in a slight frown, clasping and unclasping her fingers as if she were playing a game of cat's cradle.

'– I don't know how to say this, Mr Martin, I don't want you to get the wrong idea about me. I don't mind at all what Uncle does. But you know that the ruby necklace he is giving your lady friend belonged to Queen Uma Devi.' She stops before me, eyes widening, and her voice dropping to a whisper. '– I think Uncle has fallen in love with Katarina.'

'You think so?'

She shakes her head rapidly.

' – And Katarina?'

She moves away, clearly exasperated. 'You, Mr Martin, should know the answer to that question.'

'I suppose I should.'

'Don't you care?'

'As I said before, Katarina is a free agent.'

'I remember, I remember. How silly of me to ask the same question again!'

'Not at all. You're quite right to be concerned. It affects you, and the future of this kingdom.'

'This kingdom! – Sometimes I wish we hadn't embarked on this foolish project. I don't know how I'm going to handle this coronation business. It's embarrassing, the scale of it. I wish Uncle had settled for something less public.'

'How can he possibly do that? How else is he to let everyone in his territory know what his plans are? Besides, we all love a ceremony. We don't have much of that in this country.'

'I don't know. Tomorrow the Press will be here. I wish I didn't have to answer any questions.'

'Come, come, there's nothing to worry about. They'll love you: it's guaranteed. And Katarina will shield you if there are any problems, she's tough.'

'I really like her, you know. – And I am grateful to her. Since she arrived, Uncle is letting me out a bit more. This caged canary is allowed to fly a bit more.'

'Soon you'll feel fully free, I hope.'

'That'll be the day! – Uncle's starting to talk about marriage. He is pretty well commanding me to choose someone at the Pan-Princes' Conference.'

'So soon! – That's only six weeks away.'

'In six weeks, who knows, my fate may be sealed.'

'Will you? – Will you choose someone?'

'You think I should?'

'I didn't say that. What I meant was –'

'What did you mean?' Her face glows in anger.

'Suppose you see a handsome young Prince and fall in love?'

'What a ridiculous idea! – Impossible!'

'Such things happen. You know, love at first sight is possible, it does happen.'

'Not in my case.'

'How can you be so certain?'

She picks up a ruler and taps the end of the table and flings it down. 'Can't you see? Do I have to spell it out? – How can I ever be sure with these princes that they are not after my bank account? – How can I ever trust anyone?'

In all my romantic imaginings I had overlooked the obvious. In an instant I become aware of the gulf between us, yet I must leap across: '– I hope that doesn't include me.'

'Of course not! –You're different. You are – you are my only real friend in this place.'

I want to enfold her in my arms and smother her with kisses. Instead, I take my hat off and bow in extravagant ceremony.

'I am honoured, my liege! I am and ever shall remain at your command, your loyal and humble servant.'

She laughs. 'Stop it! I don't want this nonsense from you.'

'Allow me this, then.' I take her hand and plant a lingering kiss.

We are startled by a loud piercing ring: KDR's theatrical summons to all of us for the meeting scheduled for noon.

She pulls her hand away. 'We must go.'

'You go ahead. I shan't be long. I need to call home.'

'I hope your parents can come.'

'I hope so too.'

I have been trying to get Monica since breakfast with no success, so much so that I am beginning to worry. The phone rings and rings. I hang on. Just as I've decided to give up, Monica picks it up.

'Thank God, Monica! — At last!'

'What's the matter, son? You sound agitated. Anything wrong?'

'No, nothing. Quite the contrary. I was getting anxious about you both. Been trying all morning, no answer.'

'We had to go out early. An eight o'clock appointment with the doctor. Your father has been down with a bad bout of flu. He was bed-ridden for days.'

'I'm sorry to hear that. Why didn't you tell me? How is he?'

'Better. The doctor has ordered him to rest and take some exercise. — We got your Maharajah's invitation. We know how busy you are. Didn't want to bother you.'

'You should have. Have you got any home-help yet?'

'Yes, I have. As a matter of fact, I meant to tell you, my home-help knows you. She saw your photo and recognized you. Her name is Anna, Anna Yurisch, She says she was your neighbour.'

'How extraordinary! Poor Anna! How is she? Her husband disappeared some months ago.'

'Yes, I know. She hasn't had any news of him. She firmly believes he is alive and will return. For some reason she thinks you will be able to find him. She wanted to contact you but I didn't know if I should give your number or not. I don't know what to make of all this.'

'It is a complicated story. I don't see what I can do but you can give her my number. It's not a problem. — Monica, there's something I want to ask you. Please don't get upset.'

'Why should I get upset? What is it about?'

'It's about my mother — I mean the one who abandoned me in the sand-pit. Did she ever contact you?'

Silence — followed by a faint whimper.

'Monica! I'm sorry, but I must know.'

'Strange! After seeing the doctor this morning, your father wanted me to take him to Birdwell Park, to check if the sandpit was still there, where we found you. It's the flu, he has been very restless at night, disturbed by bad dreams. I heard him calling out to stop our Ziggy running after the waves, trying to stop him drowning. It's been a very disturbing time for me. Now it's you.' Her whimper turns into a sob.

'Please, Monica, don't cry!'

'Oh, son — I wish you hadn't asked. You have no idea how it hurts.'

'I'm sorry. I know you love me, but I must know the truth.'

'Of course. You have every right. — Your father doesn't know. Yes, I did have a letter from her once. It seemed that she'd seen you, when we picked you up from school. She must have known from the beginning we had taken you. The letter was a note of thanks. — I feel terrible concealing this from you. It was awful for me. I feared she might want you back.'

'Did she?'

'No.'

'Then there is nothing to feel bad about, is there, Monica?'

'I suppose not.'

'Do you have the letter?'

'Yes. — I do have a conscience. I knew one day this would have to happen.'

'Any address on it?

'No. —But I know where it was from, that was another reason why I didn't want to let you go.'

'What do you mean?'

'She signed herself as Jasmine in Nimbin. I don't know if it was her real name. The postmark was Nimbin. I'd heard terrible things about that place.'

'Did you reply?'

'How could I? I told you, there was no address.'

'I see.'

'I didn't tell the Reverend. I didn't want any complications. I didn't want to let you go. Please forgive me.'

'There's nothing to forgive. I would like to have the letter. Can you courier it to me?'

'Of course. — I'm sorry I can't tell you very much.'

'You have. You've given me her name. Jasmine. Jasmine in Nimbin. Thank you, Monica, you've been a great help. — Oh, before I forget, the Princess is very keen to see you both at the Coronation.'

'That's sweet of her but I'm not sure if we can make it. Your father is still very weak.'

'The change might do him do. Give him my love. 'Bye, take care.'

'I will. See you soon, son.'

Jasmine, Jasmine in Nimbin: a name, a beautiful name, the name of my mother, my own mother: no longer a nameless, voiceless, dark-glassed ghost in my dreams, but a real person with a real name and habitation. A small thread to lead me to the truth. I feel light-headed as I reach the library balcony.

Jayadev waves a friendly greeting, and pats the chair beside him. From there I can observe Katarina and the Princess seated on either side of KDR at the far end of the balcony. Ganga Rao hovers around, fetching files and folders back and forth from the library.

KDR pushes down his specs to register a silent reprimand at my delay.

'Ah! – Mr Martin, just in time. Please help yourself! I recommend the fruit-punch.' He gestures towards the spread of light snacks and sandwiches on the bamboo table. '– Well, as usual, Pundit Vembu confronts me with a conundrum. It's a delicate matter. Vembu, please explain.'

'Your Highness knows I am speaking only about the tradition of your ancestors. According to this tradition, the Coronation ceremony, the investiture, to be exact, requires the endorsement of the *ādivāsis*, the aboriginal dwellers of any land: for according to our shastras, they are acknowledged, admittedly not openly but tacitly as is appropriate, to be the earth-connected people in whom the *shakti* of mother earth resides. To put it shortly, we need Mr Billy to be present and to participate in the ritual.'

'Well,' KDR turns to me, 'you have been talking to Mr Billy. What do you think? Will he oblige?'

'I doubt it. Not if it means resigning sovereignty – which, as you know, he is fighting for with the government. I've even promised we'll help him in his fight – or so I was given to understand. I don't see how we can ask him to do something which seems to run counter to our promise.'

Vembu rolls his head side to side vigorously. 'No, no, no. There's nothing to fear. It is symbolic, symbolic only. After all, Mr Billy is knowing who is really owning these properties – Highness and the Princess.'

'As I see it, that makes it doubly difficult. Mr Billy sees himself and his people as custodians of the land. Even if we explain, it won't be easy.'

The Princess puts up her hand. 'May I interrupt, Uncle?– I have a suggestion'.

KDR waves her on. 'Of course, my dear!'

'Thank you, Uncle. As Pundit Vembu says, this ritual is symbolic only, meaning we are honouring Mr Billy as much as he is honouring us. If the real purpose of the ritual is to acknowledge that the land belongs to the aboriginals, even if we are the proprietors, then why don't we simply ask our own Felix to do it?'

'Felix?' KDR and Jayadev exclaim in unison. A troubled expression clouds KDR's countenance. 'Are you serious?'

The Princess continues undaunted. 'Yes I am. Felix is shrewder than he lets on. I heard his story about us all. Ask Mr Martin: it is a pretty telling assessment and a warning as to how we should behave. I think, in fact, he is an ideal person for this ritual. It will also show we care, show that we are not snobbish.'

KDR relaxes. 'My dear Indrani, I see your point. But there's a little problem. Felix is not from this area.'

Katarina, who has been sitting all this while somewhat abstracted, suddenly speaks up.

'But I am. I am from this area.'

Hushed silence for a few seconds, finally broken by KDR. 'If I understand you correctly, Miss Katarina Rossi, are you telling us that you are aboriginal?'

'Yeah! I am. My mother was from the Bundjalung.'

'How extraordinary, how very extraordinary!'

Vembu coughs. 'But madam, no discourtesy meant, but the ceremony needs a male representative – male only.'

At this point, I remember. 'Let's call Felix in. I think he has a Bundjalung connection. His grandmother, I think, came from here.'

KDR turns to Ganga Rao. '– Is Felix about?'

Ganga Rao checks his watch. 'He should be here any minute. He has gone to fetch our lawyers from the airport.'

'I see. Well then, I suggest we take it that Mr Martin is right, and adopt the Princess's suggestion. – Vembu? Are you satisfied?'

Vembu nods, rolling his head in a circular motion: 'Nothing is perfect in this world, especially when one is on alien soil.'

KDR taps the table with his biro, and his voice turns querulous:

'Vembu, Vembu, how many times have I told you that we must treat this soil as sacred as our own – we must *make* it sacred! –That is the whole point of this exercise, don't you understand?'

Vembu's head-shake gets distinctly faster. 'Yes, Your Highness, I understand. I am understanding it very much. Your Highness will be pleased to know that we have with us pots and pots of the sacred Ganga water to make everything sacred. I am mixing Ganga water with this Clarence water to send to all parts of our kingdom. This way we can guarantee one hundred per cent sacredness of everything everywhere.'

'Glad you have worked it out. – Now, next on the agenda is the *gaddi*. Miss Katarina, your report, please!'

Katarina spreads a piece of red silk on the table. 'What you see, Your Highness, is the material we've ordered. I rang the women's co-op this morning, they're putting finishing touches to the cushion; it will be ready in a day or two.'

'Excellent! – And the Press Conference?'

'I've struck a deal with SBS. They'll arrive tomorrow and start filming. The others I've delayed till the day before the event, to give us a breather and time for Ziggy to get the press-photos done. I thought it best if we handle the formal ones and supply some suitable captions – to make sure of a good presentation.'

'Well thought-out! Thank you, Miss Katarina.'

'Now, to our M.C., Jayadev. – How are things coming along?'

'Quite good, considering I've had so little time to adjust. I could do with an assistant. I spoke to Ray Rowlatt about it, he says he can help.'

'Good! – Let's do a quick check through.'

'Sure.'

'Elephants, carriages, transport for the V.I.P.s.'

'Fine – Felix has booked limousines.'

'Seating-plan?'

'Needs reviewing. The Foreign Office is still to reply. So also the Defence Minister. But the Governor of NSW has accepted, he is sending someone. The overseas Princes will start arriving from tomorrow; they will be staying at Resort Raja till the ceremony.'

'Protocol. Never forget protocol, the most important thing. — See me later with the guest-list.'

'Yes, Father.'

'Street parties?'

'Miss Rose is advising me on that. She's experienced in that area, and also in organising floats, and so on.'

'I see. — Now to the most important matter. My dear Indrani, have you anything to tell us with regard to those papers in Miss Rose's possession?'

'Well, Uncle, I am working on it. She has agreed but seems rather reluctant to part with them right now.'

I watch the Princess eagerly as she tries to meet her uncle's relentless interrogative stare. Clearly, KDR is not pleased with her response. There is an awkward silence during which she tries to recover her composure. She is saved by the sound of screeching brakes under the portico.

Jayadev leans over the parapet.

'They're here, Ray and Roy — and there's someone else with them, I don't know who.'

24
Jasmine and Alice

No KDR, no Jeevesamma, no servants, not even Felix, just myself at the wheel of this old Saab – and the Princess, so near yet so far.

I catch sight of her in the side-mirror, sitting demurely in the back seat. It made sense when we left: her uncle had insisted on bidding her farewell as if she were leaving the country. Now that we are well on our way, it's time she moved to the front seat beside me. She has been unusually silent, staring out of the window. My time is precious, a mere hour and we'll reach our destination. Perhaps I have been too polite.

'Shall I wind up the window? Is the breeze too strong?'

'No, I like it.'

'Do we have to talk this way? Won't you join me?'

She laughs. 'I was waiting to see if you'd ask. Of course.'

I stop the car. Before I open my door, she is out, and slides in beside me. 'Please! Will you let me drive? I never get a chance.'

'That was not part of the agreement with your uncle.'

'Bother Uncle! Nor is this, then. I'd better go back to the back seat.'

'Stop! Don't get upset. Be reasonable, these roads are tricky and I am responsible for your safety. Perhaps when we get off this main road, I'll let you have a go.'

'Thank you, thank you! I promise to be good.'

The wind gets stronger, and her saree-folds billow. She smooths them down. 'Perhaps you'd better close the window.'

'Done.'

A precious, weighty silence fills the car. A slight frown creases her brow.

'—What's the matter?'

'Nothing, nothing really. – No, that's not true. There is something. It's that boy, you know, the one Mr Rowlatt brought with him. Who is he? Do you know him?'

'Who? Max? – No.'

'Do you think he's OK? Do you think he will be a good assistant to Jayadev?'

'Why not? He's a boy-scout after all. – Don't you like him?'

'No, no, it's not that ... I don't know why ... there's something strange about him. He has wild eyes.'

'His parents are Greek.'

'Oh! —We met a Greek on our voyage out, Captain Souros. Very nice man, very courteous.'

'I bet he was. I bet he fell in love with you, like this wild-eyed youngster.'

'Definitely not! Captain Souros is married. And he has two children. He is a courteous gentleman. That's all.'

'I'm glad to hear it.'

'No, I am seriously worried about this boy. I got the impression Mr Roy doesn't seem keen on him either.'

'Bravo! You're definitely right about Mr Roy. I heard them arguing over him. The boy has been holidaying at Yamba with his parents, and getting utterly bored. So he's left them for this job. Who wouldn't, if one was his age? But you're right about Mr Roy – he hadn't been consulted and wasn't too pleased about it. Besides, what you probably haven't noticed is how smitten Mr Roy is with you.'

'What nonsense! Will you please stop telling me about all these people who are supposedly falling in love with me left, right and centre. It means nothing to me. Why can't you be serious with me for one minute?'

'I am serious, very serious about you. Otherwise I wouldn't have pleaded on your behalf with your uncle to let you come with me on this trip.'

'I don't know why Uncle dislikes Rose so much. He knows why I have to see her. Besides, she has good business-sense. She's launching a new range of products in my name to coincide with the ceremony. This is a strictly business trip.'

'Really? I'm disappointed. I thought it was my company.'

'Well, that too. You are my best friend, as I said before. When I heard you were going to see Rose, I thought "Why bother Felix who has so much to do, I might as well go with you".'

'How very considerate and sensible you are!'

'Considerate, I hope I am, but sensible I certainly am not.'

'I'm delighted to hear that.'

She fidgets, twirling the ends of her saree. 'Please! –You promised!'

'Promised? What did I promise?'

'Come on, don't pretend. You promised you'd let me drive.'

'Not till we get off this road.'

'I never get a chance to drive on a proper road. Can't I take the wheel now?'

'No. Too risky.'

'I suppose I have no other option.'

'You suppose right.'

'Bother!' She settles back exasperated. I enjoy watching her sulk. I stop the car as we swerve into the gravel road that takes us to Blue Gum Farm.

'Now you may. Take care!'

We swap seats. She drives along the twisting road with an ease that makes me suspicious.

'This is not the first time you have done this, is it? Confess.'

She laughs, wobbling her head side to side.

'– Come on! I shall never know if that wobble means yes or no.'

'You are not meant to. – OK, I confess. Yes, I have driven on this stretch a few times. I had to bully Felix. Like you, he too would allow me only this bit.'

'I see. What else do you get up to we don't know about?'

She laughs, once again, wobbling her head, as we pull up to the farmhouse.

'Pity, it was over so quickly. It was wonderful. I wish that road had gone on and on forever and I didn't have to stop. It must be in my blood. You know about my father. He was crazy about cars. So crazy, he died of it. That's why Uncle never lets me drive.'

'How did you learn to drive at all?'

'Hari, our oldest servant, he taught me. It had to be secret. Poor Hari! Always terrified that Uncle would find out and put him in jail.'

'Did he?'

'Of course Uncle found out. One of the other servants, jealous of Hari, let the cat out of the bag.'

'And?'

'Uncle didn't do anything terrible, just gave one of his severe lectures. He is too fond of Hari to punish him. But he did punish me. I was not allowed to go near the car for months, and even when he relented, I was allowed to drive only within the palace grounds.'

'No wonder! Now that I've seen you drive, I'd do the same.'

'But you are not my Uncle, thank God. You are my only friend. Promise, you'll always be, no matter what happens.'

She takes my hands and gives me an earnest, searching look. 'Is it true, what Katarina says, about you seeing things? – What do you see for me?'

'See for you? I wish I could, but I am afraid I don't see by demand.'

'Am I demanding? It was just a request, a silly request, if you like. All this business of kingdoms and coronations, now Uncle starting to talk of my marriage, on top of all that's driving me crazy! Can't you see? Are you blind?'

'I'm sorry. I wish I could see your future ... for your sake ... and mine. Perhaps we should ask Vembu.'

'Vembu? Now you are mocking me.' She pulls away her hands but I reclaim them.

'Please forgive me. You must believe me. I never meant to mock you. I am not blind. I do see how difficult it is for you. Perhaps you can see, just a little, how difficult it is for me.'

'I don't know ... I thought ... Never mind what I thought – here is Rose.'

Tantric Rose emerges from one of the railway-carriages, wiping her hands on her paint-splattered blue dungaree, and squinting her eyes against the bright light, beams a smile.

'– Hi, guys! What a lovely surprise to see you, my sweet Princess! You don't mind sitting outdoors, do you, over there?' She gestures towards the jacaranda tree by the Omega carriage. 'Make yourselves at home. I shan't be long. I bet you could do with a drink, Zig – and you, Miss?'

'Just water, please.'

'One day, you'll have to stop saying, "Just water, please". – We have to make her, don't you think, Zig? Whisky or beer for you?'

'A beer 'll be most welcome.'

Rose walks towards the house, while we head towards the garden-table under the jacaranda tree.

'I don't know why Uncle dislikes her so much. She's rough and tough but has a good heart. I like her. Is that wrong?'

'I trust your judgement. It is clear why KDR is annoyed with her. Do you know why she won't give up those papers? Is it money?'

'No, no, not at all. It's something else. She will give them when she has finished ...'

'Finished what?'

'Shh! Not now, I'll tell you later. There she is, and that poor cat! See how she kicks it, like a football! She always does that when she shuts the wire-door. I don't know why that poor creature puts up with it!'

Rose returns with a plateful of pies, a jug of water and cans of Tooheys. 'Sorry, darl! This is no cordon bleu cooking, but I guarantee these are the best pies you'd ever eat. Let's get started.'

We eat and drink. The Princess picks at her pie gingerly as if she were expecting strange creatures to crawl out of it. Rose notices and guffaws.

'Go on ! Be brave! It won't kill you. You could do with a bit more flesh on you. – A bit on the thin side, our Princess, don't you think, Zig?'

'I think the Princess is fine as she is.'

'Thank you, Mr Martin.'

'Mr Martin, is that what you call him? What's wrong with "Ziggy"?'

'I can't call him that. Don't ask me why. Perhaps I should let you two talk first. I don't mind waiting in the house while Mr Martin asks you whatever he has to ask.' She rises, her lips firmly set and her cheeks aglow. Pain or anger? Hard to tell. I must call a halt to Rose's banter.

'Please, Princess! Don't go! There's no need to. Please stay!'

My voice is pleading. Clearly surprised, she sits down. Rose pats her gently: 'There, there's my good little Princess. Now, mister, fire away!'

'As I told you yesterday, my mother called herself Jasmine in Nimbin. I worked out that she would have been in Nimbin at the time you were there. You might have run into her.'

'Jasmine ... Jasmine ... was that her real name?'

'I've no idea. I'm hoping you can tell me.'

'Blue-eyed blonde?'

I shake my head, almost wobbling it, Princess-style. Rose opens a second can of Toohey's for me.

'Looking at you, it could have been her, the one I think who called herself Jasmine. Yeah, I'm sure, the way you looked just then, rings a bell, yeah, I bet it was Janine.'

'Janine?'

'Yeah, Janine Carter. She changed her name to Jasmine.'

'What can you tell me about her?'

'A pale thin kid. Nice long hair. True Aquarian. Her Dad was rich. The Carters were an old Armidale family, big in wool.'

'So?'

'It's the usual story. Mum died, Dad remarried. Janine didn't get on with her step-mum, ran away from school, ended up in Sydney — came back to Nimbin with the first wave of Aquarians. You must have happened sometime before that.'

Happened — that's about right. I happened. One small word to cover a multitude of truths. Rose certainly has a way of simplifying life.

'Did she ever talk about how I "happened"?'

'Not a lot. But by then, she was not doing much talking, not to us, not to anyone.'

'You mean she was stoned.'

'Yeah. – But she'd sing. Lovely sweet voice, I remember. Like Joan Baez, and always those sad, brutal songs. Robbie heard her at a café, brought her home. She'd sit on the veranda by the jasmine creeper and sing to the night sky. Come to think of it, it was Robbie started calling her Jasmine. The only thing that made her laugh. We took care of her. We did try to help but it was too late. I'm sorry.'

'It's not your fault.'

'She was so pale. There was something eerie about her. Robbie found her perfect for his Ophelia.'

'You mean she modelled for him?'

'Don't know if I can call it modelling. She lay on the couch for days, barely breathing, while Robbie did his stuff.'

'What happened to the painting? Did he sell it?'

'I don't think so. I'm not sure if it's even finished. He was very fond of it. It could be still be somewhere in Omega. Let's look. We'll need to shift some heavy stuff. Ready?'

'Sure.'

'Welcome to Omega! – If Robbie's Ophelia – beg yours, I can't think of her as your Mum, Zig – if Jasmine is anywhere it's got to be in the pile behind that chest. – Give me a hand, let's move this brute out. It's time I got rid of it. A bloke couldn't pay for his commission, so Robbie got given this, ugh, ugly thing. I've never liked it.'

The Princess runs her finger over its dusty top. 'But Rose! Don't you see? It's a precious map-chest. I could do with it myself. It'd be ideal for my drafts.'

'Well, well! You're welcome to it. It's yours, anyway. Everything here is yours, I never forget.'

The Princess peers over my shoulder as I check the pile behind the chest. 'Any luck?'

'Not yet!'

I continue unwrapping the paintings, with the Princess fluttering beside me. Rose watches, her ample bosom parked on the top of the chest.

'There! That's it. That's the one. – Oh, my godfather! Look at her. She's so bloody dead, yet so alive! I'm goose-pimples all over. It's like she's still on that couch. Oh, my God! Sorry, Zig! Makes me weepy. Bugger you, Robbie! You were so good – why did you have to die like that, you bastard!'

I leave the painting half-unwrapped and assist Rose to a nearby chair.

'– Shall I get you something?'

'Thanks!'

The Princess fetches some whisky from a shelf. 'She takes this when she is painting.'

'I didn't know she painted.'

'Oh, yes! That's another story.'

A shot of whisky and our solicitude revives Rose. '– That feels better. The bastard! He could do it. – Look at it.'

I see my mother, a pale ghost with a golden halo of long hair floating on a dark, murky pool: so infested with rotting weeds and water snakes that it makes me shiver.

Rose speaks my thoughts. 'Poor Jasmine! She was too good for this crummy world!'

The Princess blows the dust off the painting. 'She's magnificent –

she reminds me of Ushas, the light of dawn. So frail, so beautiful. We must take her home.'

Rose rises. 'Yeah! Our Princess is right. This Ophelia, this Jasmine, your Mum, she belongs to you, Zig. Here, let me give you a hand.'

'Thanks! No, don't get up yet. I can manage by myself.' I overestimate my strength. The frame is heavy. I stumble.

The Princess and Rose squeal in unison: 'Careful!' They grab a painting tottering off a stand nearby. The Princess props it back and hastily covers it. Rose gently pulls her back.

'No, need to cover her, sweetie! – Put Ophelia down for a moment, Zig. I want to show you something.'

The Princess bars her. 'No, Rose! Please don't!'

'Why not, darl! I am sure Robbie would like Zig to meet her. She whips the draping off the painting. '– Let me introduce you to her, Zig: Alice Gordon!'

My fingers tighten on my painting. My heart misses a beat. 'Alice? Alice Gordon? ... How on earth ... What on earth is going on here? – She's so like you, Princess!'

Rose winks. 'You bet she is.'

'Did you paint it?'

'Let me say it's Robbie's last wish. He does it through me. We haven't finished it, as you can see. Robbie missed the Archie. He wants to have a last go at it.'

I look at the unfinished painting and at the Princess. She averts her face, then turns around defiantly.

'Yes, Rose thinks this Alice will win the Archibald prize. What do you think?'

'What do I think? I don't think I can do any thinking at present —
I've just received two shots from a stun-gun. When the shock wears
off I'll tell you what I think. — If you don't mind, I'd like to move on.
Thank you, Rose, you have been immensely helpful, far beyond my
expectations.'

'No worries. Any time. Safe driving, see yous later!'

I drive in angry silence. The Princess resolutely watches the scenery.
She is tenacious, and I am still seething. As each mile whizzes past, I
am conscious of losing my chance to clear up this matter. We'll
soon reach the Castle.

I jam the breaks and pull up at a lay-by.

'— OK. Let's get this clear. Tell the truth. Did you sit for that portrait?'

'What if I did?'

'So that's what those visits to Rose were about.'

'Not just that.'

'Did you have to strip?'

'What do you take me for?'

'It's a fair question. She's painting a nude.'

'I haven't yet. I'll have to, eventually. That's the deal with her. Only
then I'll get those papers.'

'Christ! Does KDR know?'

'Are you mad? How can I tell him?'

'Why did you tell me then?'

'Because ... you are ... because I trust you. I cannot lie to you.'

She bursts into tears. 'I can't stand it. Don't be so angry with me.'

'No, my Princess, I'm not angry.' I gather her in my arms and kiss her tears. '– Yes, I *am* angry. It's only because I love you. I'm simply jealous. That's all. The thought of you ... No. Don't do it. I forbid it. The papers are not worth it. You're not to become one more model in that den.'

'But Rose says your mother wasn't a model.'

'That's what Rose says. Who can tell what really went on? I'm beginning to feel KDR might well be right to be wary of Rose.'

'What shall I tell Uncle when he asks about these papers?'

'Leave your roots where they are. Don't dig them up.'

'But you have just ...'

'Yes, I know I'm preaching to you. But to tell you the truth, I'm not sure I like what I've found. Yes, the painting is beautiful, a golden Ophelia floating ethereally on a bed of rank weeds. Is it really the woman I can call my mother? How can I tell if it's not a fantasy of Rob Gordon's? I've seen people dying of a drug overdose, there's nothing glamorous about it.'

'I'm sorry. You're upset. And I've upset you more. How can I make amends?'

'Like this.' I kiss her cheeks.

'Please! Don't. I'm confused enough.' She struggles free from my embrace.

'I know I should apologise but I can't.'

She smoothes down the folds of her saree and speaks without looking at me: 'Just tell me what I am to tell Uncle – he's expecting me to get those papers from Rose.'

'Keep stalling him, as you have been. I'll deal with Rose.'

25
Right Royal

So Ziggy mister Martin comes back to me the very next day all bihisself, minus little Princess.

I'm not surprised to see him. What with finding his Mum, and seeing the other lady – I knew it was a gamble, showing my nudie Alice – I knew he'd figure out who did the sitting and none too pleased neither. What the shit? Don't I get pissed off working bymyself, just talking to Robbie in the ether? Don't I deserve a bit of recognition, a bit of appreciation?

As I guessed, one little Princess couldn't keep her pretty little mouth shut – those rosebud lips so cute and moist, Robbie wouldn't half have sucked them dry had he got the chance, nor me neither – I could see the green-eyed monster creeping up on our friend Ziggy mister Martin, so what? I didn't do nothing wrong. Look at the pair of them, coming to me all aglow, bright-eyed and shiny-beaked love-birds on the loose ...

And me, poor Rose, growing old, weary and lonely ... oh, ever so lonely!

So, I tell mister Martin the rest of the worst, who their precious Amy Gordon, Robbie's Mum was. It wasn't easy, I tell him, piecing together what's what from those papers. Was Robbie a real Gordon or was he a prankster? 'That's the question, isn't it,' I ask him. 'And the answer?' he says. 'Don't rush me,' says I: 'The answer? – Never simple, is it? How many royals are real royals? Come to think of it, what is so real about any real royal, anyway?' He keeps mum – too clever to rise to my bait, that Ziggy mister Martin. So I carry on. 'Take that bloke down in Jerilderie, what's his name? ... Hastings, yeah, Hastings. Bush-gossip tells me he is the bloke should be sitting on the throne of England, for he is the true planta-what-not –' 'Plantagenet, you mean,' says Zig, smiling somewhat. 'Yeah, this Hastings bloke is the true king of England, not that Buckhouse saurkraut mob ...'

'So, Robbie and his mum Amy, were they Gordons? – by contamination if you like, with this Maharajah's mob? Are you sure you want to know?'

'Sure,' says Zig, 'for the sake of the Princess.' 'Okeydo', says I. But I have to have my bit of fun, don't I? So I spin it out. 'What if –' I start. He cuts me short. 'No time for ifs and buts, Rose. The Princess can't stand the pressure. You must tell us what you know,' says he sternly, then, in a quick change, he flashes a smile. 'Come on, Rose, out with it, why fuss, it's not like you, Rose.' The cunning bastard, he knows I can't resist the soft touch. '–What's in it for me, Zig? What about my deal with the Princess? Robbie sure wants to finish the picture. One last sitting, is that too much to ask?' Zig fixes me with those ocean-blue eyes of his – so reminds me of Jasmine, she could melt your heart with that look. '– Can't you forget the deal, Rose? You know you can finish the painting without her – What's your game?' That stings me, like I got bluebottle antennae round mi ankles. '–Well, mister', says I, 'if you must know, it's payback-time. Do yous have any idea what it's like for me, Rose, I who was queen of all I survey from this Bluegum Farm, to be a pensioned-off oldie on royal hand-outs? I ain't got a crocodile-hide, I know what your Maharajah thinks of me, snobby brown bastard! – Look at me! I had everything Robbie had. Don't get me wrong, I love the little Princess to bits as much as you do. Yeah, I can see it in your eyes – but I must make a masterpiece, I must have her here till I have done it, I must win the Archie, it's mi only chance to get mi dignity back.' (I'm near choking saying all this stuff). '– Sorry, Rose, you feel this way,' says he, gently touching mi arm, 'It's not their

fault Robbie left them everything. They've done their best for you —
what's more, the Princess cares about you.' 'I'm glad you see that,
Zig,' says 1, getting moist-eyed, 'Now you see why it's difficult for
me. 1 *hate* that bugger, her Maharajah uncle, 1 adore *her*. 1 don't
want to be the one to wipe that lovely smile off her dinky little face!'
'–,All the better if you tell me, Rose,' says he quietly. 'The Princess is
a strong girl. She can handle it, whatever it is.' 'OK then – have it
your way! – Here, take a look at this, the one thing that matters.
They think I'm sitting on a mound of papers, oh, no, they mean
nothing, but this is the stuff, this little photograph, you take a good
look, you don't need no explanations.' So 1 show him the sepia
print of Amy Gordon, a tiny picture frayed on the edges. 'See what 1
mean?'

1 can't help a quiet chuckle as the penny drops. '– See what 1 mean?
Tar-brushed, that's what Robbie was. Some Gordon, 1 reckon it was
the one who stood as godfather, yeah, Edward Fitzgilbert Gordon,
he's the one 1 reckon who'd got to Robby's Mum. How could they
acknowledge her or Robbie? Look at her! Handsome, isn't she, the
way many of them were before they got fat on too much mission-
station sugar and flour. What do you reckon: half? Quarter?'

'Felix would know', says he calmly. 'Is that all?' he adds.

'That's it,' says 1. '1 worked it out. Robbie was righting a wrong, you see
what 1 mean – climbing back on to that family tree he'd been kept off.
That's why I've got to forgive the bastard for what he's done to me. Do
you reckon your Maharajah can handle this?' '–1 don't know,' says Zig,
rising. 'Depends on how much of a purist he is. He likes Billy and Felix
well enough, that doesn't mean he'd want an abo in the family. 1 could
be wrong.' '– Can he take a joke,' says 1, chuckling, 'No cheap joke
neither, comes with a Lotto-size bonanza.' '– We'll soon find out, won't
we?' says Zig, grinning as he slams his car door.

That was a week ago. What a week!

So much bustle, hustle and partying, the like of which I've never
seen in my life, not even when the Aquarians took to the streets. 1
got to do mi bit as well, got the Jacaranda Queen on to my float to

play Queen of Sheba, and that went down well with the locals. I didn't get a chance to talk to Zig till I got to my allotted seat at the Coronation ceremony – in the row behind the Lady-in-Waiting and assorted royal aunts and cousins of the Princess – not bad, says I to misself, for a pensioned off harem-girl of Robbie's – it was then I grabbed Zig for a quick word. All he could say was, it was OK. '– OK? OK! Is that all? After all the fuss and bother?' I very near yelled. '– I'll explain later', says he, with his eyes fixed on the Princess.

Poor thing! They were pouring all this goo over her – milk, curds, butter, water and whatnot – it was all explained in the hand-out, symbol of this and symbol of that – blowed if I can remember it all – it was good when it stopped and the poor kid got cleaned up and dressed again in her fantastic queenly gear, loaded with jewels and garlands – a right royal goddess she looked as they put her on the elephant and we all followed her to the temple by the river. She looked so gorgeous I forgave them everything. 'Forgive and forget, Rose,' says I to misself, as I drink the umpteenth toast to the Princess and her kingdom.

Then the unthinkable happens. There am I sitting at the grand banquet, seated between the New South Wales government's rep and a fat, chink-eyed princeling who says little but munches and blinks, blinks and munches. Then he appears, the Maharajah – a po-faced bastard if ever there was one – he sidles up to me, positively beaming. 'I must thank you, Miss Rose, for clarifying the matter we were concerned about. It would seem that our benefactor, Mr Robert Gordon, was the outcome of a morganatic marriage.' (Cunning buggers! I can't believe what I am hearing. Which one of them cooked up this cock-and-bull story? Zig? The Princess? The lawyers? Or this turbaned bloke now talking to me?).

'– Nevertheless,' he continues, 'thank you for settling our mind at rest. I fully appreciate why you hesitated for so long in such a grave matter. But, as our ancient sages say, 'Only a brave wise man dares track the sacred river to its source: he may find himself amidst the snow-peaks of the Himalayas or end by a muddy spring in some dark jungle. I am neither wise nor brave but God has granted me sufficient good sense to cease questioning and make sure that justice is done.'

Well, I've got give it to him, that was clever, yeah, clever, dignified and elegant. I suppose that's what makes him the royal he is.

26
A view from the Gallery

For the first time since she arrived in Australia, with husband Ari and baby Max, Annie relishes the mouth-filling, crackly taste of her full name: Anastasia Papadimitriopoulos, a name printed so prettily, in wavy curls on the invitation-card she is clutching – just in case anyone asks any stupid questions – not that, with son Max beside her, anyone would dare to doubt her right to be seated where she is, in the VIP gallery. There it is, her grand name alongside her husband's:

Mr Aristotle Papadimitriopoulos
and Mrs Anastasia Papadimitriopoulos:
His Royal Highness Krishna Deva Raja of Ratnapuri I
cordially invites you to attend
the Coronation Ceremony of Her Royal Highness
Princess Indrani Devaraja as Queen of Ratnapuri II,
at the Castle.

A few weeks back when her son Max – bet they call him Maximos here, as he should be called – a few weeks back when Max ran away from them while holidaying in Yamba, and husband Ari got so crook and, with veins swelling on his forehead, raged against the boy, so angry he was that Annie feared she might soon have to wear black: she didn't dream then that she'd be sitting where she is now, all dressed up as for the Melbourne Cup, right at the front, in the V.I.P. gallery. She smoothens down the creases in her fine Thai-silk green gown and re-pins her pale yellow lacy hat, for the third time. She sets it at a slight tilt above her braided hair, gathered ever so delicately at the back to show off the filigree silver choker on her elegant, wrinkle-free neck. She smiles as she checks her husband beside her: it is such a rare treat to get him out of his stubbies and singlet into a nicely pressed suit and tie. He's got a bit of a tummy with all those pies, chips and beer he has been having on his long-distance hauls, but the double-breasted, light-grey suit just about covers it. He don't look too bad, her Ari: he scrubs up good. His hair is thinning a bit at the top but he's got plenty around the half-moon, and a bushy beard to match. Her smile expands as she looks at her darling Max, so clever, so smart, sitting beside her: such a handsome boy and so cool in the new blonde streaks she's put on his black mane — everyone says her Max has got the looks and attitude to become a Hollywood heartthrob like Brad Pitt. All he needs is a little bit of luck.

Annie ruffles her son's hair ever so lightly as she cranes towards him.

'Who's the lady beside your Princess, Max?'

'Her lady-in-waiting, Mum. Miss Katarina Rossi.'

'She's lovely. I'd love to do her hair. Don't you think it's lovely, Ari?'

'Sure. — But can't you leave your salon behind, woman?'

Annie's face drops. 'Anastasia, please, if you don't mind.'

'Bugger me if I didn't forget.'

'Mind your language, Ari! Remember where you are.'

'Cool it, Annie! Don't take that tone to me! You know what I think of all this.'

'I know, I know. Still, I don't get much of a chance to dress up and be seen, do I? —What do you think, Max? Perhaps I made a mistake: maybe I should have got the blue gown I saw at D.J.'s. I like Miss Katarina's.'

Max pats her hand reassuringly.

'You look great, Mum.'

'I would love to have one like hers. Shows off her figure. I wonder where she bought it.'

'They say she's a designer, Mum, makes her own stuff.'

'Do you think that shot-silk blue would look good on me, Ari?'

'What's got into you, Annie? Who do you think we are? Filthy-rich royals? – Hear that, Max? Ever since she got this invitation, your Mum's been stalking designer shops and getting me nearly broke. Who does she think she is? – the Queen of Sheba?'

'Don't tease her, Dad! Let her have some fun! She works hard enough.'

'Holy Moses! Listen to him, Annie! Where does he get this poncey talk from, "Don't tease her, Dad!" Bugger me, if my son isn't preaching to me!'

The couple sitting behind them clear their throat in reproof.

Annie tugs at her husband's sleeve:

'Shh, Ari! Mind your language, please! – For Max's sake!'

Ari shrugs his shoulders, glares at the censorious pair, and loosens his tie. 'OK. OK! – Eh, Max, how long we've got to wait, you reckon? This suit's killing me.'

Max grins. 'Not long, Dad. Look! The elephants are here!'

A loud cheer rips through the assembled crowd as the royal

elephants amble in majestically. Decked in silver and gold caparisons, garlanded, their furrowed foreheads transformed to a mosaic of coloured patterns, Jaya and Vijaya are guided by their mahouts to face the Royal Party seated on a high platform under a colourful canopy. At a prod from their masters, the elephants raise their trunks to salute the Princess. Princess Indrani, a veritable goddess in her golden silk saree, her bosom pressed down by weighty gold-and-pearl necklaces, her jasmine-laden hair braided and crowned with a diamond tiara, descends from the platform and is helped by the mahout to climb up Jaya and take her seat.

'She's a brave lady', Annie gasps. 'So clever to get up there in all that gear. – And look! The bands! Two of them! Where from, Max? They sound familiar.'

'Newcastle, Mum.'

'How right you are! It's our Marching Koalas – what's the other one?'

'"Cesco Kids", from Cessnock. They came top, Mum. You saw it on Channel Nine, don't you remember?'

'Did I? I don't remember – I love them horses too, don't they look grand? Their mane's so silky smooth, just like in the shampoo-ads – and such a lovely brown tint too!'

'They're from the Emir's stables near Muswellbrook.'

'You know everythink, Max!' Annie caresses his arm. 'How grown-up you look!'

Max pulls his arm away. 'OK! You guys want to follow the procession to the temple or stay put? It's a bit of a walk.'

'What do you think, Ari?'

'Suit yourself, I'm not going anywhere.'

'We'll stay, Max. My heels are hurting me.'

'OK, Mum. See you later. I must go. Bye for now!'

'See you soon, Son! Take care!'

Annie exudes a deep sigh as she waves to her son, her eyes proudly following his nimble progress through the crowd to join the royal party leading the procession.

'Bless him! He's doing well, our Max, he truly is, Ari. It's all turned out good, don't you think?'

'Dunno. Have you forgotten? What about his HSC? The boy must get back to school and that double-quick. I can't let him hang out here with this royal mob one more day.'

'They pay him well, Ari!'

'For how long? There's no future in this game.'

'Max has got good friends. – Who knows what they can do for him.'

'Don't be stupid, woman. The boy's got to drop this nonsense, get back to school, get a decent education, learn a trade, get a proper job. He better or it's the strap for him.'

'Ari! How can you? Why you so mad at him? He done nothink wrong.'

'Nothink wrong? Nothink wrong? Jesus! Have you forgotten what he did? He bolts from us, saying nothink – God knows where he's gone, and you sitting up all night, weeping your heart out, driving me out of mi mind. – Done nothink wrong? I swore I'd belt him the moment I saw him. I should have.'

'Please, Ari! Don't be mad at him. He did call.'

'I'd already gone to the cops. Made me look stupid.'

'I'm sorry, Ari, I shouldn't have pushed you. But Max did explain everything. And then he got this lovely invitation to this grand do. Can't you forgive him, just a little?'

'Forgive? After what he put us through? All that worry, sleepless nights, and trips to the police station ? – You spoil him, that's what does it. He deserves a good belting. He'll come to no good, carrying on like this.'

'Max's doing a good job here, Ari. Didn't the Prince himself say so? It's good for him, and for me too. When did you last take me to a fun-party?'

'We have Christmas and Easter, don't we?'

'Always with the rellies, and cooking and quarrelling? Call that a party? Look at this! Look around! Everyone looks happy. Look at those kids waving them flags! Aren't they cute? And look over there! Look who's waving to us? Come on, Ari! Wave back, it won't kill ya!'

'Why should I?'

'Because it's our Ray, Max's good friend.'

Ari shakes his head and glowers. 'Didn't you say he's a lawyer?'

'So what? He's a very appreciative customer. He liked what I'd done for Max and wanted the same. It was difficult, the colour wouldn't take nice and easy, but I did a good job.'

'Don't like ginger-heads, don't like lawyers. Lawyers are scum.'

'A-ri! Ray fixed Max up with this job, didn't he? Why don't you ease off a bit and let me enjoy the show.'

'OK! Please yourself, but don't expect me to.'

'I should have gone with the procession, but I couldn't leave you.'

'I thought it was your heels.'

'I might have managed.'

'It's too late now. I can hear the band, they must be returning — Sorry, Annie! You missed whatever they were doing at the temple, but thanks for staying with me.'

'It's all right, Ari! I'm glad you feel better about it. Max'll be pleased. — Here they are, the royals, with our Max! And he's heading our way.'

'—Hi, Mum, Dad! How're you doing? Listen! I've got a little surprise for you.'

Annie turns to her husband, face flushing.

'See, I told you! He's a good lad.'

Ari runs his fingers through his beard, his eyes exuding suspicion:

'What's it this time, son?

'See that durbar?' Max waves towards the canopy under which select guests process to receive gifts and honours from the newly crowned queen of Ratnapuri II. '— How would you guys like to join them bigwigs?'

'No, not me, count me out, son! Your Mum might like to.'

'How about it, Mum?'

'Me, Max? You're kidding.'

'No kidding. It's up to you.'

Annie looks at Ari and then at the durbar, bewildered.

'No, Max, I don't think I can.'

'Don't worry, Mum. It's all right. I thought it might be too much for you. Don't matter. Here, take this! Something for you and Dad from the Queen. Ray arranged it.'
Max hands over an envelope.

'What is it, Max?'

'Go on, open it! I must be off. See yous later!'

Annie tears the envelope open and gasps as she reads. Ari grows uneasy:

'What is it? Lost your tongue?'

'They're giving us a free holiday, a whole week, at one of them cottages at Resort Raja, 5 star-like. – I don't know what to say – I can't believe what I'm reading.'

'Give it to me, let me check.' Ari puts on his bifocals and scans the contents of the letter. 'Bloody hell! It says here, we are to take this holiday right away while they are doing some Princes Conference! – What the hell will I do in a conference?

'But there's a cultural festival, Ari! Shakespeare an' all.'

'Shakespeare? What's he got to do with me? You must be joking. – Sorry, Annie! We can't take this up. I've got a log-delivery job.'

'Ari! How can you be so cruel? It's a lifetime's chance of a luxury holiday for us.'

'But we've just had a holiday.'

'Yamba? Fish and chips and pizzas? This is different. Max tells me the Maharajah keeps classy chefs.'

'This Rajah business has really got to you. Time you got back your common sense.'

'It's only a week, Oh, Ari! Please! It don't cost us nothink. Like Max said, it is a present.'

'Are you sure there's no catch?'

'Look! It says here, "You are invited to be our guests". Ever heard of guests paying?'

'Let me check again! – Ya, You're right. I see it now. "All expenses paid".'

'Yes, then?'

'I suppose the logs can wait a week.'

'There's my good boy!' Annie plants a kiss on the tip of his ear, and whispers: 'It'll be like a second honeymoon.'

'Is that a promise? I better spruce up.'

'You're fine as you are. I love you.'

'I love you too.'

*   *   *

'My dear Monica! If you don't mind, I'd like to go back to our room. I think I have seen enough.'

'Are you feeling unwell again, Jerome? Let me help you.'

'I'm all right, just a little tired. The heat and the noise are getting to me. All I need is some peace and quiet. But there's absolutely no need for you to miss anything.'

'I don't mind.'

'No, no. You must stay, and for Anna's sake. She might feel lost without one of us.'

Monica confers with her companion. 'Anna says she'll be all right. She can see Ziggy from here. No need to worry she says. She'll join us later.'

'I'm glad to hear that. Let's go then.'

Back in their room overlooking the courtyard gardens, the Reverend unburdens. As Monica had guessed that it was more than the heat and the noise.

'I'm afraid I can't really take all this pagan pomp and ceremony. I keep asking myself "What would our Lord have made of this?" I can't understand why our son has got mixed up in it.'

'The young lady is very beautiful and charming, don't you think? It was specially touching to hear her take the coronation oath. I must admit I got a bit emotional when she said so sweetly, "I will at all times protect this country, regarding it as divine".'

'I am sure the young lady means well but we must beware of idolatry in any form, especially as the land-worship that is so fashionable these days.'

'The Maharajah seems an intelligent gentleman. He is full of enthusiasm to do good. His heart's in the right place, wouldn't you agree?'

'His spirit still needs purifying, I would say. All this extravagance and mumbo-jumbo rituals, so pagan! It makes me uneasy. This is no place for us. We shouldn't have come.'

'But my dear! You needed a change of scene after your illness. This invitation was timely. Besides, don't forget Anna! Poor woman! This is a treat for her. She has been such a helpful companion.'

'I'm sorry, Monica, I've been a burden to you in the last few weeks.'

'Don't say that, Jerome! You're never a burden. I can cope, especially as I have Anna with me now. I am glad she's enjoying it here.'

'So am I. – Now I think I'll lie down for a while. Could you please draw the curtains a little? This light is too strong for me.'

'Of course.'

'I doubt if I can attend the banquet this evening. But you better go and give my apologies. I would like to get back home as soon as possible.'

'We'll talk about that later.' Monica arranges the pillows as the Reverend settles down and closes his eyes. She kisses him on the forehead, adding, 'When Ziggy comes'.

*   *   *

I see, and I record with my camera, the transformation of my beloved Princess into an image imperial. A bejewelled goddess in gold brocade, seated on the red *gaddi*, her seat of royalty, she radiates a serene joy, now listening, now speaking a word or two to her well-wishers. Paradoxically, the noisy rituals have placed her in an enclave of dignified silence from where she performs whatever she is directed to do with effortless elegance. Surrounded as she is by suited, bearded, turbaned dignitaries, many of them of ample girth and sullen masculinity, she reminds me of a delicate, tight-budded lotus arching its stalk towards the sun from out of muddy waters that are choked with its gaudy green discs of leaves.

A bitter sweet joy-sadness crushes me as I click away.

The loudspeakers are piping out syrupy Indian melodies. Their high-pitched lilting vies with the raucous music from the bands. Somewhere in the background, one can still hear the drone of the priests' chanting: *shanti, shanti, shanti,* peace, peace, peace.

The bands play on: brassy, shrill at times, then downright cacophonous. After a seemingly endless sequence of national anthems to welcome dignitaries from various parts of the world, they are now rendering a cocktail of popular hits. We have had 'Greensleeves', 'Granada', 'Men of Harlech', the 'British Grenadier' and 'Amazing Grace'. Now they are giving a hearty rendering of 'Waltzing Matilda', and the crowd joins in readily. When that ends, with roars of applause, whistling, tooting of horns, the blaring of trumpets and clashing of cymbals, Queen Indrani rises from the *gaddi* and begins her walkabout.

I decide to stay put. Let the TV crew rush alongside her as she meets the people. It takes a few minutes for her to realize I am not with her; then she looks up with an anxious frown and a fleeting smile. Quickly, I dive behind the camera: I know too well what a predatory journalist can do with just that one fleeting glance and smile.

I love her deeply. She warms my heart. I must keep off intruders from my sacred patch. So I glue my eyes to the lens and evade her searching.

And as I pan the scene, I see Anna, on her own. I wonder when the Reverend and Monica left.

Should I rise and leave too? — Before it is too late? My task here will soon be over: by the end of next week, once the Pan-Princes Conference is over. Would KDR want me around? Day by day he is advancing in his courtship of Katarina. And he is making serious plans for Indrani's future as the Queen of this realm. He is trailing suitors before her; and she is expected to charm the bizoids of that monstrous multinational *Vulcan*, before tomorrow's business meeting with them to discuss land-rights and profit-sharing.

And Indrani? There is no doubt as to what she wants. How does one propose to a Queen? Even if I do, can I really live here, in this make-believe world of ceremony and commerce? Am I to be just an attendant lord?

She is a child still. She plays, but her playing is in earnest. Just as it was yesterday, when we met briefly in her workroom, before dinner.

'I can't call you Mr Martin all the time, and I don't really like Ziggy either. What am I to do?'

'What would you like to do?'

'I know!' Her eyes brighten. 'You shall have a new name. In fact, I ought to knight you. I'll do it right now, right here. Are you ready?'

'Sure!'

'Kneel, please!'

I kneel. She grabs a ruler and touches with its tip my shoulders and head, saying: 'You shall no longer be a commoner, neither Mr Martin nor Ziggy. I dub you knight of my realm, Ezmar the Invincible! Arise, Sir Ezmar!'

I kiss her hand as I stand up, laughing.

'You may laugh, if you please, but I am wholly serious. You are my knight.'

'I am delighted to be your servant, my lady.'

'Of course I shan't be calling you Lord Ezmar, though I'm pretty pleased with it as a name. Quite clever of me, don't you think, to cut and paste your name like that?'

'Simply ingenious! I feel I can join the *Lord of the Rings* team any moment!'

'Heaven forbid! – You can relax. I won't be calling you Ezmar either, only EM. You should know by now we Indians live by our initials. Like Uncle is KDR, you'll be EM. Even that is to be used sparingly.'

'Thank God! – And by that logic, from tomorrow I should be calling you Q I, for Queen Indrani.'

'Makes me sound like a liner!'

'That might please your uncle, but not me.'

'You are free to call me whatever you please.'

'I've been thinking –' I pause deliberately.

'Yes?' Her eyebrows arch.

'How about Rani? For you *are* my Rani.'

'I like that. I like that very much. But we have no need of names, do we?' Her voice bubbles with joy, her amber eyes fill with expectation.

I push the door shut behind and embrace her. She closes her eyes as I kiss, and whispers. 'Don't abandon me, tomorrow, promise? Stay close, please!'

'Of course! When my camera is on you, as it shall be all the time, you are with me, don't forget.'

'I hope I am with you always.'

So I have stayed close all through this ceremony, until now. Yet all the while I feel I am caught in a somnambulist trance. As the crowd carries her away from me, I start packing my gear.

'– Hullo, Mr Martin!'

'Hullo, Anna! Enjoying the party?'

'Yes, yes. Very much. Thank you. – Can we talk now?'

'Sure!' I have been avoiding this encounter, but I can no longer put her off. 'It's too noisy here, let's go in.'

She follows me to my room. As soon as I put the gear down, she bursts out.

'–Stefan is alive. I know.'

'You mean you *think* he is alive.'

She shakes her head. 'No, no. Not think.'

'Have you heard from him?'

She shakes her head even more vigorously.

'No, no. Not hear not speak, but I know, because he ring. Five ring and stop. It's his sign, save money.'

'Are you sure it's not a wrong number or something?'

'I'm sure. I know it's him.'

'Why didn't he speak to you then?'

'He afraid, I know in my bones. He very, very afraid. Some enemy done this to him.'

'You never mentioned any enemies before. Does Stefan have enemies?'

'Not here, but in the old country. There, enemies for everyone.'

'So you think it's someone from the past.'

'I do. I find out.'

'Find out? What? How?'

'I go see boss-man in the garage. I ask questions. He get mad. He shout at me. "You bloody wogs! One minute you hug and kiss, next minute you stab and kill. That bloke came to see your husband, he bloody well look a friend, grinning and shaking hands. Who can tell what the bastard did?" This the angry boss man say. So you see!'

'Did you tell the police?'

'Police? No. Police bad. You good. You find Stefan. Please!'

'How?' My patience wears thin. I wish this woman would not pursue me. 'How am I to find your husband?'

'That day in my flat, you came, you knew I was in trouble.' She nods her head again, her dark eyes moistening with tears. 'You help me now, please!'

'What can I do?'

'Your priest-father, and Mrs Monica, they very good people, they pray for me, every day. Maybe you pray too!'

I avoid her earnest searching eyes. 'I'll try.'

'Thank you! Thank you very much!'

After she leaves, I fling open my windows. Storm-clouds on the horizon lend an outlandish, silvery-red glow to the light that streaks through them. A rumbling of thunder in the distance: it is not long before the skies will deliver a volley of hailstones on the crowd, scattering them. I see Indrani being hastily steered into a limousine, which snakes its way back to the Castle through the helter-skelter.

The rains begin in earnest during the banquet. The skies rupture, and a heavy, steady downpour begins, accompanied by sheet lightning and thunder. I am not sorry that the conversation at my table gets drowned out. As we reach the seventh course, I see an anxious Ganga Rao conferring with KDR, who rises and pauses a while, surveying those assembled as if he were taking stock before he speaks.

'Ladies and gentlemen! I have just learnt that the creeks near us have flooded and burst their banks. As a consequence, the road to Resort Raja is unnavigable. I gather some cars have been washed away. Therefore, regrettably, those of you who are staying at Resort Raja will have to forgo the comfort of that venue and stay here tonight. Please bear with us while we make emergency arrangements; and may I request your co-operation in sharing rooms? Thank you! Please continue to enjoy your banquet!'

I am asked by Ganga Rao if I could billet an elderly couple and their twin sons; I had noticed that KDR had been unusually deferential towards this couple, even urging Indrani to follow suit. It was not hard to see why: one of the handsome youths was fresh out of Harvard Business School, and the other was big in shipping. The twins were ready enough to fall in line with KDR's plans, which meant that they were brought to Indrani's attention at regular intervals or made to perform courteous errands for her under some pretext or other. Clearly KDR was confident that one or the other would win her over. His only regret seemed to be that she had to make a choice: it would have suited him best if she could have married both.

Monica invited me to join them. '– Your father should be deep asleep by now, he was very weary. We mustn't disturb him, but there's no problem otherwise. Anna sleeps on the couch. You don't mind the floor, do you? It'll be like our camping days.'

So it was. It took me back to my childhood. There was something reassuring about being near them, sleeping on the ground, while the winds whistled through the roof and rain kept roaring on.

I awoke in an hour. There was a duet of snoring from the bed, one strong, the other mild. Anna was fast asleep, curled up on the couch, with her portable CD wires dangling beside her. She looked peaceful.

'Maybe you pray': Anna's words keep ringing in my ears.

Maybe I pray.

I am out of practice. I haven't done this since I left home. The Reverend had insisted on regular family prayers. 'I don't understand why people find prayer difficult. Our Lord tells us clearly all we have to do is ask. "Knock and it shall be opened to you!" So you see, my son, it is as simple as that: "Knock, knock!"'

Knock, knock. My heart pounds. Knock, knock, knock. I retreat from the roaring outside and dive within, wading through seemingly endless tides of fatigue. Buffeted about by flashes from the past and the day's events, I am overcome by a heaviness that is neither sleep nor sorrow. 'I must keep awake, I must, I must, I must,' I chant while my eyes stay closed. I must reach the eye of the storm, the calm within the storm.

Suddenly something gives: I feel a flow of warmth spreading from my heart through to my limbs, slackening the muscles that had gone taut in my efforts to keep alert – and I hear that voice again.

'Wake up!'

'I am awake.'

'Are you sure?'

'Yes – No. You are right. I am not. I can't see my way through this.'

'I am the way.'

'But what does it mean?'

'That's for you to find out.'

'How can I? I am in a rut, back where I was. I wronged Katarina, I hurt her. I fear I am about to repeat myself. I love Indrani, but I can neither marry her nor abandon her. I am trapped. Then there is Anna. She won't give up. I hear you, yet I don't believe in you. I am persuaded that I have the "strong-eye", yet I feel that it is yet another delusion. I am weary, sick to the core. My ship has struck a reef and is breaking apart. That is the truth. That is the truth, the whole truth, and nothing but the truth. Satisfied?'

The last word emerges as a shout, startling Monica awake.

'–Is that you, son? Are you all right?'

'I'm sorry, Monica. Just a bad dream.'

'It is a terrible night. You were always frightened of thunder when you were little. – Can I get you anything?'

'No thanks! I'm all right. I hope you can get back to sleep.'

27
A Kingdom is Born

Our kingdom of Ratnapuri II is well and truly launched. My beloved niece Indrani is now its crowned queen.

Despite our misgivings, Mr Boonoo Boonoo Billy came, and, with great grace conducted a smoking ceremony, and thus solemnized our pledge to protect the land and all that dwells therein. Without his willingness to bond us to this land, truly his land, all our pomp and ceremony would have been in vain. May Bhagvan shower his blessings upon him and upon us, in this newly-inaugurated kingdom!

Though I say it myself, the Coronation was a splendid ceremony. Vembu was in his element. No compromises, no shortcuts, he had insisted — and how right he was!

Like the god Agni himself, Vembu officiated at the ritual-platform where, on a bed of paddy, he had set up the twenty-one *kalaśas* — twenty silver and one golden — all filled with sacred water, one part Ganges and three parts Clarence, all the pots festooned with garlands of mango leaves and sacred thread, and capped with coconuts. It was an impressive sight: Vembu and his team of priests, their faces and bare torsos aglow with the light reflected from the gleaming pots, and their chanting filling the air with a vibrant holiness that did not escape the most determined Philistines among our guests.

Ah, the guests!
I could not have wished for a nobler assembly. What a glittering array of remnant royals! They had come, my old friends, from home and from the wider world; from Mysore, Baroda, Bikaner, Pudokkottai, Kerala and Nepal; from Lichtenstein, Denmark, Sweden, Spain, Thailand, Laos and Japan. I was gratified to see delegates from the embassies of Canada, Argentina, Cameroun, Ireland and Zambia; even more pleasing was the presence of representatives from the State and Federal governments. This is where Jayadev had proved himself. His business contacts, the pinguid pair who had visited us many moons ago, whose names I cannot remember even now: well, my crafty Ulysses of a son had skilfully deployed them to allay the suspicions of the Australian authorities. Together with our lawyers Messers Rowlatt and Roy, those two Aussies assured their government that in no way were we infringing the laws of this country, for we neither had an army, nor claimed any rights to pass laws, nor did we claim any sovereignty. The last disclaimer puzzled them the most. 'What are you doing then and why?' asked one of the bewildered and exasperated members of the team sent out investigate what we were up to. Jayadev tactfully left it to me to explain. 'You see Mr ...' — I forget his name. 'You see, in our ancient country, until the British came and muddied the waters,' (this brought out a crack of a smile on the fellow), 'you see, before the Raj, sovereignty was not an issue with our Princely States, at least among those who preserved and persevered in the ancient ways. Kingship is a sacred understanding, a Rajah is known as the "one-sixth man", he takes one-sixth portion of a kingdom's wealth in return for his service, and the sacredness of kingship belongs to the office, not to the man. A Rajah's duty is to sustain dharma, the Law, not to create it. So we are here to protect the people in our land and promote their welfare in the best possible way.' '— And this Coronation business, what's all this about then?' he says, with barely concealed contempt. 'Ah,' I say to him. 'Come and see! You will then understand the difference between being a Rajah and a mere landowner, a capitalist tycoon, or even a philanthropist. Come to the ceremony and you will see what it is to become a sanctified trustee of a land and its people.'

So he came, having concluded within himself that Indrani's

Coronation was no more than a big party-bash, as did others, from other departments, from the Foreign Office (I am sure A.S.I.O. was there somewhere, hardly surprising if they weren't), sticky beaks from Trade and Industry, Tourism and Development, and po-faced gentlemen from the Immigration Department, just in case — and most prominently, officials from the Inland Revenue, all hovering over us like carrion-crows twitching their beaks, convinced that there's *something rotten in the state of Denmark.*

I am not sorry to have disappointed them, for it is not for nothing that I, Jayadev and Ganga Rao burnt the midnight oil with our lawyers to make sure everything was pukka and above board. Jayadev and his young assistant, I must confess, did a splendid job of pampering the tetchy bureaucrats, so much so that, by the time they were seated at the banquet and had quaffed my choicest wines, they couldn't care tuppence about what we did here and why.

Irksome as they are, our problems are not with these bothersome petty bureaucrats from the State or Centre. Governments dream on, sedating themselves with the conviction that they are in charge; but they know, as I know, what the truth is, who it is, or, rather what it is that holds the real reins of power, and how powerless we are, or choose to be, before the likes of *Vulcan*, that great monster of a multinational with its bellies within bellies swelling with the companies it daily swallows, ever gorging, and, never satisfied! They are the 'unacknowledged legislators' of our world today, here, there and everywhere, ruling all and accountable to none!

Yes, I did invite them, purposefully, and they came, those beady-eyed Vulcanites, as immaculate and clean-faced as missionary Mormons in black suits, and just as uptight and loyal to their masters. Sure enough, they were flashing their Colgate-ring smiles to start with. When Mr Billy did his smoking ceremony, I could see their twitchy smiles that seemed to say, 'No doubt this old buffoon (meaning myself) knows how to indulge the whims of the natives, keep them happy, let them do their little bit ...'

What they failed to register was the signal for battle. Our ancestors, the illustrious Cholas, crossed turbulent waters to subdue distant kingdoms in honourable wars, and they then converted their foreign loot into local charity. The faceless chiefs of the likes of *Vulcan* plunder the poor and the gullible, to fatten their own wallets and perhaps cast some crumbs towards their shareholders. Clearly there is a battle to be fought here in Ratnapuri II, and our battleground is the boardroom table.

So, when I told the Vulcanites that I had invited Mr Boonoo Boonoo Billy, whom they regard as a menace, to join our meeting next week, their smiles vanished altogether. For the first time it began to dawn on them that their friendly 'Mr Maharajah', a good investor, sound pillar of Capitalism, might well prove a thorn in the corporate flesh – if indeed one can credit this paper-borne system, this abstract piece of machinery, with something as vital and human as flesh! Soon they will see that their agenda is not my agenda; yet being a key stakeholder, they will have to listen to me, or, rather, listen to the newly crowned Queen of Ratnapuri II. What force, what scheme, what guile, what craft will they unleash to defuse our charming challenger? Exit KDR, enter Queen Indrani: *alarums and excursions!* I shall be like Prospero; I shall withdraw from the magical banquet, and watch.

'Gentlemen!' I announced, as the storm continued to wreak havoc around us in the days following the Coronation, 'Gentlemen! Since we cannot venture out, and I know how some of you are missing your golf (I myself prefer chess) may I invite you to participate in our Chess Tournament which we have arranged to while away the time till the storm clears and the roads are freed? And, by the way, chess is an apt game for this occasion, for, did you know, chess was invented in India?' With Indrani as a chief contestant, how could they resist?

It is a good thing that I had taught her well. She knows, as I know, how invaluable this ancient sport is for reading the enemy's mind like a map, especially if you watch what they do when a knight leaps to action most unexpectedly. *Once more unto the breach, dear friends, once more ...*

28
Parallel Tracks

The door is locked. Rohan can hear Ray's laughter. Should he knock or go away?

The door opens and Max emerges, his grin fading to a faint smile when he sees Rohan. 'Hi! How're you doing?'

'Not bad. And you?'

'Very busy. Dev's got loads of jobs for me still — you know, the Conference and all. Just dropped in for a quick chat.'

'How're your parents?'

'OK. They should be pleased, now that the roads are clear. Mum was getting worried she might lose her hols at Resort Raja.' Max turns around to bid a final good-bye to Ray. 'Ta for everything. See you soon. — In you go, he's all yours.'

Rohan finds Ray stretched out on the sofa. He sits up, yawning:

'How's the chess-tournament going?'

'Still going.'

'I thought you were playing.'

'I was.'

'Lost your game?'

'No. I won two games.'

'Oh! – Why did you leave, then?'

'I had enough.'

'Really? You, a chess addict? – Who did you beat?'

'The Twins.'

'That handsome pair, Romesh and Suresh? Wow! KDR wouldn't relish that. He thinks they are very smart. Clearly you are super-smart. Congratulations!'

'Nothing to coo about – I couldn't beat *her.*'

'Who? The Princess?'

'Queen. She's so beautiful, so graceful, and so clever. And to think what a fool I made of myself with one silly stupid move. Even a novice wouldn't have made it. I don't know what came over me.'

'Come on! It's only a game. What does it matter?'

'It matters to me – matters a lot.'

'My dear boy, you mustn't take it to heart. Cheer up. Let me pour you a drink. What would you like?'

'No thanks.'

'Well, I'm sorry you lost, but I'm going to have a whisky, to celebrate the fact that the roads are clear once again, and the Pan-Princes Conference will go ahead as scheduled. Cheers! – What's the matter? You look as if you are about to cry.'

'I wish I could.'

Ray picks up a magazine and, browsing lazily, yawns as he speaks:

'Come on, Rohan! It's just a game. Everything's going swimmingly. We shall get a nice bonus for all our work and then back to Sydney after this Conference, and you'll forget all about this silly tournament.'

Rohan rises and paces up and down, clenching and unclenching his fists. He stops before Ray and stoops slightly towards him. 'Ray!'

'What?' Ray drops the magazine. 'You look grim. What's the trouble?'

'I want to go away.'

'That's fine by me. Where shall we go? You choose this time.'

'No, Ray. I don't mean a holiday. I want to leave you. I've had enough. I want to quit.'

'Ro-han!– Sit down! Have a drink! Think it over.'

'There's nothing to think over.'

'What's up with you? What have I done wrong now?'

'Nothing. Nothing. It's not you. It's me. It's ... It's hard to talk about. I feel different here, definitely different.'

'I see. – Oh, God! You are in love. You are in love with that girl. Now I understand why you lost the game. She confused you. It's hopeless. You are a hopeless case.'

'You don't need to tell me. I know I'm hopeless.'

'Her uncle has plans for her. From what I've seen she's got eyes only for that photographer.'

'I know.'

'I'm beginning to feel sorry for you. What are you going to do?'

'I don't know. All I know is that I don't want to carry on as before. I know it is foolish to fall in love with her, but it makes me feel better, makes me feel clean.'

'Now that's a hit below the belt. That hurts!'

'I'm sorry. I know it's not fair – but it's the truth.'

'You bastard! You don't really care, do you, how I feel? You never did care, come to think of it. All along it has been me making all the sacrifices, adjustments, while you, you acting like a right royal spoilt brat! – You are shit! You are shit through and through!'

'Enough, Ray! I couldn't agree with you more. That's why I must leave you.'

'Bastard! – heartless, shitty bastard!'

'You won't miss me much. You have Max.'

'Do I? – What do you know? The games that boy plays! You have no idea what it is like being me.'

'Same goes for me. We run on parallel tracks.'

'Don't give me philosophy!'

'I'm sorry.'

'That's better. At least you can start being civil for all the years we've had together, and the fun! – What will you do? We still have a lot of paper-work to do here.'

'Don't worry, I shan't let you down. I will stay till the Conference is over.'

'Then?'

'Who knows?—I might quit the firm and start afresh, do something entirely different. I've always wanted to be a ranger.'

'I see. A Lone Ranger?'

'Not necessarily.'

'You're dreaming!'

'I'd rather dream. Dreaming keeps me sane.'

'You really are a fool!'

'Fool as I am, I've made up my mind. I'm leaving. I shall clear out as soon as we get back.'

'What about our house? And the garden? You love that garden. I can't see how I can keep it.'

'Find a gardener. As for the house, with all my work in the garden, it should fetch a good price; or, if you want to stay on, I don't mind waiting for my share.'

'You've thought it all out, haven't you? How long have you been plotting to abandon me?'

'I'm in no mood for another row. I think you should start taking me seriously when I say I am leaving, and that's that.'

'You'll be sorry, you'll regret it. It's a bitchy world out there – you have no idea, no idea at all what madness this is, how horrible it is to be lonely.'

'Perhaps it's time for me to find out.'

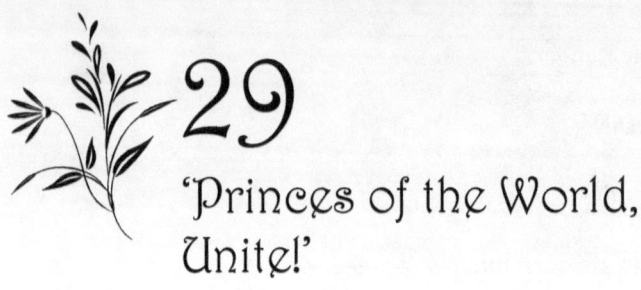

29

'Princes of the World, Unite!'

'Ladies and gentlemen! This is a great occasion, and I welcome you all —Princes, Princesses, delegates of Kings, Queens, Ambassadors, Chiefs — I welcome you all on behalf of Queen Indrani of Ratnapuri II. Our young queen is indisposed with flu and regrets that she cannot personally open this Conference. The theme of our Conference is dear to her heart and she is with us in spirit as we proceed with our solemn deliberations.

'It gives me great pleasure to tell you that His Royal Highness, the Prince of Wales, has sent us from his seat in High Grove a moving message of support, while regretting that he could not be present with us. His heroic endeavours to counteract the destructive thrust of our times in matters concerning the care of our world should inspire us. We must nail our colours to the mast, as he has done, for unless we, the royalty of the world, unite and fight the common enemy of humanity, unless we who are enriched by God's grace in varying measures lead the battle to oust the enemy within the system, unless we rid the world of the canker of irresponsible capitalism that is hell-bent on short-term gains at the expense of the very survival of the human family and its habitat, unless we undertake this heroic enterprise willingly and wisely, unless we do this, what claim do we have to our honourable status? Our concern, my friends, is to reverse this trend! Our concern is to present a united front for the rescue of our world. Our concern is to seek ways and means to move from globalisation to localisation! Let us unite in prayer to re-sacralise the world! Let us begin here and now ...'

KDR is in full Shakespearean swing. His voice trumpets through this splendid auditorium, the centrepiece of Resort Raja, designed by Indrani for the annual Shakespeare Festival with which KDR plans to put Ratnapuri II on the international map. I cannot but admire his resilience, given that this Conference nearly didn't happen.

For three days the Castle was under siege from the elements. For three dark days and three nights the skies opened and poured non-stop, transforming the Castle and its surrounds into a quagmire resembling a battlefield. All signs of jubilant celebration were wiped out within the first few hours, and soon the whole area was awash with torn buntings, sodden flags, ripped awnings, broken poles, and assorted debris of rotting garlands, coconut-branches, banana leaves, and paper cups. The weary and anxious guests were barely able to contain their fear and were eager to go home. Undaunted, KDR had turned the disaster to his advantage, working hard to rally the disheartened troops. Following the example of his favourite Shakespearean hero, King Henry V, he had gone around talking tirelessly to each and every one of his guests, and taking soundings. Seeing that he might well face some resistance to his noble ideas, he has spent hours fine-tuning this speech. I have heard him expatiate on this theme many times before, yet now his rhetoric seems to have reached a new pitch of excellence.

I could stay here listening to him once more — or I could be where my thoughts are, and sneak back to the Castle to see her. Katarina is in the front row, in rapt attention, soaking up every word. It doesn't take long for KDR to draw the rest of his audience into his dreams. I slip out unnoticed.

'— Who is it, Jeevesamma?' Indrani's voice is faint as she calls out from the inner room.

Jeevesamma holds the door half-open, pretty well barring my

entrance while addressing her charge: 'You must sleep, Lizzy Rani. I am telling Mr Martin to come later.'

'Don't do that. Let him in!'

Jeevesamma gives me a stony glare. 'Don't be talking too much, sir. She must rest. She is very tired, very weak.'

I walk past her, muttering 'Of course!'

What a contrast to the bejewelled beauty of the previous week! Lying under a white sheet covered up to her chin, my Rani looks a vulnerable, sick child. She greets me with a wan smile; her cheeks, a little more hollow than usual, highlight her fine bone-structure and make her eyes look larger than ever. Her hair hangs loose but for a few curly strands on her forehead, glued with beads of perspiration. I take her limp hand and kiss.

'– Jeevesamma! Order some coffee for Mr Martin, and will you also check if there are any messages for me?'

Having sent her minder out of the room for a brief while, she turns to me.

'I am so glad to see you. I am sorry to be like this. It's terribly tedious. How is it going?'

'The Conference? Fine. When I left, KDR was going great guns. I think by now he would have got his audience eating out of his hand.'

'Pity, I am missing everything. Uncle must be annoyed with me.'

'I'm sure he is not. His mind is on how to translate the obvious enthusiasm for his ideas into actual action. Besides, Katarina is looking after him very well.'

'I am redundant, after all.'

'Come on! Don't say that. You've done more than enough.'

She pulls a face. 'A lot was done to *me*. What did I do? I just sat there like a doll, decked up in finery.'

'You were a joy to behold, for all the people.'

'And what about you? What did you really think? Honest answer, please, Mr Chorus-Man!'

'I am not a Chorus-Man anymore. You know that very well.'

Jeevesamma returns with my coffee, and as she hands it to me, looks at her watch with intent. Indrani scowls at her.

'Don't be rude, Jeevesamma! Mr Martin has just arrived. Will you please wait in the other room till I call?'

Jeevesamma departs, leaving the door wide open. Indrani fumes.

'Look at her! She is getting worse than ever, ever since all these people from home arrived. She watches me day and night. Doctor's orders, she says, but I feel she's enjoying being my jailer.'

'Don't be cross with her. She loves you, in her own way. And she's right. You must rest, and I mustn't tire you. Besides, I must get back before your uncle notices my absence. How are you feeling? What did the doctor say?'

'He thinks it's sheer exhaustion. I think what finished me was that meeting with *Vulcan*, they were so aggressive towards Billy and I had a job getting them to be polite and listen to his case. To be honest, I'm glad to be let off this Conference. I don't think I can bear any more talk. I had to listen to so much talk while the storm lasted.'

'I noticed. I noticed how keen some of the princes were to talk to you, especially the Twins.'

'Bother them!'

'The Twins seem to think they have won you over.'

'How dare they? I've done nothing to encourage them. I never did, never shall.'

'Your uncle will be disappointed to hear that'

'Bother Uncle! Bother everybody! Bother this Kingdom! Bother you! Did you come here just to annoy me?'

Her eyes fill with tears.

It should be easy. Just a few words: 'I love you, will you marry me?' It should be dead easy, yet the words die in my throat.

Jeevesamma marches in, bearing food and medicine on a tray, and with determination sits on the bed. 'Sit up, Lizzy Rani! Time to take your medicine. You must eat a little! You must take this soup.' She turns to me sternly, 'And then she must be sleeping. Please excuse, sir.'

I rise. 'I should be going. Sleep well!'

I ignore Jeevesamma and plant a kiss on Indrani's forehead, whispering, 'I love you.'

She closes her eyes. 'Be back soon, please!'

'I promise.'

When I return to the auditorium, I find KDR hosting a discussion-panel on stage. He is flanked by four delegates on either side. A slender young man, immaculately groomed, an Oxbridge-trained Oriental Prince by his looks, is speaking with passionate intensity. '... Yes, it is true that Laotians are losing their lands daily. It is true that our government bows to pressure from the big corporations. But tell me, gentlemen, who doesn't? Everyone accuses our government of being corrupt, but I challenge you to name one government in the world which is not corrupt ... Our people make sacrifices, our government regrets what it has to do. We are ready to save our lands, help our farmers, but how? Can this honourable assembly tell us how? How are we to bring prosperity to our people without capital investment? Who is ready to invest except these corporations? Do you want us to go to the World Bank with our begging-bowls? What difference would that make? Everyone knows who they really support. We are trapped — we are trapped in this giant wheel of karma. Who can deliver us? ... Our monks lash themselves to the trees: they may save their trees — but can they save the people?'

I warm to this young man. His passionate realism is a welcome relief. The young man has thrown down the gauntlet. I am glad I didn't miss this. What will the rest say to him?

I feel a shadow beside me. Ganga Rao has crept in quietly. His face is ashen. He is trembling all over. He stutters as he speaks. 'Mr Martin! Please come with me! Something terrible has happened.'

'Where? What? — Indrani? I just saw her an hour ago.'

'No, not the Queen. Someone else. Please! Come with me.'

As we walk out into the foyer, Ganga Rao stops trembling. 'Something terrible has happened, sir. Mr Rowlatt is dead.'

'Oh, no! —Was he sick? He seemed OK.'

'Not sick, sir. Something worse. — Please come with me, sir!'

We halt before cottage number seven. Ganga Rao opens the door.'Here, sir! Ramgopal found him, sir, when he took his tea. — Like this, sir!'

Ray Rowlatt lies sprawled on the floor, his eyes staring vacantly, his blood-splattered head swarming with flies.

30

'Who Killed Cock Robin? ...'

'A murder ! – A killer in our midst ! My mind shudders at the very thought! What an outrage! – Who has inflicted this terrible blight on our auspicious activities! O ye gods, what have I done to deserve this? Why, O why? – Ganga Rao! Tell me once again exactly what happened.'

KDR is pacing up and down before cottage number seven, shaking his head vigorously to be rid of the shock. Now and then, he stops before the door of the cottage to stare at the body, gathering all his energies as if to summon the dead lawyer back to life to answer his questions.

Ganga Rao rehearses his story to us yet again. 'It was like this, Your-Highness. I was sitting at my desk in the foyer of the auditorium and making the alterations Your-Highness had wanted to the schedule for this afternoon's workshops. I am about to take my morning coffee when I see our peon running towards me, very frightened. Ramgopal is shaking all over and not speaking at all. After much questioning, I am learning this from him: Ramgopal is taking a tray of tea and cake to Mr Rowlatt as requested. He rings the bell and is waiting outside. No answer. He thinks maybe Mr Rowlatt is in the bathroom, so he waits a little longer and rings again. No answer. Meanwhile the tea is getting cold. He thinks he will have to go back to the kitchen to get a fresh pot if he has to wait longer. So he knocks on the door loudly. The door gives way. It is not locked. Ramgopal says to himself how foolish to be standing outside for so long when the door is not locked. He pushes the door open, then, he drops his tea tray when he sees Mr Rowlatt lying on the floor. He sees that Mr Rowlatt's head is bashed, and there's blood everywhere. He knows instantly some villain has hit Mr Rowlatt. So Ramgopal comes running to me. I call the ambulance and come into the auditorium thinking how I might disturb you, for Your-Highness is on the stage chairing your most important discussion. Then I see Mr Martin in the back row. Together we come to this cottage number seven. The ambulance arrives but it is too late to save Mr Rowlatt. The paramedics say that Mr Rowlatt has been dead for several hours. They talk among themselves and tell us that we must not touch anything or move anything because Mr Rowlatt has died of violence, and the police must be called at once. I am in a state of shock. Only when Mr Martin reminds me, I come to inform Your-Highness. The police are here now. The Inspector wants to start his interviews in cottage number six. Ramgopal is there right now. I must go and help, because they cannot understand him.'

KDR slumps on a chair by the door, head in hands, exclaiming. 'Who'd want to kill this poor man? Such an excellent lawyer, so hard-working! – How am I going to break this terrible news to Indrani? –Ganga Rao! You must ring her. – No! On second thoughts, don't ring her! Someone must go to the Castle. She's already weak with flu, this shock is bound to make her worse.'

As he finishes speaking, a policeman approaches him. 'The inspector would like to see you, sir.'

'Certainly.' He puts his palms together and, eyes closed, mutters a prayer, concluding, 'O Bhagvan! Be merciful to us in these dark times!'

When he leaves, Ganga Rao turns to Katarina. 'Miss Katarina! I am needed here. Would you, please?'

Katarina, who is solicitously watching KDR as he walks to the interviewing room, is caught by surprise. 'Please what?'

'Go to the Castle.'

'Me? – I am not the right person. I think Mr Martin should go. He knows her better.'

So it falls to me to be the bearer of bad tidings.

'Ganga Rao! Please tell the Inspector where I will be.'

'Certainly, sir.'

As I drive towards the gate, I nearly hit a red Cortina swinging fast round the corner. Rohan pulls up alongside and winds down his window.

'– What's going on? Why these police cars?'

'I am sorry to have to tell you. Ray is dead. It looks like murder.'

'Oh, God! – Oh, my God!' Rohan puts his head down on the steering-wheel. His back heaves as he moans. I cannot see his face.

I get out and touch him gently on the shoulder. 'Rohan! I am very sorry. It's a terrible shock for all of us – I can't even begin to imagine what it must be like for you. I am terribly sorry.'

Rohan lifts his head. His face is vacant. He takes my hand off his shoulder and stares into the distance. 'I had to go to the Castle last night. I'd left my asthma medication there. It was late, I was tired. So I decided to stay the night. To think that while I was away some bastard has done this to Ray. How stupid of me, how unpardonably stupid!'

'I understand how you feel. It's a great loss for you, that much I know.'

'Do you?' A strange twisted smile, almost a grimace, flits across his handsome features. He starts the car. 'I better go and face the worst.'

He speeds into the complex as if he is about to crash into the crowd of onlookers assembled outside cottage number seven.

As I drive towards the Castle, my head pounds with questions. Why did I not see this? Then again, had I seen it, could I have stopped it? I remember the moment of sick apprehension in Boonoo Boonoo Billy's cottage; and earlier still, when KDR took me on that helicopter ride. Is this it? Is this the serpent's sting that I feared, waiting to poison KDR's dream of a kingdom?

Jeevesamma signals for me to enter quietly. Indrani is fast asleep. I sit at a distance and watch her. May she sleep in peace, may she continue to breathe this pure air before I break my ugly news! I have no wish to wake her up. I wait, suspended in my precarious peace.

The clock strikes three. Indrani surfaces. She looks about dreamily, and seeing me, sits up smiling. 'You are back! And so soon! How long have you been here? Why didn't you wake me? – What's the matter? You look so sad. I am not that sick. I am getting better, can't you see?'

'Something terrible has happened, Rani. – Ray is dead. He was found this morning with head injuries. The police think he has been murdered.'

'Police? Murder? What are you talking about? Am I hearing right? Are you really here? Am I still dreaming? Surely this is some nasty dream, it must be.'

'I'm afraid not. Ray is dead. Murdered. I am sorry to have to wake you with this brutal, ugly truth.'

'Oh no! Oh, no! – Who'd want to kill him? Why?'

'The police are searching the orchard for the murder-weapon.'

'Murder! I can't bear that word. – Uncle is dreaming about saving the world, and we are now talking about a killer in our midst and murder-weapons. Everything's ruined, everything we have been working for – I should have known when the storm struck so quickly after the ceremony. It's all very frightening and confusing. I can't think. – What do you think?'

'I'm still digesting the facts. Nothing's clear so far.'

She pulls a face. Her mood changes from shock and bewilderment to anger.

'You are the seer, why didn't you see this?'

'Forgive me, I am a failed seer.'

'I'm sorry, I'm not being fair. I should thank you for being here with me.'

'Your uncle didn't want to break this terrible news to you over the phone. He is very worried that it might make your illness worse.'

'Poor Uncle! – How's he coping?'

'He's shocked, profoundly upset, as you can imagine. When I left, the Inspector was talking to him.'

'And Mr Roy?'

'I saw him on my way. Clearly it is a shock to him. He was here last night, he told me.'

'Yes, I remember. Jeevesamma had seen him in the corridor. She was a bit catty about him. She said he was looking a bit strange, hanging outside my room, armful of roses.'

'Oh?'

'I gather he asked after me and left this bunch for me.'

'He is rather in the habit of giving you flowers, isn't he?'

'Well, I have been sick –'

'Of course!'

'Don't tell me you are jealous of him. There's nothing to be jealous about.'

'Jealousy is hardly what I feel about him at present. It's a terrible blow to him, we must look after him.'

'He is a little strange, I don't make him out.'

'Things have been difficult for him since this boy Max arrived on the scene.'

'I met his parents. They seemed nice. His mother in particular was delighted with her little holiday at Resort Raja. Ray had arranged it. Oh, God! What they must feel now! It is horrible: poor Max, poor Rohan, poor Uncle!'

Tears flow freely. I move closer and put an arm round her. She continues sobbing quietly. For once, Jeevesamma leaves the room without any comment.

My phone rings. 'Hullo! – Ah, Ganga Rao! Any news?'

'The Inspector wants to see you, sir. His Highness is anxious to know how our Queen is.'

'She is coping; but what will happen when I leave is hard to say.'

'His Highness is asking Miss Katarina to come over to be with her, sir.'

'Good. I'll wait till she gets here.'

'Oh sir! There is some news. They have just found the murder-weapon. A fire extinguisher, it was found in a compost-pit. They are looking for fingerprints on it but so far no success – I see Miss Katarina leaving, sir. She will soon be there.'

'Thank you, Ganga Rao. Tell the Inspector I am on my way.'

31

Some Villain ...

'Ganga Rao!'

'Yes, Your-Highness!'

'Is it only three p.m.? Why is it so dark in here?'

'More storms on the way, Your-Highness.'

'I cannot bear these darkening skies. Draw the curtains and switch on all the lights. I need brightness around me — my soul is heavy with grief.'

'These are sad times, Your-Highness.'

'Do you remember the calamity that once struck our Navaratri festival in old Ratnapuri?'

'How can we forget that Navaratri, Your-Highness?'

'It is branded in my memory — that piece of flesh — human flesh as it turned out to be — how it fell from the skies amidst our guests assembled in the courtyard for the great puja! I shudder as I remember. A greedy kite had taken more than it could carry from the Tower of Silence. — The Parsis have a strange way of disposing of their dead!'

'Indeed, Your-Highness.'

'The shock and the pollution! It was like something from *The Ramayana* – that is what the *rakshasas* did to desecrate the sacrifices of the rishis. So was our Navaratri-puja desecrated by this piece of human flesh.'

'Those kites were a menace. That Parsi tower should have been closed down. Your-Highness was too considerate.'

'We cannot blame any kite this time. Some villain has done this to us, left us with a corpse in our midst – with one stroke, ruined our sacred deliberations. – Not that I don't feel sorry for Mr Rowlatt, may he rest in peace after life's fitful fever! – I myself cannot sleep for seeing his fly-blown corpse in my dreams.'

'If I may venture to say, Your-Highness might consider some medical assistance?'

'What need have I of a doctor? – I need a solution to this mystery. I need to know who killed him and why. Any news from the Inspector?'

'Inspector Muldoon has finished his interviews with our guests. He is now letting them depart.'

'At last ! For this whole week, this Resort has been a fort under siege and Inspector Muldoon in cottage number six is acting as our occupying power. I have been rendered powerless to help: our two hundred or more delegates have become virtual prisoners within Resort Raja. I can barely think or speak of the indignities they have been subjected to.'

'It is true our guests have been longing to leave, Your-Highness. But Your-Highness may take comfort in that their sympathies are with you. They understand. They appreciate the Inspector had to make sure.'

'Make sure? Make sure? How many times do I have to tell the

Inspector that they were all with me that evening in the auditorium, enjoying *Twelfth Night?* Little did any of us suspect that a killer was prowling about while we were laughing at the cruel mockery of Malvolio! – Alas, I should have known, there's a dark streak in that comedy. – Yet how could Inspector Muldoon even entertain the idea that my guests had anything to do with this sordid murder? They don't even know who Ray Rowlatt is!'

'That's precisely what Inspector Muldoon is trying to ascertain, if you forgive my saying so, Your-Highness.'

'I don't object to that, but it is his manner – Inspector Muldoon is a philistine and a bully.'

'He is a Queenslander, Your-Highness. I admit he is rough in his way of speaking.'

'Thank God, Indrani had to stay at the Castle. I cannot bear to imagine what this man would have done. –How is she?'

'Of course our Queen is deeply shocked and saddened by this tragedy, Your-Highness. She is still very weak, but Miss Katarina was able to take her for a walk yesterday. One good thing, however – her ayah has been able to confirm Mr Roy's alibi. The young gentleman has been subject to the most ruthless questioning by Inspector Muldoon.'

'Poor Mr Roy! As if he hasn't enough grief! – the shame and indignity of this investigation are boundless. Never in my life have I had to suffer such humiliation and grief. My ship has struck a reef – it is being prised apart, moment by moment. – Has the Inspector made any progress?'

'Hard to say, Your-Highness. So far he has established the time and manner of the killing. According to the forensic report, Mr Ray Rowlatt must have died sometime between 10 and 11 p.m. last Tuesday. The murderer, according to Inspector Muldoon, was probably someone known to Mr Rowlatt, for there is no sign of a forced entry or of anything stolen. The fact that the murder-weapon was a fire-extinguisher suggests, he says, an impulsive act. Clearly, the killer didn't come to cottage number seven with a weapon. In other words, the murder was very likely not premeditated. Inspector Muldoon is re-examining the Orchard staff right now. He is focussing on discovering whether anyone had seen Mr Rowlatt after supper, for that was when most of us had seen him – before the play began – he was with us in the dining-hall that fatal evening. Pity, he didn't attend the play, he might have lived.'

'Like Banquo's ghost I fear he will haunt us, until we find his killer.'

'Your-Highness!'

'Yes, Ganga Rao?'

'Shall we go? I have arranged a fleet of cars to take our guests to the airport.'

'Yes, yes, you are right. The least I can do is to bid our guests farewell – *Here's the smell of the blood still:* all the perfumes of Arabia will not sweeten the air of this, our new kingdom!'

*   *   *

As the rains start, Annie shuts the front window of cottage number ten and draws the curtains aside. 'I see cars leaving, Max! I'm packed up an' all, ready to go when the Inspector's finished with your Dad. Wiv a bit o' luck we can catch the XPT tonight. What d'you reckon?'

'Dunno – I may have to stay on a bit. I hope the Inspector lets you and Dad go.'

'You don't think he will?'

'I didn't say that.'

'Your Dad's so mad at me he isn't talking to me at all. – It's terrible, this murder! Poor Ray, poor Mr Roy, poor you! – Look at you! You look shattered!'

She moves close to Max, who is sitting by the TV, channel-hopping. She ruffles his hair. He pushes her away.

'Leave off! – What d' you expect? Ray's gone. He's been good to me. He's dead and gone. All my plans for a bit of peace and quiet gone with him too.'

'What plans, Max? What are you talking about?'

'The day before he died – was killed – he'd made me an offer.'

'An offer?'

'Yeah, a good offer. His mate Rohan was clearing out for good. Ray was no good at gardening. He asked if I'd keep an eye on it – he'd pay me, of course.'

'That would have been a nice little earner for you. What a shame!'

'Yeah, but it wasn't just the money. Ray said I could come and go as I liked – I could use his mate's room to do my HSC studies.'

'You wasn't thinking of leaving home, Max, was you?'

'What if I was? – His place is quiet, not like our flat, what with neighbours fighting, kids screaming – that room he'd give me faced the garden, lovely and quiet!'

'Does Dad know about this offer?'

'Yeah, I told him. He went mad at me.'

'Oh, Max! – What did you do that for? You know what he's like.'

'He wants me to do well at HSC, don't he? – what does he ever do to help? Always going crook at me, always shouting, threatening to belt me. – Why shouldn't I leave home when I get a chance?' Max's eyes fill with tears. 'What's the point now arguing about it? It's all over. Ray's dead. We're back in the same shit as before.'

'Please, Max, don't say that! I'm sure everythink 'll be all right when we get back. I'll make sure everything's OK for you, my pet. I'll talk to Dad, we'll move. All we need now is to get back home soon.'

'I hate home. I hate Dad. I hate –'

'Don't say it, Max! I know you're upset. But please, for my sake, bear with him. I know he has a temper but he is good at heart, he means well.'

'Is that why he hits you?'

'What d' you mean?'

'Don't think I'm stupid. I can see your black eye for all your make-up. He did it, didn't he?'

'It's nothing – he didn't mean to. He didn't want this holiday. I made him stay. Now with this murder an' all, everything's gone wrong. He'll be all right once we leave.'

'If we can leave –'

'Don't say that, Max! You scare me!'

'I scare you? –You should be scared of your husband.'

'Shh! – I hear his footsteps. Stay calm.'

Annie opens the door to a grim-faced Ari who slams the door shut and walks right past her without a word. Annie follows him.

'Look at you, poor dear, you're soaked. Here, let me get a towel and help you dry off!'

'Don't need no help.'

'What did the Inspector say? – Can we leave now? I'm all packed.'

'We can't. That bloody Inspector wants to question your son again.

– Run along, you lazy son of a bitch, before I kill you – you – you with your poofter friend, look what you've brought on us!'

* * *

'Don't be standing by the window, Lizzy Rani! Look how you are shivering! You will be catching that cold again, then where will we be? Pneumonia, flu and what not. You are still very weak, not at all well. I'm begging you be listening to me! You may be Queen now, but you are a child in my care!'

Jeeevesamma takes Indrani's hand and forcibly directs her back to bed and tucks her in.

'– The rains have stopped at last. I thought I heard a car – maybe Uncle, or Mr Martin with some news.'

'The only news I am wanting to hear is that they have nabbed the villain who killed the lawyer. Then we should all be packing and going home to some peace and quiet.'

'Jeevesamma !– Listen! What's that commotion in the corridor? Go and check, please! Quick!'

'You promise to stay in bed, I'll be going and coming back double quick.'

'I promise.'

Jeevesamma returns, highly flustered. 'She's here, your friend, that Miss Rose! I don't know what the Maharajah will say to this – the lady insists she must see you, even when I am telling her you are very weak.'

Tantric Rose ambles in, brushing the jittery ayah aside. Felix follows her, carrying a large canvas in bubble-wrap. Indrani sits up, startled.

'Rose! What a surprise!'

'How are you, pet? I heard you were sick. I would have come before but this' – she gestures towards the canvas – 'kept me busy. Besides, with Inspector Muldoon prowling around yous all – I know the bloke – I thought I'd let things settle a bit. Poor Ray! Who'd want to finish off the poor bugger? – It must be awful for you, darl, what with this murder and flu – I'm sorry, truly sorry.'

'Awful isn't the word, we are all shocked to the core. None of us can rest till we find out who did it and why. Is this Inspector good?'

'He's dogged, known for getting quick results. Any news?'

'Not yet.'

'I thought I'd come to cheer you up a bit.'

'That's kind.'

'– With this. I'm on mi way to Grafton to get it framed. Thought you might like a peep.'

'You mean you finished the portrait?'

'You'll see what we've done, Robbie and I.'

Rose starts taking the tapes off the bubble-wrap carefully, Felix assisting. Katarina enters, bearing a bunch of flowers.

'Hullo everyone! – Hi, Rose! – What's going on?' She kisses Indrani on the forehead and hands her the bunch. 'Sorry you couldn't come, it's a beautiful afternoon! I picked these for you!'

Indrani sniffs them. 'Wild flowers! I don't even know what they are.'

'You will, one day, don't worry! By the way, KDR rang to say he hopes to join us at dinner-time.'

'– Open sesame!' With that cry, Rose whips off the last layer and holds it loosely before the canvas. 'Ready, everyone? Here we go.'

Indrani rises, confused and agitated. 'Oh, Rose! It's beautiful! – But you have changed it!'

'Yeah, just a little. Last week after seeing you crowned queen – it was wonderful – I could forgive Robbie for what he'd done to me. Everything began to make sense. I was – I mean Robbie – led me to this. I've been working furiously all week to get it right. What d' you think?'

'You leave me speechless. Grandma Alice is quite transformed by the addition: it says so much!'

'That's the idea! I'm happy now.'

'–Wow! She's quite something.' Katarina walks over to take a closer look at the portrait: a nude Alice reclining on a chaise-longue, her amber eyes dreamily gazing at two miniatures facing each other on the open pages of a lace-edged Victorian keepsake-album; on the right, a gold-laden Indrani as crowned queen and on the left a sepia-tinted, shadowy image of Amy Gordon.

Katarina claps her hands in slow motion. 'Bravo, Rose! I didn't know you were an artist.'

'It's not all me, Kat. That's another story. – You like it?'

'It's great! – So Rani, this is your grandma who started it all? If I may say so, you look remarkably like her, except for your far superior brown complexion. Has KDR seen this yet?'

Rose starts repacking. 'Not yet. I want to surprise him when I win the Archie.'

'You're entering this for the Archibald Prize – as what?'

'*Dreaming the Future.*'

'Brilliant! Good luck.'

'Thanks! Bye for now. Take care. See yous later.'

As the door shuts behind Rose, Katarina draws a chair close to Indrani and sits. 'Well, well. What a surprise! I had no idea she is so talented.'

'Rose of course insists that Robert Gordon was doing it through her.'

'Clearly she has had some help from someone.' Katarina gives Indrani a searching look.

The phone beside the bed rings. Katarina picks it up. 'It's KDR!" she whispers to Indrani. 'Do you —?'

'No, no. It's OK. You take it.'

'OK. — Hullo! ... What? ... Truly ? Thank God! ... All right, all right. See you soon, then.'

She puts the receiver down. 'They've made an arrest.'

'Who is it?'

'Ben.'

'Ben? — Ben? You mean Manager Georgi's assistant ? Great God! Who'd have thought he was a killer? He's such a quiet fellow.'

'I gather he was the last person to see Ray that evening. The Inspector has decided that the circumstantial evidence points to him.'

'So he knew Ray, then?'

'So it seems. We never know what really goes on, do we?' Katarina gives her a wink as she tucks her in. 'Now you better get some rest. The killer is no longer at large. Problem solved.'

32
'To Truth!'

Ganga Rao pours me a brandy and KDR offers me a cigar. We are in the library, after dinner. It is like old times, except for the mood. A funereal pall overhangs the room, which even the presence of Indrani and Katarina cannot altogether dispel.

KDR sinks into his armchair and watches Ganga Rao prepare brandy-and-orange for the ladies. When they receive their glasses, he lifts his own. 'So at last the clouds hanging over our horizon are beginning to clear. Let us rejoice in the successful conclusion of Inspector Muldoon's investigations and the arrest of the culprit! Let us drink to the victory of truth! – To Truth!'

'To Truth!' We join in. Somehow the words ring hollow. Indrani, reclining on the chaise longue, wrinkles her brow at the first sip of her drink. 'Ganga Rao! What have you done? This tastes bitter.'

'I am sorry, my lady. A little more orange, perhaps?'

'Don't bother. I don't need it anyway.' She hands the glass back. 'Thank you. – What I can't work out is the motive. Why would Ben want to kill Ray? Whatever possessed him to do such a dreadful thing? Is it true that he keeps saying he is innocent?'

Her question is addressed to no one in particular. I hold back what I am tempted to say, as I see KDR's brows knitting in disapproval.

'Ben may well protest, my dear, but the Inspector is convinced that the man is guilty. All circumstantial evidence points to him. Ben had been seen with Mr Rowlatt that evening. A cleaner in cottage number six had heard angry voices. It's an open-and-shut case. We should be grateful that the killer has been nabbed.'

'I am sorry, Uncle. I didn't mean to upset you.' Indrani looks towards me, eyes brimming with distress. All I can manage is a faint shrug of the shoulder to indicate I am with her. An awkward silence prevails.

My phone rings. 'Excuse me!' I am glad of the chance to leave the room.

'Hullo! – Monica! Everything all right ? How's the Reverend?'

'He's recovering well, thank God! It's not about him. Something else. Anna is on her way to see you.'

'Anna? – Not again! I told her I can't do much for her.'

'I think you might be able to, if what she says turns out to be the case. She has seen her husband Stefan.'

'Seen him? Where? How?'

'Your lawyer's murder was on the 6 o'clock news. Anna was with us when we were watching. She recognized the man they've arrested. She's convinced it is her husband Stefan. She's absolutely convinced he is innocent.'

'Wait a minute. How can she recognize him? His face was covered.'

'Apparently he has a distinct tattoo on his arm, a double-headed eagle, and he walks with a slight limp. Anna was shocked, of course, but also strangely relieved. She now feels she can rescue him from whatever he has got mixed up with. That's why she's coming over. I've just put her on the night train. She'll arrive in the early hours. I wanted to make sure you were there to look after her. Please do! She is very stressed.'

'Sure.'

'God bless you! I hope she's right.'

When I return to the library, all eyes are on me, questioning.

'It was my mother. Her home-help — companion as she became, Anna — you may have seen her at the Coronation — she is arriving here tomorrow. She believes that our Ben is her husband Stefan who had gone missing some months ago. He disappeared under strange circumstances. She believes Stefan can't possibly be a killer.'

Indrani's eyes light up. 'I remember it well. The very first time you came to see us at the hotel, do you remember? — You told me about this neighbour of yours, how you had to deal with a crisis. Wasn't her name Anna?'

'Yes. What a memory you have!'

'I knew it. I knew it. There's something too neat about the Inspector's conclusions. I don't like him.'

KDR assumes a stentorian tone. 'That is no reason to question his conclusions, my dear! — Nonetheless, we drank to Truth and Truth we must have. Heaven forbid an innocent man be sentenced to a life-term! That'll only plunge us into greater depths of the evil that has fallen on us and on our kingdom. Let us help this lady as well as we can. If she's right, then Pandora's box will fly open once again. Such is life! — What more can I say, except good night? I am very weary myself, I shall retire now. May God grant us all peaceful sleep, for these are turbulent times. Good night!'

*   *   *

'More coffee for yous?'

The plump waitress, a bottle-blond matron bursting out of her stained pink-gingham apron, hovers around our table. 'You

326

finished?' She flings the question at Anna, seeing that she hasn't touched her plate of egg and chips.

Anna, startled by the shrillness of her voice, begins to eat the egg, but soon stops as she uncovers the soggy toast beneath. She pushes the plate away. 'No – no coffee for me.'

'Have some juice,' I urge her.

'– What have you got?'

'O.J.'

'O.J?' Anna blinks. '– Ah, O.J. Yes. I will have O.J.'

'And for you, sir?' I get a streak of a smile, perhaps a show of sympathy for my having to sit here with my difficult companion. Though the coffee is abominable, I give in. 'A short black, if you can.'

'Sure'.

She clears the table and ambles away. Since dawn, we have been sitting here, Anna and I, at this roadside café, *Breakfast at Billy's,* the only one open at this time of the morning. For the past two hours or so, weary-eyed long-distance drivers have been staggering in at regular intervals. Almost as soon as she got off the train around five in the morning, Anna wanted to go straight to the police station. She didn't quite get it, though I tried hard to explain again and again, that without Inspector Muldoon's approval there was no chance of seeing Stefan, and the Inspector was not likely to be on duty that time of the morning. Over breakfast, I hoped that she might open up and tell me something more about Stefan before we got to the police station. But despite my three bad coffees and persistent probing, so far I've got nowhere. Anna's English-language receptors seem to have gone on the blink. All I get in response to my queries is a silent jerky nod or a blank stare from her dark-ringed eyes, filled with fear and fatigue. She can barely speak, yet she is strangely calm, even smiling faintly now and then. She waits till I gulp down the repulsive brew.

'Can we go now?'

'It's still too early.'

'Please! – I don't like this. We wait there, not here.'

'OK.'

I pay the bill and we head towards the police station.

More waiting, hours of it, until every crack and curl of peeling paint on the walls become a familiar part of my mental screen. Hours of shuffling in our sticky vinyl seats, as the heat begins to rise. Finally, around noon we are ushered into the room where prisoners are allowed to see their relatives.

Anna is right. Now that he is shaved and his hair is cut, even I can recognize in our Orchard assistant Ben my erstwhile lugubrious neighbour, Stefan. He keeps his head down, his chin almost sinking into his breast.

Anna breaks into uncontrollable sobbing. 'Stefan, my darling, look at me, why did you do it?'

'I didn't.'

'I know. I know you kill nobody – but why did you run away from me? Why?'

He lifts his head, and his eyes dart around as he speaks.

'I didn't run away. I was taken.'

'Who take you? Why? Why you say nothing to me? Why, why?'

Stefan's head drops again. He stays motionless, eyes closed. I look at my watch.

'– Stefan! We don't have much time. You must speak up. Tell us what happened. Be quick. We can't help you if you don't.'

'It's Georgi. He got me. He bring me here to his orchard. He keep me hostage till I give the money back to him.'

'What money, Stefan?'

He drops his head again and shuffles his feet. Anna starts to whimper again. A dark haired, heavy-muscled policewoman approaches our table; eyes on the clock she taps me on the shoulder. 'Time's up.'

I beg her. 'Please, five more minutes. It's a matter of life and death.'

'Really? Tell me news.' She grins, baring a set of brilliant white teeth. A dominatrix, if ever there was one. I slip into the submissive-slave mode. 'Please, madam!'

The trick works. She looks towards the door, and relents. 'Five minutes, no more. Hurry up, before the governor skins me for this.'

I turn to Stefan sternly. 'Come on, Stefan. Spit it out. You heard her. Hurry up. It's your life on the block.'

He shudders and straightens himself, and throwing his head back, addresses me. 'OK! This Georgi – I never set mi eyes on him till he turned up that day at the garage – this Georgi has dentist brother in Balmain, pots of money, hangs out with big shots. He wants to be mayor. Why not? A very respectable gent, so everyone thinks, but what do they know? – What do they know? –Do they know he is a mass-murderer, a butcher of women and children? Back in Belgrade, that is what he was. I have papers, don't I? I have pictures to prove it. My cousin, his whole family was butchered by this doctor. My cousin, he knows nobody. He sold the pictures to me to make more money. We have a deal. He get 30%, I get 70%. Fair enough, wouldn't you agree? I'm the bloke who has to do the hard work. OK, I know it's blackmail. So what? Is that worse than butchering a whole village? I got good money from this Balmain Peter. He'd put it in the gym locker, and send me the key and I pick it up, every month. Good money, easy money, and I keep mi word, I keep mum – I tell nobody. I tell him go and be mayor if they want you, I'll do nothing, so long as the money keeps coming in for me to do what I want to do. I was nearly there. I want to surprise Anna, buy a flat, take her to Disneyland. All nice, till this Georgi turn up one day. He talk nice but he want the money and the papers or he kill me, kill Anna. He bring me to his Orchard, lock me up, torture me till I say yes. Then the real trouble begins.'

'You mean with the money?'

'Yeah. I can't get it back. Bloody lawyer! I put it with him. My boss at the garage says this Rowlatt fella – a good client – he make good money for him, so I trust him. I go see him. I give him all of it, nearly half a million. When I hit trouble, I ring – Georgi stands with a gun digging into the back of my head, I ask this lawyer. He say one week, then one week again, then two weeks, then he stop answering my calls, he no reply, nothing. I tell Georgi. I tell him he must let me go to Sydney and see the lawyer. He says no. He thinks it's a trick. He is stupid, this Georgi, he thinks if he keeps beating me he get the money. So I am stuck. Like I'm back in the old country.'

'Oh, Stefan! Why didn't you tell me anything?' Anna wails.

'How could I, Anna? What could you do?' –Then I see him, the lawyer, here. So I go to him and ask him. He don't give me a straight answer. Then I find out. He's lost it, all of it. All of mi money in some scheme that went bust. I yell at him. He throws me out. Yeah, I was angry, so angry I could have killed him. But I didn't. By the Holy Mother of God, I didn't kill him.'

'Stefan! – Don't swear by Our Lady!'

'Why not? I'm telling the truth.'

Anna, eyes brimming with fresh tears, shakes me.

'See! I told you, I told you.'

Heavy thud of boots behind us: the dominatrix is back. 'Time up!'

Her stern tone and sterner look make Anna shudder. She rises, clutching the bar that separates us from the prisoner, rocks back and forth. 'Stefan, my darling, hold on there, we'll get you outta here, I promise, love, I promise, bye!'

Stefan lifts up his face, his melancholy eyes moistening with the faintest streak of hope. 'You reckon? ... Get me outta here? Help me! I didn't kill nobody. I'm innocent, help me.'

It is late afternoon by the time we reach the Castle. I see Indrani pacing up and down the portico. Ayah is sitting in the hanging basket-chair, lazily swirling it around as she chatters. Indrani runs towards us.

'At last! – Hullo, Anna! You must be exhausted.'

'I am very sorry, my lady, very sorry to give you this trouble.'

'Not at all. Let's hope we can get your husband out. You must rest! Jeevesamma! Would you please take Anna to her room? – Now, please, tell me everything. I couldn't hear very well on the phone. Let's walk! I can't stand being a prisoner in my own Castle.'

'Where's everybody?'

'Ganga Rao is at Resort Raja, so is Felix. Since Ben disappeared, the dogs are giving trouble. There have been complaints. Billy's son rang. One of the dogs has bitten a black child. I hope Felix can make peace. Uncle has taken Katarina on Jatayu for a ride. He is teaching her to fly. I expect he too feels oppressed here at present.'

I seize her hand. 'Which way?'

'That way! You remember my first bushwalk?'

'Of course!'

'Well, go on, tell me everything.'

'You were right. Ben – I should say, Stefan – isn't the killer.'

'I knew it, I knew it. I know Uncle was angry with me for saying so, but that Inspector was too glib.'

Her tone is frenzied as is her pace. She keeps looking behind as if she was expecting something. We reach the pepper tree.

'Stop!' I take her in my arms and kiss her.

'No, no, not here. Someone will see us.'

'There's no one around.'

There may be. Who knows?'

'I don't care.'

I tighten my embrace. She yields for a moment, then wriggles free.

'Please let's move. You are right. I am agitated. Is it surprising? We've got a murder unsolved, the wrong man is arrested. We don't know who the real culprit is. Uncle has taken to consulting Vembu, as if he were an oracle! And as for Katarina, I like her well enough but I don't know if she cares for me as much. Why should she? I am sorry – I shouldn't be talking about myself at a time like this. Perhaps we should go back. I feel tired all of a sudden. This light is blinding me.'

She screws up her eyes against the sharp slanting rays. Then she starts.

'Look! Over there! So he is still here.'

'Who, Rani?'

'Mr Rohan. I thought I was imagining. I kept feeling I was being watched.'

'Has he been stalking you?'

'Not quite. He has been flooding me with flowers, red roses and white lilies. My room looks like a funeral parlour. And I can't breathe for all the pollen. I've asked Ayah to clear them.'

'Poor Rohan! Bereaved and love-sick! I need to talk to him, check out if Stefan's story about the investment is true.'

Rohan doesn't seem to notice us approaching. He stands immobilized watching something. Perhaps it is the light but when he turns round, he doesn't register my presence. His gaze is solely focussed on Indrani. His eyes are strangely glazed, almost feverish.

'Shhh! Don't move, my Princess, my Queen! Don't take one step further! They are venomous, they'll strike you dead.'

'Who will, Mr Rohan?'

'Don't you see? Black snakes! There they are, all around me, coiled, shining, ready to strike! I've never seen so many! We are in great danger. You must go back. Go back, please, let me deal with them.'

Indrani tugs at my sleeve, and whispers. 'What does he mean? I can't see any black snakes here, can you?'

'No. But do as he says. You go back. I'll deal with him. He is sick.'

I wait till she is out of sight and turn to Rohan.

'Rohan, I must talk to you.'

'Talk? Talk? What about? You've got her. They have got me. I am trapped. Look at them, beautiful, aren't they? Mind you, they are deadly. They are hissing at me. Kill, Kill, Kill!'

He starts darting around, attacking a pile of twigs with a pen-knife. I have to jump back to avoid being stabbed.

'Look at them', he swirls round, 'Do you see how they keep coming at me? Aren't you afraid? How can you stay still?'

'Hold on, Rohan! Let me try this.' I take my cigarette-lighter out and set fire to the twigs.

'You can't do that! There's a fire-ban.'

'Don't worry. I'll put it out soon.'

Rohan watches as the twigs crackle and burn. I break off a leafy branch and put the fire out. 'Now, you see, they are gone.'

'Are you sure?'

'Most certain, they can't survive that fire. Bet on it.'

'Thank you.' He brushes the soot off his clothes.

'Shall we go back now?'

'My head hurts. I can't remember what I came here for. I thought I saw her here.'

'You did. She went back to the Castle.'

'Oh!' He rubs his head and stares vacantly into the distance. 'I don't feel well. I can't remember anything. What will she think of me? What was I doing?'

'Don't worry about that. It's over now. Come, let's go back. You need rest.'

After seeing him to his room, I go looking for Indrani. She is not in her room. Ayah directs me to the workroom. The door is locked. She must still fear Rohan. I call her.

She opens the door.

'How is he?'

'He has taken some pills and is resting. He needs a doctor. But before I deal with him any more, I need this.'

I hug her close and cover her in kisses. This time there is no protest from her even when my hands stray towards her breasts. Then I sense a mood-change. She seems abstracted.

'What is it?'

'I can't stop feeling he's watching us. Then this thought keeps coming into my head.'

'What thought?'

'Promise you won't get cross!'

'Promise.'

'I keep thinking, for once, we could do with your visions now. What a pity you can't be "ordered" to see.'

I slacken. Her words sting. 'Maybe I can. Maybe I'm putting off the task.'

'The task?'

'I should be questioning Rohan. He knows the truth, that's what's making him ill.'

'Perhaps you better go and do it, and before Uncle returns. I'd rather you questioned him than Uncle.'

'You're right.' I kiss her on the lips. 'Wish me luck.'

I wait nearly an hour by Rohan's bed, watching him sleep. His face looks tranquil, like a baby's. When he surfaces, he smiles. He sits up, startled. 'Where am I? What are you doing here?'

'It's OK, Rohan. You are safe.'

'What do you want from me?'

'The truth.'

'The truth!' He laughs wryly. 'The truth. You make it sound so easy. You have no idea what it was like for me. And I did nothing. Absolutely nothing.'

'I understand.'

'Do you? How can you? You don't know Ray. You don't know what he can be like. I didn't know till then how I hated him. – I did nothing, absolutely nothing. I just stood there watching him bleed to death. That's the truth. Now leave me please, I must go back to sleep.'

'Rohan!' I grab him and shake him. 'You know who killed Ray. You saw him bleed to death. You know the killer. Who is it, Rohan? You must speak, if you are to get well.'

'I can still smell the room, stinking of cheap deodorant. It wasn't Ray's. He used good stuff.'

'Who was it, Rohan?'

'The lorry driver. What's his name? Ari, Max's Dad. He was mad with rage. Ray stole his son, you see. Ray's very good at it – stealing young men.'

'Where were you?'

'Me? I can't remember.'

'Try. You must. You know what this means.'

'I am trying, you fool, but I have this black hole in my head. I can't get past it.'

'Were you in the room?'

'No. Wait. It's coming back. I heard a heavy thump. I went to check what happened. That lorry driver ran out past me. Ray lay there, head-bashed. I just stood watching him till he died. I was gasping for air. My asthma. So I rushed out, got my car and drove to the Castle to get my medication. — Could you pass me those pills? I need more. I need a long, long sleep.'

'I've rung for the doctor. He should be here soon, Rohan.'

'Do me a favour, will you?'

'What is it, Rohan?'

'Tell her I feel free, for the first time in my life. I am happy to die here, near her.'

'Don't talk of dying, Rohan, You are young, you'll pull through this trouble.'

My hollow consolation is drowned by a most piercing shriek from outside.

I rush out. Jeevesamma stumbles out of Indrani's room, shrieking, wailing and tearing at her hair.

My stomach turns to acid. 'Rani! — Where's Rani? What's happened?'

Jeevesamma continues wailing, shaking her head and beating her breasts.

Indrani comes out, phone in hand and ashen-faced.

'Crashed. 'Copter crash. Uncle is dead. And Katarina. Crashed by Resort Raja. Bushfire. Resort Raja is burning. All burning, burning.'

She gets the words out one by one, zombie-like. I catch her as she collapses.

33
Disposals and Proposals

Santa season is upon us. That snowy-bearded red clown runs amok, while the tarmac melts in December heat. Will we ever grow out of this absurd nostalgia?

My back-seat passengers, Anna and Stefan, however, can't have enough of the tinsel garlands, plastic reindeers and all the ho-ho-hos that assault us relentlessly, as I speed towards the station. They are chattering away, planning their Christmas. A spell in prison, a near miss from death – and a sea change in Stefan. His habitual lugubriousness is gone: he pulsates with a childish joy that makes me envious.

As I bid farewell to them at the station, he gives me a hearty hug, crushing me in a profusion of thankfulness. Anna beams with pride.

'Thank you, thank you, Mr Martin. I always knew you could help us. And you did.'

'And you, Anna, deserve a medal for persistence.'

'I am so sorry for your lady. Don't leave her sad too long, Mr Martin. You make her happy.'

'How can I ignore your command, Anna?'

The train starts to move. She blows me a kiss through the window.

'Goodbye!'

'Goodbye! Safe journey!'

When I return to the Castle I find Indrani at KDR's desk in the office. Ganga Rao is with her, handing her papers to sign. She looks up, a faint smile streaking through her amber eyes, darkened by grief.

'I shall miss Anna. She is so tenacious and tender.'

'She is quite adamant that we should visit them in Sydney soon.'

'I would like to see you in your habitat.'

'It is a small, nondescript flat in a noisy suburb.'

'Italian, you said.' She pauses, and taking my hand plays with the watch strap. 'Do you miss her? What does it feel like, losing someone so close and yet not so close.'

'I used to worry about Katarina's beauty withering away for lack of love. Yet I could not love her the way I love you. I never imagined she'd die so young. I feel angry — absurdly angry on her behalf. She shouldn't have been cheated out of life, just when she had a chance of real happiness. She never had that chance with me.'

'Uncle was going to propose to her, you know, when the Conference was over. He was planning a cruise with her, stopping by Ratnapuri on the way to Europe. It was to be a ship-wedding, just like Grandfather Vikram's. And Grandpa Vikramv— he perished in flames.' She averts her eyes, brimming with tears. I put an arm around her.

Ganga Rao coughs significantly. 'I beg your pardon, my lady. This document needs to be signed here as well.' He pushes a sheet towards her. She signs it mechanically, her shoulders slumping wearily.

I stroke her hair. 'Can't all this wait? You don't look well enough to be doing so much paperwork.'

'Well enough! I can't keep the staff here much longer. They can't wait to get back home. Even Ganga Rao – isn't that so, Rao sahib?'

'I have always served Highness. I shall serve you as long as you need me, Your Majesty. When Your Majesty no longer needs me I shall be content to return to our Old Ratnapuri.'

'"Your Majesty! Your-Highness!" –You know it's all over, Rao sahib. What am I signing these papers for?'

'Your-Highness, like your illustrious uncle, is big-hearted. –We've nearly finished, madam, just a few more to go. Now if you'd be kind enough to read this before you sign, madam.' He pushes a letter before her.

I move to the window till they finish with the documents. Indrani stretches her arms, yawning:

'Thank God that's over. I am glad to be shot of it all.'

'So you are abdicating, as it were.'

'What else? This place is desolate. I can't bear to live here. Besides, I'd rather do it now. It's strangely exhilarating, giving everything away. Shall I tell you what I've done?'

'If you wish – I am all attention.'

'Jayadev gets to run the businesses. I am giving Blue Gum Farm and the Gordon paintings to Rose. Billy and Felix will be the custodians of Resort Raja – what's left of it. The land is valuable and they belong to it.'

Ganga Rao mops his dome.

'May I go now, my lady?'

'Thank you, Rao sahib – for everything.'

An immense sadness spreads over her face as she watches him leave. 'Poor Rao! He lived for Uncle. He keeps up a brave front, but he is shattered inside. He needs to go back, and live off memories. All I can do is to give him some shares. I hope they don't let him down. And did I tell you? I have set up a trust for that poor boy Max. It was the most difficult thing to do, writing to him and his mother.'

'You have done everything you can: true to your Coronation-vows.'

'Please don't remind me of that.'

'I am sorry. But Ganga Rao is right. You shall never cease to be my queen. Even more so, now that you have made yourself a pauper –'

'More or less.'

'Now that I am unemployed –'

'I thought that you were a freelancer.'

'Very free indeed.' I kneel before her. 'Will you be my own, my one and only queen? Will you marry this penniless, rootless, moody, unpredictable, delusory, ageing photographer who absolutely adores you?'

'What a question? – Rise Sir Ezmar, Ziggy, Mr Martin, EM, or whatever else you care to be called. At last I am free to do as I wish. I accept.'

*   *   *

Boonoo Boonoo Billy blows the dust off the carved box and hands it to Indrani. 'For your knick-knacks, Miss: something to help you keep us in mind and tell our story.'

'Thank you, Billy. I shall indeed.'

Billy locks up the shop. 'Okeydo! Ready, Zig? — You can drive us up to the Falls, from there it's an hour's walk. You reckon you can make it, Miss? It's hotter up there: Westerlys blowing like a furnace.'

'I must. I shall.'

When we reach The Falls, Billy points to a steep track snaking its way up through burnt-out gums. We follow him in silence. I hold an umbrella over Indrani as she climbs, breathing slowly and evenly to cope with the heat. Billy stops.

'Down there, Miss! That's where they found the 'copter bits. The fire spread quickly, as you can see, all the way down to your Resort. I'm sorry it's all gone, Miss. But I've a good mind to build that theatre back. We need a conference centre for our Council.'

'Will you, Billy? It's a great thing you can do for Uncle.'

'We could do with a bit of tourism too, Miss. We've got the dancers, the artists, and bush-craft. We'll carry on what your uncle wanted to do with this land, Miss. And I promise we put on some Shakespeare now and then. All of yous must come.'

'Thank you! We shall.'

'Now if you two stay here, I'll go down with Felix. — Ready, Felix? Got the shovel and the pot?'

'Yeah!'

We take shelter under a giant strangler-fig and watch the panoramic splendour of the seemingly endless range of hills that stretch on the far side of a great drop.

'I wonder what it was like,' Indrani pauses as she drinks some water. 'To know that you are rushing forward to meet death, as it were, when the 'copter went down. I can't bear to think how horribly they must have suffered in the fire.'

'On the other hand it's possible they were already unconscious when the 'copter hit the side of this gorge.'

'We shall never know. One thing I am certain, Uncle would have appreciated this spectacular scenic backdrop to his grand exit.'

Billy returns with two pots full of the earth from the crash-site:

'Here, Miss! Take care, they're heavy.'

'Thank you, Billy.' She passes the pots to me. 'One for Ganga and one for the Clarence.'

'That's right, Miss. I won't forget how he mixed the two. This Clarence was sacred to him. He understood what we are on about.'

'How right you are!' Indrani turns to me. 'Shall I? Or will you?'

'I think better coming from you.'

'OK then. – Just one thing more, Billy. May I ask of you a favour?'

'What can I do for you, Miss?

'It's to do with Mr Rohan.'

'Poor bugger! How's he doing?'

'They'll discharge him from the hospital soon. The doctor says it was *petit mal*, a kind of amnesia. He can plead diminished responsibility for withholding evidence. They'll let him go. He'll recover fully, given the right environment, so the doctor says. Will you help him?'

'What have you in mind, Miss?'

'He talks about being a ranger. Will you take him?'

'Sure, Miss.'

I drive in silence, admiring Indrani's calm handling of her grief. My own thoughts are tangled and my spirit is severely jangled by the visit to the crash-site. Like a demon-ghost in a Hong Kong movie, Katarina, Koori Kat, glides into my psyche, demanding attention. I had arranged for a mass to be said in the Catholic Church in Leichhardt where she used to drop in occasionally. The priest who vaguely knew her had gone. The new incumbent did his best – but his encomium, put together from my notes, fell on an indifferent, whispering audience. Her Sicilian relatives were more concerned with the forthcoming fight over who gets Café Gregorio. The whole episode left me exhausted, disappointed and angry.

I must do something for her, something to set her at rest, here, at the place where she died.

We reach Billy's workshop. '– Billy!'

'Yes, Zig?'

'May I also ask you a favour?'

'Go on!'

'It's for Kat. She came to this part of the world looking for her tribe. She found the Bundjalung but she couldn't be part of them. Now she's part of them. I want that to be recognized in some way.'

'Sure, Zig. We could do her story at the site. No worries. You let me know when and I'll get the dancers and the singers.'

'Thanks, Billy.'

Felix emerges from the interior, clutching cans of Tooheys. Billy hands them out and lifts his can:

'Let's drink to them, to the Raja and the beaut Kat! Cheers!'

We join in. 'Cheers!'

When he has downed a few cans, Felix turns to me in tipsy slur.

'Remember how I came to see you? That night when I got your wallet? You thought I stole it, didn't ya? That's what everybody thinks, blackfella he steal. Australia Felix, he never steal. He take what he find. Now we find this beaut land, we take, thanks to this great lady! You lucky fella, Zig! Thanks, mate! You didn't throw me out that night, you took me in. —He's good fella, this Zig, my lady! He look after ya, cheers! Where're yous heading, Zig?'

'Going on our own "walkabout", Felix.'

'Which way?'

'Up, down and roundabout. I've got a job with the UN Disaster-Relief mob, and Rani will be designing houses for the quake-flood victims and the like."

'Beaut, Zig! Say hullo to the world from Australia Felix. Promise you'd say a loud hearty hullo!'

'I promise, most solemnly promise!'

As we say our goodbyes, I hear thunder in the distance. A sudden gust of wind disperses gum-leaves over us. Indrani shakes them off, laughing:

'How strange! I shall never get used to this. A moment ago the wind was boiling hot, now it is cool.'

'That's because the Southerlys are here.'

ABOUT THE AUTHOR

CHRISTINE MANGALA was born in Tanjore District, Tamil Nadu, South India into a Brahmin family distinguished for five centuries as devotees of Shiva, and as Sanskrit scholars, writers and composers.

Educated in India at the Universities of Delhi and Osmania, she was the first woman to win the Nehru Memorial Trust Scholarship, which took her to the University of Cambridge for a doctorate on 'The Problem of Evil in Jacobean Drama'.

Since 1968, Christine Mangala has lived largely in the west, though maintaining regular contact with her homeland. She married a Cambridge don and raised four children, then spent twenty-two years with her family in Newcastle, New South Wales, before returning to Cambridge, where she has been active in the development of the Institute for Orthodox Christian Studies. She has taught literature in the Universities of Cambridge and Newcastle, New South Wales, but in more recent years has put her experience of eastern and western religions to promoting a better understanding of both: through lectures, broadcasts and publications, but especially in several works of fiction that 'flesh the bones', exploring what such beliefs mean in human experience.

Her first novel, *The Firewalkers* (1991), was short-listed for the Commonwealth Best First Book Prize and also for the Deo Gloria Award. The Australia Council Literature Board funded her second novel, *Transcendental Pastimes* (1997), which takes a western film-crew to South India to investigate a guru who claims to remember his past incarnations. *Looking for A Kingdom,* her third novel, now draws on her unique experience to bring India to Australia in a joyful and entertaining celebration of the meeting of two very different cultures.

Shalimar Gardens, to be published in 2014, is a murder mystery involving Hindu and Muslim extremists whose activities disrupt the centuries-old social and religious harmony of a civilised Indian city. Christine Mangala is at present preparing a scholarly study of Orthodox Christianity in relation to Hindu beliefs.